THOR & DRAGON

STEEL ARCHANGEL'S BOOK 1

R. KNIGHT

Title: Thor & Dragon

Series: Steel Archangel's MC, SAFC1 (Book 1)

Original - Ebook Copyright 2023 R. Knight

Edited - Paperback Copyright 2025 R. Knight Publications LLC

Cover by: belle âmes designs

Formatting by: Becky Hodges

Edited by: Franklin Beck

Contents

Dedication

To MY FAMILY AND friends for supporting my dreams of being an author. Thank you for everything, from bouncing ideas off each other, for helping me come up with the right phrase or saying, to putting up with my crazy characters and worlds that I frequently talk about and everything in between. Love you <3

For those who have faced trauma, whatever it may be, may you find your anchor who will help pull you from the darkness. We are not damaged. We may have a few bends, but we are not broken. Find your inner steel and may you blossom beautifully.

Acknowledgements

To MY READERS, THANK you for joining me as we learn more about the members that make up the Steel Archangel's MC as they find their women. Men who are possessive, protective alpha's who will do anything to protect their partners. Women who are kickass and strong in their own way, whether they realize it or not.

To my PA, Becky Hodges, you are an absolute godsend! I would be lost without you and the babes you introduced me to, who are affectionately named after you, Becky's Babes. Thank you all for your support, bouncing ideas around, and general shenanigans ;)

To my Alpha Team, I can't begin to say how thankful I am to have met you! You've helped name a few things in this book (including a certain device of Levi's that's introduced toward the end of the book) as well as given me quite a few character ideas. Thank you for your support and keeping me going <3

To my friend, who wishes to remain anonymous, thank you for looking over my Russian translations. You really saved me when I was fretting who would be able to verify if my online translation sites were accurate. I'm very thankful that I was given your name <3 Also, thank you for teaching me more things about your culture. I can't wait to try the recipes you sent me :)

Reading Order
Other Works By R. Knight

Steel Archangel's MC

Thor & Dragon (SAFC1)

Timber (SAFC2)

Patch (SAFC3)

Patch & Mary: A SAMC Christmas to Remember (SAFC3.5)

Reaper (SAJC1—coming soon)

Smoke (SAFC4—TBD)

Cannon & Atlas (SAJC2—TBD)

Children of Prophecy

Hell's Lost Princess, Book 1

Book 2 (coming soon)

Shifter Royalty

Mates, Book 1

Spirits, Book 2

Book 3 (coming soon)

Standalones

New Beginnings

*This is in the process of being rewritten
and rebranded. The link will be coming soon*

Content & Trigger Warning

THIS BOOK IS INTENDED *for a mature audience aged 18+. It contains foul language, violence (including torture and murder), adult situations, mention of rape as well as mention of conditioning/grooming (does not go into detail) which may trigger some readers.*

There is no cheating. While there is a bit of a cliffhanger, there is a HEA for Levi, Thor, and Dragon. Each book can be read as a standalone, but it is best read in order as the story builds on the members and their women/partners in the Steel Archangel's MC.

Steel Archangels MC Members

Forest Creek Chapter (SAFC)

Ryan Gilbert (Thor)—President

Reed Thomson (Phoenix)—Vice President

Nick Gilbert (Dragon)—Enforcer

Alexander 'Alex' Carter (Ryder)—Sergeant at Arms

Elijah Anderson (Tripp)—Secretary

Liam Caldwell (Timber)—Treasurer

Noah Banks (Judge)—Road Captain

Jaxon 'Jax' Witlock (Smoke)

Luke Morgan (Patch)

Malcolm Hart (Bones)

Michael Adams (Gunner)

Aiden Hunt (Axe)

Owen Burke (Bear)

Troy Simpson (Colt)—Prospect

Drae Black—Prospect

Steel Archangels MC Members

Junction Creek Chapter (SAJC)

Anthony 'Tony' Leyton (Reaper)—President
Isaac Lopez (Devil)—Vice President
Kai Miller (Punisher)—Enforcer
Leon Foster (Razor)—Sergeant at Arms
Tyson Manning (Smithy)—Treasurer
Grant McGee (Beast)—Secretary
Adam Collins (Loki)—Road Captain
Cole Thornton (Python)
Hunter Beck (Doc)
Ragnar Miller (Odin)
Duncan Goodwin (Atlas)
Theodore 'Theo' Harris (Cannon)
Drake Olsen—Prospect
Nathan Flynn—Prospect

Old Lady

Astrid Miller—Old Lady to Odin

Translation Glossary

BELOW YOU WILL FIND the glossary list for the Russian translations of the words and short phrases that will appear in *Steel Archangel's MC: Thor & Dragon*. You will also find translations for the first four times the word/short sentence appears in the body of each chapter so that you won't have to repeatedly flip back to this glossary list. Longer sentences will only be translated in the chapter and will not appear below.

If you see an error with any of the translations, please remember that I am human and do not speak Russian. I have researched and had someone who speaks Russian look these over. We tried to get these translations as close as possible to being accurate, but again, we are human and may miss something.

If you do spot something that needs correcting, please reach out to me via email rather than reporting the issue and I will work to get it corrected (author.r.knight@gmail.com). Thank you for your patience and understanding <3

Format:

Russian word/short phrase [pronunciation] = English word(s)/phrases/sentence.

Note: Russians tend to use **Блин** (which literally means pancakes) much like we use the word 'bugger!' when we're in a situation where cussing isn't appropriate.

Да [da] = Yes

Брат / брат [bratt] = Brother

Кухня [kuchna] = Kitchen

Сейчас [seichas] = Now

Папа [papa] = Dad

До свидания [do svidaniya] = Goodbye

Понимаешь [ponimat] = Understand

Дети [deti] = Kids

Подождите [podozhdite] = Wait

Сукин сын [sukin syn] = Son of a bitch

Семья / Семью [semya] = Family

Сестре [sestra] = Sister

Спокойной ночи [spokoynoy nochi] = Good night

Люблю тебя [lublu tebya] = Love you

Я тоже тебя люблю [ya toze tebya lublu] = Love you too

Альфа [alfa] = Alpha

Байкер [byker] = Biker

Уйди [uydy] = Get

Уносите свои задницы [unosite svoi zadnicy] = Get your asses off

Рассказывай [rasskazyvaj] = Tell me/us

Нет [net] = No

Спасибо [spasibo] = Thank you

Сёстры [syostry] = Sisters

Наши поздравления [nashi pozdravleniya] = Ours congratulations

Добро пожаловать в семью [dobro pozhalovat vie semue] = Welcome to the family

Хорошо [khoroshiy] = Good/okay

Молодец [molodets] = You got it

Позаботьтесь о ней [pozabottes o ney] = Take care of her

Очень верно [ochen verno] = Very true

Камеры [camera] = Camera's

Идиот [idiot] = Idiot

Сделай это [sdelay eto] = Do it

Конечно [konieczno] = Of course

Блин [bl'in] = Pancake

Steel Archangels MC Series Song Inspiration

Man of Steel by Brantley Gilbert
Tough Town by Brantley Gilbert
Who Hurt You by David Morris
Warriors by Imagine Dragons
Simple Man by Lynyrd Skynyrd
Ride the Wind by Poison
Miracle by Shinedown
Monsters by Shinedown

Thor & Dragon Song Inspiration

Ride the Wind by Poison

45 by Shinedown

Get Up by Shinedown

Painkiller by Three Days Grace

Synopsis

Levi Wallace

Finishing college was supposed to be a time of celebration for me, my friends, and my family. Instead, we find out demons from my past are back. And to top it off? I discovered that I'd been sold by my own flesh and blood, and I have no idea why. This time, my demons are back with a vengeance and will do anything to claim me. To my surprise, the MC that Uncle Bear belongs to offers me protection... which instantly has me on edge. However, I quickly find myself accepting. In the past, I never wanted to be *that* close any MC, so imagine my surprise when I find love in the form of a biker. And not just *a* biker. *Twin* bikers. As my demons continue to chase me, I'm grateful my men have my back because it isn't just me that I'm looking out for anymore.

Thor & Dragon

We'd given up on finding a woman who could handle both the President and the Enforcer of an MC. There aren't many women strong enough to handle two men and our kind of life for the long haul. When our club comes under threat from a previously unknown club, we try to find out their motivation behind targeting us. Imagine our surprise when we find out their motive has been a woman we've known for years. And she's all grown up now. We didn't know about the attack on her when she was a teenager, but this time... This time she has us behind her and we aren't afraid of getting our hands bloody. But our Enchantress doesn't have just us behind her. She has a whole MC army at her back who will do anything to protect their Queen.

Chapter 1
Levi

I hand in my test to the professor and make my way out into the hallway before exiting the lecture hall. As I look around the campus of Wisconsin University, I breathe a sigh of relief. It's not that I don't like it here; it's gorgeous.

Groupings of trees are scattered throughout the campus, and there are multiple benches where people can sit, relax, or study. There's also a small forest that butts up to the campus, and I frequently walk the paths. The forest was one of the major 'pluses' for this place when I visited the summer before my senior year of high school. It reminded me a little of my hometown—Forest Creek, Wisconsin.

The reason I'm relieved is because that was my last final, and I'm finally done with college! Now, it's time to make my way back home and help my dad in our family's bar and grill, Wallace's B&G, something I've always wanted to do. With a spring in my step, I head toward the parking garage.

The only thing that's putting a damper on my happiness is how things ended last night with Scott. We've been dating for almost a month. At first, I didn't want to date anyone so close to graduation, but Scott was persistent. Finally, I relented and went on a date with him, but only after he understood that I had no plans to stick around after graduation. I couldn't stress enough to him how important it was to me to go home and eventually take over my family's bar and grill from my dad someday. He told me he understood and even hinted that he was willing to move. One date led to another and then another. Before long, he was introducing me as his girlfriend.

As the weeks went on and graduation kept creeping closer, he tried multiple times to get me to change my mind about leaving. Each time I'd remind him how important the bar and grill was to me and that I'm going to be moving home. He let it drop each time. That is, until this past weekend.

Once again, he brought up the topic and practically blew up at me for not committing to him and saying horrible things about my family and me. A shudder runs down my spine as the memory of the argument washes over me. The argument ended with him throwing a mostly full bottle of beer against the wall and storming out of my apartment.

I thought that was going to be the last time I saw him, but I was wrong. He showed up at my apartment again last night, begging me to forgive him. When I told him no, things got out of hand pretty quickly. Another shudder runs through me because things had gotten very close to being completely out of hand.

"How can you be so selfish, Levi? I've given you plenty of my time over the past few weeks and yet I get nothing in return. Nothing. Not even getting my dick wet."

He walks toward me, trying to cage me into the wall as he towers over me as menacingly as he can, since he's only a few inches taller than me.

I cringe at his choice of words before I shove him back and out of my face. His breath reeks of alcohol and his body sways slightly, which proves he'd been drinking a lot before coming over here and forcing the door open.

I'd been about to leave since I'd run out of packing tape and wanted to get a few more moving boxes so I wouldn't have to pack the boxes so heavily. I even checked through the peephole to make sure no one was in the hallway, but I didn't know Scott was lurking around the corner and out of sight.

As I take him in, I can honestly admit that I don't know the man standing in front of me right now. He's the complete opposite of the Scott I'd gotten to know. Or is this who Scott really is, and the Scott I had grown to know was all a façade?

His face distorts in anger, and the bulging veins on his neck look like they're about to burst. He takes a few more steps away from me, for which I'm grateful, but he's still breathing heavily and looks like he might punch something. I just hope that 'something' isn't me. Instead of rehashing the same old argument, I focus on the words he just said.

"I'm not the type of woman to give into pleas for sex after knowing someone for only a few weeks. I'm not going to give you head just because you demand it. No one takes the choice away from me."

That should have been my first red flag when he did that a little over a week ago. However, I ignored it, thinking it was just his dominant personality.

He huffs and shakes his head. "No, you're just a fucking cock-tease that flaunts around wearing skin-tight clothes and then doesn't understand why men are upset when you turn us down or don't want to take things further."

His face softens, but after what just happened, I'm not sure if his next words are going to be an act or not. My gut is telling me to get away from him. Big time get away from him. Fool me once, shame on you. Fool me twice, shame on me. He is not going to fool me again.

"You know I care about you, Levi. I need something to go on that lets me know you're in this for longer than this next week."

I shake my head at his manipulative words, especially since he's rarely looked me in the eye during this entire conversation. No, his gaze is once again raking in my curves and as if to prove my thoughts, the asshole licks his lips and then bites his lower lip as he stares at my breasts. When his gaze returns to my face, his face darkens as soon as he sees how angry I am.

"And why would I do that, Scott? Especially when you look at me like some piece of meat to claim. No, you're just trying to manipulate me into doing whatever the hell you want. I thought you had gotten my message loud and clear last weekend, but it seems to not have sunk in. Let me reiterate. We. Are. Through. I don't want to see you ever again. I will not let anyone pressure me into something I'm not ready for. Especially when you make it seem like all you want from me is sex. And if you dare bring up the fact that I'm leaving, just remember I told you that was going to happen before we even started dating and you told me you were fine with that. Obviously, that was a fucking lie. Now, I want you out of here. Get out of my apartment before I call the police."

Making sure to not fully turn my back on him, I walk to the door and open it. Surprisingly, I see my friend Sam on the other side, his hand poised to knock. His gaze darts between Scott and me a few times before lingering on my face for a few seconds and then it returns to Scott, staying there.

"Is everything all right? I heard a lot of yelling through the walls."

I huff and shake my head, which only makes Sam's frown deepen. "No, things are not all right, but as long as Scott leaves, I won't have to call the police."

I open the door wider as my attention goes back to Scott, but it doesn't escape my notice that Sam has stepped inside my apartment and is casually leaning against the wall to the left of the door.

Scott looks between both of us a few times before his face darkens and he takes a few steps forward. He stops when Sam pushes off the wall and stands at his full height, which is more than a foot taller than Scott.

"I should have known something was going on between you two. What, are you giving him all the goods while stringing me along and giving me nothing?" Scott grits out through clenched teeth while glaring at me, whereas I'm seriously trying to understand where the hell that train of thought came from. Sam is gay and has only just recently told me that he might be bi, but there's no way I'm telling Scott that. Shaking my head, I point to the door.

"Not that it's any of your business anymore, but Sam and I are friends. Have been for a few years now. I am capable of having male friends and not fucking them. Now, as I said before, get out of my apartment before I call the police."

As soon as Sam hears that last part again, and adding in the fact that Scott hasn't budged, he pulls out his phone. A few seconds later, I hear the telltale voice saying "9-1-1 what is your emergency?"

With another glare my way, Scott moves toward the door. "This isn't over, bitch," he calls over his shoulder.

I move to step out in the hall, but Sam gestures for me to stay put and steps out himself to make sure he leaves.

In the kitchen, I grab us both a beer as I try to shake off my nerves. I vaguely hear Sam filling the operator in on what happened and hear her say the report has been logged in case something happens again.

Sam ended up staying with me for a while to make sure I was okay and to be there while I called Sasha [pronounced: SAW-SHAW] to let her know what had happened. It was difficult, but I finally got Sasha to agree not to head out tonight after pointing out that she wouldn't get here until about 3 am. Though I'm pretty sure she would have left tonight if Sam hadn't been here, but his last final is also my last final.

After hanging up with Sasha, Sam wanted to stay longer to make sure Scott didn't come back, but I was crashing hard. It was only after repeatedly promising that

I'd call him if anything else happened that he headed back to his apartment. He knew I really didn't have any backup right now since Sasha, her twin brother, Alexei [pronounced: AH-LEHK-SAY], and our two other friends, Ethan and Travis, had already moved back home a couple days ago because he helped take boxes down to the trucks. The five of us lucked out at getting apartments in the same complex. Shortly after moving in, we met Sam, and he was welcomed into the fold.

Sighing, I finish my beer, and after verifying everything was locked up; I make my way to my bedroom. The sooner I got away from here, the better. Then I won't have to see Scott again.

With a deep breath, I push thoughts of Scott from my mind and focus on the positives. I'm excited to see my dad and uncle again. I hadn't seen them since spring break a few months back, but that was only for a few days because one of my teachers decided to be a prick and gave us a huge business analysis project that was due the Tuesday after we got back from break. Asshole.

Twenty minutes later, I slide behind the wheel of my SUV, since I took a leisurely last stroll through campus on my way out for the last time. I'm about to hook up my tunes when a text from my bestie/sister, Sasha, has me perking u p.

> Sasha: Hey, girl! We're about fifteen minutes out. Can't wait to see you!! :)

Even though we had talked last night, I was totally going to ignore the little happy dance I did in my driver's seat when I saw her message. Gosh, I'm such a dork sometimes but I miss my bestie.

> Levi: Can't wait to see you either, girl! In my car now and heading to the apartment. See you soon :)

I can't wait to see Sasha, Alexei, Travis, and Ethan again. All four of them finished their finals a few days ago, so they already moved back home. Sam isn't going to be moving out of his apartment until tomorrow when his brothers come to help him move back home to Minnesota, otherwise, we'd help him load up his truck. Out of the six of us, Sam and I are the only ones that were unlucky enough to have their last final start on Friday-frickin-afternoon at 4-frickin-pm.

Yay us, I thought as I rolled my eyes.

As I drive toward my apartment, I try to focus my fried out, but excited, brain on what all I have to do yet.

Pack my everyday essentials that I had purposefully left out.

Pack up my remaining things in the living room and kitchen.

Do a final wipe-down of the surfaces in the apartment.

Turn in the keys to my landlord.

On the bright side, at least the bulk of my belongings are already packed. I've already filled the holes where I had pictures and shelves hanging on the walls, so at least that tedious chore is done.

Ten minutes later, I pull into the apartment parking lot and as I'm putting my SUV in park, the hairs on the back of my neck stand up, washing away my excitement like a bucket of ice water. My fingers itch to grab a weapon.

I know how to shoot and throw knives with deadly precision. Plus, my dad, grandpa, and uncle had made sure I knew how to defend myself since I was a little girl. When I got older, they taught me how to shoot. But throwing knives, that was all my grandpa.

My gut is in knots and, on a lark, I send off a coded text to Sasha and Alexei.

> Levi: **Блин** [Bugger]! I forgot what time we're supposed to meet. Was it six o'clock?

Translation of our code: I'm getting major bad vibes and I only have six knives on me.

Russians sometimes use **блин** (which literally means pancakes) much like we use the word 'bugger' when we're in a situation where cussing isn't appropriate. Both Sasha and Alexei frequently use the term. However, I'm a person who will always tell it as it is and I never give a shit about where I am when I say it. And both Sasha and Alexei knew that. That's why we chose **блин** [bugger] as my code word when I felt like something was wrong or off. Something that was making me feel like I needed backup. ASAP.

The one time I ignored this feeling, things went bad. Like epic proportions bad. Ever since then, I've always trusted this feeling, and it hasn't proven me wrong.

Her reply is almost instantaneous.

> Sasha: **Да** [Yes]. Though we may be five minutes late or so. **Брат** [Brother] wants to play with us tonight so he brought a deck of cards. Says he'll clean house.

Translation: Understood and they'll be here in five minutes. Both her and Alexei are fully armed, and they'll head straight to my apartment on arrival.

Putting my car in park, I purposefully drop my phone by my feet and pull out the bag I have stowed away under my seat. Trying to not act too suspiciously, I carefully tuck away all the blades. I wish I had more blades or even my gun, but they're locked away inside the safe in my apartment.

As I get out of my SUV and grab my bag out of the backseat, I carefully look around, but nothing seems out of place and I don't see anyone lurking around. Walking up to my apartment, I try to act as natural as possible in case anyone's watching me. I also know Sam isn't back yet. I checked before leaving the lecture hall, but his head was still ducked down as he worked on his final. That means Sasha and Alexei are my closest backup. The closer I get to my door, the more my uneasiness and nerves grow.

Grabbing my keys out of my pocket, I freeze for a moment before forcing myself to unlock the door.

There are fresh scratch marks on the doorknob and around the strike plate.

Fuck! Why didn't I inspect the strike plate when I moved in to see if the apartment owners had replaced the short-ass screws that came with the strike plate with the recommended longer screws?

Taking a deep breath, I unlock it only to find Scott sitting on my couch, drinking a beer with a crowbar at his feet. I scowl at him, and my gaze quickly darts around the room, landing on the stack of boxes in the corner.

Shit. I hope he didn't mess with my stuff or take anything.

Thanks to my apartment's mostly open concept, I can tell there isn't anyone else in here unless they are hiding in my bedroom or bathroom down the short hallway.

My gaze lands on him again, and my stomach sinks when I see he's wearing a cut. The most dressed down I'd ever seen him in was a polo shirt and jeans. So, to see him in a t-shirt and jeans, even without the cut, is out of character. Taking a closer look at his cut, the road name 'Fang' is patched on one side and the title 'Enforcer' on the other. I never knew Scott was part of a motorcycle club. Or that he even had a motorcycle. Which club does he belong to?

Fuck, this isn't good. I have no idea if his club is one of the good ones or the ones that are into illegal shit. I'd been around bikers all my life in my parents' bar and grill since there is a motorcycle club in Forest Creek. Not to mention, my uncle is also part of said club. I know from him and my own history that not all clubs are on the straight and narrow like my uncle's club. Some other clubs dabble in drugs and guns. Others... others I pray I'd never cross paths with. Ever again.

I push those memories aside. I'm not going to let them distract me. Scott smirks at me as he takes another drink.

"What do you want, Scott? I told you last night, *repeatedly* I might add, that I didn't want to see you again. That we were through. Not to mention you broke into my apartment and are drinking my damn beer." I'm fucking pissed he broke in, but to add insult to injury, you don't mess with a Wisconsinite's beer.

Scowling again, I cross my arms and try to keep the partially opened door in my peripheral vision. I don't know if he has more men lurking somewhere where they can ambush me, but I also want Sasha and Alexei to be able to get in easily if this goes south. My fingers land on the knives tucked into the insides of my leather jacket, ready to grab them if need be.

The sneer he gives me, along with his dark chuckle, sends a chill down my spine as he pushes up off the couch. "We're done when I say we're done, Levi. No one walks away from me. You are mine, and the sooner you realize that, the better."

I huff and roll my eyes. Something that I know will piss him off to no end.

Yeah, that's wise, Levi. Piss off the guy who broke into your damn apartment.

"I'm not a possession, Scott. You don't own me. I broke up with you last night again, since you didn't get the message last weekend. You can't force me to be with you if I don't want to be with you."

His face darkens, and he takes a few more steps toward me. "You were mine since we first started going out. I will have you as mine, and you will come back with me to the clubhouse. Whether you want to or not. I gave you more than enough time and I will take what is mine, bitch. No one, not even your fucking little friends, can stop me."

My eyes widen slightly at his words, mad that he's rehashing the no sex thing, yet again, but also getting a little scared that he may actually try to rape me or hurt my friends. Yeah, I never gave into his pleas for sex and the reason being was that I was still a virgin. I'm not a prude or saving it for marriage, but I wanted the person I lost my virginity to, to be someone special to me. Not to just throw it away on a whim or a guy that didn't give me any sparks at all when we kissed.

With a growl, he lunges toward me, and I draw my blades as I dart back from him. As he darts back toward me, he draws his own blade. While, yes, I've trained in self-defense from an early age, especially after what happened when I was almost sixteen, but by no means am I a black belt or even close to it.

As minutes pass, he starts to become winded. He often bragged about his fighting skills, especially with how proficient he was with knives, but that fact that he's winded while I'm not gives me a little hope that I'll come out on top of this fight. I've already cut him about half a dozen times, and he's yet to land an attack on me.

A commotion from the hallway draws my gaze to the door. Rookie fucking mistake.

Out of the corner of my eye, I see Scott dart toward me before I can put distance between us. Pain sears across my ribs, and he curses as my blade sinks into his arm again. He jumps back out of my reach, looks toward the hallway and then back at me, his face red with anger.

"This isn't over, bitch! I'll have what's fucking mine. What should have been mine fucking years ago," he tells me before running out the door.

I should run after him, but all I can do is stare after him in confusion. What the hell did he mean by 'years ago'? I met him for the first time a couple of months ago.

Moments later, Sasha and Alexei burst through the door with blades drawn. It doesn't escape my notice that their blades are a little bloody. Our friends and two other guys are behind them.

I bite the inside of my cheek to keep from groaning.

Apparently, Dad sent a few of the Steel Archangel's along with Sasha and Alexei. They look familiar, but in the four years that I've been in college, I hadn't been home longer than a week whenever I visited. While I had visited my uncle's house at their compound, I hadn't gone to the clubhouse. I must be remembering them from our bar and grill.

Shrugging out of my jacket, I grit my teeth as pain sears across my ribs again. My scowl deepens when I notice how much blood has already soaked through my tank top.

Dammit... I really liked that jacket and shirt. Alexei's eyes widen when he sees the blood.

"**Кухня** [Kitchen]. **Сейчас**. [Now.]"

He heads straight toward the closet that holds my medical kit while Sasha follows me to the kitchen. I try my best to ignore the two Steel Archangel's, which is hard because they are both fucking hot, especially the one with black hair.

Travis and Ethan each give me a side hug on my way into the kitchen. They each grab a beer out of the fridge and plop down on my couch. In the years that they've known us, they know to not get in the way in situations like this. I'm not as close to them as I am with Sasha and Alexei, but I still consider them my family.

Sasha sanitizes the table while Alexei sets my kit nearby. After taking a shot of Jack that Sasha had already set out, I scrub my hands and arms. I always prefer a shot of Jack rather than numbing the area if the wound isn't too serious. Though some medical people would probably chide me on that, as I'm technically thinning out my blood with the alcohol.

A deep growl comes from the taller biker as I go about my business. "What the hell do you think you're doing?"

His deep, rough voice sends tingles through me that I try my damnedest to push down. I turn around and freeze for a moment as our gazes lock and I get a better look at him.

He has to be over six-foot tall as compared to my five-foot-nine frame. His black hair is about shoulder-length, sky-blue eyes that seem like they could freeze me in place, and he has a short, neatly trimmed beard and mustache. Not to mention heavily tattooed arms and muscles to die for. His shirt strains against his chest, and his jeans hug his thighs.

Wonder what his ass looks like in those jeans...

Where the hell did that thought come from? I sigh internally as I chastise myself. He may be sex on a stick, but he's still a biker. They don't do serious relationships. That's why I always keep bikers, except for my uncle, at arm's length regardless of if they show interest or not. No matter how my body reacts to this new guy, I won't act on it. Though that thought has my stomach twisting in knots, and I'm not sure why.

Jesus-fucking-Christ girl, you just broke up with someone. Get a grip!

While there were no sparks whatsoever with Scott, I should not be drooling internally over someone so soon. Taking a steadying breath, I stomp down my emotions before walking over to the table, which already has my gear spread out on it thanks to Alexei.

Both of the bikers take a few steps closer to me and Sasha pulls out her own blades, effectively stopping them both from advancing further. Out of the corner of my eye, I steal a glance at the taller guy's cut, and the knots in my stomach tighten when I see he also has an Enforcer patch. Would he be just as bad as Scott? Glancing at the other patch on his cut, it says his road name is Dragon, which is fitting since he damn near looks like he could be one if he were a dragon shifter. Not to mention those dragon tattoos down his arm. Dammit, I should probably cut back on my PNR books.

"What's it look like, asswipe? I'm going to stitch myself up. Us three have been sparring with knives and swords since we were old enough to hold them. As a result, all three of us know how to stitch up a wound."

"At least let Patch here do it. He's a trained ER nurse as well as an EMT," Muscles says, the name I decide to nickname Dragon with for the time being.

As he crosses his arms, my gaze is drawn to his stomach. Wonder what it would be like to run my tongue over the muscular stomach I know he has to have if his corded arms and tree trunk thighs are anything to go off of?

Dammit, Levi. Fucking focus!

My gaze flicks over to Patch, the guy Muscles gestured to. He's a very good-looking guy. A few inches shorter than Dragon, with dirty blond hair and green eyes. Like his friend, he's covered in tattoos and is also fairly muscular. I shake my head and finish my prep work.

"No can do, Muscles. I don't know either of you, so there's no way I'll let either of you near me to fix me up. I have no idea what you are doing here, but you were not invited. Back. The. Fuck. Off. I'll deal with you after I'm stitched up. In the meantime, shut the fuck up so I can focus."

Muscles, i.e. Dragon, narrows his eyes at me, and his jaw ticks like he wants to argue more with me. However, with a quick glance down at my wound, he deflates a bit, and when his gaze locks with mine, his eyes almost seem softer, and I can't place the look that comes over him. He opens his mouth to say something, but Patch beats him to it.

"Fine, but will you at least let us monitor you while you stitch yourself up? Also, I'd like to look over your stitchwork afterward to make sure everything is good. I swear I am a nurse at the hospital in Forest Creek and the medic for the Steel Archangel's MC."

Narrowing my eyes at them, I quickly debate what I should do. What I really want to do is kick them out, but I need to tend my wound. Deciding to concede just a little, I square my shoulders, grab another knife from my limited armory hidden on my body, and point it at the two jackasses. A woman has to make sure her point, no pun intended, is made. I want to make sure it's clear that no man will be making decisions for me. Ever.

"Fine, but do not talk while I am doing this, and yes, you can inspect the stitches after the fact. Do not interfere with what we do, as us three have a well-oiled process we follow. Is that understood?"

They both give curt nods, and with a nod of my own, I sheath my knife and whip my ruined tank top off. Thankfully, I'm at least in a sports bra today so the ladies are mostly covered, though a lot of my cleavage is unfortunately on display.

Dragon inhales sharply, and I hear him growl as he shoots a warning look at Patch and Alexei before moving to block Travis and Ethan's view. I roll my eyes at his alpha possessive asshole behavior. He doesn't dictate who I can be around. He also has no idea what Alexei means to me.

With Sasha and Alexei already scrubbed up, they get out the mirror and cleaning supplies while I inspect the depth and length of the cut. I breathe a sigh of relief that I had on an older leather jacket which took the brunt of the attack. The cut isn't very deep, but it's about three inches long.

I get to work cleaning and disinfecting my wound while they get out the rest of my supplies and prep the needle. When I'm ready, I take the needle from Alexei while also not missing how both biker's gazes track my every movement. Dragon, once again, inhales sharply as I start my stitches, and I chuckle as I work.

"Relax, Muscles. It's not a deep cut, so this won't take but a few minutes. Either chill out or get out."

Out of the corner of my eye, I see him shoot Patch a look who nods and his shoulders relax a bit as they both turn back to watch me work.

True to my word, I have the stitches finished in a few minutes and clean the remaining blood. Looking over at Patch, I tilt my head in his direction to let him know I'm finished. He's by my side in an instant, but quickly gives me a smile.

"Nice work, Levi. However, I could tell from back there that it was fine, but I didn't think Dragon would let it slide if I didn't come over and inspect it."

He winks at me, and I chuckle when Dragon growls at him as he shoots Patch a dark look. Patch smirks back at Dragon and turns to me.

"Now, if you could please bandage it up, we'll get to moving things for you so that you don't have to lift anything. If there's something heavy that needs packing, just let us know."

I huff and roll my eyes. I know I can't lift anything heavy for a bit while this heals, but it still chafes me that he's ordering me around.

"Fine, but can you please tell me why you're both here? I knew Sasha, Alexei, Ethan, and Travis were coming. But why you two and why *patched* members from Steel Archangel's? Figured you would have sent Prospects."

"Not sure, Levi. We were about to leave when **Папа** [Dad] insisted they come with us. He wouldn't tell us why either," Alexei replies as he stands protectively nearby, scowling at Dragon.

Okay, then.

Wait a minute.

Why's he only scowling at Dragon and not Patch? Fuck, do they know about last night? No, my bestie probably only told Alexei. Maybe.

"That's mostly club business, so we can't tell you much. What we can tell you is that the club has received threats lately. Since your family's close to the club, your dad asked if someone would accompany all of you as added protection, just in case," Dragon tells me.

"Great. So in other words, you're our babysitters. One would think with our backgrounds, Dad wouldn't ask for help from the club." I roll my eyes as I get up from the table. I know I'm being bitchy, but I hate it whenever Dad pulls shit like this.

"Yeah, and look where that got you. A new scar to add to your collection."

My body tenses at Dragon's words, and before he even finishes his sentence, a heavy *thud, thud, thud* sounds out as knives from Sasha, Alexei, and myself are now embedded in the wall around Dragon's head. He stands there, stunned, his gaze locked with mine. Patch raises his hands and smirks at Dragon before backing up slightly.

Travis' and Ethan's dark chuckles and the sound of their beer bottles clinking together from the living room have both bikers looking nervous and a bit more on edge. Travis and Ethan know I'm fucking pissed, and someone's going to pay.

I pull another knife from my pouch tucked into the back of my jeans, and without breaking my gaze, step toward Muscles as I point my blade at him.

"The only reason Scott got the drop on me was because of a commotion in the hallway. I know how Sasha and Alexei operate. Their first instinct in a scenario like this would have been to slice first, ask questions later. If they were still breathing, that is. That's my MO as well. So, I'm going to guess you went all macho and made a ruckus in the hallway, which diverted my attention from Scott and led to me being hurt. How warm am I, Muscles?"

Chapter 2
Dragon

Fᴜᴄᴋ, sʜᴇ's ʀɪɢʜᴛ ᴏɴ the money with her assessment.

Well, mostly.

And the fact that she's standing here head-to-toe with me, not backing down, just makes my dick even harder than it already was.

It's been a long time since I've seen Levi, and I'm glad she hasn't lost her sassiness or backbone of steel. Last time I saw her, she was already a knock-out but had just turned eighteen and was about to head off to college. I'd kept a distance, but it was difficult. Especially whenever I heard she was back in town for a visit.

However, the older version of Levi standing in front of me blows my mind with how sexy she is now. It's hard not to stare at her gorgeous body that has *definitely* filled out. Especially in the sports bra and jeans that mold to her every fucking curve. I feel like the wind's been knocked out of me every time I look at her.

Instead of the usual rail thin body type that society thinks should be the norm for women, she has meat on her bones, and I wouldn't have to worry about breaking her when I fuck her. She has a large chest and a curvy hourglass waist that leads to her perfect, juicy ass that just begs to be held. Her stomach is soft with a bit of a pouch, which adds even more appeal. My woman enjoys her food.

She's probably a little over five and a half feet tall. Her curly red hair reaches down to her waist, and her bright green eyes are currently as sharp and hard as the blade she's pointing at me. I shake myself internally and refocus on her question.

"Actually, these two did their thing, but they missed the one coming at them from behind. It was with that one that the scuffle broke out, and that's when we were noisier than we wanted to be."

Levi's gaze flicks over to Sasha and Alexei, and with sheepish nods from them, she finally backs down and sheathes her blade.

"Fine. Let's get things done and get out of here. I never knew Scott was in an MC, but since his cut said Enforcer on it, I'd like to finish up quickly before they all descend on us."

At her words, Patch's gaze locks with mine. Shit, it's like we suspected.

"What else did his patches say?" he asks.

She gives Patch and me a curious look but still answers him. "Fang and Enforcer was what I could see. I didn't catch the club name on the back."

I frown. The only Enforcer I know close to these parts named Fang is from the Black Plague MC and they're over four hours away. What are they doing here? I'll have to see if Smoke can tap into the camera's here. Maybe he can get a clearer picture of him and his cut.

As I come out of my thoughts, I notice Levi scowling at me, and with that, I realize I hadn't moved from my spot, but the others had.

"Sorry, Levi, was just trying to figure out which club he could be with. And don't worry about not catching the club name. You had more important things to worry about with your wound."

The look she gives me is a combination of being startled and also wariness. Like she isn't sure she should trust me and dammit, that thought has me more twisted up than I'll ever admit to anyone. Still, she graces me with a small but tight smile right as fabric is thrown in her face.

"Get that on before I start my **брат** [brother] speech on this one."

I turn toward Alexei. His accent seems thicker than before and sounds a bit like it might be Russian. He walks up in between me and Levi as he glares at me. Leveling a glare of my own at him, I stare him down. Little fucker needs to know we will not be pushed around.

I will not be pushed around.

Especially by him.

I may be a bit softer with Levi, but she's the only one who will get that treatment. Although, I do respect him for standing up for her.

Both of us are soon forced to break eye contact when Levi shoves us apart. The glare she sends Alexei's way makes him pale slightly. The action makes my need for her increase. Fuck, this woman is going to be my undoing.

"Knock it off, you neanderthals! Alexei, you know I love you **брат** [brother], but we need to get done and out of here. Now scoot that ass of yours and start packing what's left with Sasha."

Hearing her say that she loves him makes my stomach twist in knots and a surge of jealousy shoots through me. Who is he to her?

She pivots on her heel back toward me and, unfortunately for her at the moment, the glare she gives me has the opposite effect. Instead of scaring me, I smirk at her. Her sassy attitude just turns me on even more, and my jeans are feeling a lot more uncomfortable. Any woman who dares stand up to me earns my attention and focus. Fuck, she's fucking perfect for me.

Her eyes widen a bit, and her breath hitches as she realizes what had just happened before her eyes narrow again.

"And you. Since my unofficial nickname for you is Muscles, get to carrying things down with Patch, Travis, and Ethan. Either put them in the truck or the black SUV parked in spot ten with the Harley emblem on the back window."

She tosses me some keys before marching off toward the bedroom where Sasha went a few minutes ago. Alexei scowls at me again, and it darkens when he sees me staring at Levi's ass as she walks away.

He seems about ready to say something, but what sounds like a foreign slew of curse words coming from the bedroom has him biting his tongue, though he seems to be fighting back a grin. Instead, he picks up a few boxes and heads out into the hallway.

I pocket Levi's keys, and as I'm picking up a couple boxes of my own, I notice Travis and Ethan trying to contain their grins as well. With another look toward the bedroom Levi's in, I wonder which one of them had been talking and what language they were speaking in. The fact that it could have been Levi and that it might have been a rant about me has my gut in a twist yet again.

Pushing that thought aside, I head out into the hallway and exit outside. As I set the boxes down in the bed of the truck, I realize I've never gotten this worked up by a woman before. Not even in my past relationships, though there were only a few since the MC life isn't for everyone.

I hear Patch chuckling behind me and quickly push the boxes forward toward the front of the truck bed. Fuck.

"Fuck, man, you're already in over your head with that one, aren't you?"

I turn on my heel and glare at him as my jaw clenches. Fucker just grins at me. "What the fuck you goin' on about?"

"She's hot as fuck and wields a blade just as good as you. Maybe even better. Not to mention she has to be seasoned with what I saw from her arms, torso, and back. No wonder you're interested."

Just the thought of all the scars covering her has my stomach in knots again. Even though I won't admit it aloud, it tore me up when I saw her bleeding because of that fucking bastard. The surge of protectiveness toward her that's coursing through me startles me even further.

Patch slaps me on the shoulder, and I turn back toward him.

"Relax, brother. She can take care of herself from the looks of it. I bet whoever gave her those scars are either those two in there or are six feet under."

I nod and hope he's right. However, I don't want those two hurting her either. They seem important to her for some reason. More so than the other two guys that came up with them.

"Let's just get this done and on the road. She's right about one thing. We need to be out of here before Fang's crew gets here. Let's just hope that it isn't who we think it is."

Patch's face grows serious, and we both quickly head back upstairs.

With both Sasha and Levi packing the few remaining things, the five of us guys make quick work of carrying the boxes downstairs while Levi supervises, since she can't carry anything. More than once, though, I catch her eyeing the wall where she stood up to me earlier.

As I grab another box, I hear her mutter under her breath about her deposit. It's then that it clicks that their marks from when all three simultaneously threw knives at me might bar her from getting her money back.

While it was hot as fuck seeing her throw a blade and purposefully missing, hopefully anyway, I don't want her to lose out on her deposit because of me and my big ass mouth. Thankfully, I'd rented an apartment while we were expanding the clubhouse years ago, since our house wasn't finished yet, and had brought something along just in case Levi didn't have any.

If it were any other woman, I'd let them fend for themselves in this type of situation, but Levi's not just any woman. Nor would I have offered to do this for any other woman—I'd probably have sent Prospects with most likely one patched brother who wasn't an officer.

She's the reason why I volunteered to be the one to accompany Patch on this trip. As the club's Enforcer, I'm deadly as fuck, and even though Patch is our medic, he's no slouch in the fighting department either. Between the two of us, I figured we'd have things covered if something went south. At least that's what I told myself, anyway. Though, the knowing smirk Thor gave me after I'd volunteered was enough to tell me he knew the real reason why I'd volunteered.

After setting the boxes in the truck, I grab the tube from my saddlebags. Back in the apartment, I head over to the wall, noticing that Levi's making her rounds through the other rooms and areas, double checking that she didn't leave anything behind. Pulling out my own knife, I widen the holes slightly and use the flashlight on my phone to peek through them. Not seeing any electrical wires, I breathe a sigh of relief and get to work filling the holes with spackle. After a few moments, I hear a small gasp behind me.

Turning around, I bite back a groan at seeing her staring at me, her jaw dropped in shock. Fuck, I really don't need to be thinking about how my dick would look sliding between those plump, pink lips of hers.

"Didn't want you to lose out on your deposit because of me being a jackass."

She gives me a hesitant smile that makes my chest warm. "Thanks, Dragon. I appreciate it."

I give her a chin lift and get back to work. She heads toward the living room, but pauses and looks back at me, her face serious and haunted.

"For the record, they aren't a collection. A few are from us three practicing, but the vast majority are from me surviving something terrible that happened in my past."

The emotions that flit across her face have my chest tightening and I want to pull her into my arms, but at the moment, I don't think she'd accept it. Instead, I give a curt nod as my mind tries to go through past events in town that could pinpoint what happened to her, but I come up blank.

"I'm sorry, Levi. I was an asshole and shouldn't have said that."

Her lips quirk up a bit as she tilts her head, and I know what's coming. "Wait, is the big, bad Enforcer biker apologizing to little 'ol me?"

I can't help the grin the stretches across my face, happy to have at least lightened the dark cloud that was hanging over her, even if it was only for a little bit.

"Don't get used to it, Spitfire. It's probably the only time you'll hear me say it."

She smiles fully at that, and damn if her smile isn't a shot straight to my dick. Just as she opens her mouth to say something, Sasha calls out to her from the bedroom. With a small smile to me, she turns on her heel. My eyes track her perfect ass as she heads toward her bedroom, and I have to bite my cheek from groaning out loud. Fuck, this is turning into a battle of willpower.

As I turn back toward the wall, I try to discreetly adjust myself and start filling the holes with spackle again. Damn, this hard-on better go down before we leave. Riding with a hard-on is not comfortable. Patch smirks at me as if he knows my issue.

"Fucker," I mutter, and flip him off. He laughs before carrying another box down to the SUV.

After a few minutes, the holes are filled with spackle, and I walk around, checking the other walls while I'm at it. Not finding anything else in need of repair, and noticing that she's already patched a few holes herself, I head into the kitchen and wash my hands. As I dry my hands, I glance around the living room, noticing there's only one box left. Pocketing the spackle, I grab the box and head down.

I'd seen Alexei grab a pile of ratchet straps from Roy's truck this morning, so I grab them out of their truck and with Patch's help, we both start securing everything in the truck bed. A few minutes later, we have everything secure and are waiting for the others.

As I lean against the truck, my mind goes back to Fang. What does he want with Levi? Why was he so insistent she go with him? I mean, besides the fact that she's fucking gorgeous. Is she part of the reason why our club's been getting threats lately?

Shaking my head, I cross my arms and wonder what the fuck is taking the girls so long. Alexei, Travis, and Ethan are chatting over by Levi's SUV. Alexei shrugs on a leather jacket as Ethan slides into the driver's seat of the SUV while Travis gets into his truck.

"Where are they?" I grumble. We need to get on the road. Patch chuckles at my annoyance, and I turn my attention toward Alexei, who's walking toward us.

"Levi went to turn in her keys. Sasha went with her to say goodbye as well. We already turned in our keys a few days ago when our classes were over."

I frown, wanting to get back on the road in case Fang's crew is already on their way. I also make note that his accent isn't as strong as it was earlier when he was mad.

Nodding toward Ethan and Travis, I turn back to him. "Doesn't Levi want to drive herself? I mean, you guys all came in the same truck."

Alexei smirks at me in response. "Oh, she'll be driving all right. Just not her SUV."

His grin grows as Patch and I share a confused look. He pulls out his phone and hands it to me. "Here, program in your numbers. I can give you the girl's numbers, too."

Despite my confusion, I give him my number and program their numbers into my phone. Just then, the office door opens, and laughter pours out of the building.

"Will do, Mrs. Adams. Tell your husband goodbye for us. Take care!" Levi calls out before she closes the door after them.

Fuck me.

She looks even hotter than she did earlier.

Levi has on a tighter leather jacket than before and leather riding boots. She still has on her skintight jeans and the tank top she's now wearing hugs her curvy figure. Her hair's pulled back into a long braid, and she has a backpack slung over her shoulder.

Patch chuckles next to me, and I realize I'd been staring at her. With a scowl, I contemplate smacking the asshole, but instead, I turn my attention back to Levi and notice Alexei walking up to her and Sasha. It's then that I realize they're all dressed similarly, and Sasha has her hair braided as well.

Levi turns toward Travis and Ethan and gives them a chin lift. "Usual formation, gents. Drive safe."

They both give her a two-finger salute, and she nods.

She turns back toward Sasha and Alexei, and they lean forward so that their foreheads touch. They murmur words that almost sound like Russian again. I stare at them in confusion about what they are doing and saying. For fuck's sake, we need to get on the road.

As they pull apart, I recognize one of the things they say as 'до свидания' [goodbye]. One of two Russian words that I know. The other being, 'да' [da].

Then, my jaw drops as they head over to three bikes in the back of the parking lot that I'd seen when we pulled in, but paid no attention to. Patch laughs next to me as he claps my shoulder, but I ignore him and the desire to punch him. Again. Should have named him fucking Chuckles instead of Patch.

Sasha laughs at something that was said and Levi freezes before her cheeks turn a little pink and her gaze flicks toward me. I grin at her and her cheeks turn a darker shade of pink. Damn, does it feel good that I can make her blush. Levi says something back to Sasha, which has her scowling again. Her scowl has both Sasha and Alexei laughing in response as they pocket their phones and zip up their jackets. He must have shared our numbers with the girls.

"Alright, enough kidding around. Let's head out." Levi gives us a chin lift, and with that, we head over to our bikes. Thankfully, both Patch and I brought our full-face helmets today so we could use the Bluetooth option if need be.

Assuming we're going to take the same formation as before, with us riding in front of the SUV with Travis in the rear, I start up my girl and pull forward a bit to wait for the trio to take the lead.

Surprisingly, Alexei pulls out first, then Sasha, and finally Levi. With the way they're lined up and staggered, Sasha's the most inexperienced rider it seems, and with Levi being in the back, she's an experienced rider who also knows at least some basic bike repairs.

Fuck.

I have to find some way to make Levi mine, cause there's no way in hell another brother is going to have her as his woman. With a groan, I adjust myself, yet again, before heading out.

Chapter 3
Levi

I GRIN AS I take in Dragon's shocked face as he stares at me on my bike. Then he smirks, and I have to bite back a groan when he straddles his own bike.

Fuck, the man is even sexier than before and is definitely going to fuel a lot of late-night fantasies with my BOB. Thankfully, I already had my toys packed before the others came to help me finish up today. I don't think I'd ever be able to face Dragon again if he had found my toys.

Shaking my head to clear my thoughts, I pull out after Sasha and let the feel of the cool spring air wash over me. It's been a while since I've gone on a long ride, and I'm definitely looking forward to some wind therapy. I normally don't wear a full face-mask helmet, just a skull cap with some sunglasses. However, with this long of a ride, and with how many people are in the group, we all wanted to be able to use Bluetooth if needed.

As we ride, I can't help but steal quick glances at Dragon in my mirrors. He shocked me earlier when he apologized and fixed my walls. I didn't expect either from him. Especially because of his rank within the MC.

While I've had my fair share of exposure to bikers, whether it was the Steel Archangel's or from clubs that were either visiting or passing through Forest Creek. I'd seen a fair amount of bikers that were chauvinistic assholes often surrounded by club bunnies who were meant to service their needs. From what I'd heard as I waited tables from some of the visiting clubs, a few of them had Old Ladies and yet they would still hook up with the bunnies. That I know of, there aren't any Old Ladies yet in the Steel Archangel's MC and I don't know them well enough for if they'd ever cheat on their Old Ladies when, or it, they found one.

That isn't what I want.

I want a man who'll have my back, be faithful to me, support my dreams, and maybe someday, have a family with. Also, he'd be someone who wouldn't be put off by my own streak of independence and ability to defend myself. As much as my body and heart want to think Dragon could be different, I doubt he'd be all of that with me. Not to mention he probably doesn't want to be tied down.

The uneasiness that settles in my gut surprises me, along with the swirl of jealousy at the thought of how many bunnies or other women Dragon has been with. Or would be with in the future. I shove those thoughts aside and try to let the road and the wind calm me.

After driving for a few hours, we pull off at a diner with an attached gas station. Whenever we make the trip back home, we always stop to eat here.

When I'm done filling up the tank, I pull up to the diner and crab walk my bike into a spot. Surprisingly, Dragon pulls up to my left and parks his bike next to mine.

Swinging my leg over, I take off my helmet and grab my backpack out of my saddlebags. Dragon dismounts, but as soon as his helmet comes off, I have to resist the urge to run my fingers through his long hair. His piercing blue eyes pin me to the spot, and from the look he gives me, it feels like he can see right through me.

"How long you been ridin', Spitfire?"

Damn, that nickname coming off his lips sends a jolt through me. This man has me soaking wet with just a look. I'm in trouble. Big time. His smirk has me wondering if he can sense my dilemma. I shake myself internally; and try, yet again, to regain control of my traitorous body.

"Had a dirt bike since I was ten and got a motorcycle as soon as I could. Plus, I've ridden with my dad, uncle, grandpa, and some other family for as long as I can remember."

His eyes widen in surprise before he smiles and damn, does my pussy clench in response.

Down, girl.

"Come on, let's get some grub."

I nod and move to follow the others into the diner. He steps up behind me and when his hand lands on the small of my back, tingles shoot through me. I fight to keep a blush off my cheeks, but judging by the wink Sasha gives me, I'm pretty sure I've failed miserably.

We all pile into a couple of booths next to each other and damn it all to hell, Dragon slides in next to me. Sasha smirks at me while Alexei eyes Dragon warily as we place our drink orders and take the menus from the server.

Dragon clears his throat and looks around at us. "How long have you guys known each other?"

"Since before preschool. Our family had recently moved to the area, and we three hit it off almost instantly. Been inseparable ever since," Sasha tells him.

Sasha, Alexei, and I were definitely inseparable growing up. They're twins and their family moved from Russia to Forest Creek when they were three. After a car accident killed their parents in the eighth grade, they ended up in the foster system. My parents tried to become foster parents so they could keep them close, but before they were qualified, Sasha and Alexei were already placed in a home.

While we were happy that they were still in town and nearby, their foster parents were only about the money. They barely did what they needed to do to provide for the twins. They weren't abusive, thankfully, just assholes.

Sasha and Alexei were frequently over at our house to escape from them, and it never bothered my parents. They were there so much that they had their own rooms. Ever since then, we'd basically been adopted siblings in all contexts but legally. When we were in high school, Travis and Ethan moved into town, instantly clicking with us, and were frequently at our house as well.

"Agreed. We're so close that we consider each other siblings. Even Dad calls them his kids, though they aren't his legally or by blood."

Dragon's gaze flicks between her and Alexei. "Are you two brother and sister?"

They both nod in response.

"Unfortunately, been saddled with this one since conception. Been a thorn in my side ever since," Alexei said as he dodges a head swat from Sasha.

"Aya, you're lucky I love you, **брат** [brother]."

I chuckle at their antics, but Dragon looked slightly confused.

"...Russian?"

"**Да** [Yes], we rarely speak it since mainly Levi and Roy understand. But if it's just us four, we'll sometimes slip into it," Alexei replies.

Sasha nods in agreement before she narrows her eyes and points her finger at Dragon. If we weren't in a restaurant, I'm sure she would have used a blade rather than her finger. "However, you piss any of us off enough, you most likely will have Russian rant directed at you. Possibly even knives. Fair warning. Also, only warning you get. **Понимаешь** [Understand]?"

I bite my lip to keep from chuckling, even though I can hear Travis and Ethan laughing quietly behind me. Her accent had thickened, and whenever that happens, she slips a bit more into her broken English. Same with Alexei. Honestly, I love when their Russian comes out. That usually happens whenever they're emotional, but then again, I also love to speak Russian almost as much as they do.

"Fair enough," Dragon says, though he does seem slightly worried.

I smile at the twins and open the menu, even though I already know what I want. We've been here often enough that I really don't need to look, but I need something else to focus on instead of the heat coming off of Dragon. Also, it's not helping that his leg is damn near touching mine, which makes it extremely hard to focus.

A few minutes later, the server brings us our drinks and we place our orders. My usual is their house burger with fries. It's drool-worthy good.

While we wait for our food, we chat, and gradually, I can see Alexei becoming more relaxed around Dragon, which surprises me. And he isn't the only one.

Everything's going well, all things considered, until Dragon puts his arm behind me on the back of the booth and my body immediately tenses up. I hate when guys do that unless we're dating. Even then, I found it barely tolerable. I shift a bit more to the left and forward as I try to put more distance between us.

Dragon seems oblivious to my discomfort, but Sasha picks up on it immediately. She's about to say something, but I subtly shake my head. I don't want an argument to possibly happen and have things get out of hand in here since I don't know Dragon very well. The owners are already leery of bikers, and I really don't want to be the reason behind bikers, in general, being banned from the restaurant.

Thankfully, our food comes a few minutes later, and he moves his arm. My body relaxes and out of the corner of my eye, I notice a frown on his face as he glances at me but says nothing.

We tuck into our food and as the first bite of the burger hits my tongue, I moan at how good it is. It's like an orgasm for your mouth. A mouthgasm. Haha... Yeah, I'm a dork.

As I open my eyes, the twins are trying to keep from laughing and Dragon has me pinned with a heated stare.

I look between them, confused. "What? Their burgers are awesome. You don't like me expressing how happy my tastebuds are, then either don't listen or go sit somewhere else," I say as I wave them off and take another bite of my burger, purposefully moaning again.

The twins' shoulders shake with their silent laughter whereas Dragon makes a soft, weird, almost strangled sound. I glance at him in confusion again. What the hell is his problem? He shifts in his seat and that's when I realize what his problem is. Oh... I take another bite of my burger to hide the grin on my face. Gonna suck for him when he gets back on his bike.

However, the thought that I cause the same reactions in him that he does to me makes my chest warm and my cheeks burn. Though on the flip side, that thought also scares the shit out of me, since I know he could never be mine. I'm not a hit-it-and-quit-it kind of girl.

After everyone finishes their meal, pays, and has a bathroom break, we head back out to our bikes. As we near our bikes, some other bikers roll up and my gut is instantly in knots as the hairs on the back of my neck stand up. They're eyeing our group closely and make no attempt to hide the fact that they're basically eye fucking Sasha and me.

"**Блин** [Bugger]," I curse under my breath, and Sasha looks at me before her eyes widen and she turns to look closer at the other group. She nudges Alexei and both of them give me a chin lift.

If you weren't looking for it, you wouldn't have noticed us three getting ready for a potential fight. Jackets remain unzipped to access knives if need be. Hands are lowered and bodies loosen up, ready to respond. Eyes instantly harden and sharpen.

Dragon must have sensed a change in us. His gaze flicks toward us and widens slightly before he looks more closely at the newcomers. With a subtle chin lift to signal he notices it too, he quickly glances at Patch and some sort of similar silent communication takes place between them. The newcomers stop when they see Sasha and me approaching our own bikes; hers being the one on the other side of mine.

"What the hell is the world coming to that bitches ride their own sleds amongst bikers?"

Sasha and I freeze momentarily before we step toward the asshole. Without even looking at her, I know she has the same murderous look as I do.

"Ones who think for themselves and aren't owned by anyone," I grind out as my body vibrates with anger. This is one of the main reasons I keep bikers at arm's length. I hate the way some of them treat women.

"Just because we're women doesn't mean we're supposed to solely warm beds and sate the needs of men," Sasha spits out.

The three of them laugh and the one who spoke actually adjusts himself as he licks his lips and eyes us hungrily. My lip curls in disgust as I look them over closer, as well as looking for any possible weapons.

All three of them are old enough to be our fathers and definitely nothing to write home about. They're greasy, dirty, and seem slimy as fuck. None of them are wearing a cut, but that doesn't mean anything. They could belong to a club and took them off while riding through another club's territory out of respect or wore something that said they had permission to pass through their territory. Though, I doubt these three asswipes know anything about respect, especially with the way they're treating us. Both Dragon and Patch had previously said their

President called the other clubs and got permission to wear their cuts as they passed through.

"Feisty. Just how we like them. Seems to me like you two need to be taken down a few pegs and broken in," the lead asswipe sneers as he once again grabs himself.

Instantly my fist flies to his nose, and I smirk when I hear the satisfying crunch of bone. Blood pours out of his nose and his buddies step forward but stop suddenly, their scowls deepening.

Hands wrap around my waist, and I'm pulled back into a hard chest. Out of habit, I step slightly forward, making it easier to move if things go south. Dragon's left hand slightly squeezes my left hip twice, though I don't think it's because he's mad at me as his grip still remains loose but doesn't move from my hip.

Out of the corner of my eye, I see Alexei pulling Sasha back as well. Gritting my teeth, I see why. Fucking cops have pulled up and are eyeing our group.

Dragon pulls me flush against him. At first, I think he's mad that I moved away slightly until he leans down and I can feel his breath on my ear. A shiver rolls through me before I can stop it, and I feel my skin break out into goosebumps.

"Easy there, Spitfire. Much as I'd love to see you wail on these guys and teach them a lesson, I don't want to be bailing you two out of the slammer."

To emphasize his words, he shifts so that my ass rubs against the bulge in his jeans. Damn, I have to bite my tongue to hide my surprise. Much like I guessed, he's big, and my body hums with need. But fuck am I unhappy about not being able to beat down on these jackasses.

"It'd be in your best interest to learn how to respect women," Alexei says, his voice cold and icy. His hand tightens around Sasha's shoulder. I'm sure she's just as livid as I am that we can't do more.

"Fucking bitch! You need to teach your woman her rightful place. On her back with her legs spread. Just like a split-tail should be." The guy spits blood on the cement and Dragon's hands grip my waist tighter.

"Nah, I like her just the way she is. She's perfect."

My cheeks warm at his words, but my mind reels with my insecurities and the past. I also don't miss that he didn't correct him when the guy said I was his woman.

"And the only reason why I'm not letting her pummel your ass into oblivion is because of our audience. As he said, learn the correct way to treat a woman. Next time, I won't save your ass."

With that, Dragon turns and steers me back toward my bike, his hand still wrapped around my waist. I peek over my shoulder and see the fucktards head into the gas station. I hate showing my back to an enemy.

"Fuck, I need a target or to work out or something," I say through gritted teeth, my body still shaking in anger.

"I know, Spitfire, but for now, let's just focus on getting back home safely, and then you can take out your frustrations however you need to."

I nod and it's then that I notice he's been rubbing my arms in a soothing motion. Being in his arms feels safe. Something that's uncommon for me unless I really know the person. Surprisingly, a lot of the tension in my body starts to fade as he continues to rub my arms. He must be able to sense when I'm in a better headspace because he leans forward and kisses my forehead. Fuck, this man is going to be my undoing.

"Come on, Spitfire. Get that sexy ass on your bike and let's roll," he says as he playfully taps my hip.

I can't help the chuckle that escapes, though even I can tell it's strained. Then my cheeks start to heat when I realize he just called me sexy.

Shaking myself internally, I grab my helmet and put it on. Throwing my leg over my baby, I start her up and we're soon on the road again. We only have a little under two hours left to ride and then I can soak in my tub at Dad's place.

As the scenery flies past, I think more and more of the bar and grill. I'm looking forward to running it with Dad and eventually taking over for him when he decides to retire. Both Sasha and Alexei already have jobs lined up at the tattoo parlor where they'd interned the last couple of summers, so they're set as well. Plus, Travis and Ethan landed jobs at the local construction company. For now, my plan is to stay at Dad's house, but my mind wanders to where I could get a place to live in the area when a call interrupts my thoughts.

"Hey, Spitfire."

Immediately, I know something's wrong as Dragon's voice is strained and tight instead of his usual smooth and deep voice. My gaze darts to my mirror and I notice his previously relaxed riding posture has been replaced with one that's coiled and ready to react to danger at a moment's notice. He's seriously on edge and his head is swiveling more than before to watch our surroundings more closely.

"What's wrong?"

A strained chuckle comes across the line and my gut tightens. *"Some of my brothers are going to be meeting us in a few minutes to ride with us the rest of the way back. I need to take all of you to the clubhouse."*

I grit my teeth at the thought of going to the clubhouse. It's Friday. I don't want to be around club bunnies. *"Why the fuck do we need to go to the clubhouse? And don't give me that fucking 'it's club business' line because if you do, you and Patch might as well go ahead to meet up with your brothers by yourself."*

He sighs and I can tell he's debating on whether to tell me the truth or not. *"I can't tell you the details right now. It's a conversation that all of you need to hear. Not to mention not a good one to discuss while most of us are on bikes."*

"Dragon..." My jaw's starting to hurt from grinding my teeth together as I somehow manage to keep from pulling over right now and demanding that he explain.

He sighs again. *"There's been a threat... against you specifically. And a warning for the twins."*

Fuck, fuck, fuckity, fuck, fuck, fuck! If Scott is behind this, I am going to enjoy skinning the bastard. Alive.

"Talk to me, Spitfire."

"We'll go to the clubhouse. For now. But you better keep me involved, Dragon. If there's anything pertaining to my safety or the twins' safety, we need to know. None of this 'club business' bullshit."

"I'll do what I can, but it will be up to my brother ultimately. Your dad is already there."

"Your brother?"

"Yeah, he's the Pres."

"Fuck my life," I mutter to myself, but judging by the sigh I hear, he heard it. *"I'm gonna let the others know the change in plans. I can already hear the rumble of*

more bikes in the distance, and I want them to know before they get here. Especially Alexei, since he's in the lead."

"Sounds good. And just so you know, we'll be going straight to mine and my brother's house on the compound instead of the clubhouse. No reason to have this conversation around loose ears."

Well, at least that's one worry off my shoulders. *"Got it."*

His head bobs in my mirror before he hangs up without saying goodbye, and I quickly dial up the group.

"FYI, more Steel Archangel's will join us in a bit for the remainder of our trip. We won't be heading home, but rather to their clubhouse. Or more precisely, the President's house, which is on the compound."

"What the fuck for?" Sasha bites out.

"There's been a recent threat... against me. And a warning for Alexei and Sasha."

Silence meets my ears, but I can practically see the fumes rolling off the twins.

"Fine, but I don't like this," Alexei grits out.

"I don't either, but we need to know what they know." At least, they better tell us everything. I bite my tongue to keep from adding that bit in.

"Do you think they'll tell you? You know how they are with club business," Travis says, and I sigh.

"I said something similar to Dragon when I demanded at least we three are kept in the loop since it's regarding our safety. He said he'd try, but it's ultimately up to his brother."

"Who's his brother?" Ethan asks.

"... The President."

"Fuck," Sasha mutters.

"Yeah. Let's go along with it for now and later we'll make a more informed decision. Okay?" Ethan replies and I see Sasha and Alexei bob their head in front of me.

A chorus of yeah's and да's [yes] ring out before I sign off.

Minutes later, I notice ten other bikers in the distance off to the side of the road waiting for us. As we approach, five pull out in front of us, and I assume the other five will take up the rear. Gritting my teeth, I stew as we ride the last half hour of the trip. Fuck, if this shit keeps up, I'll probably end up cracking all my teeth.

Driving down the road, there are woods to my right and a long cinderblock wall on my left. While I remember hearing a rumor that after an issue at the clubhouse a few years back, they put up a cinderblock wall for extra protection; I didn't think it went this far back from the entrance.

The speed of the bikers in front of our group slows, so we must be getting closer to the gate. After pulling into the compound, they lead us along a winding road. This is definitely bigger than I remember. Either that or they've cleared some land recently.

As we pass the clubhouse, we get a lot of stares from the few non-club members and the club bunnies. Guess only the members knew we were coming. I also don't miss the glares and interested looks Sasha and I get when they realize we're women.

At the thought of the bunnies, I scowl. Fucking patch-chasing bitches. I shake my head and focus on where we're heading, in case we need to get out of here quickly.

Patch and eight of the men who joined us peel off and park by the clubhouse. The remaining two lead us back toward a house that's tucked into the woods.

It's a big, nice-looking, two-story house with white siding and black shutters and what looks like a wrap-around porch. A detached three-stall garage stands next to it. Though with how big the house is, I wonder who all lives there.

The two men in front come to a stop and the rest of us park as well. As soon as I rip my helmet off, I glare at Dragon and stalk over to him.

"Spill, Dragon. What the fuck is going on that we all had to detour here instead of going home?"

A throat clears behind me, and I turn my glare to the newcomer, only to throw my hands in the air.

"Fuck me sideways. Now I have to deal with two alpha assholes."

The new guy, whom I'm assuming is the President, smirks, and winks at me. My scowl deepens as I try to ignore my traitorous libido. Why do they both have to be so fucking hot? They have to be twins because the new guy is basically a complete carbon copy of Dragon, except the new guy has darker blue eyes than Dragon. At first glance, everything else seems to be identical about them. If I'm going to be here for very long, I'll have to figure out some other ways of telling them apart.

Wait. Where did that thought come from?

"Well, true to Dragon's words, you are definitely a Wildcat. I'm Thor, President of the Steel Archangel's MC. This is Phoenix, my VP. How about we take this conversation inside?"

I turn my scowl back at Dragon, who just smirks that sexy as fuck smirk in response. What the fuck did he tell his brother about me?

"Fine, but you better have alcohol in there, otherwise my knives are definitely coming out to play," I tell them before turning and starting down the path that leads to the house.

"Same here, **сестра** [sister]," the twins say in unison and as they fall into step behind me, I don't miss the shocked looks on Thor or Phoenix. I hear Dragon's deep chuckle behind me, and I can't stop the grin that forms.

"You two will have to go back to the clubhouse..."

Before Thor even finishes his sentence, three knives are embedded in the dirt at his feet. His shocked face soon turns tight with anger as he stares down the twins and me. I slip another knife out of its sheath, stalk toward him, and stand toe-to-toe as I point my blade at him.

"They go where we go for the time being or we all walk. They're with us regardless of your opinion on the matter. You don't separate family. Once we know what's going on, we can make a better decision on who goes where. So, it's decision time for you, big guy. We staying? Or are we riding out of here? Cause I gotta tell you, my gym is calling me, followed by a nice soak in my tub. What's it gonna be?"

His nostrils flare, and I know I'm taking a big risk calling him out in front of his VP, Enforcer, and any other of his club brothers that may be lurking around, but he needs to know that we won't be pushed around. Ever.

"Inside."

His voice is hard and cold, but damn, does it still send a shiver down my spine. Just like Dragon's voice does. His eyes widen a bit before he smirks when he sees the effect his voice has on me.

Sheathing my knife, I give him a smirk of my own. After retrieving our knives from the ground, I pivot on my heel before striding toward his house like I own it, flipping a blade in the air. Fucker better learn quick not to mess with me or my family, otherwise he might lose some appendages.

"At least it was you this time and not me," I barely hear Dragon say before he laughs softly and claps someone's shoulder, most likely Thor's.

"Fuckin' hell," someone mutters. I decide to ignore them and instead continue up the stairs and through the front door.

Once inside, I have to do a double take. It isn't as bare, messy, or as uncoordinated as I thought a place owned by a couple of bikers would look like. This place is gorgeous. Wood floors, leather furniture, open concept with what looks like a professional kitchen as well. And damn, they even have a fireplace. Definitely not what I was expecting in a place mostly full of men.

"**Дети** [Kids]."

I turn around and realize that I'd somehow missed that my dad was in the kitchen during my gawk session. There are a couple beers on the counter nearby and he raises his hands, which hold another four beers. I chuckle. The twins and I walk over to him, take a beer, and we all stand together in a hug as we rest our foreheads together. Our usual family greeting and goodbye.

Instantly, I know something's wrong with Dad.

He's holding us tighter than he usually does, and his muscles are all taught under my hand. I pull back and really look at him. His face and eyes are haunted, and I know things must be really bad.

"Dad?"

He shakes his head, but I don't miss how his hand goes to his necklace. The necklace Mom gave him a few months before she died. He always clutches it when he thinks of her or of what happened leading up to her death. My stomach sinks as Dragon's words echo in my head.

"No, no, no, no. They can't be back."

My voice is a whisper, but Dad hears me anyway. His gaze locks with mine and he nods, a grim look on his face. I stare at him in disbelief. The twins look at him in shock before their worried gazes turn toward me.

I don't realize I've backpedaled until my back hits a muscular chest and hands grip my waist. Someone takes the untouched beer that's now dangling precariously from my fingers. Dad's about to speak when a voice booms from the front door.

"You better let me in, Prospect, unless you want to be six feet under. My family's in there!"

"Thor said no one else was to enter," another voice responds.

I'd know that voice anywhere and damn, do I need him right now. I quickly rip the hands away that were on my hips and make my way to the entryway with the twins hot on my heels. Through the door window is the unmistakable figure of my uncle. Well, adopted uncle.

"Bear!" all three of us shout in unison.

The Prospect is roughly shoved aside, and Bear hastily opens the door. Seconds later, he wraps all three of us in a giant hug. When he pulls back, he cups my face and damn, my tears almost fall at that point.

"Uncle Bear, please say it isn't true."

Chapter 4
Dragon

Fuck, I'm not sure what the hell's going on, but seeing my Spitfire near tears is gutting me.

Wait, *my* Spitfire?

That thought shocks the shit out of me, but damn, does it feel right.

The surge of jealousy at seeing her in Bear's arms is almost too much. Thor seems to be in the same boat, which is a comforting feeling. Both Levi's dad, Roy, and Phoenix eye us suspiciously, but I don't give a shit. Levi's my only focus as I try to keep from ripping her out of Bear's arms.

The only thing that slightly calms both of us is when she whispers, 'Uncle Bear'. Last I knew, he didn't have any family. Bear rests his forehead against hers and whispers something to her. She nods and takes a deep breath, squaring her shoulders as she meets his eyes again.

"That's my Little Ninja. Now, let's sit down and get all the deets. Then, if you want, I can show you where the gym is, and we can spar or I can set up some targets for you."

She gives him a small smile, and her shoulders relax a little before she follows the others to the living room.

Bear turns toward Thor, and anger radiates off him as his eyes narrow at him. Normally, Thor would have ripped into a brother for this sort of disrespect, but instead, Thor's just standing there, taking Bear's ire. Also, surprisingly, Phoenix doesn't seem concerned by Bear's outburst. Almost like he was expecting it. Now I'm getting pissed. What do they know that I don't?

"You shouldn't have kept me out, Pres. You know they're my family," he growls. There's a reason Bear has that road name. He's a mountain of a man at six foot ten inches tall, almost three hundred pounds of pure muscle. You do not want him pissed off and coming after you.

"I wasn't expecting you back until tomorrow, otherwise you would have been with us on the ride."

"As soon as I heard, I came back. They aren't getting her, Pres. Not again."

Something passes between them and dammit, I want to know what the hell is going on. Especially if it involves Levi.

When Thor called earlier, he didn't give me much info other than there was a very serious threat to Levi and a warning for the twins. Thor gives a chin lift to Bear and, with a look back at me, we all head to the living room.

I know that look. If I still have questions after this, he'll fill me in. Also, I know we're on the same page.

We both like Levi.

A lot.

Thor and I are extremely close and right, wrong, or indifferent, we've always wanted to find a woman that we could share. It's just the way we are.

As we walk into the living room, I notice everyone else is sitting down except for Levi, who's pacing behind one of the couches. Bear and Phoenix still stand somewhat behind us, but off to the side a bit.

All eyes are on Levi, as if they can sense she's close to snapping. You can feel the nervous and angry energy rolling off her. I didn't realize I'd started to move toward her until Bear's hand lands on my shoulder, and with a grim look, he shakes his head. Finally, she stops pacing and grips the back of the couch before she looks over at Thor.

"What's the threat?"

Thor glances at Roy, who nods somberly and goes to the kitchen. When he comes back, he looks almost defeated. In his hands is a box and, after pausing a moment, sits it down on the coffee table. With a heavy sigh, he opens it up.

I inhale sharply.

It's filled with pictures. On the top of the pile is a note and I can tell that some of the pictures are of a woman who's been severely beaten and her throat has been slit.

Levi's strangled cry has everyone's heads snapping toward her. She shakes her head and keeps muttering 'no' repeatedly as she steps backward until her back hits the wall. Her face is as white as a ghost, and I can see her body trembling from across the room as tears stream down her cheeks.

This is not the same spine of steel woman who stood up to Thor and me earlier. Something traumatic happened to my Spitfire in the past and I plan to keep it from touching her ever again.

"No, this can't be happening again. It can't. No, no, no, no."

She keeps repeating those words as her gaze stays glued to the box, almost as if she's in a trance or something. Once again, Bear's hand lands on mine and Thor's shoulders, his face grim as he looks back at Levi.

"She's trapped in her memories. I know you want to help her, but if you approach her right now, you'll likely end up with a knife in your body."

"It's a chance I'm willing to take. I'm just going to try to talk to her and see if I can bring her back to us."

With a last look at Levi, he nods reluctantly at me. Normally, I'd chew his ass out for stopping us. Bear's a patched member, but he isn't an officer. However, with him being Levi's family, I bite my tongue. Plus, this isn't the right situation to have that kind of a talk.

I slowly step forward and raise my hands. Even though I can tell Thor's torn and wants to help her, he doesn't approach. She knows me better out of the two of us. Something that will hopefully change soon.

"Spitfire, it's me. Dragon. Remember? You gave me the unofficial nickname of 'Muscles' earlier after you and the twins damn near took my head off. Come back to us, Spitfire."

She continues to shake her head as she stares at the box, tears still streaming down her cheeks.

"No, no, no, this can't be happening. Not again."

"Come back to us, Spitfire. Your family's all here and we all have your back."

"No, no, no. I can't go through that again. I can't. I'd kill myself before I went through that again. Not again. Not again."

Her words gut me, and I don't even recognize the strangled sound that comes out of my mouth. Out of the corner of my eye, Bear and Roy are looking between both Thor and me in confusion, and I bet I wasn't the only one that made that sound.

"Babe, we're not going to let them get you. You hear me, Spitfire? Thor and I won't let that happen. Come back to us, Spitfire." At that last part, I step into her line of vision. "Come back to us, Babe."

Her gaze snaps to mine and the pain and heartache I see in her eyes almost brings me to my knees.

"Come here, Spitfire. You're safe here."

I hold my hand out and after a few moments; I see her walls crumble and she rushes into my arms. She clutches my cut, and I hold her as more tears come. Thor's instantly at my side and wraps an arm around her as well, so that she's sandwiched between us. She shifts a bit so that her head is against both of our chests, and we hold her as she clings to us.

Thor's gaze locks with mine, and I know the rage in his eyes matches my own. We'll tear down anyone who so much as touches a hair on her head. Levi is ours and we'll protect her till the end.

Once her tears subside, she pulls back and wipes her face. Thor grabs the nearby box of tissues, and she gives him a weak, watery eyed smile as she takes a few.

When she appears a bit more composed, I take her hand and lead her over to an empty couch. Sitting down, I pull her onto my lap. Thor sits down next to me, picks her legs up and drapes them over his lap.

I place a kiss on her temple and rub her arms and back, hoping to ease some of the tension in her body like I did earlier at the diner. Thor does the same, rubbing one of her legs while the other is still holding her small hand in his. Once again, I purposefully ignore the questioning looks Roy, Bear, and Phoenix are giving us. Not to mention the twins, Ethan, and Travis.

"Talk to us, Spitfire. You're worrying us."

With a heavy sigh, she leans against me and takes my hand in her other one, grasping it tightly. Glancing down, I can tell she's holding Thor's hand just as tightly as well.

"About a month before my sixteenth birthday, Mom and I were out shopping in town. It was one of the rare full days off she had from the bar and grill. I'd had a weird feeling all day, but I ignored it because I selfishly wanted to spend the day out and about with her. That was the one time I ignored my gut, and we paid heavily for it."

She closes her eyes, and as she takes a deep breath, a tear rolls down her cheek. Thor leans forward, and when he wipes it away, neither of us miss how she leans into his touch. She takes another deep breath and when she opens her eyes, she gives us a small, weak smile, and squeezes our hands.

"The last place we went to that day was the grocery store. As per our norm, we always cook out on Saturday nights, so we went to stock up on food. Sasha, Alexei, Uncle Bear, and Grandpa were all supposed to come over. Dad's shift was almost over at the bar, and then he was going to head home. As we walked out to our car, we didn't see a van pull up next to us until it was too late. They grabbed both of us and before I could even pull a knife, a cloth was held over my face."

A shudder runs through her body, and I hug her tighter. A pit forms in my stomach as I worry about what she has been forced to endure and witness. Then I remember what she said back in her apartment. That her scars are from surviving something terrible in her past. Fuck... Are her scars and those pictures related? Is she one of the people pictured in the photos? Suddenly, the pit that was growing in my stomach gets bigger and at the same time, a feeling of dread washes over me. I share a concerned look with Thor. No matter what she tells us, it'll be a far cry from what she experienced firsthand.

"We woke up in a dimly lit room. The windows were mostly boarded up, but through the cracks in the boards, we could see that it was near dusk. I had no idea how much time had passed to tell if it was still the same day that we were taken or not. Both of us were chained to dirty, smelly beds. They had taken my boots and belt, so I was left without any weapons.

"We laid there for a long time and Mom kept saying positive things. That Dad, Grandpa, and Uncle Bear would be looking for us and they'd find us. That we'd be okay. I heard the waver in her voice, though. She was worried they wouldn't make it in time. The sun had just set when we heard boots overhead."

"You don't have to say any details you don't want to, Sweetie," Roy says. She nods weakly before taking another deep breath.

"If they are back, I'd rather say this once and only once."

Roy nods, but judging by his pain filled face, he doesn't want her to have to relive any of this.

Levi takes another shaky breath and squeezes Thor's and my hands. We squeeze back.

I know my brothers would probably give me shit for being all sappy and shit, but if what I'm doing is what Levi needs, then that's what I'm going to give her. It surprises me that in such a short amount of time, this woman has completely gotten under my skin. And there's not a damn thing about it I would change.

Levi pauses and Sasha gives her a nod, as if encouraging her and giving her strength. Their gazes lock as she continues.

"Four of the men had masks on and had something to alter their voices. They called each other by letter rather than using names—*A, J, K* and *F*. They were dressed in head-to-toe black. I couldn't see a tattoo or any other identifying marks on any of them. A couple of the masked men stalked toward me and unhooked my chains before roughly dragging me to another room. I heard Mom call for me before the door slammed shut behind us, muffling what she was saying.

"They chained me up so that my arms were above my head and my feet were chained to the floor. They kept asking me for information on the Steel Archangel's MC, but I didn't have anything to tell them. I'd never been to the clubhouse since I was just under sixteen. Sometimes, I would see club members at the bar and grill, but that was limited to mostly saying hello and waiting on your tables. I said I saw you guys around town, but other than a wave or another short hello, that was it.

"Other than Uncle Bear, I didn't really know anyone in the club very well. They thought that with me working at the bar and grill, and with Uncle Bear coming to our house a lot, that I would know something useful, but I didn't.

"They didn't believe me and started cutting me or whipping my back. After a while, they brought Mom into the room. They'd done similar things to her. She had cuts all over her body and bruises were already starting to form. They threw her down on the bed and chained her down. Tight. She couldn't move at all."

Tears roll down her face as she stares at a spot on the couch in front of her.

"They asked me questions again and again, but when they didn't get a different answer, they tortured us more. That... that went on for a long time before they'd had enough. Said if I didn't give them what they wanted, then they'd take what they could get. *F* cut off the remainder of my clothes and Mom begged them to take her instead of me."

A violent shudder runs through her body and her hands start to shake. Thor's gaze locks with mine, both of us worried about what she's going to say next.

"*A* raped her and continued to torture her in front of me as the others groped me. They wouldn't let me close my eyes or look away. They made me watch and said this was what happened to those who stood against them. Then, they carved 'BP' into Mom's stomach while *K* carved 'BP' into my thigh. When *A* was done raping her, they tortured me again, asking if I suddenly remembered anything useful. I thought about lying, but I didn't even know what to lie about.

"Three more times that happened—*J*, *K* and then *F* each raped her. After *F* finished, he asked me the same questions again. When I didn't give a different answer, he went over to Mom and yanked her head up so she could see me.

"*F* stared at me while he told Mom that she'd served her purpose and not to worry. That she'd be seeing me soon after they had their share of me. Then... then he slit her throat as she tried to thrash against him, yelling a bunch of curse words at him before..."

She shudders violently again as her tears came harder, her grip on our hands tightening like vices.

"He... He came over to me and smeared her blood from the knife on me. Said it was my turn. And only when each of them had had their fill of me, as many times as they wanted, then I'd see my mom again. He was just about to rape me when Uncle Bear, Dad, Grandpa, Alexei, and Sasha burst through the door.

"In the shock and confusion, they quickly overpowered *A*, *K*, *J*, and *F*. Once they were tied up, Dad gave me his shirt to cover up. As soon as I had it on, Uncle Bear picked me up and quickly left the room. As he carried me upstairs, I noticed the bodies of the rest of the men laying on the floor motionless. They were either shot or had their throats slit. Looking over Uncle Bear's shoulder, I saw Dad carrying Mom's body behind us, wrapped in a blanket.

"Uncle Bear took us all out to Grandpa's farm and since Grandma was a nurse, her and Sasha helped clean and stitch me up. Uncle Bear and Grandpa wanted to kill *A*, *K*, *J*, and *F* for what they'd done to us. To make them bleed and beg. Even though they knew Mom's wishes, they still wanted revenge and to take their lives for stealing hers.

"Since our family is close to the club, Mom had told us time and time again what was to be done if something happened to her if an enemy of the club had gotten hold of her. They could be beaten, threatened, tortured, branded, or whatever she had endured, but we could not kill them. She wouldn't have us killing someone and have that on us or on her memory. So, they weren't killed, but I bet they sure as hell wished we had killed them. They were later dumped on the edge of Steel Archangel's territory and in the middle of nowhere."

Silence meets her words as she slumps against me, emotionally drained after telling us what had happened. I tuck her head under my chin and hold her, occasionally dropping a few kisses on the top of her head. After a few minutes, she turns toward the coffee table.

"What's the note say in the box?"

Bear's gaze shoots to Thor, who gives him a chin lift.

Just as he's about to reach inside, Sasha puts a hand on his arm, stopping him. "**Подождите** [Wait]. Shouldn't we check for fingerprints?"

Thor sighs and shakes his head. "Ryder already checked for fingerprints. Only ones he found were on the outside of the box, which didn't bring up any leads. Prospect said a teenage courier dropped off the package. He was most likely paid to drop it off and knew nothing of what was inside."

With a sigh, Sasha nods and lets go of Bear's arm. He picks up the note and his sharp intake has my stomach in knots.

The note shakes in his hands, and his gaze goes back to the box before he sifts through the pictures. He sets aside some of them face down, most likely the ones of Levi's mother, and his gaze bounces between Thor and me. Rage fills his eyes and is practically rolling off him.

He stands with the box in his hands and walks over to us. After a few seconds, he hands it to Levi, but he doesn't let go right away.

"This time, if we catch the fuckers, they will die."

Levi looks up at him before sitting up straighter. Her eyes harden as rage rolls off her. "If those four lived and are coming after us again, death will not be immediate. Those fuckers will be tortured, and I *will* have a hand in the torturing and killing."

Bear's gaze shoots to Thor, and she turns her stare toward him. No one says anything for a few moments before Thor sighs and nods. Fuck, I'm not sure I'm okay with this.

"As much as I don't want you to have to witness anything like that again, Baby Girl, I know you need to do this."

Thor's gaze locks with mine, and we both nod.

I didn't miss the nicknames he's given her either, but I don't think she's noticed due to the range of emotions she's reliving. I'm sure he didn't miss the nicknames I'd given her earlier; truth be told. Levi's ours and we won't stop until she's tied to us in every way. Though if she truly doesn't want anything to do with us, we would back away even though it would kill us. But based on how she seemed just a bit ago, that might not be the case.

Levi nods to Thor, and lifts her legs off his lap, shifting slightly on my lap before standing up. I bite my lip to keep the groan from escaping when she shifts on my lap. Fuck, this woman's going to be the death of me.

She paces in front of the TV before taking a deep breath and opening the box. Her eyes widen and her hands tremble as she picks up the note before she flips through the photos.

"**Сукин сын** [Son of a bitch]," she whispers violently as her gaze darts around at the contents.

"Spitfire?"

She turns toward me, and I freeze at the pissed and murderous look on her face. There must be something wrong with me, because seeing her like this is fucking turning me on.

"He's mine to kill," she grinds out.

With that, she thrusts the box into my hands before she rushes out the front door.

A moment later, we can see her through the windows, practically running across the wrap around deck to the backyard with a bag slung over her shoulder. Shit, I bet she's gonna bring her knives out.

Fuck.

I bet she's fucking hot with blades strapped to her gorgeous curves. I shake myself internally to get a grip on myself. This is not the time to be getting worked up like that.

Taking a deep breath, I flip open the box and am surprised by the number of pictures still inside. Rage fills my veins as I sift through them. When I read the note, I can't believe the fucking piece of shit.

I look up at Thor and the others before clearing my throat. I know Thor, Phoenix, Roy, and now Bear know the contents, but the others don't.

"Fuckers been stalking her for years. There's dates and ages on all of them. They started when she was seventeen. There's some from Roy's house, at the bar and grill, inside her apartment, some out and about with Sasha and Alexei, of you guys with some other guy, and of her in class. Some of the pictures look like they could be from Sasha's or Alexei's apartment. There are even ones from when we packed up her place earlier today. Fuckers obsessed with her."

"What's the note say?" Alexei asks, though I notice his jaw is tight and fists are clenched. My jaw tightens again as I look down at it, clutched in my hand.

I told you earlier that I'll get what's mine, bitch. What should have been mine years ago. You won't be able to hide from me, as I've proven by these photos. Those Steel Archangel pussies won't be able to protect you. You'll scream for me once again, just like your mother did. Only this time, your punishment will be worse. Keep running from me and your little friends will endure the same punishment. You'll watch as they are tortured and killed. No one messes with us.

~ Fang, though you may remember me as F

P.S. A, K, and J and are looking forward to meeting you again as well. Sweet dreams, Princess.

Dropping the box on the table, I stalk to the kitchen with Thor right behind me. I'll have to talk to Thor later about the last attack and if he knew what Bear had done. Bear's family. We could have helped them.

I shake off my thoughts and refocus. That talk can happen later. Right now, my Spitfire needs me. Knowing she'd probably need something to help take the edge off, I grab some drinks out of the fridge and head toward the back door.

Chapter 5
Levi

THRUSTING THE BOX INTO Dragon's hands, I make a beeline to the front door.

I can't break down in here.

I can't break down in here.

I can't break down in here.

Outside, I slip past the Prospect and stalk straight toward my bike before grabbing my backpack out of my saddlebags. Heading back up the porch steps, I try not to run as I make my way to the backyard. Hopefully, the Prospect doesn't follow me and that no one's on patrol back here.

Taking a look around, I wish I could take a moment to appreciate the beautiful backyard, but my gaze focuses on the trees at the edge of the backyard before snagging on one that'll be perfect for me.

My fingers tremble as I slip off my jacket, unzip my backpack, and strap on my sheathes. Walking back twenty paces, I turn and face the tree. Grabbing two blades, I twirl one in my fingers as my emotions threaten to boil over. Moments later, blade after blade sink into the bark of the tree in front of me.

One of my demons from my past found me and tricked me into going out with him.

Oh, my God! I kissed and made out with him!

Bile rises in my throat, but I push it down and imagine Scott, no Fang, strapped to the tree as my blades sink into him repeatedly. To make him pay for the pain he caused me and my family. For what he'd done to my mom. To make him hurt for coming after me again and trying to seduce me.

Once all of my blades are embedded in the tree, I stalk toward it as I angrily wipe away the tears that continue to fall. Numbly, I sheath all the blades and step back twenty steps again to repeat the process. Later, when I'm alone, I'll get out

my black journal and pour out more of my emotions, but this will have to do for n
ow.

I don't know how long I've been throwing knives when I hear the back door open as I sheath the last of my blades and step back for another round. I ignore whoever came outside and start throwing again. As they start talking, I realize it's Dragon and Thor, and my fingers almost slip when I release a blade. They must not realize how much their deep voices carry back here. My fingers work on autopilot as I listen to them, and I can't believe what I'm hearing.

How can they feel that way about me? Didn't they hear that my ex-boyfriend is actually Fang? Why aren't they disgusted by it like I am? Shaking myself internally, I tune them out as I focus back on my blades. Hopefully, the cold feel of the steel will help me process my whirlwind of emotions.

Chapter 6
Thor

As I follow Dragon outside, I'm not prepared for the sight before me.

Levi's taken off her jacket and has sheaths strapped to her back and thighs, as well as a few pouches on her hips. My guess is that she most likely has some hidden in her boots, too.

Knife after knife she flings into a tree trunk. The sight sends a surge straight through me and damn, does my dick take further notice of her. I thought she was sexy before, but she's even sexier like this.

"Fuck me," Dragon mutters, and I nod in agreement before turning to him.

"Just to make sure we're on the same page, you serious about pursuing her?" I make sure to keep my voice low so that neither Levi nor the others can hear if they're near the back door.

"Fuck yeah, I am. You seem to have taken an almost instant liking to her as well. You serious?"

"Hell yes, I am." As my attention goes back to Levi, a sigh escapes as a concern I have keeps bothering me. "I just hope she's okay with both of us. Hope she doesn't run."

Not many women can handle one of us, let alone both of us. They may think they can, but shortly into the relationship, they bail because they can't. But somehow... Somehow, I feel like Levi would be able to handle us. Maybe she needs both of us just as much as we need her.

"I don't think she'll run. She went toe-to-toe with both of us and stood her ground multiple times."

A chuckle coming from behind us catches both of us off guard. We both spin around to find Sasha sitting on the railing, cleaning her nails with a knife.

"Levi can definitely handle both your stubborn asses. You treat her right, like an equal, and she'll do same. You belittle her, talk down to her, or treat her like possession; she'll be gone so fast you won't realize she's castrated you in process. She's not a hit-and-quit girl. You treat her like that, and I'll make sure no one finds your bodies."

I notice her accent has thickened, and that she's slipped into a more broken English than she had been speaking earlier. "She's lucky to have a friend like you. But I knew from the moment I saw her she wasn't a hit-it-and-quit-it type of girl. She's ours."

"Agreed, knew Spitfire wasn't that type of girl either. She's the one for us," Dragon tells her.

Sasha narrows her eyes as she looks between us. "Make sure stays that way or I'll make good on threat. **До свидания** [Goodbye]."

She slides off the railing and walks back around to the front of the house. As we turn around, I notice Alexei leaning against the railing, flipping a knife and Dragon curses.

"Fuck's sake, you two are like ninjas."

"Us three like ninja's," he says as he gestures to Levi as well.

Like Sasha, his accent has also thickened.

"You do her wrong, break her heart, and they won't be your only nightmares. I'll be helping hide your bodies. That's what **семья** [family] do." With that, he looks at Levi one last time before heading inside.

"Damn, brother. Think we need to learn Russian."

Dragon grunts in agreement as we turn back toward Levi as she continues to throw.

After a while, she pauses and stares at the ground with her hands on her hips. She shakes her head and stalks toward the tree. She sheathes her knives and I decide to take a chance. Hopefully, I won't find a knife in my body as a result.

When I clear my throat and her head whips toward me. "Need a break, Wildcat?"

I raise a beer and after a moment, she nods before grabbing her bag and making her way to the deck. I hand her the beer and she cracks it open. As she takes a long draw, I try to gauge how she's holding up. Her eyes still have that haunted look, but there's also determination shining through.

"How you doin', Spitfire?" Dragon asks.

Wildcat shrugs as she takes another long drink before setting the beer, now half empty, down on the banister. She starts taking off the sheaths that run across her back, along with the pouches on her waist, before tucking them into her backpack. It doesn't escape my notice that she keeps on the ones that are strapped to her thighs. Fuck, that's still sexy as shit.

"As well as I can be after reliving that shit and seeing most of what was in that box. Among other things."

She picks her bottle back up and drains the last half of her beer quickly, which tells me the rest of how well she's handling this. She's probably just barely holding herself together, to keep from falling apart, but she won't do it in front of us.

I motion for her to follow me and open the fridge we keep outside. She whistles as she looks through our selection. We like good beer, which includes craft beer, so we always have a nice selection at the house as well as the clubhouse. Also, we live in Wisconsin, which has a lot of damn good breweries. Beer is practically a given in this state.

With new beers in hand, we sit down in three of the many chairs scattered around the backside of the deck and I hand Dragon a beer. Levi sighs as she leans back and eyes the house.

"Is it just you guys that live here?"

"Yeah, it's just us now. Dad used to live here with us after Mom died five years ago. A few years later, he started to develop Alzheimer's, but we wanted to keep him with us as long as we could. Last winter, it got really bad, and we had to put him in a home. He passed away earlier this spring."

"Sorry to hear that."

We both shrug it off. We were actually glad Dad didn't have to live years with it because it was hard on him. He couldn't understand why we never brought Mom with us when we visited. Tore both of us up pretty bad whenever he would bring her up. It still hurts that he's gone, well, that they both are, but at least he's not suffering anymore.

Clearing my throat, my thoughts go back to the problem at hand. "We'd like to have you stay here, Levi, while we hunt down Fang and his club. With all of us here, we can help protect you all better."

Her body visibly tenses, and she narrows her eyes as she looks between both of us. "I won't be a prisoner here. I have a job waiting for me."

Dragon shakes his head quickly to set things back on track. "Never said you were a prisoner, Spitfire. As for the bar, I work security there. I would prefer that you only worked when I'm there so that we can make sure you're safe. As for staying here, you can have the master, since that's the biggest room. Figured you'd want all the stuff that you moved back with you. That includes anything you might need from your dad's place. That would be the best room for you."

Her gaze darts back and forth between us again. "Where do you both sleep?"

"Our rooms are on either side of the master. Just so you know, though, we had Timber put in adjoining doors back when Dad lived there so we could keep a better eye on him. They also don't have a lock for that same reason." Her eyes narrow again, and I raise my hands in surrender. "We won't enter without your permission. We don't treat women like that. If you want, we can change out the doorknobs so that you have a lock."

She relaxes a little and gnaws on her lip as she seems to think over everything. "What about the twins? They have jobs at the tattoo parlor in town. Where would they stay? Also, what about Travis and Ethan?"

"Our brother Axe runs the tattoo place. One of the Prospects works there, too. That shouldn't be a problem. As for where they'd stay, here would be the best place for Sasha. Don't want her staying in the clubhouse. Not sure if Alexei would want to stay here, too, or if he'd want a room at the clubhouse. Travis and Ethan, we'd put up in the clubhouse. They both work for Timber at our construction company, so we should be okay in that aspect if they become targeted later on."

Her shoulders slump in what appears to be defeat. As she takes a long draw of her beer, I try not to show I'm anxiously awaiting her answer.

Another selfish reason that I want her close to us is so she can get to know us better. Be more comfortable around us. Yeah, it's a bit of a dick move. We could have posted guards at her place and the twins' place, but all my brothers live within the compound. Even the Prospects. If they were all here, it's true that we'd be able to protect them better. It would be harder if we had to spread everyone out amongst multiple locations.

"Okay. Can my stuff be put in your garage for now? I want to go through everything to make sure there's no cameras on anything before they come inside. Or something else. I don't know if Scott messed with my stuff when he broke into my apartment."

I nod, relieved she's thinking along the same lines as I was about her stuff. "We can have Smoke come over tomorrow to see if he can get a read on anything transmitting a signal."

"We'll have to talk to the others for their take. Though, they should be making their appearance known soon," she says before chuckling lightly.

"Wha—fuckin' ninja's, the whole fuckin' lot of ya. I swear someday I'm putting a fucking bell on you, Bear," Dragon mutters as everyone steps out of the shadows, grinning at us.

Fuck, I never knew Roy could move so quietly. He isn't as big as Bear, but he's built. Even Travis and Ethan hardly make a sound.

"Fuck's sake, Bear. That shit is meant to be saved for our enemies. Not for scaring the shit out of your brothers," I say as I run a hand through my hair.

Bear chuckles darkly at me before his gaze lands on Levi. "You think I'm bad? Just wait for that one. She's better than the rest of us. Combined."

A wicked grin spreads across Levi's gorgeous face as she wiggles her eyebrows. "I sense we could pull some serious pranks here."

Her grin deepens as I glare at her. Both Dragon and I speak in unison, our voices heavy with warning.

"Spitfire."

"Wildcat."

She looks between us and starts laughing.

"Gonna tan that ass of yours if you try anything, Baby Girl," I mutter, but don't miss the shiver that runs through her and if I wasn't watching her so closely, I'd have missed how her legs clench together. Damn, I almost cum in my pants at that combined with the saucy look and wink she gives us.

"Not much of a deterrent, gents."

"Fuck," we both curse, and her laughter rings out as the others join in.

Roy's the only one not laughing, and gives both Dragon and me a hard look as if to say, 'I'll beat your asses if you hurt her'.

As the laughter starts dying down, Levi moves to get up, but I stand with my hand out for her empty bottle. She hands it to me and gives me a small smile as she leans back in her chair. As I head toward the fridge, I discreetly adjust myself, but don't miss Phoenix's grin.

Shit. I'd almost forgotten that he was here, even though he's my best friend. Then again, the man is usually quiet, but whenever he does speak, you damn well better make sure to listen. Also, the fucker is almost as bad as Bear with how sneaky he can be, which has me on edge if these five are as good as Bear says they are.

Beers in hand, I head back to the group and give Levi hers before plopping back down in my chair. We chat for a while, and everyone relaxes more as we get to know each other better.

Around eleven o'clock, Levi seems to be getting quieter and quieter. Periodically, she stares off into space and either picks at her nails or twirls a knife. Though I'm amazed at how well she can twirl a knife subconsciously and not injure herself in the process.

Occasionally, she chuckles at something someone says or engages in conversation, but she doesn't say much. I glance over at Sasha to see if it's just me noticing it, but she also seems worried as she keeps an eye on her friend.

By the time midnight rolls around, Levi seems to be fully trapped in her head. She hasn't said anything, laughed, or smiled at anything for about twenty minutes or so. I'm getting more and more worried about tonight, hoping she won't have nightmares after reliving that shit. Catching Sasha's eye, I subtly nod toward Levi, and she gives me a worried nod back. She claps her hands together and stands up. The abrupt change startles Levi, and she jumps a bit in her chair as her hand snaps out to grab the hilt of her blade.

"I'm gonna head in. Come on, **сестра** [sister], you look dead on your feet. How about you show us our rooms, boys?"

With a nod, I get up and hold out my hand to help Levi to her feet. She hesitates, but eventually takes it. Giving it a squeeze, I start back inside, but stop and turn back toward the group. "Phoenix, can you show the others where their rooms are at the clubhouse? Prospects should have them all prepped by now."

"You got it, Pres."

The others turn to follow him, but Alexei stays back as he watches Levi anxiously.

"You go, **брат** [brother]. I'll help **сестра** [sister]. Besides, these two won't let anything happen to her."

His worried gaze flicks to us for a few moments before he turns back to Sasha. "Warn them."

When she nods, he turns and follows the others.

Dragon's concerned gaze meets mine, and I frown. What did they need to warn us about? It's then that I realize Levi hasn't pulled her hand away and is still in mine. I give it a little squeeze. As I look at her to gauge her reaction to what Alexei said, I notice she's already lost in thought again, her eyes slightly glazed over even though she's only had four beers tonight, and the last one she finished an hour and a half ago.

Giving her hand another squeeze, I lead us back into the kitchen and give them a quick tour of the downstairs before heading upstairs. There are four bedrooms for guests, plus the master and our bedrooms. Sasha picks out which room she'll use and then I point out which rooms are ours before stopping where Levi's room will be. When we open the door, Sasha's jaw drops.

"Damn, I think you have the best room in the house, girl!"

Levi looks around the room in shock as she nods slightly.

After Dad passed away, we redecorated the room. Like most of the house, this room also has hardwood floors. We repainted the walls and sparsely decorated it. With Dad's hospital bed gone, we put in a big, king-sized bed in hopes we'd someday find a woman that was right for us. There's a sitting area in front of the TV, and we have another fireplace in here.

Levi opens and closes her mouth a few times before she shakes her head slightly. "You guys keep surprising me," she murmurs as she runs her hand over the handmade bookcase that runs under the windows.

Dragon's chest puffs out, and I know he's happy that she likes his handiwork. I keep telling him he should open up a custom wood shop, but he always says he'd rather have it as a hobby. That doing it for a living would suck the fun out of it. Squeezing the strap of her backpack on her shoulder, she turns slightly but doesn't make eye contact with anyone. Not even Sasha. Shit, I wonder how badly she's freaking out.

"I'm going to change real quick," she all but whispers.

We nod, and she quietly makes her way to the bathroom.

Once the door's shut, Sasha sighs heavily. "I need warn you. She sleeps with her blades. Tucks few under pillows and few under mattress on any open side." She sighs again as she looks over at the bathroom door.

It seems that whenever she or Alexei get emotional or worried, their accent thickens, and they slip into their broken English.

"She'll probably have nightmares next few nights. Always happens when something brings up memories or around anniversary of Emily's death. **Позаботьтесь о ней**."

I frown, wondering what that means, but Dragon beats me to it.

"What's that mean?"

With a small smile, she turns back toward us. "Take care of her."

Warmth fills my chest at her words. She's trusting us with her friend or sister to use her words from earlier when I'd asked what **сестра** meant. We both nod. The bathroom door opens and as I turn toward the door, I instantly forget how to breathe.

Levi has on a dark blue tank top that hugs her curves and short, black boy-shorts that show off her long legs. Her hair is now hanging loose and nearly reaches her sweet ass. Fuck, it's going to be hard to not kiss her senseless and hold her tight.

Sasha walks over to her and wraps her in a hug.

I shake my head to clear my mind and notice Dragon doing the same. I don't want to scare her away by coming on too fast. Especially after what all happened tonight.

"**Спокойной ночи** [Good night]. **Люблю тебя** [I love you]," Sasha says as she rests her forehead against Levi's.

"**Спокойной ночи** [Good night]. **Я тоже тебя люблю** [I love you, too]."

As the girls pull apart, Sasha waves to us good night and lets herself out. Turning back to Levi, I point out our doors in case she missed it earlier, when she seemed like she was still in a daze.

"My room is through that door and Dragon's is through the one over there. Let us know if you need anything. You may have already noticed, but there are fresh towels in the bathroom."

I step closer to her, taking her hand and rub my thumb over the back of it, praying I'm not being too forward, but I need to touch her. She blushes slightly and bites her lip as she looks down at our joined hands. It takes everything in me to keep from freeing her lip and kissing her. Her brows furrow, but her gaze stays locked on our joined hands.

"How can you still touch me after learning I'd kissed and made out with him? That he ended up being one of the demons behind our torture and Mom's death?"

She tries to tug her hand free, but I tighten my grip at the same time that Dragon steps forward, taking her other hand.

We need to nip this in the bud, but telling her how we feel might be too much on top of everything else she's been through tonight. "He tricked you, Wildcat. I'm sure if you had known who he truly was, he'd be dead right now. There's no reason to feel dirty or that you're less of a person because of what he did."

"Agreed, Spitfire. Knowing what he did to deceive you doesn't change how we think of you. Or how we feel about you. All it changed was that his punishment will be even greater when we get our hands on him."

She looks between us, stunned, before she eventually nods. I don't know if we've fully erased her doubts, but time will tell. Deciding not to lay anything heavy on her right now and possibly send her running, I decide to focus back on her stuff.

"When you go through your stuff tomorrow, feel free to put it wherever you want in here. We want you to feel at home here. Comfortable. If you need anything for the room, just let us know. Okay?"

She nods and looks between us, giving us a soft smile. "Thank you, both of you, for what you said and for helping me. I'm sorry if I seemed ungrateful earlier, but

I do appreciate the club protecting my family. I hate feeling trapped or cornered, so I was worried that we'd be kept under lock and key while we were here."

Out of the corner of my eye, I can see Dragon squeezing her hand slightly. "That's completely understandable, considering what you shared with us earlier. We'll show you around the clubhouse tomorrow, so you're more familiar with the place and introduce all of you to the rest of our brothers. We want you to feel comfortable here."

"And if any of the bunnies give you trouble, let us know."

She cocks an eyebrow at me, but I'm not backing down on this.

"I mean it, Wildcat. If they're purposefully stirring shit in my club, they'll be reprimanded and potentially kicked out. Even if you take care of the issue yourself, we still need to know about it."

She nods in understanding and Dragon clears his throat before spearing her with a look.

"Just try not to put too many knife holes in our clubhouse or spill too much blood in the process, Spitfire."

With that, her posture relaxes and we all chuckle. Almost as if we'd orchestrated it, we both step closer and kiss her forehead. She tenses at first but quickly relaxes before she squeezes our hands.

"Good night, Wildcat."

"Good night, Spitfire."

When we pull back, I notice she has a slightly dazed look on her face, but different from before, and her cheeks are a deep pink.

"Good night."

She squeezes our hands one last time and we each head to our respective rooms. Leaving the door slightly ajar, I head to my bathroom. I need a shower and to take care of the hard-on I've had almost all night.

Chapter 7
Levi

I DON'T MISS THE heated stares both Dragon and Thor give me as they each head to their rooms. Damn, it's getting harder and harder to resist them. They've heard the deepest, darkest part of my past and are still looking at me that way. Every time one of them touches me, tingles shoot through my body like a current. Did they really mean what they said? That they don't see me as less because of what Fang did to me?

I can only imagine what it would feel like to have both of them caressing my body all over and both of them kissing me. Groaning, I shake my head.

What the hell am I thinking? There are two of them! I can't be with both of them! But the thought of possibly choosing one only to turn away the other guts me.

With another groan, I gather a few knives from my backpack, tuck them away under the edges of my mattress and pillow before flicking off the light and crawl into bed. Almost in sync, the showers start in both of their bathrooms. Even separated, they seem to think the same. Images of both of them naked and wet have my core heating and my legs clenching together.

Fuck, I'm not going to get any sleep like this. Pushing my nerves aside, I lower my hand, slipping it under my shorts and underwear and start stroking my clit.

Images creep into my mind of both of their rough hands caressing my skin and both of their mouths on my body have me moaning with need as I stroke faster. My other hand roughly grabs my breast, tweaking my nipple through the thin material.

Remembering how it felt to have Dragon pressed up against me outside the diner has me shivering. Would Thor be just as big? I've always fantasized about having a man pounding my pussy from behind while I suck off another man. The mental image of Dragon and Thor doing just that has me peaking as my thighs clamp tightly around my hand. I bite my tongue to prevent myself from crying out loud as I come harder than I'd ever come before.

As I catch my breath, I realize I'm screwed.

I want both of them.

I'm just not sure if my heart will survive it if they both leave me.

With a groan, I roll over and fall into a fitful sleep.

"Told you those pussies wouldn't be able to protect you. That I'd have you again, bitch."

Pain sears across my cheek as my head whips to the side from the force of Fang's slap. I bite my tongue to prevent my cry from escaping, knowing he gets off from hearing my pain.

He roughly grabs my chin and makes me look at him, chuckling darkly as his grip tightens, no doubt leaving even more bruises than I already have all over my body. Bruises that are already dark purple.

"I'll beat and fuck that strength and determination out of you, Levi. Bet your pussy's tight. You better not have given it away to those fuckers. Cause if you have, your punishment will be severe. Very severe."

Fang runs a knife through the material of my shirt, letting my breasts come into view. He groans when he sees the lacy black bra that I'd purposely worn for my date tonight with my men. He quickly does the same thing to my pants, leaving me only in my bra and thong, spread out on a dirty mattress with my wrists and feet tied to the bedposts.

The dark look on his face as his gaze rakes over my body has me struggling harder in my restraints, trying to get them loosened enough to where I could slip my wrists and feet out.

He traces patterns over my skin with the knife and I try not to cry out as the knife bites into my skin, but when he occasionally cuts deeper than the others he's already marred my body with, I can't stop my cry of pain. His eyes gleam brighter at the sound.

Bringing the knife up to his mouth, his tongue darts out, licking my blood off the knife. I can't stop the shudder that runs through my body.

He turns around and soon I hear a rip before he turns back to me and slaps some duct tape over my mouth. My struggling intensifies and I try to yell as tears stream harder down my face.

"Can't have you screaming and alerting anyone. When we get to where we're going, we'll have more time to play, and I can enjoy those pretty little screams of yours even more."

He quickly pulls off his shirt and drops his pants as he speaks.

More tears roll down my face as I realize they won't get here in time. He tears off my thong and bra, holding a knife to my face as he leans further over me.

"Time to see how bad your punishment will be, Levi."

My eyes widen as he roughly shoves his fingers inside me. I thrash and try to pull away.

No, this can't be happening!

"That's my girl. No one's been here yet. Don't worry, I'll fuck the thought of those Steel Archangel's out of your head. This pussy is mine. Only mine and my brothers. Time to take what should have been mine six years ago."

He lines himself up to me and I thrash harder, trying to scream through the tape. No! This can't be happening!

His hands grip my hands hard over the rope as I try to further pull away from him.

"Levi, Spitfire! Wake up, Babe!"

"Come on, Wildcat, open those beautiful green eyes. You're safe, Baby Girl. Wake up, Wildcat!"

My eyes fly open as I try to catch my breath. Dragon's holding my right hand and Thor has my left, a blade gripped tightly in each of my hands.

"There you are. You're safe, Spitfire. It was a nightmare. You're safe, Babe."

Dragon's hand cups my cheek as his thumb wipes at my tears, drying them. My eyes drift shut as I try to calm my frantic heart. I barely pay attention when they slip the blades out of my hands. Mainly because they're here and they make me feel safer than my blades at the moment.

The bed shifts, and I open my eyes again. They've both scooted closer and are looking at me with concern. They don't speak, but both are stroking the back of my hands in a soothing pattern. I have a feeling they know what my nightmare was about, and I'm glad that they aren't asking about it. But right now, I need them closer. To feel that safe feeling I had felt in their arms earlier.

"Hold me. Please."

Instantly, they both get up, slip under the covers, and lay down next to me. Both of them drape a heavy arm around me and as I snuggle in closer to them, they both tighten their grips around me.

Dragon presses a kiss to my forehead, and Thor places one on my neck. I shiver at Thor's touch and feel his smile against my skin as he kisses me again.

"Rest, Wildcat. We're here to keep you safe."

"Sleep, Babe. We've gotcha and won't let anything happen to you."

I nod and close my eyes. This time, I fall into a restful sleep, safe in their arms.

I wake as dawn's first light peeks through the curtains and freeze when I feel a heavy weight draped over me. As I blink away the sleep, it suddenly comes back to me that it's just Thor and Dragon. I bite my lip as that thought sinks in.

Just Thor and Dragon.

It shocks me at how that doesn't bother me. Instead, my body lights up with excitement, even though I'm nervous that they didn't really mean what they said about Fang. Shaking my head slightly, I try to untangle myself, but their grips just tighten in response. I damn near swoon when Thor snuggles my neck and Dragon tucks my head under his chin.

"Where you goin'?" Thor asks, his gravelly voice heavy with sleep as he kisses my neck. Once again, his kiss sends shivers down my spine. He moans before shifting, and my eyes widen as I feel his erection press against my ass. Dammit all to hell, he's huge, too!

"I have to go to the bathroom."

They both grumble but release their grip. As I untangle myself, Dragon smacks my ass. My pussy clenches and I have to bite my lip to keep a moan from escaping.

"Hurry up and bring that sexy ass back to bed, Spitfire. It's still early."

My cheeks heat, and I quickly turn away before they can see how much they're affecting me.

Once I relieve myself and wash my hands, I check my bandage, but it's still secure and there are no signs that I need to change it yet. I'll do that after my shower later this morning.

As I smooth my tank top back in place, I stare at myself in the mirror. My cheeks are still flushed and my nipples are pebbled. Just thinking about Thor and Dragon sends another shiver down my spine. A knock on the door has me jumping slightly as I wipe my sweaty palms on the towel.

Gripping the doorknob, I open the door before freezing, barely stopping myself from smacking into Dragon's chest. Taking a step back, I swallow thickly at the sight of both of them as they lean against the door frame.

Their long hair is tousled from sleep and their eyes blaze with heat. I bite my lip as my gaze roams their wide chests covered with ink and muscles. Their shorts hang low on their hips and my eyes widen as I notice the huge bulges in their shorts. Swallowing hard, my gaze lifts and I feel myself blushing even harder.

Shit, they caught me ogling them. They both smirk at me, which just makes them even sexier.

With a scowl, I shove past them. I need to escape their sexy, near-naked bodies so I can think straight.

However, they're quicker than I am and Thor catches my hand, twirling around to face him. I curse as I stumble at the change, and my hands fly to his chest to catch my balance. His hands land on my waist and his callused thumbs brushing against my stomach. The hair on his chest tickles my hands and without even thinking, my fingers move through his hair. A pleased hum escapes his lips as he closes his eyes. A moment later, there's another set of hands on my waist. Dragon nuzzles my neck as I continue to watch Thor's relaxed face.

"See what you do to us, Spitfire?"

They both step closer, and a moan escapes me before I can stop it as I feel both of their erections pressed tightly up against me. They both roll their hips, and my head falls back against Dragon's chest as my eyes close. My breath hitches and picks up as Dragon starts to kiss up my neck.

Thor shifts and soon I feel his lips on the other side of my neck. Another moan escapes as they both suck on my skin where my neck and shoulders meet. No doubt I'll have hickeys later.

My moans seem to spur them on as their grips tighten and their kisses become harder. Thor claims my lips, and as Dragon's hands slowly slide around to my stomach, a whimper of need escapes me. His fingers are teasingly close to the top of my shorts.

"Spitfire, we want to make you feel good. Will you let us?"

My body tenses and freezes at his words. Thor pulls back from the kiss, and he cups my face in his hands as our gazes lock.

"We won't do anything you don't want to, Wildcat. You say the word and we'll stop. If you don't want this to go any further right now, that's fine, too."

I bite my lip as I debate about what I really want and how far I want to go. My body and heart want this, but my mind is still resisting.

Suddenly, I'm extremely nervous. I've never done this before. What if they don't like having sex with me? I'm not experienced like they are. What if they get bored with me and ditch me afterward? Do they really want me with this new information about Fang?

"Hey, Baby Girl, what's with that look?"

At Thor's words, Dragon comes around and cups my other cheek with his hand. My cheeks heat with embarrassment, and I try to turn away, but their firm grips won't allow it.

"What's wrong, Spitfire?"

I swallow hard and focus on Thor's chest rather than meeting their eyes.

"I, I've never..." I pause as I swallow again, unable to finish the sentence.

"You're a virgin?"

I nod and tears prick my eyes as I try to turn away again. I'm sure they'll push me away now that I've admitted it. That they'd find someone more experienced to fill their needs.

Thor lifts my chin and forces me to look at them. I'm not sure what I expected to see, but it wasn't the loving, caring looks that I found. A gasp of surprise escapes and Thor traces his thumb along my lower lip.

"Wildcat, we don't care if you're a virgin or not. And we meant what we said last night. We're interested in you. Both of us, if you couldn't tell."

He smirks and I can't help the little nervous chuckle that escapes. Yup, I *definitely* felt how interested they are in me.

"We'd love to be your first lovers, and if we have our way, your only lovers, and to expose you to new things. If you want to share that with us, that is. Like Thor said earlier, anything you don't want to do, just say the word and we'll stop. It's up to you, Spitfire. This all goes at your pace. If you aren't ready, that's fine, too."

I bite my lip again as I look between both of them. I didn't miss the 'only lovers' bit, and I'm strangely not freaking out about it. Instead, it's amped up the desire that's coursing through me, but I also need to make sure they know my limits. I can't believe I'm about to suggest this, but I want to take that jump. I want them to be the first men that I'll be with, but before I make that jump, I need to know a few things first.

"How would this work? How do we do this with both of you and me? Are you going to just throw me away after we have sex? Because if that's what's going to happen then, no, I don't want you to be my firsts."

Their gazes soften, and they pull me closer. I hadn't realized I'd stepped away from them during my panic.

"You'd be our woman, and we'd be your men. Other than us three, we wouldn't see anyone else. No sharing outside of us," Thor says, and Dragon nods in agreement.

"You better mean that because if I find out you've slept with another woman, even if it's just oral, I'll skin you both alive and bury you where no one would find you." Surprisingly, they both chuckle at my words. I narrow my eyes at them and frown as my anger grows. "What's so funny about that?"

"Just that the twins already threatened to kill us and offered to help hide our bodies if we ever hurt you, Spitfire."

My cheeks heat as my jaw drops. By the twins doing that, they'd given Thor and Dragon their approval. My cheeks heat even more, and they chuckle softly.

"I love how you blush for us, Wildcat."

They both lean forward and place gentle kisses against my temples as their hands caress my back and hands.

"What do you say, Spitfire? Want to be our woman and see where this goes?"

As I stare into their faces, I realize my previous feelings are still true. I want to at least try to see if this would work. Not just sex, but to be with them. To not let my nerves about Fang tricking me rule my life.

Turning toward Dragon, I go up on my toes and kiss him, a moan escaping him when I run my hands through his hair. After a few moments, I pull back, turn toward Thor, and give him a kiss.

Breaking the kiss, I'm shocked by how intense and heated their gazes are. I nod as I swallow the nervous lump in my throat and they both grin widely at me.

"I'll be your woman and you'll be my men."

"When it's just us three Spitfire, call me Nick," Dragon says.

"And me Ryan, Wildcat."

"All right Nick, Ryan. No cheating, just us three."

They nod and their faces light up with their sexy smiles. I really hope that this will all work out, because I'm pretty sure I'm well on my way to losing my heart to them already.

Nick grips my waist and hoists me up in his arms, bridal style. I squeal in surprise and quickly wind my arms around his neck, afraid that he'll drop me. "You're going to hurt yourself carrying me around. Put me down, Dr... Nick!"

He laughs as he shakes his head. "Babe, I can bench press more than you weigh. It's nothing to carry you around. In fact, I'd never put you down if I could get away with it."

My cheeks heat at the thought, but before I can say anything, Ryan grumbles and nudges Nick's shoulder.

"You can't carry her everywhere, because then I wouldn't get a chance to carry our woman."

Nick sighs. "Alright, we'll both take turns carrying our Enchantress around."

I scoff and smack Nick's chest playfully.

"Will you both stop it? I am more than capable of walking. Plus, in no way will I allow you both to keep me from doing what I want." Ryan gives me a look and I groan slightly. "Okay, I realize I might not be able to do *everything* I want with that psycho, Fang, making my life hell, but you guys know what I mean. Besides, what if we have kids someday and I'm all huge? There's no way you'd be able to carry me then."

They both stop and stare at me. Their eyes darken even further, and it's only then that I realize what I just said.

Oh, fuck.

Why the hell did I say that? I tend to ramble when I'm nervous, and now I just might have shoved my foot in my mouth and lost them before I really even had them.

"You want kids, Babe?" Nick asks and I swear my tongue feels like it's cotton.

I open and close my mouth a few times, trying to get the right words out so that I don't scare them even further away. "Well... I mean... I didn't..."

Nick lifts me slightly and spins me around so that my chest is pressed to his. Instinctually, I wrap my legs around his waist and his large hands cradle my ass. He rests his head against my forehead, and it's only at that point that I realize he's breathing heavily. Ryan moves and places his chest to my back and rests his hands on my hips.

"You want kids, Spitfire?" Nick asks again.

I swallow the lump in my throat and decide just to put it out there. "S-Some-day. I'd like to have kids, eventually. I'm sorry, I shouldn't have brought it up. When I'm nervous, sometimes I ramble, and I don't want to scare you off when I only just got—"

Nick's mouth slams down onto mine, breaking off my ramble. At the same time, Ryan's mouth latches onto my neck, most likely making the hickey he gave me earlier even worse than it was. Or if there wasn't one, there probably is now. Nick's tongue duels with my own and I moan as his hands start to knead my ass.

"Baby Girl, did you think the thought of kids would scare us away? Feel what you do to us, Wildcat. We'd love to fill you so full of our cum that you'll always have a baby in you."

To emphasize Ryan's point, Nick lowers me slightly and I moan when I realize they both feel even larger than before. *Holy fuck.* My breath hitches and another moan escapes me as they both roll their hips.

Hearing my moans, they roll their hips again and again as they both start kissing me harder. Nick continues to knead my ass while Ryan's hands tease my nipples and squeeze my breasts. My body feels like a current is running through it. My whimpers grow as I press my aching clit harder against Nick.

Both Ryan and Nick pull back, almost in sync, and another needy whimper escapes me when Nick lifts me slightly so that my core is now pressed against his stomach. They both chuckle, and Ryan steps back.

Before I can protest, Nick lowers me onto the bed and then lays down beside me. Ryan claims my mouth, ravishing it like it's his last meal, his tongue dueling with mine. I moan into his mouth as Nick kisses down my neck. Heat spreads through me again, and once again I can't believe how wired I am from just their touches.

"I love how responsive you are to our touch, Spitfire."

His hands go to my waist and under my shirt before he pauses. When I don't stop him, he continues until he cups my breasts. His thumb runs over my nipple, and when he tweaks it, I moan deeply into Ryan's mouth as I tug on his hair. The growl that escapes Ryan sends goosebumps across my skin.

He nips at my lip and pulls back slightly. "I think she likes that, brother. Her moans are so sexy."

"Damn straight they are. I want to hear more of them."

They both shove up my shirt, mindful of my bandages, and each takes a breast in their mouths. My hands fly to their heads as another moan escapes. Their tongues tracing on my skin while flicking my nipples. They have me feeling like I'm on fire. When I tug on their hair, needing more, they both moan. The vibrations against my skin send shivers through me, and I squirm as my pussy throbs for attention.

As if they read my mind, two hands trace down my stomach and tease me through my shorts. My hips buck off the bed as one hand teases my clit and another traces over my lips. With how wired I already am, I can already feel my orgasm building again.

"More, harder."

My panting grows louder and, right as I'm about to cum, they both pull their hands away and let go of my nipples with a pop. I whimper in protest, but they kiss down my stomach instead, chuckling at my impatience.

"I want to taste you as you cum for the first time tonight, Spitfire."

My cheeks heat and I look away, not wanting to admit that I'd already gotten myself off earlier to images of them. They both chuckle again, and Nick teasingly slides his tongue under the top of my shorts. His fingers skirt around my pussy, and I desperately try to move so that his hand is where I want it.

"I think our woman may have already pleasured herself tonight," Ryan says, his deep voice wrapping around me, sending shivers down my spine.

I feel myself blushing and they chuckle, yet again, in response. God dammit, if they don't stop chuckling and get their hands and mouths on me soon, I'm going to take this into my own hands.

"Tell us what you were thinking about when you pleasured yourself earlier, Wildcat."

My mouth goes dry, and it's hard to swallow. Licking my lips, I try to focus on the words that struggle to come through the fog of desire they are creating. "I... I was on my hands and knees. One of you took me from behind and the other I took in my mouth."

I wasn't sure it was possible, but their gazes turn even more heated. Nick positions himself between my legs and, as he looks up at me, runs his tongue over my core through my shorts. I shudder and try to move closer to him.

"Tell us who was where, Spitfire. We'll make your fantasy come true."

My pussy clenches at his words, and I moan. "You were in my pussy and Ryan was in my mouth."

They both moan deeply, and descend on me in sync, quickly pulling off the rest of my clothes. Ryan takes my nipple into his mouth again as he kneads and tweaks the other. Nick licks my slit and moans again.

"She tastes like honey, brother."

Ryan moans around my breast, and Nick takes my clit in his mouth, nipping it.

"Oh, fuck! Yes!"

I can't believe how good it feels to have someone go down on me. I've given some of my past boyfriends blow jobs before, but none of them ever went down on me.

When Nick adds a finger as his tongue continues to tease my clit, my hips buck hard. I tug on his hair, wanting him closer. When his finger moves in a come-hither motion, I grind harder against him. He hums in approval and my thighs clamp around his head as the vibrations send me over the edge. His tongue continues to lap up my juices as he keeps fingering me.

As I come down from my orgasm, he pulls back and crawls over me to kiss me. Surprisingly, I don't mind my taste on his tongue. Ryan lets go of my nipple with a pop and smacks my thigh lightly.

"Up with you, Wildcat. My turn to taste you."

I look at him in confusion, but they just smirk those sexy smirks at me. Nick pulls me up and Ryan lays down on his back.

"Sit on my face, Baby Girl."

Nick helps steady me as I get in position, since my limbs still feel like limp noodles. I hold on to the headboard as I lower myself onto Ryan's face. His tongue darts out immediately and his hands grip my thighs, pulling me tighter against his face.

An almost feral moan escapes my lips at the difference and my hips roll against his face. He growls, and the vibrations cause another moan to escape me.

"That's right, Spitfire. Ride his face. Take your pleasure."

Nick smacks my ass as he kisses my neck. I grip the headboard tighter when I suddenly feel a finger by my puckered hole and when he applies pressure, my hips buck even harder against Ryan's face. No one's ever touched me there before, but when he does it, it sends tingles through me.

"I think our woman likes that. Someday, one of us will take you back here while the other is in your pussy. What do you think about that, Spitfire?"

Holy shit, does that sound fucking hot!

I nod and his hand disappears, but a moment later, I feel his finger running through my slit and then a wet finger presses harder against my hole as his other hand grips my breast roughly. The tingling increases as he presses harder against me.

"Y-Yes! More, harder."

Nick groans as he claims my mouth and finally pushes his finger inside of me. It stings a bit at first, but damn, does it feel good. I rock harder against Ryan's face, careful not to move too much to pull at my stitches, and he groans deeply as his fingers clutch my thighs harder. I'll probably have bruises tomorrow from his fingers, but I don't care. This all feels so good. I don't want it to stop.

My thighs start to tremble when Nick adds another finger and pumps in and out of me faster. They both must have sensed it because they both pick up their movements. After a few moments, Ryan sucks on my clit, nibbling a bit more than before and I cum hard.

I lean forward, resting my head against the headboard after my orgasm fades. My whole body feels like jelly.

Nick's arms encircle me and gently lifts me off Ryan before laying me down, sandwiched between the two of them. Ryan rolls on his side and kisses me hard. Once again, tasting me on his tongue doesn't bother me. I think I'm actually starting to like it.

Chapter 8
Dragon

FUCK, I CAN'T BELIEVE my Spitfire is naked and in my arms. She's ours and we're never letting go. Kissing her neck, I massage her breast and tweak her nipple. She moans into Ryan's mouth and fuck, that sound is so sexy. I hate to pause what we're doing, but I need to know. Damn, I wish we'd discussed this in the beginning.

"Are you on birth control, Spitfire?"

She pulls away from Ryan, her eyes half-lidded with desire. She seems slightly confused, and I hope she doesn't freak out.

"Yes, it helps with my periods. Why?"

"Because I'd like to go bare and feel your sweet pussy."

She tenses and turns a bit more toward me. No doubt her mind is going to my past. "I'm clean, Babe. I had a test a couple months ago and I haven't been with anyone since then."

Her gaze flicks to Ryan, and he nods as well.

"I'm clean too, Wildcat. Been a few months since I've been with anyone as well."

Her gaze darts between us, and I hope like hell she doesn't ask. I don't want to get into that right now. She lets out a shaky breath and nods. She's nervous. I don't want her to be nervous, and I open my mouth to reassure her, but Ryan beats me to it.

"We can glove up if you want us to. We won't do anything you don't want us to."

She shakes her head and blushes. "I want to feel you, too. To do this with nothing in between us."

I lean up and claim her lips as my hand goes to her pussy. She's soaked and my finger easily slides in. I add another and work to stretch her.

Her hips buck, and she arches her back off the bed. She moans and I feel Ryan's hand brush against my chest as he massages her breasts. When his grip tightens, she starts to grind against my hand. Fuck, she's so responsive to us. And I love it.

When I pull my hand away, she whimpers and pouts, but as we both stand up, her mouth drops open when we strip out of our shorts and boxers. I fist my cock, and she licks her lips as she eyes us hungrily, which quickly turns to nervousness as her eyes widen.

"Oh my god, I don't know if you'll both fit..."

Her gaze shifts between us as she bites her lip nervously. Both of our cocks are thick and long. The only main difference between us is that Ry's cock curves a little to the left while mine goes to the right.

"They'll fit, Spitfire. We'll make sure you're prepared for us. Is this still what you want?"

I try to keep my body from tensing up as I wait for her answer. I don't want her to say no. I want her to be mine. To be ours.

"Yes." Her voice is breathy and a bit lower than usual. Her breasts start to heave a little as her breathing picks back up.

"You still want us to act out your fantasy, Wildcat?"

She moans and bites her lip as her eyes light up. "Yes, so you better get those sexy asses back in bed with me."

I climb over her and kiss her as I line up with her entrance. Leaning on my elbows, I keep most of my weight off her torso so I don't aggravate her stitches. I enter her slowly and when she hisses; I pause to let her adjust to my size as I continue to claim her mouth.

"Fuck, you're so tight, Spitfire. Your pussy feels so good."

I feel Ryan's hand in between us as he tweaks her nipples and kisses down her neck. When I reach her barrier, she tenses slightly, and I deepen the kiss.

"Just relax, Wildcat. It'll hurt for a bit, but then it'll feel really good. Trust us, Wildcat."

She nods and when he tweaks her nipple hard; I thrust at the same time. She cries out and damn, does my chest tighten when I see her eyes get misty from the pain.

After a few moments, she nods and rolls her hips. I slowly thrust in and out of her and soon, she's clawing my back. Her moans grow louder, and I lean up on my hands. With the new angle, I'm able to thrust deeper and Ryan claims her mouth as he continues to tease and tweak her nipples.

Mid-kiss with him, she looks up at me and the saucy woman winks at me. I feel my balls start to tighten, but there was no way I'm coming yet.

With a smirk, I grab her hips, lifting slightly, and start thrusting faster. Her eyes roll as she gasps for air and tugs on Ryan's hair. I feel her legs start to tremble, but I don't want her to cum just yet. Pulling out, she whimpers in protest, and I smack her thigh, smirking at her.

"On your hands and knees, Enchantress."

Her eyes light up and she quickly changes positions. As I reenter her, she moans deeply at the change. Ryan comes over by her head and when he moans, I know she's taken him in her mouth.

"So hot, so tight. Fuck, Wildcat!"

God, her moans are so sexy, and damn, seeing her take both of us sends a jolt through me. Tightening my grip on her hips, I thrust into her harder. After a few thrusts, I feel her pussy clamp down on me as she screams around Ryan's cock.

"Fuck, you're like a vice, Babe!"

I start to feel my own orgasm climbing, but I want her to cum at least one more time. Staring down at her, my gaze goes to her curvy ass. Running my hand over it, I smack her ass and grip it hard. She moans again and starts thrusting back harder against me. Both Ryan and I moan in unison and I smack her ass again. His cock slides from her mouth as she cries out.

"Fuck, that's so hot, Nick. Give me more, Babe. Smack my ass."

A shudder runs through me at her words. My hand comes down harder on her ass and her pussy clenches around me. When she cries out, I'm worried that Sasha might hear us on the other side of the house.

"Fuck, that feels so good! Mmm, bring your dick back over here, Ryan. I'm not done with you yet, Hun."

We both moan again, and he quickly does as she asks. He pulls her hair away from her face, and she looks up at him as he thrusts into her mouth.

"You like that, Wildcat? My brother's dick in your pussy and mine in your mouth?"

She hums her agreement, and she wiggles her ass against me, causing me to moan. I thrust harder into her and feel close to coming.

"Can't wait till one of us is in your pussy and the other is in your ass. Both of us worshipping your body like the Enchantress you are."

Reaching down in between us, I run a finger through her juices and then press against her ass. She squirms as she moans, but soon relaxes and lets me in.

"You like that, Spitfire? You want us both pounding into you and giving you orgasm after orgasm? Filling you full of our cum?"

Her pussy clamps around my dick as she cums, and with a roar, I cum inside her. From Thor's matching roar, my guess is he just came as well. I can't believe how hard I cum, or how much I'm filling her. I've never cum this much before.

Pulling out, I walk over to the bathroom and quickly clean myself up. Wetting another washcloth for her, I head back into the bedroom. Ryan's already picked her up and laid her down toward the top of the bed, and I notice that she's already half asleep. I quickly clean her up and when I see the blood on the sheets, I make a mental note to do a load of laundry later today. I may be a biker, but our mom insisted we know how to take care of ourselves. Fuck, I can almost hear Mom's voice now.

"My boys will not be irresponsible men. You will both know how to cook, clean, do laundry, and such."

She must see us rolling our eyes, even though her back is to us.

"Trust me, boys. In the future, the woman you find will appreciate it. Especially when you have little ones underfoot. Mark my words, your lady will love you for it."

She somehow knew, even at the age of ten, that we'd want to share a woman in the future.

After throwing the washcloths in the hamper, I climb into bed beside Spitfire. She's snuggled into Ryan's chest, and they're both almost asleep.

Well, Ryan isn't really asleep, but I know he'll need time to settle his mind. Out of the two of us, he's always been the one that worries about things more. Not to mention he's the more logical and cautious of the two of us. Most of the time, it's a good thing. Don't get me wrong, he has a wild side that even I'm scared of when you piss him off, but his level-headedness is good for the club.

Snuggling up to Spitfire's back, I hold her tight and drift off.

Chapter 9
Thor

THE BED DIPS AND I feel Nick slip in behind Wildcat as I pretend to be asleep.

My mind is going a million miles a minute and my worries are coming back to the forefront. When Nick's breathing evens out, I open my eyes and look at the woman in our arms.

She's gorgeous with her wild red curly hair, bright green eyes, full lips, and curvy figure. Fuck, her curves are to die for. I never wanted a woman who was rail thin and always ate rabbit food. One that was too scared to eat an ounce of fat. From what Nick told me of their supper at the diner, our woman has no qualms about eating whatever the hell she wants.

While I hate the fact that those fuckers hurt her, and that she might still feel insecure about them, her scars aren't a deal breaker for me. If anything, they're hot as fuck. Proof that our woman is as strong as steel. Though if I had anything to say about it, no one will dare to lay a hand on her or hurt her ever again.

Brushing a curl that had fallen to her face behind her ear, I sigh.

She shifts in her sleep and whimpers as her forehead scrunches up. Surprisingly, I notice that Nick kisses her neck about the same time as I place a kiss on her forehead. She settles down almost immediately and snuggles closer to my chest. Tightening my arms around her, I kiss her forehead again.

I never thought I'd be one to settle down. I mean, I'd hoped it would happen, but as the years went on, it seemed like we'd never find a woman that would want to be with both of us.

Nick and I are so close that it never felt right when we'd individually see other women. The women always hated it too, since we always wanted to do everything together. Needless to say, the relationships we had never lasted long. But seeing Levi laying in both of our arms tonight feels right.

Thinking back, I smile as I remember the first time I saw her at Roy's bar and grill years ago. She lit up the room and would happily chat with everyone. She was gorgeous beyond belief but at that time, was still in high school. The last time that I saw her was at a party her dad threw for her, the twins, Travis, and Ethan, before they went off to college. Like Dragon, I'd kept my distance on purpose. She was eighteen and way too young for us at that time.

I sigh and tighten my grip around her. My hope is that as she gets to know us better, she'll want to stay rather than leave. Even after we solve the issue with Fang and Black Plague. At least she isn't completely new to the MC world, so that should help. The bunnies will cause problems, I'm sure of it. Granted, she'd be able to handle anything they dish out, but we both have been with most of the bunnies. Some at the same time. If the bunnies cause too many problems, though, it may drive her away.

Then there's the age gap. During our conversation tonight, we found out that she's twenty-two, almost twenty-three. We're thirty-eight. It didn't seem like it was an issue for her, but she could have just not said anything. With another sigh, I close my eyes, but I'm surprised when she tightens her grip around my waist and kisses my chest.

"Rest, Hun. Your brain is on overload and it's keeping us up. We're good. If you still have worries, we can talk in the morning."

"What she said," Nick grumbles as he kisses Levi's neck. She shivers in response but still doesn't open her eyes. I chuckle at his smirk when he looks up at me as he places another kiss on her neck and she shivers again.

"Sleepy time is now, otherwise I'll get my knives and send you both back to your own beds," she hisses, but her smiling lips give her away. Chuckling again, I kiss her forehead again and try to go to sleep.

Someone stirs next to me, and I blink away the sleep. It takes me a moment to remember where I am, but then I smile as I look over at my Wildcat. She's starting to wake up and the little noises she makes when stretching are so damn cute. Nick laughs next to me, and she glares at him.

"What?"

"You're just too beautiful, Spitfire. That's all."

Her face softens, and I lean over and give her a soft peck on the lips. Her stomach growls, and we all laugh.

"We best get ready Ry, so we can get our woman some breakfast. Seems she somehow worked up an appetite." He winks at her and her cheeks flush.

"Speaking of, how are you feeling, Wildcat?"

The pink on her cheeks gets a little deeper and I can't help the smile that plays on my face that we can still make her blush.

"A little sore, but other than that, perfectly fine."

Her stomach growls again, and she laughs. "Okay, okay, I'll get ready, miss bossy stomach!"

Laughing, I get up and stretch. Nick's chuckle has me turning around, and I smirk when I see Wildcat staring at me, biting her lip.

"Later, Wildcat. We need to get you fed." When her eyes darken, I correct my statement even though I don't want to. "Real food, Wildcat. And the train of thought you just had will be coming true later. That's a promise." I wink and playfully swat her ass as I walk toward my room. A gasp has me turning around and I see Levi looking in a mirror.

Shit. We left a lot of marks on her last night. Nick comes up behind her and kisses one of the hickeys on her neck.

"Gotta show all our brothers that you're taken, Spitfire."

She huffs and rolls her eyes as she walks to the bathroom, muttering about 'possessive alphaholes', but her voice is missing the edge I'd expect if she were really mad. Not to mention, I saw the small smile she was trying to hide. She's not as upset as she's trying to lead us to believe. With a chuckle, I continue to my room and hop into the shower.

I quickly get ready and head downstairs to make some coffee. I need to talk to Nick. We have Church today, which means we have to tell our brothers more about the threats against Levi and the twins. I don't want to give away everything Levi told us unless we have to. Not to mention, I want to make sure he's on the same page before we talked to her.

Just as the coffee finishes, I hear his heavy footsteps coming down the stairs and pour a second mug. He rounds the corner and grins when he sees me walking toward the table with a mug for him. As he slides into his usual chair, I set the mug down in front of him and sigh as I sink into a chair next to him.

"You're thinking too much about this, Ry."

I cock an eyebrow at him and frown, shaking my head. "I'm just worried that once she sees more about our life that she'll leave. Especially if the bunnies continually stir up trouble. It's not like we've been saints. We've both been with most, if not all, of them. Not to mention we're fifteen years older than her."

He frowns as he stares at his coffee. "We know the bunnies will cause problems. The best we can do is to not let them cling to us. We'll spread the word that we're off-limits. But we need to decide how many strikes to allow before they're gone because we both know it won't be a one-time incident."

"I was thinking three strikes and they're gone. I have no delusions that with the first strike, they'll try the *'no one told me'* spiel. Especially because it's not one of us off limits, it's both of us."

He nods and chews on his lip. "We should make an announcement. Do it tonight toward the beginning of the party once most everyone's there. I mean, we can tell the bunnies that are here already on cooking and cleaning duty and we can tell our brothers at Church. They'll probably figure it out at breakfast, but yeah, I'm sure they'll have questions."

I nod in agreement and sigh before taking another sip of my coffee. "Do you really think she's okay with our age gap?"

He huffs and shakes his head at me. "If she said she doesn't have a problem with it, I believe her. From the little I've been around her, if she has a problem with something, she would have told us. Relax, Ry." He pauses and his face hardens as his grip around his mug tightens. "Speaking of Church, we need to talk to Levi and see how much she wants us or Bear to share. I don't want to overshare if she doesn't want us to."

I nod in agreement and, as I hear footsteps coming down the hallway leading toward the stairs, I try to force myself to calm down the anger that had risen at the thought of what she'd been through.

As they round the corner, I freeze as my Wildcat comes into view. She's dressed in a semi-tight-fitting t-shirt with a respectable v-cut. Two hickies peek out around her collar, one on either side of her neck, and my chest warms that she didn't cover them up. Her jeans mold to her curves perfectly, and she has on her black riding boots. Her curly red hair is loose and her green eyes light up when she sees both of us. Sasha clears her throat, and I shake myself.

"Do you ladies want coffee now or to wait till we get over to the clubhouse for breakfast?"

"Need coffee before meeting **альфа байкер** [alpha bikers]," Sasha grumbles before winking at Levi and heads over to the coffeepot.

Levi bites her lip as she tries to hide her smile, and she blushes when she looks over at us. I shake my head and get up, kissing her temple before getting out the creamer and sugar. I'll ask later what she said, but I have a pretty good guess as to what it meant.

"Not sure how you like your coffee, but here's some sugar and creamer. If there's something specific you like, just let us know and we'll have the Prospects get it on the next grocery run."

Levi shakes her head but grabs a mug off the hook before filling it and sitting down without adding anything to it.

Huh. Would not have guessed she liked it black. Sasha, on the other hand, pours in so much creamer that I'm wondering how much coffee is even in the mug. After adding a couple cubes of sugar, she sits down next to Levi.

"So, what's on the agenda today?" Levi asks.

"We'll head over to the clubhouse, show you around and then have some breakfast. We have Church later at ten." Nick pauses when we both notice Levi tensing up. She knows we're going to have to talk about the threats. He quickly looks over at me and clears his throat before continuing. "After Church, we're pretty open, so we can help with looking for cameras and move your stuff upstairs to your room. There is a party at the clubhouse later tonight."

Levi tenses even further at the mention of the party and if I have to guess, it's because of the bunnies. She takes a deep breath and Sasha grabs her free hand, squeezing it lightly. Levi hesitantly looks up at us.

"Am I going to have to repeat what happened to your brothers?"

Her voice is strong, but I still catch the waver in it. Instantly, we both shake our heads.

"No, Wildcat, you don't have to if you don't want to. We can share the details with them if you want us to. We do have to give them some details about what happened so that they know what to prepare for, but if there are parts that you don't want to share, we won't."

Nick nods in agreement. "We can give the cliff note version if you would prefer."

Levi relaxes slightly, but after a moment, she shakes her head as her jaw and eyes harden. "As much as I'd like to keep some things left unsaid, I don't want anyone to get hurt when you all go after Fang and his club. You can tell them everything. It's best if they know what they're capable of." A shudder runs through her before her face hardens further and her eyes fill with rage. "Make sure they understand Fang is mine to kill, and I get a hand in torturing all four of those bastards for what they've done to me."

We both nod, even though I know neither of us like it. While I don't want to add to her nightmares, I understand her need for closure. But killing a person changes you. I just hope she'll be okay if she really does go through with it.

Sasha clears her throat and grins as she looks at both Nick and me. "So, are you three an item then?"

She wiggles her eyebrows at Levi, who blushes beat red, and I swear I see a tinge of pink on Nick's cheeks. We both look over at Levi and smile. Even with having a few reservations, I still want to pursue a relationship with her. Last night I was already feeling an insane protectiveness toward her and want to make sure no one harms her ever again. Levi smiles shyly at us before turning toward Sasha.

"Yeah, we are."

Sasha squeals and wraps Levi in a hug. My grin widens at her words and a weird feeling tugs in my chest. Shaking it off, I glance at Nick. The skin around his eyes seems a bit tight as he rubs his chest, but his grin never wavers as he looks at Levi. Maybe he's feeling the same thing? As Sasha turns back toward us, her eyes narrow, and I have a feeling she's silently reminding us of her threat.

Chapter 10
Dragon

I PLACE OUR MUGS in the sink, figuring I'll wash them later. Turning back toward the group, I pause when I see Levi staring at the sink with a weird expression on her face.

Walking over to her, I pull her in for a hug, needing to touch her. "What's wrong, Spitfire?"

She shakes herself slightly before frowning as her gaze goes back to the sink. "Um, don't take this the wrong way, but who cleans your house?"

I pause, not expecting that question from her. Understanding dawns on me in an instant before I smile down at her. "Thor and I do. We do our own laundry, too. Same as cooking if we aren't at the clubhouse. No bunnies are allowed in here and they know they aren't allowed."

My thoughts instantly sour as I think back to a few months ago. I try to shake off the feeling and my anger, but it's too late. A dark shadow crosses her face and I sigh.

"We might as well tell her, Dragon. She's gonna find out soon enough, and it's better to have her hear it from us rather than from someone who wouldn't tell her the full truth."

Levi stiffens in my arms, and I notice Sasha bristling, but neither says anything as their gazes dart between us. Thor leans against the island and we both sigh heavily. Thankfully, he starts speaking because I'm barely containing the rage in me right now.

"About a year ago, Dragon and I started hooking up occasionally with a new bunny, Monica. We made sure she knew it was only a hook-up, nothing more. But over time, she got it in her head that it was more than that. She kept dropping hints that she wanted to be more with us, but we always squashed it immediately.

Each time it happened, both of us reminded her again that it was just hookups. We didn't keep it a secret that we also hooked up with other bunnies because we didn't have a serious relationship with her, nor did we want one with her. She started going ballistic on the other girls and causing fights. Because of the problems she caused, we eventually kicked her out. Told her never to come back. That was three months ago."

"But that didn't stop her," I grind out through clenched teeth. My body shakes with anger as the few memories I have bombard me. I hate retelling this story, but he's right. She needs to know, and it's better for her to hear the truth rather than a fabricated story littered with lies.

Sighing, I run a hand over my face. Levi tucks herself under my arm as she lazily draws patterns on my chest. I relax a bit and kiss the top of her head as Thor continues.

"A couple of months ago, we were celebrating the club's anniversary. A bit after midnight, Dragon decided to turn in. I was talking to an affiliated club President at the time and said I'd be home soon. It wasn't even half an hour later when I headed to the house. When I opened the door, there was a trail of women's clothing leading upstairs. We've never brought a woman to the house for sex before. We always took them to our rooms at the clubhouse. They all knew they weren't allowed in here."

I shiver as fury courses through me. Not being able to take it anymore, I step away from Levi and sink into a nearby chair in an effort to avoid punching a hole in the wall and scaring both of them. Leaning forward, I clench my fists to rein in the rage. Levi crouches in front of me and cups my cheek. I kiss her hand and sigh. I *hate* this part.

"What happened, Dragon?"

I sigh heavily again before pulling her up onto my lap and laying my forehead in the crook of her neck, inhaling her sweet jasmine scent. "I came home because I wasn't feeling well. That rarely ever happens, but my head was spinning like crazy. I grabbed some waters, went up to my bedroom, and stripped before crashing on my bed."

A shudder runs through me, and she tightens her grip around me. I open my mouth and close it a few times, not able to get the words out.

Thor clears his throat and from the corner of my eye, I can see the rage and anger radiating off him. Sasha's eyes widen and are starting to get watery, most likely guessing where this is leading. Thor clears his throat again and continues.

"Following the trail of clothes to his bedroom, I saw Monica about to have sex with him, but he was barely conscious. After restraining her, I called Patch. Turns out she had a friend drug his beers. She got past the Prospect at the gate, somehow, and snuck into our house. While restraining her, I also noticed she was wearing our mom's wedding ring. We eventually got it out of her that she went through our things and found our mom's ring tucked in Dragon's dresser. She'd heard from someone about it being a family heirloom and that it was now in our possession, since Dad had recently passed. She got it in her head that we were serious with her and that the ring should be hers. Along with being our Old Lady. Needless to say, we called the cops, and her ass was hauled out of here." Thor shakes his head, and I hold on to Levi tighter.

"So last night when you said that, was she the one you both had meant?"

We both nod and shame rolls through me. I hate that she'd gotten the slip on us. On me.

Levi's hand lifts my chin until I'm looking into her gorgeous green eyes that are misty with unshed tears. Eyes that also hold anger burning deep in them, but somehow, I can tell that her anger isn't directed at me.

"None of that was your fault, Dragon. She drugged you and was about to take advantage of you. You both did what you could to make sure she couldn't come back after she waved her crazy flag."

I can't help the chuckle that comes out at that last part before she continues.

"But even the best setup and security can be thwarted by a driven, crazy, psycho bitch. Honestly, I'm going to guess we haven't seen the last of her. Especially if she has friends that are still bunnies here. If they find out I'm your guys' woman, word will get back to her and I'll bet my best blade that she'll make an appearance at some point. Probably sooner rather than later. Especially if she really does think you guys were serious about making her your guys' wife and Old Lady."

My body tenses as fear rakes through me, and I notice Thor's body going rigid. *Fuck...*

"I'm right, aren't I? She has friends that are still here?"

Thor and I lock eyes and nod.

"Yeah, Wildcat, there are four girls that are still here that she was really close to. Pretty sure she's still friends with them. As soon as one of them hears the news, she'll probably know in less than ten minutes."

Levi scoots off my lap and stands up, pulling me to my feet in the process. She looks over to Sasha, and the pair grin as they chuckle darkly.

"Well, then, I think you should show us a picture of the bitch so that we know who to watch out for. Looks like our blades will be having fun soon."

Sasha cackles at Levi's words. Straight-up fucking cackles.

Both pull a blade out and flip them. Levi looks back at me, and damn, I almost kneel at the look she gives me. Thor pulls out his phone and shows them a picture of Monica before texting it to them as well.

"Don't worry, Dragon. That bitch will regret doing that to you and damn, are my babies looking forward to meeting her."

Levi grins evilly and flicks her tongue against the blade before sheathing it.

Fuck. Part of me thinks there must be something wrong with me because there's just something about seeing my Spitfire handling her blades that has me hard as a rock each time I see it.

I pull her to me and crash my lips to hers. Thor groans, and when she pulls back from my kiss, he spins her around before pulling her in for another bruising kiss.

As they separate, Sasha gives her a wicked grin. "We need to bring Alexei up to speed. His blades will want to play, too. No one messes with our **семья** [family]."

A huge grin spreads across my face and my chest warms at the fact that Sasha considers us as part of her family. Damn, am I happy that they're on our side and not having to go against them.

We lock up the house after the girls grab their sweatshirts, since it's still chilly this morning, and walk to the clubhouse. Along the way, we point out Bear's house, but not surprisingly, they already knew where it was. Besides us and Bear, Timber and Phoenix are currently the only other brothers that have a house built within the compound walls. Though, a couple of our brothers are in the late stages of finalizing their designs with Timber for their own houses.

Both girls are beyond excited about the pool and hot tub, but damn near drool when we show them the basement which houses the gym and target range.

Apparently, they hadn't seen or taken advantage of them before when they'd come to see Bear.

In the gym, we notice that Alexei, Travis, and Ethan are working out with Colt and Drae [pronounced: DR-EY], our Prospects. As I watch them, a little tension releases that they seem to all be getting along, and for that, I'm thankful. Especially since both Thor and I are so serious about Levi. I don't miss how Colt's eyes light up at Sasha's presence, but I don't say anything.

Turns out, I didn't need to.

Without even looking at each other, both Levi and Alexei cock an eyebrow at Sasha. Her cheeks turn a little pink, but other than that, she doesn't give any other indication that she likes Colt. Well, at least an indication that I could read, anyway. They seem to have their own little way of silently communicating between each other, much like my brothers and I do.

After showing them around the gym, we all head upstairs and toward the kitchen, including Alexei, Ethan, Travis, Colt, and Drae. I groan internally when I see Tiffany, Ashely, Trixie, and Roxy finishing up with putting out breakfast. Tiffany, Ashley, and Trixie are three of Monica's friends. The three of them already have their faces caked with makeup, their hair styled and are wearing skimpy clothing that barely covers anything. I can't see them, but I also bet they're wearing their sky-high heels. Their gazes are locked on my other brothers, but as soon as we enter, they flick to us and widened when they notice Levi's hands in ours. My grip tightens automatically, and Levi squeezes back. These bitches better not try anything.

"Help yourselves to whatever you want for breakfast," Thor tells the rest of the group. Turning back to Levi, he grins, and I catch a mischievous glint in his eye. He brings Levi's hand to his mouth and presses a quick kiss to it with a wink. "Sit with us when you have your food, Wildcat."

I lean in and press a quick kiss to her lips and don't miss the whimper when I pull back. I wink at her and grin. "Later, Spitfire."

Heat flares in her eyes and dammit, I wish it was just us three in the kitchen. I'd have her suck my cock while Thor took her sweet pussy. With another wink, I lead her over to the pass-through counter.

As we get our food, Roxy, our newest bunny, comes over and says hello. Well, bunny is a bit of a stretch. She doesn't service the guys, though a few of them have given her appreciative looks. She needed protection, and we gave it to her in exchange for her help with the cooking and cleaning around the club. She's still pretty timid and spooks easily, though I've noticed she's been slowly opening up to us the longer she's here.

"Are you guys going to introduce us to your friends?" Roxy asks, though I don't miss how her gaze roams over Alexei appreciatively.

"This is Levi, Thor's and my woman. The twins are Sasha and Alexei, that's Ethan, and last but not least, Travis."

I make sure I'm talking loud enough for the other bunnies to hear and internally smirk when I see Tiffany, Ashley, and Trixie's shocked faces, which soon turned red with anger at the mention of Levi being our woman. Roxy smiles at our group.

"Well, welcome everyone. If there's anything you need, just let us know."

Once again, I catch her gaze lingering on Alexei, and this time, both Levi and Sasha smirk at him with a raised eyebrow. He blushes slightly and looks back at Roxy.

After everyone has their plates and drinks, we all sit together at one of the tables. Levi sits in between Thor and me, and I have to suppress my smirk when Colt sits next to Sasha. She blushes and gives him a small smile. Alexei grins at her and the tension in her shoulders relaxes. Guess he approves of Colt for her.

I'm also surprised when Roxy hesitantly asks if she can sit with us, which is a first for her. We immediately make room for her and, not surprisingly, Alexei pulls a chair over for her next to his. Phoenix, Smoke, and Judge join us shortly afterward and before long, everyone's talking like they're old friends.

We're almost finished when hands snake across my upper back and I freeze. I know for a fact that it isn't Levi, because one hand is on her coffee mug while the other holds her fork, frozen about halfway to her mouth. Out of the corner of my eye, I notice Thor's body going rigid as well when arms snake around his neck.

"Why don't you come with us, and we can have a little fun before you have to run off to your meeting?" Ashley purrs in my ear. Tiffany tries to rub her chest against Thor's back while Trixie runs her fingers through his hair. He shoots to his feet and turns around so quickly that they stumble in their stripper heels, damn near falling in the process. At the same time, I push to my feet and shove Ashley away, glaring at all three of them. Judging by their nervous faces, they know they fucked up.

The room goes quiet. We have a rule that we don't hurt women or children, but there's no way I'm letting these bunnies try to lure me away from Levi.

Key word—try.

"Guess you three decided to ignore what Dragon said earlier about us being taken. Levi is our woman, which means we're off-limits. This is strike one for you three, because I know you heard him," Thor growls as he shoots them scathing glares.

He glares again at each of the bunnies that are here in turn. "This goes for all of you. If a brother is seeing anyone, you do not approach them for sex and cause trouble. Three strikes and you're kicked out of the club. We'll be making another announcement later tonight at the party for the bunnies that aren't here."

A glint catches my eye and I glance over my shoulder, grinning darkly when I see Levi sitting on the table, flipping a blade in the air. The twins are both turned and watching with sharp eyes, but I know their hands are already on the hilts of their hidden blades.

An angry shriek brings my attention back to Tiffany, Ashley, and Trixie. Their gazes dart to Levi and their lips curled in disgust as they roam over her curvy body. My body tenses at the action. I don't want anyone looking that way at her. Tiffany looks back to Thor and a sly smile slides over her face.

"We used to have so much fun, Thor. She can't please you like we do. She isn't cut out for this life." Tiffany turns toward him and starts reaching out to him when suddenly a loud thud sounds and she shrieks as she jumps back, nearly knocking over Ashely and Trixie in the process. I can't stop my dark grin when I see a blade is now stuck in the wood floor just inches from where she just stood.

Levi steps forward and stands between both of us. I snake an arm around her waist and feel Thor doing the same. When she pulls another blade from somewhere under her shirt, I catch a glimpse of some sort of sleeve around her waist and what seems like a pocket of blades that she's flipped down for easy access. Fuck, it's so sexy seeing her armed.

Wait, how the hell did I not feel that pouch or sleeve earlier?

She pulls a second blade and starts flipping one of them in the air, never taking her eyes off the trio. "Keep your skanky hands off my men, bitch, otherwise more of my knives will come out to play. I'd hate to mar those pretty little faces or pop those balloons you call boobs."

Their faces turn red with anger as they glare at Levi. From the sound of it, a few of my brothers are trying to stifle their laughter. And yes, two of them did get boob jobs in the hopes of snagging one of us from what I hear, but I think Trixie had it done before she came here. Tiffany steps forward, crossing her arms across her chest, which pushes her fake boobs up even higher.

"You don't belong here. You aren't cut out for this life, bitch! Why the hell would they both want to waste their time on your fat ass when they could have us? Thor and Dragon will tire of you soon enough, and then they'll be back in our beds."

"You and the other bunnies were just a means for a release, but I can assure you, I will never be tapping you again. Neither Thor nor I will ever be tapping any of you ever again. Why the fuck would we want you or any other club girl when we have someone like Levi."

"She still isn't cut out for this life!"

A hard thud sounds again before she shrieks and hops backward. Everyone in the room stills further except for the twins, Thor, and me. I smirk and kiss Levi's forehead, giving my blessing for her to continue.

"What the fuck are you—ah!" Tiffany shouts in surprise again as another hard thud has her jumping further back as Levi throws another knife in front of where she just stood.

"You don't know anything about me other than your preconceived notions about my appearance, so how the fuck do you know if I'm cut out for this life or not? I will say this again. Stay away from my men." Another knife flashes before Tiffany shrieks and hops back again, damn near falling on her ass. She would have too, if Trixie hadn't caught her.

I step up behind Levi, grabbing her hips and leaning down to place a kiss at the base of her neck.

"Damn, Spitfire, you keep bringing those knives out to play and I'll bend you over this table and take you right here." I roll my hips in emphasis and damn near groan when her tongue darts out and licks the blade she's holding. Fuck, that almost has me coming in my pants like a teenager. There must be something wrong with me for getting riled up by seeing her handling a blade like this.

"Promises, promises," she purrs as she grinds her ass against me for a moment before sauntering forward toward Tiffany.

"Fuck, Dragon, she's the mirror image of you wrapped in a female body," Bones says as he laughs, and our brothers join in as well. Fuck... He might be right.

Spitfire twirls a blade in her fingers, staring down the trio as she walks forward, collecting the rest of her blades and sheathing them. When she picks up the last one, she points it at them one last time. "You and the other bunnies should pay attention to my warning. Hands off my men. They're mine."

With that, she turns and walks back to us. Thor pulls her in for a bruising kiss. When she pulls back, I spin her and kiss her hard as my hands run through her silky curls. I pull back reluctantly when catcalls ring out and Levi chuckles, flipping them off without even looking. Laughter erupts throughout the room. Taking her hand, I lead her over to the couches where the others had congregated. Sasha brings over Levi's coffee and settles on the couch opposite us.

Ryder plops down and grins. "So, are you assholes going to introduce your woman?"

I scowl at him, but Levi just chuckles darkly.

"I'm fully capable of introducing myself, asswipe. I'm Levi Wallace. You going to introduce yourself, or do you need your mama to come by and make you play nice in the sandbox?"

Those in hearing distance howl at her words. Ryder laughs so damn hard, he damn near falls off the couch. "Fuck, you'll fit right in here, Sweetheart," he gets out between fits of laughter. A low growl escapes me at his term of endearment for her, but he just smirks at me.

"How long have you been throwing knives?" Timber asks once he's recovered from his fit of laughter.

"Since I was five. I always loved watching my grandpa throw. One day, I found some of his knives and started throwing at a target I'd made in the backyard. Soon as he found out I liked throwing, he got me my own set and some targets. He started training me and I've been doing it ever since. He also trained Sasha and Alexei."

Timber freezes as he stares at her in shock. "Wait, is Richard Wallace your grandfather?"

Levi grins at him, and Timber's jaw drops.

"Care to share the significance, asshole?" Ryder asks as he looks between them.

"Rich threw knives in competitions and won many awards. His accuracy was better than any of his competitors, that is, until Levi came on the scene. She quickly dominated the sport and became pretty well known herself."

"Well, hot damn, Wildcat."

Thor places a kiss on her temple, and I do the same. Pride swirls through me at what she's accomplished. Not to mention holding her own with our brothers and hitting it off with them so well. We fall into conversation, but I don't miss Tiffany and a few of the other club girls giving Levi the stink eye. Thankfully, they steer clear of us. For the time being, anyway.

As we're talking, more of my brothers trickle down from their rooms or wherever they were last night and get their breakfast. Phoenix comes over and gives Thor a chin lift. Levi sees the signal and gives us each a kiss, but I catch the nervous look in her eyes and posture.

"You guys go on in for Church. We'll stay here with Colt."

I give her another kiss and get up. My gaze locks with Colt, and he gives me a chin lift. He'll make sure they're okay while we were in Church. Bear stops when he sees Levi and they talk quietly for a bit. Whatever he whispers in her ear seems to help calm some of her nerves. She gives him a hug, and he nods to me over her shoulder as Drae goes out to man the gate.

Chapter 11
Thor

EVERYONE FILES INTO CHURCH after leaving their phones in a basket near Colt, myself and Phoenix excluded, and I close the door before standing at the front of the table. Banging the gavel, I call the meeting to order.

Timber gives us an update on the financials and, one by one, each of my brothers that oversee our businesses report on how things are going and if they have any issues or concerns. Judge runs the car and body shop, Axe runs the tattoo parlor, Smoke runs the security company, Timber runs the construction company, and Tripp oversees our apartment buildings and house rentals.

Once we get through the usual business, I look over at Dragon and he gives me a chin lift as he sits up straighter in his chair, his body tense. Looking over at Bear, he does the same. I'm about to speak when Bones speaks up.

"So, is it true that that little lady out there tamed the big bad Thor and Dragon?"

He grins when I scowl at him, and I'm sure Dragon has the same scowl on his face.

"Her name is Levi Wallace. Keep your fucking hands to yourself."

A shocked look crosses his face before he grins again and holds up his hands in surrender. "Sorry, Pres, meant no disrespect. Are you two claiming her?"

"Yes," both Dragon and I say at the same time. I know it's fucking fast, but she's it for us.

A few of the guys look shocked before grinning. They're no doubt remembering some of the times when Dragon or I have said we didn't want to have an Old Lady. We'd given up on finding someone that we could both be with. But that was before Levi rushed into our lives like a whirlwind. Bear grins at both of us and some of the tension that was on my shoulders eases. I'd been worried about what he would think of us being with Levi, especially since she considers him part of her family.

I give a chin lift to Phoenix since I can't technically lead the vote on this one. He clears his throat to get everyone's attention.

"All those in favor of Thor and Dragon claiming Levi as their Old Lady, say 'aye'."

A chorus of aye's rings out from everyone, and Dragon and I grin at each other.

Ryder straightens in his chair and his gaze darts between Dragon and me. "Wait, is she the one that the threats are against?"

We nod and the tension in the room instantly increases.

"Yeah, Levi's the one that the main threat is directed at. However, there's also a threat to the twins, Sasha and Alexei, that if Levi keeps running from them, the twins will be tortured and killed in front of her. The threat comes from an Enforcer named Fang and three others, *A, J,* and *K.*"

Everyone's posture goes rigid, and I can taste the rage and anger filling the room. Our club doesn't hurt women or children. Clearing my throat, I turn toward Smoke, our tech guy.

"Were you able to get the images that we asked about yesterday?"

"Yeah, Pres."

He clicks a few buttons on his laptop and I step to the side, pulling down the projector screen. After a few moments, there are side-by-side pictures projected on the screen. One of Fang's face, and the other picture is of the back of his jacket as he fled yesterday. Thankfully, Smoke got an image where it appeared that Fang was looking over his shoulder to verify it was the same person and not a decoy.

"Here's our man, Scott Black, aka Fang, Enforcer of Black Plague MC. The Black Plague MC is mostly made up of members of the Black family.

"Fang's grandfather, Scar, started the club. He had two sons, Boar and Ghost. He passed it down to his son, Boar, who in turn passed it down to his son, Archer. Archer took over about ten years ago. Here's a list of the current Black Plague members and the most recent pictures I could find of them."

Black Plague MC
Eric Black (Archer)—President
Ryan Black (Joker)—Vice President
Scott Black (Fang)—Enforcer
Vince Black (Korso)—Sergeant at Arms
Dax Princeton (Dogg)—Secretary
Anthony Black (Leo)—Treasurer
Evan Black (Snake)—Road Captain
Derek Roth (Chainsaw)
Jason Black (Skunk)
Travis Black (Diablo)
Hector Giles (Butch)
David Combs—Prospect
Clint Blackwell—Prospect

"As you can see, Black Plague is a heavily family-oriented MC. The Pres, VP, Sergeant at Arms, and Enforcer are all brothers. The Road Captain, Treasurer, and Medic are brothers and cousins of the first four officers. The first four are Boar's sons and the latter three are Ghost's sons. Black Plague deals heavily in illegal activities like drugs, weapons, and even human trafficking."

I look through the list, quickly scouring for the three other possible attackers. I curse and soon hear Dragon and Bear curse as well.

"Pres, it's got to be Archer, Joker, Korso, and Fang that attacked Little Ninja. They're the only *A, J, K* and, *F's* on that list," Bear growls through clenched teeth.

"Who are *A, J, K,* and *F* again? Why are they threatening them?" Judge asks.

I sigh and my shoulders tense at having to retell Wildcat's story. My gaze goes to Bear's and then Dragon's as I try to rein in my anger.

"Last night, Levi told us what happened seven years ago, about a month before her sixteenth birthday. Dragon, Bear, Phoenix, myself, and of course Roy, Sasha, Alexei, Ethan, and Travis were present. We talked to Levi this morning about how much she wanted to share about what happened during that attack.

"For everyone's protection and so everyone knows what we're going up against, she said she wants all of you to know the full story. She doesn't want anyone to get hurt by leaving out some of the information as a way to keep some of the details private about what happened. We said we could retell it so that she wouldn't have to say it all again, especially in such a short time span. This does not go beyond these four walls."

I level everyone with a hard stare, even though I know it isn't necessary. I trust these men with my life and know they'd protect Wildcat and her family.

Exhaling heavily, I recount what Levi had said last night. Every now and then, Bear or Dragon speak up with more details. When we're finished, my brothers are barely containing their rage.

"I mean no disrespect, Pres, but are you sure you're okay with letting Levi take part in the torture of all four and then with the killing of Fang?" Timber asks, his jaw tight but his eyes are filled with concern.

"I don't like it, but I understand that she needs this closure."

He nods, but still seems worried. Turning back to Smoke, I frown.

"We know their club is based four hours northwest of here in Minnesota. I doubt they'll be too far away from her. They must have some place that they're using as a base near here. See if you can track them down."

"You got it, Pres."

"All right, meeting adjourned. Smoke, Tripp, Dragon, hold back a bit."

The others file out of the room, and I turn to Tripp.

"Need you to order a cut for us, Tripp."

"No prob, Pres. I can get it in, in about a week, maybe two. The lady that normally does them has some people out on vacation and she's swamped. What do you want it to say?"

I turn to Dragon and we both grin, knowing the perfect name for her. Once we get the details ironed out, he leaves, and we turn our attention to Smoke as he lays a bag on the table.

"You can use these scanners to detect if anything is emitting a signal. I've got three of them. Keep in mind, it will only work if they have the device turned on, on their side.

"A couple of days after she's gone through her stuff and put things away in your house, it'd be a good idea to discreetly walk around with the scanner to see if you can pick up any other signals. Maybe have her put it in the pocket of a hoodie or jacket. There are some new Bluetooth earbuds in there that are paired with the scanners. She could walk around while dusting or something so that if they are watching her, they won't be tipped off as quickly that she's looking for more devices."

He pauses and looks between us as he frowns.

"Just make sure to be careful of what you say in case there are more devices that aren't on now but could be activated later. Make sure she's aware of why you may not be fully explaining things so that she doesn't get all pissed off at you both and we find you full of knives or something."

Dragon feigns shock as he clutches his chest. "Damn, Smoke, sounds like you actually care about us."

Smoke shakes his head and tries to hide his grin. "Fuckers, the both of you," he grumbles, but pauses as he looks toward the main room when laughter breaks out and then looks back at us. "She seems like a nice girl and already I can tell that she's perfect for you both. Don't fuck it up."

With that, he grabs his laptop and heads out to the main room, with both of us staring after him in shock.

"I don't think I've ever heard Smoke say anything remotely positive about a woman before," Dragon says as he shakes his head in disbelief.

Sighing, I shake my head. "Not my story to tell, but there's a reason behind why he steers clear of women." Clapping him on the shoulder, I pick up Smoke's bag. "Come on. Let's go and get our woman."

Heading out into the main room, I pause by the bar and take in the scene. Everyone's laughing at something Sasha and Levi are saying. Grinning at Dragon, we both make our way over to her.

Chapter 12
Levi

MY STOMACH'S A BALL of knots when everyone goes into Church. Even though I'd given permission, I still don't like that all the patched members will know that part of my past. I don't want them treating me like I'm made of glass after this or looking at me with pity. However, I want them to be safe if Fang comes here, and to do that, I need to swallow my pride for their safety.

"So, how long have you guys known each other?" Colt asks, and as I look at the four people who I consider my siblings, the five of us grin.

We go on to tell him about growing up together, and of course, the conversation eventually steers to embarrassing stories. Sasha turns to Alexei and grins mischievously. Shit... What are they going to dig up now?

"Remember when Levi served us her first drink at the bar?" She wiggles her eyebrows at me, and I groan loudly, covering my face as I feel my cheeks heating from embarrassment.

"Seriously? You guys have to bring this one up?"

They laugh and I groan again, my head falling back against the couch.

"Before opening that night, she was nervous even though she'd been slinging drinks whenever we would get together. All four of us were there for her. What she didn't know was a new guy started a few days prior," Alexei starts.

"Dante," I say with another groan.

"Right, Dante. So, earlier in the day, Roy had him stock the liquor shelves. Levi starts mixing us a drink but runs out of vodka. She grabs the next bottle in line and finishes making our drinks," Sasha says.

"Oh, no..." Colt starts, and I nod, lifting my head off the back of the couch.

"Yeah. Turns out Dante didn't pay too much attention to the labels and put an ouzo bottle in with the vodka bottles. They were both clear, both had foreign words on them, and the bottle size and shapes were similar. Everyone took huge swigs of the drink because it's one I always made for them. Needless to say, they were sputtering and soon I was wearing their alcohol."

We're all laughing by now, including me, even with still being embarrassed by the story.

"I hate the taste of ouzo," Sasha said with a grimace as she wrinkles her nose.

Alexei gags at the memory. "We're Russian. Don't ever mess with our vodka."

"You all had so much to drink trying to get the ouzo taste out of your mouths. I still haven't forgiven you for ruining my favorite hoodie, Sash." I mock glare at her and then wink. I don't give a shit about that old, ragged hoodie, and they know it. We all laugh harder.

"I had forgotten about that! Sasha threw up in Roy's car on the way back to your house and the hoodie caught the brunt of it," Ethan says between fits of laughter.

"Yeah, so after I got all your sorry asses into your rooms and the guest rooms, I had to clean it up and then had to take care of your hungover asses the next morning. Dante got an ass chewing for mixing up the drinks, and I always look at every label, even if it is in the same row."

"Yeah, but you love us," Travis says as he gives me puppy dog eyes and leans over on my shoulder. I roll my eyes, still chuckling.

"Yeah, I do, but sometimes I really wonder why."

I laugh again as I smack the bill of his ball cap so it hits his nose and then twist his nipple since he can't see me. This causes another bought of laughter just as the door opens and everyone starts filing out of Church.

"What's so funny, Little Ninja?" Uncle Bear asks before he leans down and kisses the top of my head. We give him a highlight overview as a few more guys join us, and soon they're all laughing with us.

Out of the corner of my eye, I see my men walking over to me and I can't stop the smile that breaks out across my face. I bite my lip when I see the heat in their eyes. Damn, I hope we can get more alone time today because I definitely need them again. They both lean down and give me quick, but heated, kisses.

"How are you doing, Spitfire?" Dragon sits down to the left of me, and I chuckle when he pulls me onto his lap. Thor sits down where I was previously and beams at me as he pulls my legs up onto his lap.

"Good. We were just getting to know one another a bit more and, of course, the twins had to share a few stories." I mock glare at them again, but they just smile in return. "What's in the bag?"

"Smoke gave us some equipment to help us go through your stuff, Wildcat. But before that, let us introduce you to the rest of our brothers."

Hearing about the bag, my mood sours instantly, but I try to push it to the back of my mind for now.

One by one, they rattle off their names and I'm thankful everyone has on their cuts. It's going to take a bit to remember everyone's names. They have a fairly decent-sized club. I'd seen a lot of their faces over the years, but there are some new ones that I've never met before. It seems like they have almost fifteen members just off a rough head count.

"Wildcat, can I have your phone? I want Smoke to install something on it. That way, if Fang calls, maybe we can trace the call."

Nodding, I dig it out of my pocket and unlock it. "Sure, Hun. Here."

I hand him my phone, which he passes off to Smoke. He gives me a chin lift and sits down at a nearby table, opening up his laptop.

After introductions, we chat for a bit with some of them, while others go off to play pool or darts. I finish the last of my coffee and move to slide off Dragon's lap to get more. Instead, Thor plucks the mug out of my hands and slides out from under my legs. He leans down and places a quick kiss on my lips. I chuckle softly and I lean back into Dragon's embrace. If these two have their way, I'll always be in one of their arms it looks like. While it's sweet some of the time, they better not do this all the time.

"Well, who would have thought we'd see you both whipped?" Uncle Bear teases as he winks at me, and everyone laughs.

"You'll be eating those words when you find your Old Lady, Bear. Maybe watch and learn a few things," Dragon says as he places a hot kiss on my lips.

My heart flutters at hearing him say Old Lady. I knew they wanted me to be their woman, but did they want me to be their Old Lady, too? Dragon pulls away just as Thor gets back and hands me back my mug.

"Thanks, Hun." I tug on his cut, and he leans down to give me another hot kiss. He pulls back and sits back down, pulling my legs back on his lap, and massages my calves again.

"Dragon's right. Take a few notes on how to treat a woman right."

He winks at me, and his statement starts up more trash-talking about them being whipped, but I just chuckle and lean deeper into Dragon's arms as I sip my coffee.

We chat for a bit longer and when I finish my second mug, Thor picks up the duffle bag and we head out toward the house. They fill me in on what Smoke said about the cameras and I hate the thought of them not telling me things due to the possibility of missing cameras or microphones during our search. At least it'll only be temporary until we think we have found all the devices.

In no time at all, I realize we're already back at their house and am staring into their garage at my SUV and Travis's truck that holds my belongings. I'm not looking forward to this.

With a sigh, I turn to the guys. "I'll go in and grab the keys to move the vehicles so that we have room to go through stuff in the garage before taking things inside."

They both nod and start unhooking the ratchet straps on the truck.

As I jog up the stairs to my room, the hairs on the back of my neck stand up like I'm being watched. Looking around, I don't notice anything out of the ordinary, but as the feeling grows, I grab my keys and quickly make my way back down to the garage. My face must have shown my nerves because as soon as the guys see me, they pause unloading the truck.

"What's wrong, Wildcat?"

I frown as I glance back toward the house, unsure if it's paranoia or something else.

"Spitfire?"

I shake my head and turn back toward them. "I'm not sure. It could just be paranoia, but... I swear it felt like someone was watching me as I went inside, and it intensified when I was in my room."

Thor takes my hands, and it's only then that I realize I'd been wringing them together. They both exchange a look before turning back to me.

"How about you stay out here with Ry and I'll take one of these inside to look around?"

I nod as he takes out one of the scanners and pairs the earbuds to it. Pulling on a hoodie, he tucks the scanner into the pouch and heads inside. I stare after him until Ryan comes up next to me and pulls me into a hug, kissing the top of my head.

"Don't worry, Wildcat. We'll get all of them and then we'll be able to relax again."

I nod and exhale heavily. Leaning up, I give him a quick kiss, smiling up at him. "Thanks, Ryan."

Pulling back, I head to my SUV and back it up until it's parked just outside of the garage doors, while Ryan does the same with the truck. Apparently, he'd snagged the keys from Travis at breakfast. Spying a couple of card tables against the back wall, I set them up and decide to start with the boxes that Ryan and Nick had already pulled out of the truck.

Scanning through the instructions Smoke left us, we switch on the scanners and get to work, trying to see how many boxes are sending off a signal to see if we can narrow any down.

I instantly scowl. Out of the ten boxes that were already unloaded, every single one of them sends off a signal.

"God damn fucker," Ryan mutters as he hands me a box while he takes the next one.

Opening my box, my stomach sours instantly. Inside is a bunch of my bras, panties, and lounging clothes. Sneaking a glance at Ryan, I'm slightly relieved that he's focusing on his own box.

Pulling out a few of my bras, I wave the scanner over the first one and it goes off where the cups join in the front. Frowning, I do the same to the next one. And the next one. And the next one.

"Fuck…" I mutter and Ryan's head snaps up, frowning, before he smirks at me.

"Can't wait to see you in some of those, Wildcat."

"Yeah, well, I'm not sure I want to wear them anymore," I say, my voice dripping with disgust and anger.

It takes a moment before realization dawns on him. He scowls, picks up his scanner, and walks over to me. With each bra that he looks at; his scowl deepens.

"Baby Girl, what would you say to getting new clothes? All of these have some form of device in them, and I don't like the idea of you wearing something that fucker has touched. Especially when it's something like these."

"I was already thinking of that, but in the meantime, I'd like to take out a couple of the devices until I can get to the store. After I get new ones, I'll toss these." Dropping them on the table, I gasp and then look down at my clothes. "Oh, fuck, what about what I'm wearing now?"

Ryan curses, and I step back a bit from the table. He waves the scanner over me, and I groan when I hear three beeps go off. One at my bra, my belt, and then my boots.

Immediately, I pull off my belt and sit it on the table before taking off my boots. Not wanting to totally expose myself in case someone comes up to the house, I step over to the garage door that's still closed and quickly take off my hoodie, shirt, and sleeve before ripping off my bra. Pulling out a knife, I make a small slit in the material and remove a small, circular device. Ryan immediately crushes it with his boot. Picking my scanner up off the ground, I breathe a sigh of relief when it doesn't register any other devices on my clothes.

I'm about to put my bra back on when suddenly I'm in Ryan's arms and he has me pressed up against the wall. My skin shivers from the cool feeling of the drywall as his lips crash down on mine.

"Fuck, Wildcat, you're so damn beautiful."

I moan as he cups my breasts and tweaks my nipples. He lifts me by the waist, and I wrap my legs around his waist. Feeling his hard cock against my pussy has me moaning again as I rock against him.

"I need you," I gasp out and Ryan immediately lowers me down to the ground.

I quickly shimmy out of my jeans and panties. As soon as they hit the ground, he lifts me by the waist again and I can't contain my moan as he teases my pussy with his fingers. He's already pushed his jeans down his thighs and, damn, do I get even wetter feeling his cock rub against my slit.

"Fuck, I love how you're always wet for us. I need to be inside you, Wildcat."

I cry out as he enters me in one stroke before he starts thrusting into me hard and fast.

"Fuck, I can't believe how tight your pussy is, Baby Girl. This is gonna be quick. I need you too much."

I don't recognize the noises coming out of my mouth as he works me through two back-to-back orgasms. All I can focus on is the pleasure that he's giving me. I crash my lips to his and whimper as he nips at my lip before he trails kisses down my neck. I know I'm leaving scratch marks on his back, but I don't care.

His hands tighten on my ass, and he cums inside me at the same time as a third, powerful orgasm racks through me. I swear my vision blacks out around the edges for a moment. Ryan kisses me as he continues to hold me up while we recover. The gentleness of his kiss is in contrast to just a moment ago, but damn, do I want more of them.

"Fuck, that was hot."

I open my eyes and see Nick with his dick in his hand and cum coating his fingers. I can't help the giggle that comes out as I wink at him. "Glad you enjoyed the show, Babe."

Ryan pulls out of me and slowly lowers me to the ground, holding me while I get steady on my wobbly legs. Nick comes over with some shop towels and cleans me up. Once I'm more steady, I start to get dressed again as Ryan pulls up and re-buckles his pants.

"So, what spurred on the love fest?" he asks us with a smirk, which soon turns to shock at our scowls.

"Fuckers put some sort of device into each of her bras. She ducked over here to remove the device from the one that she was wearing. There was also one on her belt and boots."

Nick's face darkens at the news and he shakes his head before frowning at the pile of clothes on the table. "Well, fuck. Looks like we'll need to take you shopping later, Spitfire."

"Yeah, I don't want to wear them longer than I have to, but I also want to go through the rest of my things to see what else I may need to buy. Maybe we can go shopping tomorrow or Monday depending on when we get done?"

"Sounds good, Wildcat."

Giving them each a kiss, we get back to work.

As the afternoon wears on, I've already taken devices out of all my jackets, purses, and a few more bras to tide me over until I can get some new things. I set aside all of my shoes, as that will take some work to get those out without ruining them.

The guys insist I can buy new ones, but I love my boots, and I want to see if I can easily remove the devices first. Thankfully, the devices were sewn into the sidewalls of my boots, so those are easier. My heels and sandals... that's going to be way more difficult. I managed to save a few of my favorites but finally cave on the rest, saying I'd buy new ones. The guys are a huge help and we make good progress.

I'm working through a box of electronics when I feel a change in the guys. Looking over at them, they seem frozen as they both stare into a box that's in front of Ryan.

"What's wrong?" I walk over to them and freeze.

Fuck.

It's my box of toys. Nick hands one of the vibrators to me and with a shaky hand, I lift up my scanner.

It gives off two pings.

Swallowing the bile, I look it over more closely. There's a device hidden in the battery chamber. Furrowing my brow, I continue looking over it again to figure out where the other one is. That's when I notice Ryan holding a small box that I don't recognize.

Looking up at them, they both look royally pissed off as they stare at the box. My stomach turns in knots as I lean closer to see what's inside. Ryan turns the box in his hand and a flash drive along with a note comes out. With shaking hands, I pick up the note and freeze.

> *You're so beautiful when you cum, Princess, both inside and out. Can't wait to see you coming on my dick. Have fun watching.*
> *~ Fang*

Dropping the note, I sprint outside, barely making it three feet before throwing up.

Chapter 13
Dragon

THE FURY COURSING THROUGH me at Fang's note and what I'm guessing is on the flash drive damn near has me seeing red. As far as I'm concerned, all her toys are going in the trash. We'll buy her new ones if she still wants them. The only thing that's keeping me from losing it completely is the fact that my Spitfire needs me. Needs us.

Once she's done throwing up, Ry sweeps her up into his arms and carries her inside. She looks so pale, and her hands are shaking. Following them inside, I make a pit stop in the kitchen and grab some bottles of water and a bowl in case she needs to throw up again. Not that I blame her one bit. That fucker took intimate and private moments of hers and recorded them. No doubt he used the videos for his own sick pleasure.

Levi's sobs shake me out of my thoughts as Ry lays her down on the bed, toes off his boots, and lays down next to her. She instantly rolls toward him and buries her head in his chest. After setting the bowl and waters on the nightstand, I kick off my boots and crawl in behind her, wrapping an arm around her. We both hold her, pressing soft kisses to her forehead and shoulder as we try to help her calm down.

"We'll get him, Wildcat. And when we do, he'll pay for what he's done to you."

"Damn fucking straight, Spitfire."

"He... he is so... g-getting s-skinned... a-alive," she hiccups as she tries to catch her breath.

"Sounds like a plan, beautiful," Ry says as he kisses her forehead.

"Did, did you... f-find any cameras... in the house... e-earlier?"

I sigh, my gut tightening just thinking about them. Placing a kiss on her shoulder, I tuck my face into the crook of her neck. "Yeah, I found a few that weren't ours and gathered them up. Prospect took them to Smoke. Our cameras are mainly external, but we also have a few scattered throughout the house as a 'just in case'. While they do always record, they aren't monitored unless we need to look into something. I don't know how they got them in our house or how long they've been here, but we'll be looking into that."

Levi nods but otherwise doesn't say anything. Raising an eyebrow at Ry, he subtly shakes his head and frowns before kissing her forehead again. After a few moments, her breathing levels out some, and her hiccups cease.

"What's going through that beautiful mind, Wildcat?"

She sighs and wipes her eyes.

"Just furious beyond hell that he recorded something so intimate of me. Not to mention I'm embarrassed. I mean, I know he already had cameras that pointed to my bed due to the pictures we saw, so that means he saw *everything*, both external and internal. God, he probably jerked off to them, too. What if he decides to post them somewhere? I don't want anyone other than you two to see me like that."

I freeze at her statement. As the rage rises inside me, I have to fight down the urge to pummel something into oblivion.

She starts crying again, and her whole body shakes with each sob. We need to find Fang and the Black Plague fast. And when we find them, their torture will be long and painful. I have a feeling both Ry's and my demons will be unleashed when we find him. There's a reason why we have the road names we do.

After a few minutes, Levi's tears subside as she falls asleep. We lay there for a few more minutes to make sure she's okay. Ry nods toward the door and we both carefully slip out of bed. I quickly write her a note that we'll be downstairs before following Ry out and quietly closing the door. I head straight to the kitchen and Ry hands me a beer as he takes a long pull from his.

"This is so fucked up. He is so fucking dead," I mutter before taking a swig.

"Agreed. Beyond fucking pissed he violated her like that," Ry growls as he leans against the counter, hands gripping the edge.

"Not now or tonight, but we need to talk to her about finding out what exactly is on the flash drive. If he has some sort of message on there, we need to know what it is."

"You're probably right, but fuck, I'm not sure how she'll react to watching it or if she wants us to watch it. There's no fucking way anyone else is watching her do that."

"Damn fucking straight. No one else is gonna see that."

He drains the last of his beer and slaps my shoulder. "Come on, man, we can't do anything until we get more intel on them. Let's keep looking for bugs while she rests. Least we can do for her, to ease some of the weight on her shoulders."

"Sure, but I'm gonna quickly check on her first. Meet ya out there in a few."

I down the last of my beer and quietly make my way back upstairs. Levi is still cuddled up on the bed and thankfully, isn't showing any signs of nightmares. Picking up a nearby blanket, I gently lay it over her before giving her a kiss on her forehead.

"Nick," she says softly as she snuggles deeper into the blanket.

My chest warms when I realize she can tell us apart, even when sleeping. Grabbing our boots, I quietly make my way back downstairs and out to the garage, knowing that I'm probably grinning like a fool.

"What are you so happy about?" Ry asks as he nudges my shoulder.

I give him his boots and feel my grin growing wider. "Just that when I covered her up with a blanket and gave her a kiss, she knew it was me. Don't know how she can tell us apart when she's sleeping, but apparently, she can."

He grins as well and pats me on the back. Very few people besides our parents could ever tell Ryan and I apart. The fact that Spitfire can tell us apart makes me believe we might be able to make this work after all, and my chest warms even more at the thought. After lacing up my boots, I set an alarm for an hour and get to work.

We both make pretty good progress through Levi's belongings. Still, it seems like every box has something in it that has some sort of device in it, so we make sure we're thorough. We don't want to miss anything and have any repeats of what's most likely on the flash drive.

"Hey, sorry I passed out."

Turning around, Levi's standing in the door, rubbing the sleep out of her eyes. Her hair is still a little tasseled, and she looks cute as shit.

Walking over to her, I pull her to me and give her a kiss before Ry does the same.

"Don't worry about it, Wildcat. It was a huge shock, so it's completely understandable."

Her cheeks tinge pink as she gives us a little half-smile, but I can tell that it's still weighing heavily on her.

"Um, this morning you mentioned there's a party tonight. What time does it start?"

Knowing she's trying to change the subject, I nod. I don't want to push her on this, especially right now.

"They usually start around 4 pm. We're having it catered tonight, so food will start showing up between 4 and 5pm."

At that, she freezes and looks at her watch. Seeing that it's already 3 pm she looks around at the boxes in a panic.

"Crap! I've got to find my bathroom stuff so I can get ready and then change!"

She frantically starts looking through the boxes and breathes an audible sigh of relief to find it amongst the boxes we'd already gone through.

"Which boxes do you need us to carry up, Wildcat?"

She jumps and blushes, apparently not having heard Ry walk up behind her.

"Oh! Um, these two, and then I'll need my boxes of clothes that have already been gone through."

"Head that sexy ass of yours upstairs, Spitfire, and we'll bring everything up for you. Is Sasha getting ready with you?"

"Shit! I should text her. She'll probably want to borrow some of my stuff unless she was able to get stuff from her room at Dad's place."

"The twins live with you guys?"

"Yeah. It's a big house that has four extra bedrooms. Mom and Dad always wanted a bunch of kids, but unfortunately, they couldn't have any others after me. When the twins started hanging around our place more and more, Mom and Dad gave them each a room so that they had their own space when they needed to get away from their foster parents."

"Well, if they didn't get their stuff today, we'll see to it that they can get it tomorrow. Same with Travis and Ethan," Ry says and I make a mental note to talk to him about this later. I'm guessing Levi's going to want to live close to the twins, so we'll need to account for that at some point.

After a few minutes, we carry everything that she needs upstairs. As we're setting down the last of the boxes, Sasha appears in Levi's doorway.

"**Уйди** [Get]. We need time to get ready. **Уносите свои задницы** [Get your asses off]."

I chuckle at her words, guessing that whatever she said means that she's kicking us out. After giving Levi a kiss, I head back downstairs with Ry.

Chapter 14
Levi

SHAKING MY HEAD, I try and fail to hide my smile at Sasha kicking the guys out. I know the literal translation of 'уносите свои задницы' is 'get your asses off' but in English, she's basically telling them to scoot their asses out of here. I bite my lip to keep a chuckle from escaping at the looks my guys give her.

Once the door shuts, she pounces like I knew she would. "Okay, now that we have girl time, **рассказывай** [tell me]. How're you doing?"

Walking to the bathroom, I sigh as I start combing my hair and debate how much to tell her.

"**Нет** [No!] Whatever, put that frown on your face, **рассказывай** [tell me]! If those assholes did something to hurt you, they'll be tasting my steel!"

I spin around, ready to tell her she's jumped the gun, but seeing her standing there, wearing a shit-eating grin, has my body relaxing as a strained chuckle escapes. Should have known she wasn't serious since she hadn't slipped into her broken English.

Sighing again, I turn around and make myself focus on my hair as I try to not cry, or throw up, and fill her in on what Fang's done this time.

"I mean, how the hell did he know exactly which box he needed to put his box with the scan drive into? I rearranged those boxes so much because I had stupidly boxed up some stuff I needed, so I had to search through them. Besides—very few boxes were labeled. I wish I knew how long he was in my apartment before I showed up."

"What time did you leave before your final?"

"A little over an hour, so I wasn't gone for long. I was done with my final in about forty minutes. I stayed in all morning for last-minute cramming."

"Okay. Different topic so your eyes don't get any redder," she says.

I breathe a sigh of relief and then smirk at her. "So, Colt, huh?" I grin when she blushes and bites her lip.

"He's very nice for a **байкер** [biker]. We talked for a while when he was working behind the bar earlier. Sucks that we can't hang out tonight. He has to guard the gate." She pouts and I chuckle.

"How long has he been Prospecting?"

"Almost nine months, so he's close to patching in. If they all vote 'да' [yes], that is."

"Do you think anyone would vote no?"

"I don't think so. From the little I've seen so far, everyone seems to like him. Granted, he does get some shitty jobs from the bit that I saw this afternoon, but he doesn't gripe or complain in the least."

"That's good. I like Colt but don't know Drae that much. Apparently, he just started Prospecting about four months ago."

"I didn't get much of a vibe off him yet. He hung around while we talked, but that's about it. He was always just on the sidelines."

Sasha has an uncanny ability to read people, and I always trust her judgment. I frown as I've also noticed Drae on the sidelines earlier too when we were eating. He kept eyeing our group weirdly.

"Not to mention, he was watching you very intently when you were going off on those three bitches."

Her words make me pause. My mind goes back to Fang's note from last night and then the other cameras that Nick found inside the house earlier. Does Fang have someone planted here? I set my brush down and turn toward her.

"Intent how?"

She shrugs one shoulder. "He sat up straighter and his eyes tracked every movement. He seemed very interested in the sleeve and pouches you wear under your shirt for your blades."

I frown again and make a mental note to keep an eye on him to see if it's just curiosity or if he's going to be a possible problem in the future. I don't want to bring something up to the guys if I don't have proof. Shaking my head, I decide to change the subject.

"What's your feel on Roxy?"

"She's nice. I talked to her a bit when Colt was doing something for one of the guys. She cooks and cleans for the guys. Sometimes she works behind the bar at parties, but that's it. She doesn't have sex with them. I get the feeling she's been hurt in the past cause I saw haunted looks cross her face every now and then. Not to mention, she's jumpy around loud noises. That being said though, she and Alexei were talking for a bit. I think he likes her, but I don't know if he knows she doesn't sleep with the guys. He wouldn't go for someone like that."

As we finish our makeup and hair, we chat about the tattoo parlor, the bar and grill, my men, and everything in between.

When we're done, I walk over to the boxes and started pulling out clothes, debating on what I should wear tonight. Sasha opens the box next to me and starts digging around in it.

"Oh, Levi, you have to wear this one tonight!"

I turn toward her and know she's right. In her hands is my favorite black Harley Davidson halter top. It has a built-in bra and shows a bit of cleavage, more than what the guys have seen me in so far, but not to the point of them practically spilling out of my shirt. I'm not one to put the ladies on full display.

It sinches under the boobs and the bottom flows out a bit rather than being snug. Perfect for hiding a few blades if need be. It'll show my scars, but with the guys already knowing my story and having seen them the night before, I'm not worried.

"Okay, but you need to wear this one."

I turn back to the box I was going through and toss her a dark blue one-shouldered tank top that I know she loves. With her blue eyes and long blond hair, she looks beautiful in it whenever she wears it. Since we're roughly the same size, we tend to share clothes a lot.

"Да [Yes]! Спасибо [Thank you]!"

I chuckle and strip out of my clothes. Knowing my men will be excited later, I put on one of my thongs before putting on my tank top and shorts since it's supposed to be pretty warm this evening. If I do get cold, there are multiple fire pits we could stand nearby. As always, I make sure to put on my sleeve that I wear around my waist for my blades. Rummaging through my shoes, I pull out my favorite wedges that I managed to save. Once we're ready, I glance at the clock and

realize we're done just in time. Not seeing the guys downstairs or in the garage, I
start a group text as we head out.

> Levi: House is locked up. Sasha and I will be at the club-
> house in a few minutes.

> Dragon: Thanks, Spitfire. Head to the backyard by the fire
> pits and look for me. Ry's waiting with Phoenix at the front
> for our brothers from the Junction Creek chapter that are
> supposed to be here any minute.

> Levi: Will do.

> Thor: Can't wait to see you, Wildcat. Be there in a few.

I send back a kiss emoji and pocket my phone.

"That look looks good on you, girl."

I look over at her and blush at her smirk. She shoulder bumps me and I can't
help the chuckle that escapes.

"I'm happy that you finally found a man, well men, that make you happy. You
deserve it."

"Thanks. I'm hoping you find a man that makes you happy, too." She blushes
at my words and her gaze flicks over to the direction of the gate where I know
Colt is. "Dragon says to meet him back by the fire pits. Thor will join us after the
Junction Creek guys get here. Maybe later we'll walk over and talk to Colt at the
gate."

She blushes further, but nods.

About halfway to the backyard of the clubhouse, I hear the roar of bikes
approaching. My nerves start acting up again. Will they bring more bunnies that
have been with Dragon and Thor? Is it just Monica and her group that I need to
worry about? Or is there more?

A few minutes later, we round the corner of the clubhouse and I pause as my
gaze scans the crowd. My heart skips a beat when I spot Dragon near the firepits.
His jeans hug his ass like a glove and even from here, I can see the strain his shirt
is under to contain his muscles. Looks like he's talking to Alexei, Travis, Ethan,
and Ryder.

They seem to be deep in conversation, and a smile breaks out at how well my brothers are getting along with Dragon. However, before I can take another step, strong hands grip my arm and I'm twirled around. Out of the corner of my eye, I notice another guy has Sasha in his hands as well.

"Well, aren't you a pretty little thing? I swear all the best pussy is here. How about we go and get acquainted?"

Pulling a blade, I fist his shirt and press the blade to his neck. "I'm not a fucking club whore, you fucking jackass! Before you start feeling a woman up, you might want to ask if she's here with anyone!"

"A feisty bunny, just my type. Everyone knows that none of the Forest Creek brothers have a woman or an Old Lady, so you and your friend are fair game."

I notice another flash of steel out of the corner of my eye and then a growl as Sasha presses her blade into the neck of the biker holding her. "You assholes may want to get your hands off us. I'm taken and so is my sister. Unless you want to piss off the President and Enforcer, that is."

The guy I have held at knifepoint seems confused by what Sasha says, and his gaze darts between us before settling on something over my head, and I'm pretty sure I know who's behind me. His body tenses and the movement causes my blade tip to nick his skin and a trickle of blood runs down his throat.

"What the fuck are you doing with your hands on our woman and her sister?" Thor growls.

"What the fuck is going on?" another deep voice rumbles from behind me. "Care to explain why you two are at knifepoint?" Whoever spoke must have heard Thor, because while his voice carried a tone of annoyance, it also held amusement.

"These assholes didn't believe us when we said we weren't bunnies. Nor did they believe Levi's your woman," Sasha spits out as she presses her blade harder against the idiot that had grabbed her. He's close enough that I can see his face pale and sweat starts to bead on his forehead.

"We meant no disrespect, Thor. This isn't the first time we heard a bunny claiming to be someone's woman, so we thought it was another instance like that," the guy that I have at knifepoint tells him.

Dragon steps closer, and soon I feel one of his hands gripping my waist. "Well, let's clear the air. Levi is our woman. Her sister, Sasha, is also taken. Neither of them are bunnies, so keep your fucking hands to yourself," he growls.

"Sorry, Dragon. Won't happen again." His gaze flicks between my men and me, and after a few moments, I step back and lean against one of my guy's chests, Dragon's most likely, since his hands have a rougher feel to them. I keep my gaze locked on the two men as I flip my blade in the air. Thor places his hand on my hip as well and squeezes slightly. Sasha steps back slightly but then tenses as another set of arms wrap around her waist.

"Babe, you alright?" Colt asks, and Sasha relaxes against his chest before sheathing her blade, turning in his arms, and planting a kiss on his lips.

"Just dealing with some grabby assholes that didn't want to listen. But, wait, why are you back here? You said you had to man the gate tonight?"

He places a chaste kiss on her lips before grinning at my guys. "Drae's currently watching the gate. Dragon texted me to come back here for a bit because your blades already came out to play," he winks at her and she blushes before turning to us.

"**Спасибо** [Thank you]."

"No thanks needed. You're family to Levi, which means you're family to us. Besides, if anything happened to either of you, I'm pretty sure your brother would be sinking a blade into us," Dragon says as he chuckles.

"Damn straight, **брат** [brother]. You okay, **сёстры** [sisters]?" Alexei asks as he comes up to our group.

"No offense, man, but I wouldn't call the Pres or Enforcer of this club a 'brat'. Show some fucking respect," the other man spits, the one that approached with my guys. Looking at his cut, his name is Reaper, and he's the President of the Junction Creek chapter.

Alexei rounds on him, his eyes darkening to near black. "I spoke no disrespect. **Брат** is Russian for 'brother'."

Seeing Alexei clenching his fists, I step forward and put my hand on his arm before looking back at Reaper.

"How about we fully introduce ourselves? I'm Levi Wallace. This is Alexei and Sasha Petrov, and yes, they're originally from Russia. Later we can introduce you to Travis West and Ethan Mills, who are over by the firepit. They are all part of my chosen family. As is my Uncle Bear."

Reaper glances down at me, his brows furrowing. "Wait, Levi... as in Rich Wallace's granddaughter, Levi?"

I grin. "The one and only."

Reaper's face shows even more shock, and now I'm wondering exactly how he knew Grandpa. Also, what the hell did Grandpa say to everyone about me? His gaze darts between Sasha, Alexei, and me as some sort of recognition dawns on him. He shakes his head and turns back to the two that had grabbed us.

"Fuck guys, you really are lucky that they only held a knife to you rather than having a knife sticking out of you," Reaper mutters as he runs a hand over his face.

Both of his men are frozen with shock as their gaze's dart between Sasha and me. They seem like they're trying to figure out how their Pres knows about us, and honestly, I'd like to know more myself. Reaper gives my men a chin lift before turning back to his men.

"Cannon, Atlas, how about you guys go grab a beer, and maybe some food," he pauses and looks back at Thor. "Are these the only two women who are off limits?"

Hands tighten around my waist and I see Colt's arm tighten around Sasha.

"Them and one other named Roxy. She's not a bunny, but she does work and live here. She's working the bar inside tonight. The bunnies will be here later and they can get their dicks wet then," Thor says.

Cannon and Atlas nod, but before leaving, they turn their attention to Sasha and me.

"Sorry ladies. It won't happen again," Cannon says and Atlas mumbles something similar before they both walk off. I pull away from the guys slightly and sheath my blade.

"Fuck, Spitfire. Even with that little speech, you're gonna have to make sure you stick close to us tonight. Especially when you're sexy as fuck in that outfit. I don't want any brothers getting ideas and making moves on our woman," Dragon says before he pauses and he looks down at my stomach. "How many pouches you have on that sleeve, Spitfire?"

Shock freezes me for a moment before I relax and smile up at him. "I take it you two saw it earlier this morning and maybe just now, huh?"

"Yeah, Wildcat. We both caught a glimpse of your sleeve."

"Sleeve?" Reaper asks as his gaze darts between us, and I smirk before lifting my shirt a little and pulling the clasps attached to the sleeve. Since I have on a looser shirt around my stomach, all four pouches flip forward, revealing eight small, handmade blades in each pouch. Whistles ring out from the guys along with the twin's laughter. Turning back to my guys, I give them each a quick kiss.

"I only have eyes for you two. If someone gets out of hand like those two did, I won't draw blood unless I have to. However, I won't tolerate anyone disrespecting me and as a result, disrespecting either of you. Just so you know, Sasha has a sleeve similar to mine as well, whereas Alexei had to get a bit more creative with hiding his weapons. Though all our riding boots share the same features as his."

As I speak, Sasha undoes her clasps and four pouches also slip out from under her shirt. Then all attention turns to Alexei, and whistles sound out once again as he triggers his toe and heel blades and pulls out the hidden blades from the sides of his boots.

"*Gambler's Daggers* is what they're called. We've sewn sheathes for four blades into each boot. So, if we're going anywhere where there's a metal detector, please let us know so we can switch out our gear."

Laughter rings out at his words and Reaper's guys that are nearby looked shocked and, frankly, a little nervous. Reaper, however, is currently doubled over, laughing as his hands rest on his knees. His other men that are spread out around the yard look over at us in curiosity and amusement at seeing their President nearly crying with laughter. I'm sure he'll be getting a lot of ribbing later.

"Fuck, Thor, these three are lethal, especially since I know of their history from Rich," Reaper says as he straightens and runs a hand through his dark brown hair. As his laughter dies down, he looks at Sasha and me. "Apologies for my brother's words and actions, ladies. I won't make excuses for them, but they both have a hard time trusting women. However, that still doesn't condone their actions. I'll speak to them later about that."

Something shifts in me slightly as I glance at Atlas and Cannon's receding backs. While I hate that someone has caused both of them enough pain that they don't trust women, I still can't ignore the fact that they didn't back down right away when we made it clear we weren't interested.

As I secure my pouches back into their hidden position, I vaguely hear my guys whispering behind me. Glancing up at them, I catch Thor nodding at someone. Following his line of sight, I notice Phoenix getting up and heading inside.

"What's going on?" I ask quietly.

"We have a couple of club announcements that we need to make in a moment, Wildcat. How about you ladies go get a drink and some food? Alexei, go with them. Until word spreads that they aren't to be touched, I'll feel better knowing you're with them."

Alexei nods, and I give both of my guys each a quick kiss, though it doesn't escape me that Alexei seems to stand taller at Thor's words.

"I gotta head back to the gate, Babe. Text me if there's any more trouble," Colt tells Sasha. She nods, and he gives her a quick kiss before heading back to his post. She links her arm through mine, and we make our way to the buffet table with Alexei right behind us.

Chapter 15

Levi

THE TWINS, TRAVIS, ETHAN, and I, are talking with Ryder, Timber, Reaper, and a few of his men—Devil, his VP, and Punisher, his Enforcer—when the back door opens, and the club bunnies come strutting out. Four of them are barely dressed in crop tops and short ass skirts that damn near show their hoochies. The other two have a bit more clothing, barely, but at least they cover the important b its.

"I wish they had minimum clothing restrictions. I get that they're here for entertainment for the uncommitted guys, but yeah, I don't want to see that," I mumble as I try, and apparently fail, to contain my grimace based on some of the guys' laughter. Though what surprises me is when a couple of the guys look up and grimace right along with me.

"Those four are always the worst at parties like this," Ryder says as he shakes his head.

Reaper seems about to say something when an ear-piercing whistle sounds from across the yard. Looking in the direction that the whistle came from, Thor and Phoenix are standing together near a firepit. Phoenix is holding something behind his back, but I can't tell what it is.

"I'd like your attention, assholes and ladies!" Thor calls out before waiting a few moments for the chatter to die down.

"Earlier today, there was a request that was entered. We met with the other officers and have come to a decision. Can I please have Alexei come forward?"

Confused, I turn toward Alexei and notice that he's fidgeting nervously as he gets up from his seat and walks toward Thor.

Thor nods to Phoenix, who pulls a box from behind his back and hands it to Alexei. He opens the box and flashes a huge smile at Thor, which he returns. My jaw drops when he pulls a cut out and slips it on before turning back toward the crowd. Well, shit. My brother was just accepted as a Prospect in the club.

"Welcome to the Steel Archangel's, brother."

A smile forms as I cheer with the others. Ever since he started apprenticing at Steel's Ink, he's been talking about joining the club. Sasha beams up at him as she cheers.

Thor holds up a hand to silence everyone. He scans the crowd, almost as if he's looking for someone, and nods.

"We also have another announcement to make. Some of you heard it this morning, but I'm going to repeat it for those that weren't here earlier. We've established some new rules in our club for the bunnies. I will be talking with other chapter Presidents about what we're doing so that they're aware as well. Even though Forest Creek is the mother chapter, each chapter will be making the call if they want to implement the same changes or not. Though I will be highly recommending the changes so that they're in effect for whenever they need to fall back on them."

Looking around, I don't miss the glares directed at me from Tiffany, Ashley, and Trixie. The other three bunnies just look confused and slightly nervous.

"There is a three-strike policy that went into effect this morning. If a brother becomes involved with someone, you will not go around creating trouble. You do not approach them for sex. If you do any of these things, you'll get a strike against you. Three strikes and you're kicked out of the club. This also means that you aren't able to work at any of our club businesses. If you live in one of our apartments or houses, you will be required to pay the rent that a non-club member is expected to pay. If you don't want to pay the full rent, then you'll be moving your ass out.

"Three of you already have a strike against you after this morning's little stunt when Dragon and I informed you that we are taken. You will treat our brother's women and Old Ladies with the respect that they deserve. Is that understood?" He glares at each of the bunnies in turn. Tiffany seems ready to spit nails, but thankfully, she doesn't say anything.

"All right then. Enjoy your evening everyone. Church is at ten tomorrow." Thor clasps Alexei on the shoulder and they head toward us, with Dragon close behind.

I'm out of my seat quickly and pull Alexei in for a hug. "Congrats!"

A moment later we're almost knocked off our feet when Sasha throws herself at us, wrapping us both in a hug. "**Наши поздравления** [Ours congratulations]!"

We chat with the others as the night goes on. Needing to excuse myself, I go up on my tippy toes and give my guys each a kiss.

"Going to the restroom. Be back in a minute."

"I'll go with you," Sasha says as she gets up.

I nod, but as I turn away, a hard smack on my ass has me yelping, and I twirl around to see Dragon smirking at me. Rolling my eyes, I blow him a kiss and head inside toward the restroom.

After doing our business, we head into the main room since I want to check in on Roxy and make sure she's doing okay. I don't think any of Reaper's guys would pull a stunt on her like they did earlier with Sasha and me, as I'm sure word has spread since then, but still, I wanted to be sure.

"Hey Roxy, how're you doing?"

She gives us a small, nervous smile, and I make a note to check in on her more tonight. Her gaze keeps darting around the room, and her posture is tense. "Doing okay. You ladies need a drink?"

"Yes, please. Beer for me."

"Beer for me, too."

With a nod, she grabs us two beers from the cooler and cracks them open in front of us. As she pulls her hands back, I don't miss the tremble in them. Taking a chance, I smile at her.

"Hey, Roxy, would you like to go shopping with us tomorrow? I need to get a few things and Sasha never turns down a shopping trip."

Sasha grins at me and rolls her eyes. "You never seem to complain when I find cute shirts and shit for you," she teases. I bump shoulders with her and laugh. Roxy giggles and gives us a tentative smile.

"Yeah, I'll go shopping with you. I cook for the guys though, so maybe after lunch? I'd need to make sure I'm back in time to start supper, though."

"Don't worry about it, Roxy," a deep voice says as he rounds the corner to the bar. Roxy jumps, but she relaxes a bit when she sees its Phoenix. Even though his voice is quieter than the other guys' I'm still surprised he startled her. I heard him purposefully walking louder down the hallway just a moment ago. She turns and grabs a beer from the cooler for him, and he gives her a chin lift.

"You're here every day and rarely leave the compound. We can order in tomorrow night for supper. Have fun with the ladies. A couple of Prospects will go with you three to make sure everything is okay." With that, he silently heads back the way he came, and I bite my lip to keep my giggle in at her shocked look.

"I should be used to how quietly some of them move around by now, but I'm still constantly surprised by it," she mutters before she laughs and we join in. Pulling out my phone, I unlock it and hand it to her.

"Here, put in your number and I'll text you, so you have my number."

"Oh, same for me," Sasha says before she hands her phone over as well.

When Roxy hands me back my phone, I send her a text with my name. "Sweet! Let's meet up after lunch here in the main room then, okay?"

"O-Okay."

I smile at her and she returns it with a more natural smile than the one I'd seen earlier. Grabbing our beers, we head back outside and toward my men. Halfway there, skinny arms snake around Dragon's waist, and I freeze when he doesn't push them away right away.

"Is that?" Sasha asks, and when I see the woman's smug face looking at me, I'm pissed.

"Yeah, it is," I grind out and make my way over to my men.

Stopping in front of them, I cock my eyebrow at them as I fold my arms across my chest. Conversation around us grinds to a halt. The bitch's arms tighten around Dragon's waist, and it's then that he realizes I'm not the one next to him.

"What the fuck?" he yells as he turns around. He stares at her in shock before his face darkens. "Monica. What are you doing here? How'd you get in? You're banned from all our properties," he says darkly through gritted teeth.

"What do you mean, Baby? I'm right where I'm supposed to be. Next to you and Thor," she purrs as she tries to rub her boobs, which were obviously paid for, against him. He pushes her off him and she stumbles in her stripper heels. Do all these bitches wear stripper heels? Do they get a group discount or something?

"We want nothing to do with your skanky ass. You have never been and will never be our woman," Thor says as he moves to my side, wrapping his arm around my waist just as Dragon does the same. Monica's face turns red as her gaze tracks their movements. Her lip curls up in disgust as she looks me over from head to toe.

"Her? Seriously? Why would you choose that scarred, fat pig over me? She'll never be able to handle you both the way you like to be handled. She isn't cut out for this life," she sneers as she straightens her shoulders and tries to put a sweet smile on her face as she bats her eyes at my men. My body tenses at her mentioning my scars before I force myself to relax. Rolling my eyes at her, I shake my head.

"Are you done with your rant, little girl?" I ask, my voice heavy with boredom.

She scoffs and her face turns redder. "Little? You're calling me little? You look like you're barely legal, whereas I'm the same age as Thor and Dragon. We went to school together."

"Age is just a number. While, yes, I am younger than my men, I can definitely handle both of them as they have proven repeatedly," I purr, and both of my men chuckle as they press kisses to my temples.

"There's no way that you would be able to please them with your fat ass! Dragon, please Baby, let's get out of here and I can remind you why we're so good together," she says as she sidles up to my man.

I stare at her blankly. Did she really just do that? I look at Dragon and then to Thor, who looks like he's trying really hard not to bust out laughing.

"Um, Monica?"

She turns toward me smugly and I point to the name on the cut of the man she's clinging to.

Thor.

She blanches as her mouth opens and closes.

"Can you seriously tell me that you can't tell Dragon and Thor apart? And for that fact, can't you read? Their names are on their cuts. I mean, even without their cuts, I know who's who," I chuckle, and she narrows her eyes at me.

"Everyone gets things mixed up every now and then," she sputters as she tries to backpedal.

"Yeah, no. They both walk differently. They both talk differently. They both kiss differently. They both fuck differently. Their tattoos, scars, how their eyes change color, how they wear their hair. It's all different. The fact that you hadn't noticed any of that and I've been able to pick up on all of that in the short time that I've been around them is pretty fucking telling. So, get your fucking hands off my man and get the fuck out of here. They are mine and will never be yours."

She stumbles back a couple of steps as her gaze goes from me to my men and back to me. Fingers grasp my chin, lifting it up, and Dragon places a searing, hot kiss on my lips. I moan as I lean into him. When he pulls back, he spins me and Thor's lips crash down on mine for another scorching kiss. Fuck, these men's kisses are lethal.

When he pulls back, a throat clears, and we turn to see Ryder and Smoke smirking as they hold Monica's arms, preventing her from charging at us.

"I checked the cameras and turns out that Monica was able to sneak in because she was in disguise—wig and all. She changed in Ashley's room before making her way out here. Ashley, Tiffany, Ginger, and Trixie all hid her as she made her way over to you so that none of us would realize she was here," Smoke says as a dark smirk crosses his face.

Yikes, I wouldn't want to be any of those girls right now.

"Well, I think they need a little punishment, then." The cold tone in Thor's voice should have bothered me, but it doesn't.

I grin as I look up at him. "Is there any chance that part of their punishment could be to be fully clothed? With how little they wear, it would probably irritate the hell out of them."

Thor's lip twitches, and Dragon chuckles behind me.

"I think that can be arranged, Wildcat," he says before placing a kiss on the top of my head. He gives a chin lift to Ryder, who returns it and gestures behind us. Looking over my shoulder, Judge and Phoenix are practically dragging Monica's friends over to us.

"You four are confined to your rooms the rest of tonight and until we come to get you tomorrow morning after Church is done. We'll vote on your punishment tomorrow. Someone will bring you breakfast in the morning."

At that, Phoenix and Judge drag them, kicking and screaming, inside.

Thor turns toward Monica and she pales at the dark look on his face. "You are never to come here again, Monica. If you do, I can guarantee you won't like the outcome."

Ryder spins her around, shoves her forward, and makes no move to help her as she stumbles.

"You can't treat me like this, Ryder. I'm their Old Lady!"

"If you were really someone's Old Lady, your ass wouldn't be banned from our clubhouse, our businesses, and our housing units. Give it up, Monica. No one wants your stretched out, loose as shit, pussy."

I can no longer hear the rest of her argument as they round the corner, and I'm thankful it's over. For now, at least.

Shaking my head, I lean against Thor's chest. "Wow, she really is a special kind of crazy," I mutter.

His chest shakes with laughter and he kisses the top of my head. I feel Dragon's lips on my neck and immediately goosebumps break out across my skin. He steps closer and I bite my lip as I try to stop a moan from escaping.

"You should know better than to keep those moans from us, Wildcat."

"I know, but I didn't think you would want your brothers to hear them, too," I whisper as I clamp my legs together. Fuck, these two are going to be the death of me.

Thor steps closer and when I feel him against me, I don't hold back the moan this time, but I make sure it's quieter than usual.

"I think Spitfire wants us, Thor." They both grind their hips at me and my knees damn near give out as desire pools in my belly. I nod my head, but then shake it as I take a deep breath and try to tamp down my libido.

"As much as I want you both, I don't think that's a good idea right now. Later tonight, definitely, but you two shouldn't disappear just yet. I mean, Reaper and his guys got here not too long ago. From the sounds of things, you guys don't often get together. Shouldn't we stay for a little longer?"

Twin smiles beam down at me, even though their eyes burn with lust.

"You're perfect, Wildcat." Thor leans down to kiss me, cutting off my scoff.

"Definitely not perfect. I'm sure you'll start to notice that the longer we live together, but thank you." I go up on my tippy toes to kiss him again as I try to ignore the fact that their grips on me have tightened, and their eyes darken even further. As I pull back, Dragon spins me and kisses me.

"Perfect for us, Spitfire."

My cheeks heat as I lean against his chest, tucking my arm around his waist. Looking past the guys, I see Reaper and a few of his guys watching us with amusement. Smiling, I wave them back over.

"Sorry about breaking up your talk earlier. Do you need me to step away if it was about club business?" I worry my lip and pray I haven't overstepped or made a mess of things already, but there was no way I was going to let Monica get away with what she did. And to be fair, that bitch started it all by sneaking in here.

Reaper grins and shakes his head. "Sweetheart, you can interrupt us any day. And if these bozo's ever mess up, you call me, and I'll come kick their asses for ya." He pauses and winks at me as my men grumble. "Your grandfather was a good friend of mine, and he talked about you frequently. It's an honor to meet you in person."

My breath catches and tears burn my eyes. I have to blink repeatedly in an attempt to keep them from falling. Grandpa passed away last year, but sometimes the pain seems as fresh as it was the day I heard he had collapsed from a heart attack.

"Thank you," I whisper, and Dragon growls.

"Reap—stop making my woman cry."

I laugh and playfully smack his chest. "Oh stop, N... Dragon." My cheeks heat at my slip, which has all the guys laughing.

We chat for a while and the more I learn about these men, the more relaxed I'm becoming. I'm confident that I made the right decision to trust myself with Thor and Dragon. A couple of hours later, the conversation comes back around to me throwing knives.

"Say, how about a little demonstration? Or maybe a little friendly competition? With how much Rich talked you up, I'd love to see you in action." Reaper asks as he gestures to my stomach, no doubt meaning the sleeves hidden beneath it.

I shake my head and lift my now empty beer bottle, the fourth one tonight. "Not tonight—I don't throw when I've been drinking. But how about this? We can set up a friendly competition for a later date and then have another party in the evening?"

Cheers go up around us, and I look over my shoulder in surprise. I hadn't realized almost everyone had been listening in when Reaper asked about that. Surprisingly, Tripp jumps to his feet and walks over to a man I haven't met yet, but per his cut, his name is Beast.

"Looks like Beast and Tripp will work out a date when we can all meet up again," Devil says as he laughs.

Shaking my head, I smile. I've never been as accepted or as welcomed as I'd felt here at Steel Archangel's and now, with Reaper's crew.

Sure, in the past I've put on a happy face, but that doesn't mean I didn't hear the whispers about my size or what I've been through. Here though, neither of those things seem to matter except to a few bunnies, who I suspect would be bitchy to anyone the club brothers brought here as their woman. Or man, if that was what they preferred. Now that I think of it, I'll have to ask the guys to make sure that's okay here. I'd hate for anyone to be discriminated against because of who they loved.

Shaking myself internally, I grin at Reaper. "Well then, starting tomorrow, I guess you guys had better start practicing."

Roars of laughter surround me, and my guys tighten their grips on me. Looking up at Dragon and then Thor, something crosses their faces that I can't decipher before their eyes darken yet again. Thor pulls me into his arms and claims me with a searing kiss. Dragon steps up behind me, places his hands on my hips, and kissed my neck. My legs damn near buckle when I feel both of their erections pressed tightly against me. When Thor pulls away, I whimper but pause when I see a sexy smirk lighting up his gorgeous face.

"Let's get you home, Wildcat. We have naughty things planned for you."

Even with my lust-filled brain, I still remember I didn't come here alone. Looking over my shoulder, Sasha winks at me and waves goodbye before walking over by Alexei. Between him and Colt, I'm sure she'll get back okay later.

Thor says a hasty goodbye and says we'll see everyone in the morning at breakfast. Catcalls follow us and when all three of us, without discussing it, raise our hands and flip everyone off as we head home, laughter erupts once again out of everyone.

Chapter 16
Levi

Five Weeks Later

The last few weeks have felt like I've been walking on a cloud. A couple of days after arriving, I went with Sasha, Roxy, Colt, and Alexei to replace the parts of my wardrobe that I couldn't save. While we were gone, the guys watched the scan drive to make sure Fang didn't have a message hidden on it. Luckily, there wasn't a message from Fang and let's just say that after seeing me play with toys, the sex was pretty hot and heavy afterward for a few hours.

In less than a week after coming to the clubhouse, I was back to working at the Bar and Grill and the twins were settling in nicely at Steel's Ink. Things are also going smoothly with Travis and Ethan at their jobs at Steel Construction. Everyone is still staying at the compound and I'm starting to wonder if Ethan and Travis will want to Prospect with the club. They've been watching things more closely as of late, and I'm kind of hoping they do. I'd love to have them here and close by.

Dragon, Thor, and I have settled into a routine. Both guys moved into my room the day after we made things official, and they give me at least two orgasms before we head over to the clubhouse in the mornings.

Each morning, Sasha and I help Roxy whip up breakfast for all the guys and the bunnies. The bunnies are supposed to be on rotation to help us, but really, only Sarah and Amy help when it's their day. After breakfast, Thor heads into his office at the clubhouse while Dragon and I head to the bar and grill if it's a weekday. They still don't want me to be unescorted because of Fang, so we rearranged m y office so that Dragon could have a desk in here too when I have to come in to do paperwork. After my shifts, we head back to the clubhouse. Like with breakfast,

Sasha, Roxy, and I usually make supper with occasional help from the bunnies. Evenings are spent either at the clubhouse or relaxing at the house.

Today's Saturday and the guys have just gone into Church. Yesterday, Sasha, Roxy, and I decided that we'd whip up pancakes, sausage, eggs, and bacon for breakfast this morning. Heading over to the pantry, I grab the pancake mix and frown as I take in the state of the shelves. Looking over my shoulder, I notice Roxy grabbing the bacon and eggs from the fridge.

"Hey, Roxy? You said you went to the grocery store yesterday with a couple of Prospects, right?"

She turns, placing the items on the counter and I notice her frowning, too. "Yeah, we did. We loaded up four carts full of groceries and I can't find half of what we bought for the fridge stuff." It's obvious when she notices the lack of food in the pantry behind me, because her eyes go wide and her fists clench. "Those were stocked full! What the hell is going on?"

I have to bite my cheek to hold in my smile at her outburst. I've gotten to know Roxy pretty well these past few weeks, and I'm happy to see her coming out of her shell.

"Let's grab out the supplies we have and if need be, we'll send a couple of Prospects to get the rest before the guys get out," I say and pull out one and a half boxes of pancake mix and four syrup bottles from the pantry. Sasha and Roxy pull out four dozen eggs, two packs of sausage, and three packs of bacon. For the fruit, we only have a few apples, two containers of strawberries, one container of raspberries, one bag of grapes, and a couple of oranges.

"Okay, we really need to send someone out." I exhale heavily and grab the pad of paper off the shelf, frantically writing down what else we need for breakfast while Sasha calls over the Prospects.

"Guys, we need one or two of you to make an emergency run to the store!"

"We just went yesterday," Drae groans.

Sasha huffs and points angrily at the pantry. "Well, then groceries are growing legs and walking out of here because Roxy said those shelves were stocked full yesterday. Same with the fridge," she growls.

Their eyes widen before narrowing when they look at the pantry. The doors are still open so they're able to see how bare the shelves are.

"I'll mention this to Thor later, but we have to get breakfast going with the supplies that we have. Can you run and get this so we can finish breakfast? We'll worry about the other stuff later," I say as I hand the list to Colt. He reads it over, nods, and turns to Drae and Alexei.

"I'll get this. You two stay with the ladies."

"Thor said no one should ride alone right now," Alexei says as he looks up from the laptop in front of him.

I bite my lip. We only have three Prospects, but Travis and Ethan should be somewhere on the compound. Thor always wants all three Prospects in the main room when they're at Church. No one should be entering the compound, so the gate doesn't need to be manned. One of them also helps watch the cameras on a laptop from the common room, which is what Alexei's currently doing. At least the bunnies aren't out here right now. I don't want to deal with their crap on top of the missing groceries. Even though it's Ginger's day to help us in the kitchen, she's nowhere to be found, like usual. The other bunnies are probably still in their rooms.

"Alexei, since you're on laptop duty, can you please text Travis and Ethan to come up to the main room for a bit? I know they aren't Prospects, but they both know how to fight. Drae, you go with Colt."

Colt nods at my words and Drae rolls his eyes at me but gets up. Colt's and Alexei's eyebrows rise as they share a look at Drae's behavior. Colt nods to me again, his lips in a flat line and his hand raises to snatch the SUV keys Roxy just tossed to him. Both of them leave, and I have a nagging feeling that something isn't right.

Frowning, I glance at Alexei to see his take on the situation, but he's also frowning and staring at the door the guys had just gone through. Maybe I'm not the only one that's been thinking Drae's been acting differently for the last couple of weeks. Looking over my shoulder, the ladies are also frowning before going back to their tasks. Yup, definitely not just me.

Sighing, I start prepping the pancakes. As we're cooking, a wave of nausea comes over me and I start to feel a little lightheaded. Shaking my head, I steal a few bites of fruit that Sasha's cutting up. She raises her eyebrow in question, and I nod. She moves the bowl of fruit she's already cut up closer to me and I take a few more bites. For the last few days, I've been feeling more drained and hungrier than normal. I figured it was just the stress getting to me about Fang. Either that or I'm coming down with something again. Sighing again, I get back to work on the pancakes.

I put the last pancake under the warmer and clean up my supplies. Hopefully Colt and Drae will be back soon, so we can finish making breakfast. I just put my dishes in the sink, planning to wash them quick so I'll be prepared to keep cooking once the guys get back when my phone rings.

It's an unknown number. That's odd. I have everyone's number in the club programmed into my phone so I know it's not Colt or Drae. I let it go to voicemail and slip it back into my pocket. Maybe it's spam or someone claiming my car warranty is about to expire. My phone beeps, letting me know a message was left but I'll listen to it later.

Not even five minutes later and my phone rings again. Once again, it's the same unknown number, so I slip it back in my pocket.

"Not gonna answer that?" Roxy asks.

I shake my head and shrug. "No idea who it is, so I'm letting it go to voicemail. Probably spam."

She nods and I start prepping what's left of the fruit that Sasha's been cutting up.

The front door swings open and Colt's carrying a dozen or so bags. His face is tight in anger, and I'm wondering what happened while they were gone. Drae's right behind him with only a couple of bags. He drops them roughly on the pass-through counter and walks over to the pool table.

"Drae, get your ass out here and help carry in the rest of the food!" Colt barks as he leaves the kitchen. Drae slams the cue he'd been holding on the table and follows Colt outside, grumbling under his breath. Roxy looks at me, shock written on her face, and I shrug. I don't know what the hell's going on with him, but I'll definitely be mentioning something to Thor and Dragon later.

We quickly unpack all the groceries and get back to work. I don't know if we'll have everything finished before the guys get out of Church, but I doubt the guys will complain. They've been loving the meals we've been making.

Just as I finish mixing more pancake batter, my phone rings again from the same damn number. Frustrated, I answer the call.

"What?" I bark into the phone. All eyes snap to me at the harshness of my voice.

"Now, that's no way to answer the phone, Princess. Didn't your mother teach you any manners? Do you miss me yet? Maybe I should teach you some manners when I see you again."

The chuckle that comes through the phone sends ice down my spine and freezes me in place.

Fang.

A hand wraps around my arm and I look up in shock to see Colt motioning with his hand to keep talking, and then he steers me toward the door to Church.

"Of course, my mother taught me manners. But why would I waste them on you, considering what you did to both of us last time?"

Colt motions for me to stay at the door, and he quickly enters before shutting the door. A moment later, he reopens the door, motions me inside, and then shuts the door behind him as he leaves. Thor mouths for me to put the phone on speaker. That's when I notice that Smoke's typing away furiously on his laptop.

"And as for missing you, why the hell would I be missing you? I dumped your ass two months ago. Not missing you in the slightest."

A growl comes across the line, and I wince as something smashes in the background.

"You'll pay for that little stunt when I get my hands on you again, Princess! You're mine. Not anyone else's. You were promised to me, and I will be making sure that promise is fulfilled. Your virgin pussy is mine. No one else's."

My blood runs cold at his words. I was promised to him? By who? Then the rest of his words register and I smirk.

"Well, sorry to disappoint you, but this non-virgin pussy does not belong to anyone but me. Who I give it to is up to me and me alone. I don't know who the hell promised me to you, but I don't give a rat's ass. I chose who I want to be with, and it certainly isn't your scrawny ass."

More things smash in the background and I smirk. It's almost too easy to get under his skin.

"If you let one of those Steel Archangel bastards touch you, you just made your punishment all the more severe, you little bitch! You'll regret giving them what was mine to take. What should have been mine years ago. You'll watch as I slice up those two Russians and that other woman you've been hanging around. You'll watch as they're tortured, raped, and then killed before your eyes. Next will be whoever you let touch you and that will be gruesome. Then it'll be your turn. What we do to them will seem like a walk in the park compared to what we'll do to you. Sweet dreams, Princess. Hope you like my little present I left for you." He cackles before the line disconnects.

I stare at the phone as his words sink in. Did I provoke him too much? Is that why he threatened the twins the way he did? Does he mean Roxy as the other woman? Not to mention threatening my men. Have I just signed all of our death warrants because of my sassy mouth?

Chapter 17
Thor

"THAT'S GOOD NEWS ON all the businesses. Smoke, were you able to find anything out on Fang?"

He nods and types something into his laptop. Suddenly, the door flies open and Colt motions to keep quiet before he quickly shuts the door.

"Sorry to interrupt and not wait, Pres, but Levi just got a phone call from an unknown number. From what Alexei overheard a bit ago she's gotten a number of them this morning. Whoever it is, she turned deathly pale and looks unsteady on her feet. I figured you'd want to hear what was being said and probably trace the call."

Tension fills the room and my gut twists. Is it Fang? "Get her in here quickly. Everyone stay quiet. Smoke, trace the call."

Smoke starts typing away and Colt brings in Levi. Her hand is clenched so tight around the phone that her knuckles are turning white. I point to the phone and mouth to her *'put it on speaker'*.

She nods and smirks before she sasses off to him. He's getting riled up at her words, and I smirk at how easily he's coming unhinged.

My eyes narrow when he says she was promised to him. Looking at Levi, her brow is furrowed in confusion. I glance at Dragon, the confusion also apparent on his face. Who promised her to Fang? And why?

When the phone call cuts off, Levi pales even further. Fuck, I bet she's blaming herself for what that fucker said about Sasha, Alexei, and I'm assuming Roxy since those are the three she mainly hangs out with. Not to mention the threat to Dragon and me. I quickly pull her in my arms and sit down before tugging her down on my lap. My chest tightens when I feel how much her body is trembling.

"Take a deep breath, Wildcat. It will be okay."

She shakes her head, and a tear escapes. "No, I pushed him too far. He's gonna hurt everyone even worse now. I can't let that happen. I can't lose you, Dragon, or them. Maybe it would be better if I just went to him? Then he wouldn't be able to hurt anyone else."

A growl rips from me and I'm pretty sure I hear one coming from Dragon before a chair falls to the floor with a bang. Levi jumps at the sound and jumps again as Dragon suddenly appears, kneeling before her.

"You aren't turning yourself over to that fucker," Dragon growls.

I put a hand on her arm and look at Phoenix before nodding toward the door. He gives me a chin lift and motions for the others to step out for a few minutes. After we get her settled down, I'll call them back in here so we can discuss things further. When the door closes, I cup her cheek and dry a few more tears that had escaped.

"Agreed, Wildcat. You won't be turning yourself over to Fang. This isn't the first time we've been targeted, and it won't be the last. Yeah, we'll have to take extra precautions, but that's expected in situations like this."

Tears pool in her eyes as she shakes her head, her hands fisting in her lap. "But I brought this situation to your doorstep. You wouldn't have to deal with them if it weren't for me." She sniffles and Dragon reaches up, cupping her jaw to turn her to face him.

"Spitfire, Fang and the rest of the Black Plague were already on our radar before we knew you were a piece of this puzzle. They'd already made a few threats to us before we moved you back home, so we were already planning on dealing with them. You coming here and being with Thor and me only gives us more motivation to take care of them."

He leans forward and kisses her. When he pulls back, I lean in and kiss her as well. It kills me that she thought she'd have to sacrifice herself to save everyone else. Seems we need to bring her up to speed on a few things later.

"We'll talk more later, Spitfire, but know this. We love you and will protect you and everyone else here. Neither Fang nor any of the other members of his club are going to get their hands on you. All right?"

Her eyes go wide with shock. "You love me?"

Grinning, I pull her close and kiss her deeply. "Yeah, I love you, Wildcat."

Dragon leans forward and kisses her just as deeply. "I love you, too, Spitfire."

A huge smile breaks out across her face. "I love you both, too."

Grinning, I kiss her again. When she pulls away, she has a confused look on her face.

"What do you think he meant by the 'little present he sent me'? I haven't gotten anything in the mail. You don't think he'll go after Dad, do you?"

I pause and realize we never had someone with Roy. Glancing at Dragon, he seems to realize the same thing I just did.

"Let's send Drae over to watch him," Dragon says and Levi stiffens before she grabs his arm.

"Don't send Drae!"

Shock courses through me at the urgency in her voice. Has something happened that we don't know about?

"Why shouldn't we send Drae, Wildcat?"

She bites her lip and studies us both. "I've been noticing that he's been acting off for the last week or so. Today he had a bit of attitude when we had to have Colt and him make an emergency run to the store for us. He barely helped Colt carry in any of the groceries and had a little tantrum when Colt ripped into him for trying to play pool instead of helping carry in the rest of the groceries. All of us were shocked at how disrespectful he was being."

My eyebrows shoot up in shock and I exchange a look with Dragon. This is news to us. We'll have to keep an eye on him because that sort of behavior is not be tolerated.

"We'll keep an eye on him, Spitfire. But next time you think something is off, don't wait. Tell us as it could be something that we can help with. Now, back to the groceries. Why did you need to send them to the store? Roxy went yesterday with a couple of Prospects to stock up."

She sighs and shakes her head. "I was going to talk to you guys later, after Church and breakfast, about it. For both Drae and the groceries. At first, I thought it was only me thinking something was off with him, but everyone else was also confused by his change in behavior this morning, too.

"As for the groceries, I think we need to have Smoke look at the cameras. When we went to start breakfast this morning, the pantry, fridge, and freezer were almost bare. We didn't check the deep freezers, so I'm not sure if there's food missing out of there or not. Someone must be taking the food because Roxy said they got four cartloads yesterday. There's no way the kitchen would have been that bare after only one day. Thank God none of the bunnies were down here because I didn't want to have to deal with their bullshit on top of the missing groceries and Drae's attitude problem this morning," she says as she frowns and rubs her temples.

Wait, why wasn't a bunny helping? They're each on rotation in the kitchen for breakfast and supper.

"But if someone from the club needs food for someone or their family, why didn't they tell us? Depending on the situation, we could have helped them." She frowns again and I can see the wheels turning as she tries to figure out who it could be.

I kiss her temple and smile. She'll make a great Old Lady with trying to figure out how to help whoever's involved in this situation. Speaking of which, we need to talk to her soon about that.

"We'll talk to Smoke and see what he can find out about the food. Now, how are you feeling? We still need to finish up Church, especially now with this new news about Fang. We'll need to discuss how we're going to go about the extra protection until we get our hands on Black Plague."

She tenses slightly, and her eyes harden. She cocks her head to the side and narrows her eyes at me. "I'm not even going to be able to know what's going on, am I? Even though this pertains to me as their primary target."

"Sorry, Wildcat, but that's club business."

Her eyes blaze with anger at my words and she hastily slides off my lap, stepping back from us. "So, I seriously won't be able to know anything about what you'll be doing to keep me safe? What will be done to find Fang and his club? Wouldn't I be safer if I knew even the cliff note version so that I can keep a better eye out?" She looks between both of us as she crosses her arms. "Did you even mean what you said about me being able to help torture them and be the one to kill Fang?"

"We don't like it, but yes, we meant what we said about that. The rest is club business to keep you safe. The less you know about our methods to go about that, the—"

She huffs, cutting us off, and stalks toward the door. We both reach out to her, but she raises her hand to stop us. "Nope. Should have known you two would go all caveman."

My chest tightens and dread fills me.

She pauses at the door and turns back toward us. Her hurt-felt gaze bores into both of us as she shakes her head. "This is my life. I should at least know some of what's going to be going on. I'm not saying that you had to tell me every detail, but I should have at least been able to know the gist of what was going to happen. I won't be a prisoner in my own life, and I won't let anyone control every aspect of my life. No matter how much I love you both."

She opens the door and leaves. While she doesn't slam the door, she does close it roughly. My chest aches at her words, and I rub it as I stand staring at the door. Did I just mess up the best thing that came into our lives?

The door opens and Bear's angry gaze settles on us before he closes it behind him. "You are my Pres and Enforcer, but Little Ninja is my family, and she comes first. What the fuck did you two say to her that had her storming out of here like she was going to light someone's ass on fire and then cut them up to feed to the wolves?"

Narrowing my eyes at him, I barely resist chewing him out for talking to us like that. "Honestly, that's between us three, and we'll talk more with her later about it."

Bear shakes his head and crosses his arms. His gaze hardening even further. "Let me guess. She wanted to know about what would be done regarding hers and the others' safety. Knowing you two numbskulls, you probably pulled the club business line on her, didn't you?"

My jaw clenches as my anger grows. It really is none of his business what we discussed, even if he is her family.

"You two probably just messed up royally with your woman. You'll be lucky if she even speaks with you again."

The dread that was filling me earlier grows even heavier at his words.

"Do you think your dad never talked to your mom about club business?"

I look at Dragon and we both shake our heads. In all the years that Dad was in the club and then later as their President, we never heard him discuss anything with her. Bear shakes his head at us and frowns.

"I know for a fact that he did because I was there for some of it. She was his sounding board sometimes. Others, she helped him through some of the rougher things he had to do. Not to mention she helped him with what he saw when his sister was taken."

Bear shudders at the memory and my breath hitches. I remember Dad talking to Mom about when Aunt Ella was taken and what had been done to her. I just hadn't known it was something he did with the club when he went to search for her. Then again, we were only five when that happened, so we might not have known it was club business that they were talking about. Bear's humorless chuckle has my attention returning to him.

"I see you both are now starting to realize things a bit more. Let's get the guys in here and discuss a few things. The women are still cooking and when I walked in here, Levi was heading into the kitchen. Even as pissed as she is at you, she'll still finish making breakfast. If you're lucky, we'll finish in here before she makes a run for it."

Panic fills me that she'd leave, especially after all the things Fang spewed at her earlier. "Call the others in."

Bear gives me a chin lift, and I risk a glance at Dragon as Bear heads out into the common room. He's as nervous as I am that Levi might leave while we're in here.

"We gotta make this right, Ry. I can't lose her. We can't lose her."

"Same. No way in hell am I gonna lose her, either. She's the best thing that ever happened to us."

He nods and goes back to his seat as the others filter back in. I love Levi and can't live without her. Sure, she could probably do better than two alpha asshole bikers, but we're selfish and don't want to let her go.

When everyone's back in their seats, I turn to Smoke. "Did you get anything from the phone call?"

He nods and, after a few clicks, a map comes up on the wall. "The call was made from somewhere around this area, which is about a half-hour northwest of here. There are a couple of houses close together, so it's hard to pinpoint exactly which house the call came from. With a little more digging, I can probably find it out. Might not be a bad idea to get a few eyes on the area and see if we can learn anything else. As for Black Plague as a whole, they seem to have been pretty busy. There are reports of a lot of women in surrounding towns going missing. Reports also state that a lot of men wearing Black Plague cuts are seen in the areas prior to the abductions. Fuckers are doing this in our backyard." Smoke pauses before he looks at me. "You aren't going to like this, Pres, but most of the women that have gone missing resemble Levi—red hair, green eyes, and a curvy figure."

He presses a few more buttons and pictures of the missing women appear on the wall. Rage fills me with what's happening to these women. Women who were most likely ripped out of their lives because they looked like my Wildcat.

"Pres," Phoenix says quietly.

When I look at him, he nods at the table. I glance down and realize I've gripped the edge so hard I have blood dripping down my hands. Cursing, I wipe my hands on my pants, thankful that I wore black jeans today. Patch gives me a chin lift and grabs the kit that's stored in here before pulling a chair up next to me and getting to work on my hands.

"We need eyes on those four houses. Smoke, figure out who owns or rents those houses. Maybe we'll get lucky and find clues to where Black Plague is hiding those women." Pausing, I think back to the phone conversation and what Levi had said about Drae. "Keep things close to the chest regarding Black Plague. I'm not sure how Fang knew that Levi was becoming good friends with Roxy, but I'm guessing that she's the other woman Fang referenced in the phone call. Roxy, Sasha, and Levi have become really close, so she has to be the third woman. Also, we need to keep an eye on things around the clubhouse."

I fill them in on everything Levi had told us about Drae and the missing food.

"Do you think he could be a mole, Pres?" Bones asks and I frown.

"I don't know, but we need to be careful about what we say outside this room pertaining to club business. We should also see if there's anyone else that would like to Prospect. If Drae is a mole, then that only leaves us with Alexei and Colt as Prospects. With Fang's threats, we'll need to take extra safety precautions, especially with the women. Remember, no one rides alone. Always pair up."

Timber gives me a chin lift, indicating he has something to say.

"Pres, both Travis and Ethan have voiced that they'd like to Prospect for us. They've been living at the clubhouse since these threats started and have learned a lot about the club. They want to help protect everyone, especially Levi and Sasha, as they see them like family."

I nod at the thought of them becoming Prospects. They're good men, and I think they'd do well. I also know Smoke has done background checks on them from when they had applied at Steel Construction and that he hadn't found anything amiss or suspicious. "All in favor of having Travis become a Prospect? We need a unanimous vote for this."

One by one, everyone agreed to have Travis become a Prospect.

"Alright, all in favor of having Ethan become a Prospect?"

Once again, aye's rang out around the room.

"Sounds good. Let's have a gathering tonight and they can get their cuts. Since it's short notice, let's see if we can get it catered in rather than having the women making everything. We'll meet again after we learn more about the houses and what else Smoke can pull up on those bastards. Also, after Smoke digs into the camera feeds around the clubhouse regarding this morning and the food."

With the meeting adjourned, I'm anxious to find Levi and talk to her. We really need to beg for forgiveness because there's no way in hell I'm going to lose her. Patch finishes bandaging my hands, and I look at Dragon. He gives me a chin lift, and we head out to the main room.

Chapter 18
Thor

OUT IN THE MAIN room, I look through the pass-through and sigh in relief. Wildcat's setting out the food as she laughs at something along with Sasha and Roxy. I frown when I realize it's only the three of them in there. Which bunny was supposed to be on rotation today? Seeing Alexei nearby, I figure he might know and maybe can gleam a little info about the situation for me. Pulling a chair out next to him, he gives me a tight smile.

"Pres."

Shit. From his tone, he knows something's up with Levi, but damn if I'm going to talk to him about it.

"Do you know which bunny is supposed to be on the rotation today?"

He snorts and shakes his head. "Pres, only Amy and Sarah help out on their days. The other bunnies sneak in at the last minute and act like they've been helping all along. Usually, it's right when the food is ready, and the guys are already in line. Look, here comes Trixie."

He points to his laptop, and scooting closer, I angle the laptop so that I can see it better. Sure as shit, Trixie is coming down the hallway and slips into the kitchen from the back. The other women are already taking the lids off everything on the counter, and I see Levi scowling at Trixie when she realizes she's in the kitchen. Rather than confront her, she turns to finish her tasks.

"How long has this been going on?"

Alexei looks a little nervous as he glances up at the kitchen. "Not too long after Levi and Sasha started helping Roxy, so a little over a month. None of those three say anything because they don't want Trixie, Tiffany, Ginger, or Ashley in there anyway. None of them can cook and they've tried having them do simple tasks, but they just bitch and whine the whole time. It's more of a headache than anything and they can get stuff done quicker without them in there."

I frown. I'm going to have to talk to Levi about this. If this is true, we need to figure out other tasks that those four can do. They're supposed to have chores as well as being there for the men when they wanted them to be able to live here with free room and board. Not to mention, they get a small wage for spending money. If they aren't pulling their weight, they'll be gone. Clapping Alexei on the shoulder, I stood.

"Thanks, brother. I'll talk to Levi about it and get her take on it."

He nods, but still seems on edge. Heading toward the kitchen, I notice Levi's fixing herself a plate. Dragon steps up beside me and we both head over toward her. She turns around and stops when she sees us. Her jaw tenses and she pivots to go around us. I quickly catch up to her and place a hand on her shoulder.

"Can we sit with you, Wildcat? We'd like to talk and apologize."

The hardness in her eyes softens slightly as her gaze darts between us, but her body is still tense under my hand. "Fine. Get a plate and we'll talk."

Nodding, we get in line and quickly make up our plates. Honestly, I'm not even paying attention to the food I pile on my plate with how nervous I am. Grabbing a mug of coffee, I head over to the table she's at, but it doesn't escape my notice that she picked one that's a bit further away from the others.

I sit down beside Wildcat and can still tell she's tense as hell. A moment later, Dragon sits down on the other side of her. Her eyes keep darting around and I'm starting to wonder if anything else happened while we were still in Church. Taking a sip of coffee, I turn to face her.

"We'd like to start by apologizing, Wildcat. We shouldn't have tried to keep information from you. Especially since you are the main target of Fang's threats."

She frowns but says nothing.

"We won't be able to tell you all the specifics though, because if we do get blowback from what we do, we don't want you caught up in the crossfire, Spitfire. We can give you a general idea, but we also need to protect you."

"You mean like plausible deniability?" she asks, and both Dragon and I chuckle.

"Yeah. You mean everything to us, Wildcat, and we don't want to lose you. We've never been in this position before where we had to discuss how we handled club business. There will be times when you ask us something and we won't be able to answer your questions. In those situations, please try to remember that we're doing that because we're trying to protect you. Not to control, restrain, or belittle you in any way."

She sighs and nods, some of the tension in her body lessening. "Thank you. That means a lot that you both said all of that. As much as I'm still so mad at you guys, I love both of you. I'm pretty new to this relationship thing, too. Let's all agree to work on our communication and if we have another argument, we either talk about it right away or after we cool off. You both mean everything to me too and I don't want to lose you either."

We both nod and the rest of the tension leaves her body. She gives me a quick kiss before turning and giving Dragon a kiss, too. We dig into our breakfasts and as we talk, I realize Drae's sitting a few tables away from us. He's texting someone on his phone but keeps looking up at us periodically. A chill goes down my spine when I realize it's Levi that he's watching. Looking over at Smoke, I'm relieved when I see that he's working on his laptop while eating. Pulling out my phone, I quickly type up a message to him as I keep my phone hidden from Drae's line of sight.

> Thor: Can you pull up Drae's phone records? He's been texting someone all through breakfast and keeps looking up at Levi to watch what she's doing.

> Smoke: On it, Pres. Will have the info to you in a few minutes.

Glancing up, our gazes lock and I give him a chin lift before going back to eating my breakfast.

"Spitfire, can we ask you a couple of things?"

"Sure, what's up?"

"I saw Trixie slipping into the kitchen right as everyone was getting in line. Are the bunnies pulling their weight on the rotations?"

Levi pauses chewing and glances around before swallowing. Sighing, she pushes her now empty plate forward and grabs her coffee mug. Leaning forward, she rests her elbows on the table.

"I was wondering when this conversation would come up. I was waiting to say something until I had an alternative idea to tell you about and recently finalized a few of them." She pauses and takes a deep breath before looking at both of us. "I've been trying to figure out what I can have them do differently, and I have a few ideas. Trixie, Tiffany, Ashley, and Ginger can't cook. We've tried having them measure out ingredients to help out that way, but they even mess up that. We then tried having them do a little prep work, like chopping fruits and veggies or cutting up the meat. They are extremely slow and I'm not sure if it's on purpose or if they're slow because it's something new. Of course, throughout all these different jobs, they constantly complain and whine that we were ruining their manicures. Not to mention how much better they could please you sexually than me and all your favorite positions and things you both liked to do with them."

My fork freezes midway to my mouth as I turn to look at her. She's staring down at the table as she swallows thickly. Her eyes are misty, and she blinks repeatedly to keep them from falling.

"Those fucking bitches," Dragon mutters as he runs a hand over his face.

Levi chuckles weakly before smiling at him. "I shut them up pretty quick each time, but it still hurts to hear all the things you've both done with them. I know that was all in the past, but it's something I have to learn to deal with. Well, I should say Sasha and I have to learn to deal with," she says quietly before taking another sip of coffee.

I hate that she feels that way, but I can't take away the bunnies without a vote from all of my brothers. And I'm pretty sure they still want them around for their own releases. Wait a minute. "They're saying things to Sasha, too?"

She nods, and I feel the anger rising up in me.

"Does Sasha know that whatever they are saying about Colt isn't true?"

Levi looks at me in shock and I'm guessing Colt never told that tidbit of information to Sasha. I'll have to give him a heads-up later so he could ease some fears that Sasha may now be having.

"One of the rules for Prospects is that they can't have sex, either physical or oral, with the bunnies. Period."

Her eyes widen and a moment later, her shoulders relax. "I don't think Sasha knows that. The stuff they were saying that Colt did with them was pretty wild, and I know she's got some reservations about their relationship as a result."

"We'll give Colt a heads up so that he can put to rest some of her worries."

Levi squeezes my hand and gives me a small smile. "Thank you, Thor."

"Back to the bunnies and cooking, Spitfire. We've always seen them when we come up to the food line. Are they sneaking in and trying to make it seem like they were helping?"

Levi frowns and nods. "That's exactly what they are doing. With the exception of Sarah and Amy. Those two can cook, and Sasha, Roxy, and I get along pretty well with them. There were some hiccups in the beginning, but we worked through them pretty quick.

"As for Tiffany, Ashley, Ginger, and Trixie, I was going to talk to you about having them do cleanup duty in the kitchen instead and pulling in Sarah and Amy more into the cooking rotation. We purchased extra-long gloves so that they wouldn't mess up their manicures or dry out their perfectly moisturized skin," Levi says as she rolls her eyes and makes quotation marks with her hands.

Both Dragon and I shake our heads at the ridiculousness, but then again, Levi found a way around their stupid ass complaints so that they wouldn't be able to play up those excuses anymore.

"We can show them how to work the dishwashers, but if they can't figure them out, then they can hand wash the dishes. There are two big sinks so two of them could wash the dishes while two dried them. If we three, plus Amy and Sarah, are always cooking, then those four can always clean up.

"They're also shirking on their laundry and cleaning duties around the rest of the clubhouse according to Roxy, Amy, and Sarah. What if we put Roxy in charge of those tasks since she's here all day, whereas Sasha and I have jobs in town? If Roxy is in charge of those areas, has random check-ins with them, and we give clear direction for who is doing what on which days, then they'll know that they'll get busted if they don't do what they are supposed to. As of late, Roxy's been busting her ass along with Sarah and Amy to cover the other four girls' areas. I know the Prospects have their respective cleaning things to do, but I assumed that that would still fall under your guys' authority."

Nodding, I can tell by the set of Dragon's jaw that he's just as pissed as I am that those four girls are causing so much trouble.

"What the hell do they do all day?" Dragon growls and Levi shrugs.

"From what I can gather, they are either in their rooms, shopping, getting their nails or hair done, or fucking your brothers. Though from some of their complaints, I think they're mad that they aren't getting much action from the guys. That's another thing they are blaming on us. They got laid all the time before we came here, but lately, your brothers aren't having sex with them very much. However, from what Sarah and Amy have said, nothing has changed much in that regard for them."

As angry as I am at the bunnies, I'm proud of Levi for bringing together this plan. Things need to change and if the bunnies don't pull their weight, we'd have to make a decision as a club about what to do with them.

"Sorry if I dropped so much on you guys at once. You are both so busy that I was trying to figure out a solution before I came to talk to you. This seemed like something that I could do for both of you and maybe take something off your shoulders for you."

We both grin at her and as I glance at Dragon, he nods while tugging on his cut. Grinning, I pull out my phone and text Phoenix quick. I'm just about to put my phone away when it dings again. However, the text isn't from Phoenix, it's from Smoke.

> Smoke: Not sure why they did it, but guess which four bunnies snuck into the kitchen last night and threw out most of the food that was bought yesterday?

My phone pings again and there are pictures of them throwing the food into trash bags and then hauling them out into the dumpsters.

"Ryan?"

I look up and notice Levi looking at me worriedly. I don't miss the fact that she used my real name, but my argument dies on my tongue when I see exactly how worried she is.

"Sorry, but you didn't answer to Thor, which is why I said Ryan. Are you okay? You bent your fork. Also, why are your hands all bandaged up?"

Glancing down at my hand, I drop my now bent in half fork. "I'll be fine, Wildcat. The bandages are because I gripped the table a little too hard after learning some stuff earlier. Patch took care of me, and yes, we'll fill you in later."

I look over at Dragon and nod. Turning back to Levi, I grin at her. "Back to the bunnies. Your ideas are perfect and I want to implement them right away. However, first, we need to make a different announcement."

She looks between us worriedly, but she doesn't need to be worried.

"Don't worry your pretty little head, Spitfire. Your ideas are fantastic, and I think our brothers are going to love them. The bunnies will either need to get with the program or they'll suffer the consequences. They can't be shirking their duties, especially since they get a wage and free room and board."

Her eyes widen before they narrow, and she clutches her mug so hard I'm afraid it might break and she'll burn or cut herself.

"They get a wage, too? Fucking bitches! If I had known that, I would have tried to come up with a solution sooner! Bitches should have to pay back some of their wages for shirking their duties and give it to Roxy, Sarah, and Amy, since they've been picking up the slack," she growls, and I grin.

"That's not a bad idea, Wildcat."

Standing up, I give her a quick kiss before walking over toward the open part of the common area. Phoenix hands me a box and with a chin lift, I turn toward everyone, whistling loudly. Chatter soon tapers off and everyone turns toward me

.

"I have a couple of announcements to make. Wildcat and Dragon, can you please come up here?"

My brothers grin at me, knowing what's in the box I'm holding. Wildcat steps up beside me, looking nervous and worried sick. Hopefully, we'd be able to ease her nerves in a moment.

Turning toward her, I hold the box in front of me. "Wildcat, you mean the world to both Dragon and me. Would you honor us by becoming our Old Lady?"

She stares in shock at us, but when Dragon lifts the lid and she sees her property cut, her whole face lights up as she smiles. "Yes!"

Grinning, Dragon lifts her cut out of the box and she laughs when she sees her road name, Enchantress, stitched on it. After the first time we'd called her that, she asked why we called her it. We had always said it would take a special kind of woman who would be able to enchant both of us and she did that to both of us at first sight.

As she slips on her property cut, I don't miss the daggers that some of the bunnies are sending her way. She leans up, giving both of us a kiss. As Dragon wraps an arm around her waist, I clear my throat as I look around the room.

"For our other announcement, we're going to be making some changes to how some things are done around here. Could I have Roxy and all of the bunnies come up front? Sasha, you can come up too since I know you're already itching to hug our Old Lady." I wink at her and she grins before darting out of her chair.

Both her and Roxy hug Levi as they congratulate her. Sarah and Amy also give her a quick hug as they say their congratulations, which has the other bunnies glaring at them.

"Since Levi is our Old Lady, and since I am the President of the Steel Archangel's, that now puts the bunnies under her charge." As suspected, four of the bunnies' faces turn red with anger, probably knowing that their free ride is about to end.

"Wildcat, care to share the changes we just discussed and approved?" I ask her as I look down at her.

Wildcat stares at me in shock for a moment before she realizes what I mean. She smiles at me, and I wink at her. She clears her throat as she turns and looks at the bunnies.

"Over the past few weeks, we learned that there are four of you who cannot cook and refuse to help. You have been sneaking in at the last minute so that it appears that you were there the whole time. That ends now. I will be dividing up the kitchen labor differently. As work schedules allow for breakfast and supper, Sasha, Roxy, Amy, Sarah, and I will continue to prepare and cook the food. Amy and Sarah can choose to either be on a rotation or to both help every day.

"Lunch will remain as usual during the week. Since most of us work off the compound, those of you that are here will continue to grab your own lunch and clean up after yourself, which includes doing your dishes. That could be as simple as putting them in the dishwasher or handwashing them. For the weekends, us five will have a rotation so that three of us will cook and the other two will have the weekend off. Since us five will be cooking, that will leave the cleanup of the prepared meals to Ginger, Tiffany, Ashley, and Trixie. We'll make a rotation for you four for the weekend as well." She pauses and pulls Roxy forward.

"As for the laundry and cleaning duties that the bunnies do for the clubhouse, I'm placing Roxy in charge of those duties, and she will report to me."

Roxy looks up at her in shock before smiling widely, which Levi returns.

"She'll make up the schedule for who will be cleaning what area and who will be doing laundry for a given day. She will be checking in with each of you periodically throughout the day, so if you aren't pulling your weight or your area isn't clean, she'll know that you didn't do your tasks that day. The times that she'll be checking in will be random. If it is found that someone is not doing their tasks, she'll bring it up to me and those in question will have a little chat with her, me, and possibly even Thor." She pauses again as she looks at each of them.

"I recently learned that you all get a wage as well as room and board in exchange for doing these chores, in addition to being here for the single brothers. Well, with the exception of Roxy on that last part. It's in your best interest to make sure you do your allotted tasks so that you can still earn those things."

Four faces pale as Amy and Sarah try to hide their smirks. Oh yeah, those two are really happy with these changes. I also don't miss Alexei's shocked look when he realizes Roxy isn't a bunny that is here sexually for my brothers. I think I may have been correct in my guess that he likes her. Levi squeezes my hand, and I take that as my cue to step in.

"Now, it has come to my attention that four of you have been severely shirking your duties. Tiffany, Trixie, Ashley, and Ginger. For the last few weeks, you've been making the others pick up your slack while you went off and went shopping or got your nails done or whatever the fuck it is you were doing. That ends now. If we find out that anyone is shirking their duties in the future, they will get a warning and their wages docked. If you receive a second warning, you will lose a week's pay. If you receive a third warning, you're kicked out and are no longer a club bunny." I pause as I look at each one of them, making sure my words have sunk in.

"For my last announcement, Trixie, Tiffany, Ashley, and Ginger, please step forward." Their faces pale further. Tiffany looks at me defiantly while the others are trying to hide their nervousness.

"Before I continue, is there anything you want to tell me about what happened last night?"

The girls exchange nervous looks while Tiffany glares at Levi. Ashley steps forward and when Tiffany sees her, she looks ready to spit nails.

"What the fuck, Ashley? Get back in line!"

Ashley turns on her, pointing angrily in her direction. "Fuck you, Tiffany! There's no way I'm getting kicked out of here because of you! Unlike you, I have nowhere else to go if I get kicked out."

She turns back toward me and takes another step forward. Ginger steps forward to join her and takes her hand. Looking at me, Ashley takes a deep breath before speaking.

"Us four are the reason for the groceries going missing."

Shock shows on all my brothers' faces before turning to anger. Not going to lie, I hadn't expected them to turn against the others, but they are the two that really don't have anywhere to go if they get kicked out of here. At least they seem to be willing to right some of their wrongs.

"Why did you throw away most of the groceries that Roxy and the Prospects stocked up on yesterday?"

"Tiffany wanted Levi to look bad in front of you and Dragon. She wanted you both to see her fail in preparing meals for the club. She had planned to do this randomly and before big meals. Especially if any of the other clubs were coming over and we weren't catering," Ashley tells me.

"There were also other things that she had planned to do that would have made Levi look unworthy of being the President's and Enforcer's woman. Well, now Old Lady," Ginger says as she looks sheepishly toward Levi.

"Shut up, you fucking bitches! Can't believe I ever fucking told you cunts any of—" Tiffany yells before she's cut off.

Looking over at her, I notice Phoenix has gagged her and Bear's holding her arms behind her so that she can't get away. Judge and Ryder have Trixie's arms in their grasp, but so far, she's without a gag.

With a chin lift of thanks to them, I turn my attention back to Ginger. She's turned pale once again at seeing Tiffany restrained and her hands tremble. Glancing at Levi, she's staring at them in shock with her hand over her mouth. I can tell by Dragon's grip on her hip that he's keeping her back, even though she looks like she wants to comfort the two women who seem about ready to faint from anxiety.

"What else did she have planned?"

"On the nights where we were going to provide food when other clubs were here, Tiffany was going to slip something into the dishes that Levi had made. Then whoever ate those dishes would get food poisoning. She also had plans to trash the common rooms and kitchen before big events. That way Levi would have to spend time cleaning things up and then be rushed in preparing the food."

Chapter 19
Levi

THOSE FUCKING BITCHES! WHY the fuck would they do any of that?

While I do have a little sympathy for Ashley and Ginger with them coming forward, it doesn't fully dampen my anger. My guess is that Ginger's in the same boat as Ashley of having nowhere to go if they're kicked out.

Narrowing my eyes at Tiffany, I rip Dragon's hand off my waist and stalk over to her. Yanking the gag out of her mouth, I get right in her face.

"What the fuck did I ever do to you to make you want to do all of that to me?"

"They should have been mine! I was the one that they preferred since Monica was kicked out. It should be me wearing their cut, not you, you fucking bitch!"

I grin as I grip her chin hard, but not hard enough to bruise. "Do you honestly think any one of these men want to take a club bunny who has had sex with all of their brothers as their Old Lady? Do you really think they want to have someone who has had all of their holes filled by each and every one of their brothers? No, they don't. And if you had managed to pull off all that shit with the food and trashing the clubhouse, don't you realize that I wouldn't have been the only one that looked like a failure to the other clubs? If that shit did happen, it would reflect poorly on the club as well."

She balks, shock evident on her face before she masks it again with anger. Damn bitch really hadn't thought the whole thing through.

"How the fuck do you know that none of them want us as an Old Lady, bitch?"

"If they had wanted you as an Old Lady, wouldn't you already be one by now? If memory serves, the last one of all of you to join the ranks was Roxy, and that was almost a year ago. You're the bunny that's been here the longest at four years. If being an Old Lady was your goal, I would think that if you haven't become one in that amount of time, then it most likely wasn't going to happen."

Tiffany screams at my words as she tries to escape from Uncle Bear's iron-clad grip. I release my grip on her chin, but don't step back. I doubt she'll manage to get out of Uncle Bear's grasp, but if she does, I'll be prepared. *Fuck*. My cut will make getting to my blades harder. I'm going to have to make some modifications to my armor.

"How about we answer this question once and for all?" Axe calls out as he stands, and all the bunnies turn their attention to him. "Levi's right. None of us want an Old Lady that has been with every single one of our brothers."

"If that was your goal when you signed up to be a club bunny, then you might want to seriously consider packing your bags and leaving," Timber says, and the other men voice their agreement with him.

Turning back to the bunnies, there are a few that look like their hopes have been dashed but surprisingly, most don't look all that shocked by the revelation. Taking a few steps back, I feel both Dragon and Thor wrap their arms around my waist. I look at each of the bunnies in turn before I speak again.

"Take some time to think about the changes and what all was said today. I expect all of you ladies to meet back here at 10 am tomorrow after breakfast. If you are here, then we'll go over your rotations and any questions you may have. If you're absent from the meeting, then I *will* take that as your decision to leave the club. Anything that is left in your room after the meeting will be boxed up. If you do not claim the items within three days, they will be thrown in the trash or burned. Any questions?"

Of course, Tiffany chooses to speak up.

"Yes! Why do *we* have to change what we've been doing? That bitch comes in here on her high horse and suddenly changes everything! Why should we have to listen to her?"

Growls come from behind me and judging by how rigid both of my men are standing, they're barely containing their anger toward her.

"Bitch, if you'd take a look at your Pres and Enforcer, you'll realize you're a breath away from being kicked out of the club and possibly even banned if you keep talking about their Old Lady like that," Judge tells her.

Tiffany looks at Thor and shrinks back a bit before standing up straight. "What I said still stands. Why should we have to listen to her when we've been around longer than her? She's been here for five weeks and now we have to obey her every demand? She should be listening to the one that's been here the longest. This is bullshit!" she cries as she stomps her foot like a child. Laughter erupts across the room, and I shake my head in disbelief.

"Fucking idiot," Sasha says as she laughs. "You're a club bunny. You honestly believe a club bunny would be ranked higher than an Old Lady?"

Tiffany pauses before puffing out her chest. "Yes, whoever is the most senior should be the one in charge."

She juts out her chin and Trixie side-steps away from her, looking down in shame. Well, she steps away as much as she can with Judge and Ryder's grips on her arms. Laughter erupts once again from around the room, and Tiffany looks at them in confusion.

"Bitch, a bunny is at the bottom of the fucking ladder in any MC. It's always that way, no matter how long you've been here. Old Ladies and girlfriends of the brothers are cherished. Same with any kids of the brothers," Smoke says as he glares at her.

Tiffany turns redder, and I'm actually starting to worry if she'll have a heart attack or burst a blood vessel or something.

Trixie clears her throat and looks at me pleadingly. "May I please say something?"

I nod, and she takes a deep breath.

"While I do have somewhere I can go if I am kicked out, I'd rather not. It... It isn't a safe place, and I'd be dead by next weekend, most likely, or sold to some sick fuck. I know I'm probably already on strike two and this mess might have me at strike three, but..." she pauses as she worries her lip before looking at me. "Is there any way I could have one more chance? I promise I won't fuck it up."

I still at her words. What kind of family does she have that would kill her or sell her off if she went home? Thor clears his throat and squeezes my hip. Fuck, I hope that means we'll at least be able to talk to her and that he isn't kicking her out.

"Trixie, after this and before we make a decision, we'll meet to discuss a few things with you. I want to understand what you just said better," Thor tells her.

She nods but hangs her head as she shrinks in on herself. Glancing around at the rest of the guys, they all look pissed and I'm pretty sure it's directed at whoever the hell her family is, and if they really would do something like that.

"Tiffany, this is considered your third strike. Especially since you've just shown that you won't change your ways. Phoenix, Bear—escort her to her room so she can gather her shit. Don't take your eyes off her," Thor says. They both give him a chin lift and drag Tiffany away as she shrieks for someone to help her.

"All right, let's finish up with our breakfast and the rest of our day. There'll be a party tonight and we'll cater in since it's last minute. Not to mention it seems we'll have to get more groceries to replace what was lost."

I gasp and look up at him. "Are you sure, Hun? I don't mind cooking, even if it's on short notice."

He smiles down at me and places a quick kiss on my lips. "I'm sure, Baby Girl. Figure out what needs to be replaced and make up a list. The Prospects can go and get what is needed once you have it all ready." He pauses as he looks over my shoulder. "Besides, I think there are six ladies that look like they want to talk to you. First, how about everyone finishes their breakfast? Then we'll have the chat with Trixie before you talk to all the girls. I'm not sure how long that will take."

I nod in agreement and when I turn back around, I'm surprised to see Smoke and Ryder gripping Drae's shoulders. Ryder leans down and whispers something into Drae's ear. His body visibly tenses and a look of panic crosses his face. Smoke gestures to his phone, his gaze locked on Thor. He must have sent a text about something while our attention was focused on the girls.

Thor pulls out his phone, and his body instantly goes rigid against me. Dragon looks over his shoulder at the text and his body also goes rigid. I almost step out of their arms at the terrifying looks on their faces.

"Thor... Dragon... What's going on? What's wrong?"

They both look at each other, some sort of silent communication happening. Dragon nods before kissing my forehead and heads down the hall, following Smoke, Ryder, and Drae. I start to say something, but Thor silences me with a kiss. He rests his forehead against mine as his hands grip my waist.

"We have to take care of something with Drae, Baby Girl, and I'd rather tell you about it when I have all the information. For now, I need you to trust me. Finish your breakfast, if you're still hungry, but don't leave the clubhouse for now. We'll talk to Trixie after we take care of this mess."

I look up at him and nod as I bite my lip. Looking around, there aren't many people nearby, but I don't want anyone else to hear what I have to say. Taking his hand, I pull him over to the corner for a bit more privacy. Thankfully, he follows without resistance.

"I know you won't be able to tell me everything, but if he's tied to how Fang knows about Roxy and things going on here, I want to know why. Even if it is a summarized version. Why is he betraying the club? Why is he selling me out to Fang? If there is a problem and he's being blackmailed, why didn't he come forward? We could have helped him. Find out the blackmailed part first before they start beating him to a bloody pulp." I pause as thoughts and situations race through my mind, my anger rising at what he could also be doing. "However, if he did this intentionally and is double-crossing our club, our family, our home? Beat away and make sure to get in a good punch for me."

Chapter 20
Thor

I LOOK DOWN AT Levi's face as it flips between concerned, worried, to pissed off. I know I won't be able to tell her everything, but am also relieved that she asked for a summarized version. A grin slides across my face as the rest of her words sink in.

"I love that you said we're all your family, Wildcat."

Her face lights up in a stunning smile, and I crash my lips to hers. Reluctantly pulling away, I place another kiss on her forehead. "I gotta get downstairs, Baby Girl. We'll be back later. Stay in the clubhouse."

She nods, walks to our table, grabs our empty plates and mugs, and then walks over by Roxy and Sasha before heading back into the kitchen. She pauses at the entryway and looks back over her shoulder. "Trixie, Ashley, and Ginger, please come into the kitchen after you're done eating and we'll show you what needs to be done." The three women nod and tuck back to the rest of their food.

Colt and Alexei are sitting together, so I head in their direction.

"Stay in the clubhouse with the women. One of you keep an eye on the cameras. No one should be coming to the gate, but you never know. If they do, go out together, but see if Travis and Ethan will sit in here with the women."

"You got it, Pres. I take it Levi mentioned Drae to you?"

Nodding, Colt frowns as he looks over his shoulder toward the hallway that the guys took Drae down a few moments ago.

"I noticed a change in his behavior a few days ago. At first, I thought it was just my imagination, but this morning was when it really hit home. I should have told you sooner and I'm sorry, Pres. It won't happen again."

"I noticed it about a week ago and, like Colt, I thought it was just my imagination. I'll speak up right away next time. Sorry, Pres."

I give them both a chin lift, but I still need to make sure they understand things could have been much worse.

"Go with your gut if something feels wrong. Next time, if something seems off, bring it up right away. We're lucky that nothing serious happened this time, but next time that might not be the case."

Turning, I give a chin lift to the rest of my brothers and nod toward the hallway. They all get up and follow after me. Thankfully, I notice that Ethan and Travis are sticking around the main room. I don't know if they heard me, but at least they're already thinking like Prospects. Heading down the hall and then down into the basement after scanning my hand, I weave through the hallways until I come to our interrogation room.

Scanning my handprint again, I enter the room and am glad Drae's already tied to a chair. A large sheet of plastic is on the floor under him. Seeing us all pile into the room, his face pales as fear creeps in. He's already sporting a shiner, and his lip is swollen and busted. Looking at Dragon, who's standing nearby, I cock my eyebrow at him.

"He tripped down the stairs. Needs to learn to keep his shoelaces tied."

A few of the men chuckle, and I shake my head. Moving to stand in front of Drae, he swallows as he looks up at me.

"Care to explain this?" I ask as I show him the screenshots Smoke sent me of his messages.

> Drae: Yes, she's still here, but she's never alone.

> FB: Find a way to get her alone, asswipe! Message me when you have her and we'll coordinate a handoff.

> Drae: I'll see what I can do.

> FB: You'll do better than that. You get my girl or else I'll be taking yours and having fun with her before I sell her. Her and your little daughter. She'll pull in a ton of money with how sweet and innocent she is. Use her two friends if you need to, but get my girl!

His face pales further as his gaze darts around. Pings sound from around the room as Smoke sends the screenshots to everyone. Tension and anger grow in the room as they read the messages.

"I'm waiting, but I won't be patient for much longer. Explain."

"I... I didn't want to be part of Black Plague. I knew I never wanted to be, but when you're born into it, there isn't much choice. I was never a Prospect with them and as soon as I graduated high school, I split. Only my mom and sister knew of my plans to never join the club, and they were relieved. I've talked to my mom now and then since leaving, but it was always short, and I never say where I am. I didn't want them to find me."

"Wait, are you saying you're a Black Plague Prince?"

Drae hangs his head and nods. Shock courses through me. How did we miss that when we ran his background check? A glance at Smoke has me frowning as I see the same shocked look on his face. How did he hide that piece of information from us? Smoke is so good, sometimes the government taps him for jobs. For someone to pull this off and for Smoke to *not* be able to spot it, they had to be damn fucking good.

"Not by choice. My name is Jason Drae Black or Ice to the club. My dad is Ghost, brother to the past president, my Uncle Boar. Dad was Uncle Boar's VP. I wanted to be a part of a club that didn't deal in drugs, weapons, women, or kids. I'd seen what Black Plague did over the years and I wanted nothing to do with that.

"I wandered around after leaving and when I was down to my last $100, I pulled into Forest Creek. I had heard that you were based here, and that you were legit. All the way. I wanted to join your guys' MC and make a difference. I saw a sign at your garage that you needed a mechanic and I applied. Shortly after that, you accepted me as a Prospect."

He pauses and worry swirls in my gut as I steal a glance at Dragon. What the hell can of worms did we open by allowing him to Prospect?

"That's why we didn't know about your tie to Black Plague. You said your name was Drae Black and there was nothing in your background tying you to them. Did you get an alias set up? If so, who did it?" Smoke asks him.

Drae nods and hangs his head. "I hated the name Jason. The only ones that used it were my mom and sister, well, sort of. They both called me JD. I wasn't part of the club even though I was born into it. I didn't really think anything of using Drae Black when I asked to Prospect because most everyone called me Drae. The rest called me Ice, which I also hated. I honestly didn't mean to make an issue with you. I had a friend of mine wipe some of the information tied to me about the club because I didn't want anything to do with them or have anything *they* did come back to bite me in the ass.

"About three months ago, Dad called and demanded I come back home. I refused and hung up on him. A month later, he face-timed me. He had my mom tied to a chair and her whole body was already black and blue. Said if I didn't come back, he'd kill her. I knew she wouldn't want me to go back. Even though it killed me, I refused. He put a bullet in her head right there. Said I was a sorry excuse of a son and that my mother would be ashamed of me." He pauses and a sad smile crosses his face. "Thing is, Mom was dying of stage 4 lung cancer."

Swallowing hard, he looks down and shakes his head. No one speaks or moves as we watch him. He shakes his head again as he collects himself and exhales a shuddering breath.

"The doctor had given her months to live, but she made me swear to never let Dad use her against me. She must have known something was going on because she said she'd rather be killed than have to waste away in pain, both from the disease and his abuse. The bastard didn't know about her cancer and when I told him on the phone call that he actually did her a favor, he didn't believe me. I thought that was the end of it until my cousin reached out to me a few weeks ago."

"Was it Fang?" Dragon asks and Drae nods.

"Yes. He said if I didn't cooperate, they'd kidnap my girlfriend and sell our daughter. I had sent for them after I got settled here. They live in an apartment here in town. I've tried to keep them safe and away from Black Plague. Jane knew about my family and that I wanted no part of them other than my mother and sister. She's still leery about your club, so I never brought her around here. I didn't know what to do when Fang said they'd take them.

"Fang told me that he already had this place bugged and proved it by explaining what had happened earlier that morning as well as things that had happened the past few weeks. Said he would know if I talked to you guys for help or if I tried to warn Levi. If I did either, he'd take Jane and make what he did to Levi's mom look like child's play. Then he proved that he had eyes on their apartment as well. I... I couldn't risk it. She and Lindsey are all that I have left now. I'm sorry." His shoulders shake as tears run down his face.

Looking up at Dragon and the others, they give chin lifts. Drae doesn't even look up when I move closer, crouching in front of him.

"You said you only have Jane and Lindsey left. What happened to your sister?"

His shoulders shake harder, and the pit in my stomach grows.

"S-She was the oldest of us, seven years older than me. When I was fifteen, I came home from school one day and her room was cleaned out. I asked Mom where she'd gone, but she wouldn't answer me. Fang walked in and grinned at Mom. She started crying and quickly left.

"That's when I knew. He'd finally gotten to her. It didn't matter that we were first cousins. He was always groping her and trying to get her to sleep with him. From his sadistic grin, I knew he took and had his way with her. Probably my other cousins as well. I later found out she was then sold to a sick fuck who enjoyed raping and abusing children and women. Hell, sometimes even men. I couldn't find where she was sent, just that she was sold to him. That was five years ago." He shakes his head as his shoulders slump.

"We'll help you with protection for Jane and Lindsey. I'm not sure if we'll be able to find your sister... but we can look into it. What's her name?"

His head snaps up in shock, and then his eyes narrow in suspicion. "Why? I gave information to Fang, confirming Levi was here and a few other things. Why?"

With a sad smile, I place a hand on his shoulder. "Because you're a brother, and while yes, you royally fucked up, we don't tolerate women or children being beaten or abused."

Once again, he looks at me in shock before slowly nodding. "Thank you. Her name is Carolina Joy Black. I always called her CJ."

With a chin lift, I look up at Dragon and then Smoke before turning back to him, a frown crossing my face. "I'm not sure if we'll be able to find her, but we'll look. Who was she sold to?"

"Sanchez. Alejandro Sanchez."

You could have heard a pin drop in the room. Alejandro Sanchez's a sadistic fuck. He's like a ghost. The stories you hear about his victims are beyond terrifying. If a body is ever found, it's on purpose. To send a message. The body is mutilated beyond recognition and limbs are usually cut off. No evidence is ever found on them which ruins tying the murders to the sick fuck even if everyone knows it's him.

Clearing my throat, I swallow thickly. I pray we won't have to deal with him, but if we do, we'll have to be extremely smart about it.

"Back to Fang. What all did you tell him? Remember, being honest will get you a lot further than lying to us. Though, you'll still have to be punished no matter what," I growl.

He nods as he swallows hard and takes a deep breath. "I don't know who placed the cameras, but he says he has them everywhere. Even in your guys' house. He knows that you took down the ones the day after Levi and her friends came here. He said his inside person placed more during one of the parties shortly after that. I don't think he has anything in a secure room because he kept asking me if I was patched in yet. I kept telling him that I just started Prospecting about five months ago. And that's if you guys decide to patch me in at a year. That you could make me Prospect longer or kick me out if I screw up."

He pauses as he turns to look at Smoke. "I don't know which club the person was in or with, but it was when we had two or three of them here at the same time for a party. Fang eluded that they placed the camera's again when they were here. Like I said, they have access to cameras inside and outside the clubhouse as well as in Dragon and Thor's house. He kept saying 'she' but I don't know if it was one of our bunnies, one of our hang arounds, or a woman who was brought here by the other club. But that might narrow things down for when you're looking at the video timestamp records."

Smoke nods and Drae turns back toward me, looking nervous.

"Fang wanted to know Levi's daily patterns. He already knew she was going to be working at her dad's bar and grill. He wanted time frames, who she went with, did she ride or did she take her car? Everything. Around the clubhouse, he knows the girls cook breakfast and supper. Also, sometimes the food for the parties. He knows which bunnies help cook and which don't.

"However, he most likely doesn't know about what Levi mentioned this morning about the changes in the routines unless he has someone monitoring the feed. Fang knows that she's tight with Roxy, and especially Sasha. He wanted me to use the girls to lure her outside the complex for a girls' day or something. He'd then take her and the other two. Said he'd use them to teach us a lesson for taking his girl. She'd been promised to Fang years ago, and he thinks that her dad got close to the club as a way to protect her."

Confusion hits me, and crossing my arms, I absorb what he just said. Who promised Levi to Fang? Also, that doesn't sound like something Roy would do. He would have asked for help in guarding Levi if that were the case, like he did a few weeks ago.

"Wait, you said someone promised Levi to Fang. That's the second time we've heard that. Do you know who promised her to Fang?" Phoenix asks as he steps forward to stand next to me.

"Her uncle."

Everyone's attention turns to Bear, who's suddenly cursing up a storm and looks like he's about to snap. He picks up a nearby chair and hurtles it at the wall. Ryder and Dragon both step closer to him and grab hold of his shoulders.

"Bear, cool it down, brother," Ryder says, though I can tell our Sergeant at Arms and Dragon are preparing for the worst. Combined, I know they're able to bring him down, but I don't want it to come to that.

Taking a few deep breaths, Bear turns back toward the group, though you can tell he's barely keeping things under control.

"Roy's brother, Sean. That's the only other Uncle she has. Her mother, Emily, was an only child. He'd been estranged from the family for years after he kidnapped Levi as a little girl and was arrested."

I freeze. Her own uncle kidnapped her before? Bear nods as if he knows the thoughts running through my head.

"Yeah, her own fucking uncle kidnapped her. She was six years old. He picked her up from daycare early that day. She barely remembers it, thank God," he says as he runs his hands through his hair.

"She thought she was taking a ride with him to go out to the family cabin. Said they'd be meeting up with the rest of the family there. Only when they got there, it was just the two of them. As the day went on, she kept asking when her mom and dad would get there. Sean kept telling her that they got delayed, but each time, his voice would rise higher and she was getting scared. He finally fed her something, and that's the last thing she remembered before waking up in the hospital." He takes a deep breath, running his hand over his face.

"Her parents were frantic when they went to pick her up from daycare, only to find her long gone. They searched everywhere and called me to help find her. That's when we remembered the family cabin. It was the only other place that they knew of for where he might have gone. When... when we got there..." He takes another shuddering breath and Ryder and Dragon squeeze his shoulders. He nods and takes another breath.

"She was unconscious and sprawled out, naked, on the bed. Sean had tied her little arms to the bedposts. He was kneeling over her, stroking himself. He was just about to penetrate when I ripped him off her."

Bear damn near looks close to tears as he sinks into a nearby chair, cradling his head in his hands. White hot fury rises in me at how close Wildcat had come to being raped. Fuck, I want to find this Sean when he gets out and beat his ass.

"She... She doesn't know the whole story. At least that I'm aware of. When she woke up in the hospital, she was confused as to why she was there. Her parents told her she got sick after supper and then she fell asleep. They asked what she had eaten. She said Sean had cooked burgers, and he put a special sauce on hers because she was his special little girl. She ate it but said that it tasted funny.

"When she asked why Sean wasn't with them at the hospital, they said he had to go away for work and that he'd be gone for a while. She was sad, but didn't ask much about it. I'm not sure if she ever inquired about him after that. Sean got twenty years in prison for it, plus all the child pornography he had at his house."

He looks up at everyone before looking at Dragon and then settling his gaze on me.

"Roy got notification yesterday that he's getting out in about two weeks. Apparently, a few years were shaved off because of 'good behavior'. He was going to come over this weekend to talk to Levi about it."

"Fuck," Dragon and I say in unison, and Bear nods. After a few minutes, Smoke speaks up.

"But that doesn't explain how she got promised to Fang."

Drae clears his throat, and all heads turn back to him. "I don't know what he was in for, but from what I've heard, Fang met Sean in prison. Fang had a short five-year stint but got out in two for good behavior." Drae snorts and shakes his head. "I bet his dear old Dad paid someone off to get him out early. Anyway, a friend of mine that is still, reluctantly, in the club called me after overhearing a conversation about Levi. Fang had repeatedly bragged about having me under his thumb, but that soon he would have Levi in his arms again. He figured that I would know where she was since Fang said our names a lot over the phone and wanted to give me a heads up.

"Fang said he'd help her uncle again and that the two of them were going to make Levi pay for getting him sent to prison for twenty years and for leading Fang on and refusing to give him what he wanted. Fang still wants his payment for his help. He was promised her virginity again. Sean only asked that he get a couple of rounds with her when he got out. Fang didn't care as long as he got to keep Levi for himself.

"Sean apparently knows what Fang likes to do with women from the short stint that they were in prison together and is actually looking forward to the pain Levi will be suffering. I don't know about the first plan that happened years ago that was mentioned, but Fang referenced it and was pissed you guys rescued her. Pissed that you guys beat him and his brothers' asses before leaving them to die. This time around, they plan to be even more aggressive with her."

"You said your friend is still reluctantly with Black Plague. Why is that?"

Drae scoffs. "He, Dogg, was born into it too. His old man forced him to Prospect. He's got an Old Lady and she's pregnant. Honestly, the only thing that's probably keeping others from going after his woman is the baby, otherwise, they'd probably take their piece of her even if she is his Old Lady."

Locking eyes with Dragon, I know he's feeling the same anger and rage that I am. Stamping it down, I take a deep breath. I have to keep my head and find out whatever else Drae knows. Then we can make a plan. Maybe this Dogg guy might be willing to help us?

"Was there anything else that you told Fang?"

Drae shakes his head. "No. He was already familiar with your patrol rotations from his cameras, he said, but if any changes come up, I'm supposed to notify him. Same for if there are any changes in Levi's and the girls' routines. He wants Levi for when Sean gets out of prison. He's gonna have Korso, I mean his brother, Vince, go and pick Sean up from prison and then take him to wherever they plan to hold the women. And before you ask, he hasn't told me where that would be. I was supposed to get the girls to him, otherwise he'd tell his buyer that he'd soon have my daughter in his possession and that he'd be enjoying Jane before selling her off."

Drae hangs his head. I'm pissed as fuck with him, but still wish he'd have come to us when this whole thing started.

"You're not getting out of a beating, Drae. No if ands or buts about it." I pause, and he nods weakly, most likely already suspecting it. "You will help us get Fang as well as feeding him the information that we want him to have. Nothing else. I want to know as soon as you hear from him going forward. If he starts getting suspicious due to the camera feeds, we'll make something up that you're helping us with. I'm adding on an additional six months that you'll Prospect for and if you don't fuck up, we'll take a vote about patching you in."

He looks up at me in shock, his mouth hanging open. "Y-You mean there's still a chance I can patch in?"

"While you should have come to me about this the instant this whole fucking shitshow started, we don't condone hurting women or children. And while I'm pissed as fuck at you, you're also lucky as fuck that nothing has happened to Levi or the other women here." I pause as I let him see the beast caged inside me. There's a fucking reason why I have my road name. "If anything had happened to Wildcat, or the other women, we'd be having a *very* different conversation where you'd get a front row seat to how I deal out punishment to those who would hurt my family. Not to mention, you'd also be getting a front row seat to how Dragon deals out his own form of punishment before you'd be taking a dirt nap."

Drae visibly swallows hard as his gaze bounces between us.

"Or mine. Levi's my Little Ninja, but now she's our Queen and you don't mess with an MC's Queen," Bear's ominous voice sounds from behind me. Then, I'm reminded once again of our brotherhood as each of my brothers make their own pledges to protect my Wildcat, our Queen.

"Yes, I'll do whatever you ask," he says as he nods frantically. Fuck, I hope we aren't opening a huge can of worms with this mess.

"Do you have a picture of Carolina?" Smoke asks.

"Yeah, it's in my wallet."

I motion for Dragon to let him up and he fishes it out of Drae's pocket, tossing it to me.

"Flip up the flap and that's CJ. Well, that's the last picture I have of her, that is."

I pull it out and take a good look at it. She's beautiful. Long blond hair, blue eyes, and a curvy figure. But there's something about her face that's familiar. I just can't put my finger on it. I hand it to Smoke, and he takes a picture of it, the same confusion soon crossing his face. This woman is familiar to us. But how? Slipping the picture back into place, I set the wallet down on the table.

Nodding to Dragon and Ryder, they untie his arms, and he rubs his wrists where the ropes have left a bit of a visible burn. He moves the chair out of the way and then turns back toward us. Taking his shirt off, he tosses it on the chair before squaring his shoulders and shaking out his limbs.

I smirk at him and nod. Kid has guts. But he also knows the rules. Everyone gets in a punch and he has to stay standing. As the President, the first shot's mine. I'm about to strike when a thought hits me. The cameras.

"No dick shots as usual but keep it to where he can cover the bruises with clothing until they heal. Can't help the ones on his face already, but we don't want the cameras tipping Black Plague off that we're onto Drae."

Grunts sound in response and I land a blow to his side. Stepping back, the rest all take their shot. I notice Smoke's fingers flying across his keyboard and it looks like he's already checking the camera feeds. When his turn comes, he lands a blow to Drae's gut and immediately goes back to his keyboard, a smirk on his face, which then turns into a scowl.

Bear's the last to get in his punch and the force of it royally knocks the breath out of Drae. He heavily stumbles but doesn't drop. Bear grunts and pats his shoulder hard. Drae winces, but wisely doesn't say anything. Nodding to him, he puts his shirt back on and tucks away his wallet.

"Pres, we need to get Tiffany back in here." Smoke says.

Sighing, I run a hand through my hair. "I probably already know, but why?"

"She's the one who helped the other woman place the cameras. Still trying to figure out who she is. Tiffany showed her the high-traffic areas, but she also didn't know that we had our own cameras. I don't know if the mystery woman spotted them or not." He pauses and then frowns. "I also took a peek to see what she was doing recently. No one use the condoms from the communal jar. Looks like she snuck out and poked holes in them last night. I'll dig into this deeper to see what else she could have done, but it might be better to just keep your own box of condoms hidden in your room."

"Can I see who the other woman is? If she's tied to Fang, she could be a plant in whatever club it was that visited or maybe even from Black Plague," Drae asks and Smoke gives him a chin lift, zooming in on her face. Drae sucks in a breath and groans as he scrubs a hand over his face.

"That's Melanie, a Black Plague club bunny that will do anything to be Fang's Old Lady. She's not very smart but will do whatever someone says. Especially my cousins."

Smoke chuckles and shakes his head. "You're right about her not being very smart. The cameras are in fact in high-traffic areas, but she wasn't paying much attention when she mounted them. A lot of them are crooked or were angled downwards in the process. It doesn't appear that they capture audio, just video. But still, keep sensitive conversations to only in Church. That door has a handprint scanner so there should be no cameras in there. I'll check after this just to make sure. Your office should be okay, Pres, since you also have a scanner, but I'll check it out as well."

I nod and head upstairs, the rest of the guys following me.

At the bar, Colt passes me a beer, and I scan the room. Drae comes in and as he looks at the women, a confused look crosses his face. He shakes himself and asks Colt for a water. As Colt hands Drae the bottle, his gaze shoots to mine in question, and I give a chin lift that everything's all right. He returns it and smacks Drae on the shoulder, smirking as Drae tries to hide his wince. Taking a swig, Drae looks over at the women again, and that same puzzled look comes over his face.

Sliding onto a stool next to him, I nudge him. "What's wrong?"

He shakes his head, glances at me, and then back at the girls. "It's just that Trixie looks familiar, but then again, not. I noticed it as soon as I came here, but I just can't place it. It's been bugging me ever since."

As if feeling my eyes on her, Trixie looks up, which has Levi looking up as well, smiling widely when she sees me. Grabbing Trixie's hand, they walk over toward u s.

"Is now an okay time to talk with Trixie, Thor?"

I give her a chin lift and drain the last of my beer, grabbing a fresh one from Colt. Taking Levi's hand, I lead the way to my office. Smoke is just exiting, and he gives me a chin lift. My shoulders relax a bit knowing that my office is clear of any unauthorized devices.

Sitting at my desk, Levi sits next to Trixie and takes her hand, squeezing it. I frown, wondering what they had talked about while we were in the basement for her to be so supportive of her suddenly.

Chapter 21
Levi

"It's okay, Trixie. Why don't you start by telling Thor about why you went along with Tiffany?"

Trixie nods, squeezes my hand, and releases a shuddering breath.

"At first, when I got here, she seemed nice. She showed me around and introduced me to everyone. We started becoming friends. During our free time, we would hang out together, get our hair or nails done, or whatever. However, about a month before Levi came here, she started to change. She became more violent and aggressive."

I look up when I hear a rumble come from Thor and notice his eyes have darkened dangerously and his jaw ticking like crazy.

"Did she hurt you or any of the others?" he asks.

Trixie shakes her head, but then nods as she bites her lip.

Looking back over to Thor, he seems ready to burst out of his seat. I squeeze her hand, and she takes another deep breath.

"At first, she didn't hit us, but she would often grab our arms when she was trying to get us to do whatever it was that she wanted us to do. She'd squeeze hard, but not to the point of bruising. She was verbally abusive and manipulative to all of us as well. Especially Roxy.

"I honestly was worried that if we didn't do as she said, that she would hurt us. She said we had to do whatever she said because she was here the longest and that Thor said she was in charge of the rest of us. Since Roxy didn't service the guys, Tiffany said that she was at the very bottom of the ladder. She would make Roxy do the worst chores that we were given.

"Us girls would often whisper about trying to go to you about her, but each time she would catch us. I don't know how she knew we were talking about her, but she did. That's when she would hit us, but she always made it so that clothing would cover it or she... she would pull up our skirts and smack our asses or pussies really hard so that if someone saw it, they would probably just think it happened when we were with one of the guys. Sometimes she would grab our breasts hard and twist our nipples painfully. She'd do that until we swore to never talk to anyone about how she was treating us."

Thor suddenly stands, throwing his chair back in the process. Trixie jumps and looks about ready to bolt or possibly faint. I squeeze her hand and whisper that he isn't angry at her, that his anger's directed at Tiffany.

Turning back to Thor, I bite my lip. He paces behind his desk as he runs his hands through his hair. When he pauses and looks at me, I nod subtly at Trixie, and his face instantly relaxes as he realizes he scared her.

"I'm sorry for scaring you, Trixie. I'm not mad at you—it's Tiffany I'm fucking pissed at. Yes, I wish you or the other ladies had come to me, but we'll take care of things going forward. Please continue."

She nods, keeping her gaze down, and squeezes my hand again. I hate that she has to relive this shit, but he needs to know what's been going on in the clubhouse. We needed to talk to her anyway, so she volunteered to be the one to relay the information to Thor since she was already on the chopping block so to speak. Her words, not mine.

It was bad enough that Colt, Alexei, Ethan, and Travis also heard how Tiffany had treated them. I had to order them not to go down and get Thor. I was only able to get them to relent when I reminded them that I'd be talking to Thor later anyway about the changes, and that was when Trixie offered to tell Thor everything. Besides, Thor had to deal with Drae first. I just hope whatever they found out wasn't too serious. I don't want anyone getting hurt over this. Not to mention, I did get along with Drae before his sudden change. He even showed me pictures of his girlfriend and daughter, promising to bring them to our next gathering since Jane was starting to warm up to our club.

"When the rest of us started getting more attention than her from the guys, she got more violent and manipulative. Once I saw her filling a second bowl of condoms and putting it under the bar. It was right before another club was coming to visit, so I figured it was just in case the first jar ran out. But then she pulled a couple of handfuls of condoms out of her purse and tossed them on top of both jars.

"That was when I remembered something from a few nights prior. I got up in the middle of the night to get a bottle of water. When I walked by her room, her light was on, and the door was slightly ajar. I saw her repeatedly poking something into whatever was in her hand. It looked like a piece of cloth, so I didn't think anything of it at the time. But seeing her at the bar doing that made me remember there were packets all around her on the bed. That's when it dawned on me that she was poking holes into condoms and was just using the fabric as a backing to protect her hand.

"When she stepped away from the bar, I waited a few minutes and then ducked back there myself. Not wanting her to catch me, I pocketed a couple of the condoms on top and then quickly dumped the contents of both jars into the trash before tying it up. I put fresh condoms into the bowls so she hopefully wouldn't notice.

"I was just putting in the new trash bag when she came back around the corner. Her gaze flicked from me to the bowl that I'd just re-filled and then smirked as she looked back around the room. I stepped into the bathroom and then looked more closely at the condoms I grabbed. I was able to see that she entered the bag near where you would normally tear it open. She must have just maneuvered a needle around some as she poked a few holes in each one."

She pauses and looks at me sheepishly before looking at Thor and then at the ground. Nerves swirl in my gut, knowing what she's about to say. I knew my men weren't saints before they met me, and I was going to do my damnedest not to hold that against them.

"She went up to you, trying to rub all over you, and then started unbuckling your pants. You pushed her off of you, and she scowled before seeing Dragon a few tables over. She tried to do the same to him, but he pushed her off, too. Phoenix came into the room and then she started hanging all over him. He grabbed a couple of condoms out of the jar before taking her to his room.

"About a week later, I found a bunch of pregnancy tests in our joined bathroom's trash. From what I could see, all of them were negative. She was in a really bitchy mood that day and ever since then. I caught her doing the same thing a few times, and I always waited till the coast was clear to dump them and replace them with new ones." She swallows hard and looks sheepishly up at Thor. "Sorry for wasting so much money, but I didn't want her to trap any of the guys."

Thor comes around his desk and kneels in front of her, gently placing a hand on her shoulder, even though I can tell his muscles are tight, coiled in anger.

"No, thank you for protecting the guys. I know some of them want kids when they find the right person to settle down with, but to be tricked into having a kid with someone like Tiffany would have been a nightmare. Smoke recently found footage of her putting defective condoms out, so there will no longer be a communal jar. Each of the guys will have their own stash in hopes of preventing something like this from happening again."

Her shoulders sag and she nods. Thor gets up and sits back down.

"Now tell me about what you said before. Why do you think you'd be killed or sold once you went home?"

Her whole body stiffens, and she starts to shake. While we were waiting for the guys earlier, we didn't talk about what Trixie had said about her family, even though I knew the others wanted to know. I figured she had her reasons and if she wanted me in there when she talked to Thor, I would offer my support.

I pull out my phone and quickly text Colt to bring me crackers, water, and some ginger ale. Within minutes, there's a soft knock on the door before he opens it. He sets the items down on the desk and steps back out, shutting the door behind him. Grabbing the ginger ale, I open it and hand it to her.

"T-Thank you," she whispers.

"Trixie, we'll do what we can to protect you, but we need to know what happened to be able to do that," Thor says.

She bites her lip as she stares at the can gripped in her hand. Taking a deep breath, I squeeze her hand.

"I don't know if you know this Trixie, but I was kidnapped by a MC when I was just shy of turning sixteen. They also kidnapped my mother."

Her head whips toward me in shock. I nod and give a small, sad smile as I turn my back toward her and take off my shirt. As I pull my hair to the side, I hear her sharp intake of breath.

"They all wore masks, so I had no idea at the time who they were. They tortured us for what seemed like hours. All of the cuts and burns all over my body? They did that."

Turning around, I show her the ones on my stomach and chest, then put my shirt back on.

"They carved the club initials into my thigh, which I later got a huge tattoo to cover it. Well as best as they could anyway, due to the scarring. They carved the club initials into my mom as well. Then they raped and killed her in front of me." I pause as the memories wash over me, and this time it's her taking my hand, squeezing it in support. Even though my throat's tight, I swallow thickly. Looking at her through teary eyes, I give her a small smile of thanks.

"They were about to rape me when Sasha, Alexei, Dad, Uncle Bear, and Grandpa rescued me. Then just a few months ago, I met a guy who I thought was nice. His name was Scott. We went on a few dates, but I never gave in to his demands for sex. I knew he wasn't the one for me long-term and I broke it off when he tried to take things too far. I found out later that Scott was one of the ones that had kidnapped me before, and he was threatening me all over again. Knowing what they did last time to me, Dad asked the club to protect me and I'm forever grateful that he did."

I smile and turn to Thor, my chest bursting as we lock eyes, him smiling back at me.

"I met the two most perfect men for me that I want to spend the rest of my life with." Turning back toward Trixie, I squeeze her hand again. "My point is... these men can protect you if you let them. All you have to do is trust them."

She takes a shaky breath and nods. She raises her head, her eyes filled with fear and nervousness. "Before I go into my story, can I ask what club those other guys belonged to?"

I turn to Thor, raising my brow in question. He nods, and I turn back toward her.

"Black Plague MC."

Her eyes widen in fear and the can of ginger ale slips from her fingers, falling to the ground. She starts hyperventilating so badly that I'm worried she'll faint.

"Sweetie, you have to try to slow your breathing down."

Her body starts to shake, and her breathing quickens even more before her eyes roll back and Thor rushes to her side, since he'd previously stepped back while I was talking about what they'd done to me, catching her just in time and preventing her head from hitting the floor. I jump off the couch, racing to the door and fling it open. Colt and Drae are at the bar, but I don't see Patch.

"Colt! Get Patch—quick! Have him bring his kit just in case. Drae—toss me that rag and grab some more."

Colt darts off toward Patch's room and Drae reaches under the bar for the stash of rags that we keep there. Phoenix follows me back into the office, followed closely by Drae. Thor lays Trixie down on the couch as Drae and I drop to our knees to clean up the mess so no one would slip.

As we finish, I look up and see Drae staring intently at something behind me. Pivoting on my knees, I look between him and Trixie. It doesn't escape my notice that the guys are doing the same.

"Drae?"

He drops the rag on the floor, walks over to the couch, and kneels next to it. Turning her head so she's facing him, Drae just stares at her. After a few moments, he smooths her hair back away from her head, tilts it, and looks closer at her ear. Thor steps nearer, and they both suck in a sharp breath.

"Thor? What's going on?" My voice is shaky, and I'm starting to get really worried that something's wrong.

Instead of answering me, Thor looks toward Drae, raising his eyebrow in question. Something flits across his face that I don't recognize.

Drae looks between Thor and Phoenix just as Patch and Colt come into the office. "Have any of you been with Trixie intimately?" His voice is harsh, but shaky.

Patch, Phoenix, and Thor nod.

I swallow thickly and Thor gives me an apologetic smile.

"Does she have a tattoo of butterflies on her right hip?"

Confusion crosses their faces and Drae's breathing starts to become irregular as he stands up. Patch pushes closer to him, but Drae steps out of his reach.

"Please, just answer me. Does she?" He's almost yelling as he looks between the guys, almost frantically.

Colt pulls me to my feet and pushes me behind him slightly. I grip his arm as I look between them all. What's happening? Did Drae and Trixie know each other previously? If so, why didn't they recognize each other sooner?

After a moment, it's Patch who speaks up. "Yes, she does."

Drae sinks to his knees next to the couch and he places his head against Trixie's shoulder as he clutches her hand, tears streaming down his face. "CJ," he mumbles.

Thor, Phoenix, and Patch all suck in a breath and then blinding smiles light up their faces as they each clasp Drae on the shoulder.

"Drae, can I get near Tr—I mean CJ to check her out? Then we can wake her up and talk to her some. I think we'd all like to know how both you and your sister ended up at Steel Archangel's MC without realizing the other was here."

I gasp and Thor looks at me, nodding.

Drae gives Patch a chin lift and pulls back slightly but doesn't release her hand. I step out from behind Colt and walk over to Thor, wrapping my arms around his waist. He kisses the top of my head and wraps his arms around me tightly.

Patch checks her pulse, listens to her heart, and then looks into her eyes.

"I think she's wearing colored contacts, but we can ask her for sure when she wakes up. Time to wake up, Sweetie," he says as he waves smelling salts under her nose.

She jerks awake and looks around in a daze before her gaze lands on Drae. She looks at him in confusion, tilting her head slightly as she studies him closely. He kneels in front of her and then ducks his head. When he looks up, I realize he'd been wearing colored contacts. Whereas before he had green eyes, he now had dazzling blue eyes. Trixie sucks in a breath.

"Try to picture me with light brown hair, without a beard, and really skinny. Also having scars here, here, here, and here," he said as he points to various places on his face and neck. Her eyes widen before she lowers her head and, like Patch suspected, takes out her contacts. When she looks up, she no longer has brown eyes but dazzling blue eyes to match Drae's.

"JD, oh my God, I can't believe I finally found you!" she cries as she flings herself into his arms, both of them instantly in tears.

Chapter 22
CJ (i.e. Trixie)

I CAN'T BELIEVE IT! My baby brother's been right in front of me for months and I didn't know it! To be fair, he's changed so much since I last saw him five years ago, not to mention he'd also been wearing colored contacts like me. I cling to him tightly but pull back when he sucks in a pained breath.

"Easy, Sis, I took a beating today for my fuck up," he says with a tight smile.

Alarmed, I pull up his shirt and see the bruises already forming. JD grabs my hands and shakes his head, silencing the words I was about to let fly. I'd seen him beaten enough when we were kids. I didn't want to see him beaten anymore.

"Trust me, CJ, I deserved these bruises and then some. Are you feeling well enough that we can talk?"

Was I ready to share my story? Especially with my brother? Looking up at Levi, she gives me a small smile and nods. Yes, she's right. I can trust these men. Especially since I now know my brother trusted them enough to Prospect with them. He wouldn't have done that if they were anything like Black Plague.

"Yes, but I'd like Levi in there too. I—I think I'll need her while I," I pause as I swallow the lump in my throat. "While I tell you my story."

JD looks up at Thor in question, and he gives everyone a chin lift in approval. Thor pulls out his phone. His fingers fly over the screen and a few moments later, everyone's phone dings.

"Church in five, everyone. Let's all grab a drink and head in there."

Thor kisses Levi, and I blush as I look down and pick at my nails as everyone else leaves the room. I wish I had a love like that. She even found two loves.

Jealously swirls in my gut, but I stomp it down. With everything that she's gone through, I'm glad that she's finally been able to find happiness. And I only saw what they did to her on the upper part of her body. But my scars... My scars are mostly internal, though no one would know it. I had to have plastic surgery on my face, chest, and other parts of my body because of what they'd done to me. Shaking my head to clear my thoughts, I look up and see JD looking at me in concern.

"No one's gonna harm you again, Sis." He leans closer and what he says next sends a chill down my spine. "Just so you know, do not act differently toward me after we leave this room. Fang had help from Tiffany and Melanie, the bunny from Black Plague. They put cameras up around a lot of the compound. We don't think they have audio but be careful just in case. If you want to put more colored contacts in, duck your head as you make your way to your room. When you're ready, come down to Church. I'm gonna put mine back in too. Do you want me to grab you anything to drink?"

I take a deep breath and nod. "Can you grab me a ginger ale and a beer? I'll put the contacts back in for consistency's sake. I don't want to tip them off or anything. When this is done, I'll probably stop wearing them."

He nods and stands, holding out his hand. Taking it, he helps pull me up and off the couch, grabbing my shoulder to steady me. Giving him a small smile, I tilt my head up at him. God, I can't believe he's now taller than me.

"You know, it's going to be so hard remembering to call you Drae now that I know you're really JD."

He laughs and grins. "Same, Sis. For one, I can't call you 'Sis'. And two, gotta call you Trixie and not CJ."

Grinning, I duck my head as we leave Thor's office and quickly make my way to my assigned room. Opening the door, I gasp as I look around.

"Thor!" I yell, tears threatening to spill yet again.

Boots stomp down the hallway, and soon my room is filled with a bunch of men, and not in a good way.

Arms encircle me and I know JD has me. Turning toward his chest, I let the tears run. Someone has trashed my room. Pictures are torn, my bedding's ripped apart, and it looks like someone has ejaculated all over my bed. My closet's torn apart, my clothes lying in shreds. Who could have done this? Murmurs have me pulling away slightly and drying my eyes. Turning around, I see Thor and Smoke huddled over a laptop.

"D-Do you know who it was?"

Thor turns toward me and frowns before nodding. "One of them, yes, but let's take this to Church. Everyone inside—even the Prospects, Travis, Ethan, and the women. Someone go get Roy. As soon as Roy gets here, we'll start. In the meantime, Smoke, grab an extra laptop and have Alexei help you with the cameras while we're in Church. I don't want them sneaking in again. Bones, Ryder, grab your laptops too, in case something comes up that you need to start investigating."

Thor pauses and looks over at me, his face softening. "Trixie, salvage what you can and pack it up. I won't ask you to stay in this room after this. There's an empty room near Colt and Drae that you can have if you want."

Relief floods me. Guess that means they aren't kicking me out. "Y-Yes, please. Closer to J—Drae if it's possible."

The corner of Thor's mouth lifts in a slight smirk as he nods. Fuck, it's going to be so hard not to call him JD now that I know for sure it's him. Movement behind him catches my eye, and I notice Patch scooping up some of the sperm on my bedspread.

"I'll take this to the lab after we're done with Church to see if I can get a hit."

Thor nods, clasping him on the back as the guys start filtering out. When they've left, the women come in, their arms full of boxes and a couple rolls of garbage bags. As they set everything down, they all descend on me, giving me a group hug. I'm still tentative about getting close to them after everything, but Levi really broke down a lot of the barriers we all had when we talked earlier. Tears spring to my eyes at the gesture, and I blink hard to keep them from falling.

"Okay, ladies! Let's see what we can salvage. Definitely keep the pictures, even if they're torn. We might be able to put them together well enough to scan and reprint them. We'll create a pile of things that can't be salvaged but focus on what can be saved. I'd like to have Trixie all packed up before Church starts, if at all possible," Levi says, smiling at me and she gives me another hug. Fuck, her hugs remind me of my mom's. I'm going to have to ask JD about how Mom's doing later on.

"Thank you, ladies. This means a lot to me."

They all wave me off and get to work.

Each one of us tackles a different area and we quickly make headway through the disaster. By the time there's a knock on the door, I'm packed, and what is ruined is already bagged up. Opening the door, I smile up at JD, I mean, Drae. Fuck!

"How are things going?"

"Thanks to these lovely ladies, everything that's able to be salvaged is already packed. Unfortunately, it wasn't a lot."

He frowns at my words, but nods.

"Don't worry about that, Trixie. We'll do some online shopping after Church, and you'll be set up again in no time!" Levi says with a smile and I'm instantly panicking.

"I... I don't think that's necessary. I can get a few things at the store and that will tide me over for a while."

Swallowing hard, I turn around and pick up one of my bags. I don't have much money in my account. Thanks to Tiffany forcing us to do a shitload of things with her, the meager wage that I get from the club barely covered the expenses. At least now I'll be able to save my money for what I really want.

Hearing giggling, I look behind me to see Levi standing with her hands on her hips in front of me as she shakes her head.

"Nope! We're doing online shopping and Thor said to use the club card." I start to object but she holds up a hand. "Honey, this happened on club property and because someone broke in."

The other ladies grin, and Sasha mouths 'just go with it'. Chuckling, I nod and Levi quickly embraces me with another hug.

"Okay ladies! Let's grab a drink if you need one and head into Church," she says as she hands Drae the other couple of bags.

Yeah, I'm definitely grabbing a beer. Things have gone a complete one-eighty for us bunnies in such a short timeframe that my head's still reeling. Not to mention what just happened to my room and my stuff. It is so weird that Levi and Sasha are being nice to us bunnies, but I'm also grateful for the change. And that Tiffany's no longer here.

Drae shakes his head, no doubt thinking something similar based on how he's been looking between Levi and us bunnies. He slings my other bags over his shoulder and gestures for me to follow him. We head down the twisted hallways and he opens a door, setting my stuff down on the bed. He takes a moment, looking around and checking the windows.

It dawns on me that he's making sure no one's in here and that nobody can get in through the window unless they break it. My chest warms at someone taking the extra effort to care for my safety like that. It had been years since someone cared enough for me to do that. Taking my hand, he leads me out into the hallway, shuts the door, and locks it before handing me the key.

"My room is right next to you here, and Colt is next to me on this side. Travis and Ethan are in these two rooms. If you need something and we aren't here, go to them. They aren't officially part of the club, but Levi considers them her family, so they're under protection as well until we get this mess with Fang wrapped up." He pauses as he cocks his head to the side. "Actually, they'd make good Prospects. They're both hard workers and would be a good addition to the club."

I smile and nudge his shoulder. "You should mention it to them and Thor."

He smiles and winks at me. "Think I will. Now, let's get some drinks and head on into Church."

I nod and grab a ginger ale from the kitchen and then a beer from behind the bar. As I step into Church, I'm a ball of nerves again.

Levi waves me over to an empty seat next to her and from the looks of it, they've saved the seat next to it as well for JD, er, Drae. Fuck, that's going to be a hard habit to break.

"All right everyone! We have a lot to go over. For Roy's and the ladies' sake, we'll recount what all has happened today. I want to make this very clear to the women, bunnies, and Prospects, since this is the first time we've allowed you in here. You will not repeat anything you hear in this room. If we find out that you have, that's grounds for immediate removal from the club and possibly an ass-kicking. Am I understood?"

Everyone agrees, and Thor nods.

"All right, let's start with what happened over breakfast this morning."

Thor looks at Levi and winks at her. Roy's gaze follows his line of sight and then his eyes widen as he looks at Levi, no doubt noticing her cut for the first time.

"Get your butt over here, girl, and give me some love! Congratulations, Sweetie!"

Everyone starts clapping as she practically flings herself into her dad's arms. Over her shoulder, he gives a hard look toward Thor and Dragon, that reads loud and clear. Break my girl's heart and I'll kill you.

"Thanks, Dad," she says before kissing his cheek and then she kisses each of her guys before sitting back down.

Thor goes over the changes for the bunnies and then what they learned when they talked to Drae downstairs. A gasp escapes me, and I can't keep the tears from falling when he talks about Fang threatening Drae's girlfriend and daughter. He squeezes my hand and gives me a tight smile before his attention goes back to Thor. How could they think of doing that to a little girl? To his girlfriend? Holy shit, I'm an aunt!

Thor then tells them about Tiffany and how she'd been treating all of us. The anger in the room is palpable. I shift nervously in my seat, and I notice that Ashley, Ginger, Sarah, Amy, and Roxy do as well.

"I'd like to repeat what I told Trixie earlier. Our anger is not directed at you ladies. It is directed at Tiffany and what she's put you all through. However, I want to make myself very clear about this. If you ever feel unsafe here or if someone is hurting you, I want you to let me or Phoenix know. If you can't find us, tell one of the other brothers and they'll let us know. You will not get in trouble unless, of course, you're just trying to start shit on purpose. The sooner we know about issues, the sooner we can address them. Am I understood?"

"Yes," I say, along with the other bunnies.

"Now, before we get to Trixie's story, let's talk about what happened in her room. Smoke?"

Smoke clicks a few buttons on his laptop, and an image comes up on the wall. "Looks like Melanie, the bunny from Black Plague, and this man came in from somewhere on the back property. No idea who the guy is because he's covered basically from head to toe. They came in while we were all down talking with Drae. They headed straight to Trixie's room and then left about the time Trixie fainted in Thor's office."

I cock my head as I stare at the image of the man. He seems familiar somehow. Broad shoulders, slightly overweight and you can tell that his clothes are a little worse for wear. His hands are big and rough. I hear a chuckle and look at Patch in confusion.

"Sorry, it's just you two are mirroring each other and not even noticing it. Knowing what I know now, it's easy to see the similarities between you two."

A few others chuckle and Drae squeezes my hand again. Smiling at him, I turn back to the image and frown.

Wait. What is that?

A gasp escapes me, and I feel the pit in my stomach getting bigger.

"S-Smoke?"

He looks over at me and I swallow thickly before looking again at the man's hands, praying I'm wrong, but I don't think I am. "Can you zoom in on his left hand?"

He clicks a few buttons and Drae curses next to me. You can clearly see the tattoo on his middle finger.

"Korso," we both say in unison.

"Explain," Thor says, his jaw ticking in anger, and I nod.

"Anyone of the Black family that are in the club, get that tattoo when they patch in, as well as the club logo, though the logos usually on their back. 'B.P.' is for Black Plague and 'K.B.' is Korso Black. Drae and I are the only Black's that didn't get the tattoos. Then again, I don't know if Dad made Mom get one."

Drae sighs and nods, his fists clenching in front of him. "She did. Dad forced her to get it when he had his property mark inked on her. She didn't want to get them because she's terrified of needles. Dad and Uncle Boar strapped her down on the table so that Rabbit could do the ink." Looking at the image again, he shakes his head. "What I don't get is why would Black Plague's Sergeant at Arms be the one to come in and trash Trixie's room? Why not send someone who isn't an officer?"

I swallow the bile that's threatening to rise.

"Because he wanted me. They all do," I say as I blink back the tears as memories flood me. Looking up, I nod to Thor. "Guess it's time to tell my story."

Taking another deep breath, I begin.

"It happened five years ago. I had just turned twenty-two. I hated living at Dad's house on club grounds, but I needed to save up enough money to make my escape. I just needed one or two more months of wages and I'd have a good stash to get out and make my own way.

"I came home late one night after bartending and was ready to crawl into bed. Unfortunately, because I was so tired, I didn't pay too much attention as I came into the house. One of the other girls had called in so we were stretched thin that night. I closed my bedroom door and before I could even turn on the lights, someone grabbed me from behind, holding their hand tight over my mouth so I couldn't alert anyone. It was Fang that had a hold of me and Archer, Joker, and Korso were in front of me, grabbing themselves as they leered at me. Fang said he was tired of me being a little cocktease and that he was done waiting. That they all were done waiting." I pause as a violent shudder runs through me.

"Wait," Ryder interrupts. "Aren't they your cousins?"

Swallowing hard, I nod. "Yes, they are. Previously, they'd always try to grope me or press themselves against me if we were in tight spaces. It got to the point where I avoided them as much as possible. I knew I couldn't go to Dad for help because he's seen them doing it and didn't stop them. In fact, he encouraged them. Uncle Boar, too. JD, I mean, Drae stepped in whenever he saw what they were doing and rescued me on a number of occasions. Of course, it always led to them beating him up each time since they were older and stronger than him."

Drae clenches and unclenches his fists, no doubt remembering what they'd done. I hate that I'm bringing up those painful memories for him, but I have to in order for Thor and the others to know what happened.

"They gagged me and then dragged me out to an old building on the property. There was another man in there, but I didn't know who he was at the time. They tied me down to a makeshift bed that was in the middle of the room and the guy walked around me like he was inspecting me. He said that my cousins picked a good *specimen* for him," I spit out. Anger courses through me as memories bombard me of what he'd done to me that night and over the years.

"Apparently, my cousins sold me to that man. My virginity. That he could have me, but they also got to take me before he left with me. The man passed them a briefcase and Fang hastily cut off my clothes. The man raped me and then my cousins each took a turn."

My breathing grows faster as the memories fully come back. The degrading things they said to me and what they did to my virgin body. Tears stream down my face and suddenly I'm picked up and sandwiched in Drae's arms as I sit on his lap. Black dots dance across my vision. I hear someone calling my name, and then I see Patch kneeling in front of me. Levi's next to him, holding my hand.

"CJ, I need you to focus. Take a deep breath and try to let it out slowly. If you don't control your breathing, you're going to pass out again, Honey."

I nod and try to do what he says. After a few minutes, I'm able to get my breathing under control. I nod again, and he smiles, squeezing my knee before pulling out a chair and sitting nearby. Most likely in case this happens again. My cheeks heat in embarrassment.

"Hey, none of that now, CJ. That was a completely understandable reaction to remembering what they did to you. There's nothing to be embarrassed about," Levi tells me as she squeezes my hand. "We're all here for you. You don't have to give every detail, but what you can tell us might be able to fill in the gaps and help us capture these assholes."

Nodding, I take a deep breath.

"After they were done, they told the man how to get off the club property without alerting the rest of the club. That we had to be gone before 2 am because that's when my dad was due back, and it was also when the patrols were going to be switching out."

I feel Drae tensing underneath me, and I look up in confusion, only to shrink back at the look of anger on his face.

"Drae? What's wrong?" When he doesn't answer, I try again. "JD? You're scaring me. What's wrong?"

"Please get up, CJ," he whispers. Levi pulls me into her arms and Drae gets up, pacing as anger practically rolls off him. Hands grab me before Levi and I are pulled quickly behind Patch, as he stands protectively in front of us.

Drae roars in anger, punching his fist through the wall. I break free of Levi's grasp and dart around toward Drae, but Patch catches me, pulling me close to him. I struggle against him, not flinching as he glares at me. The others get up, standing close by, poised to leap into action if need be. I only stop trying to get out of Patch's grasp when I hear Drae's hurt-filled voice speaking softly.

"He knew. The fucker knew what they were going to do to you." He pauses and turns toward me, tears pooling in his eyes. "He literally dragged me to go with him that night for the deal. He had to have known that I always stayed up until you got home. If I wasn't there, then they would be able to do what they wanted."

I push against Patch again, and this time he lets me go. I run into Drae's arms, wrapping my arms around his waist, and burying my face in his chest.

"You can't blame yourself, Drae. They would have done it sooner or later unless I had managed to get away. Though, knowing them, I figured they'd probably have Chainsaw looking for me." I look up at him and know it'll be a long time before he's really able to believe that it isn't his fault.

"But they did, and I wasn't there to try and stop them. Sanchez had you for years, and I know he did something terrible to you because your face isn't the same as it used to be. The bone structure's all wrong."

I swallow thickly and nod. "It was after I'd tried my last escape. I was free for three days before his men found me. They dragged me back to him and he beat me damn near to a bloody pulp. I honestly thought I was going to die. It wasn't until his daughter told him that if he wanted to really punish me, he should stop and let my body heal. Then sell me to Creed. Creed was a new associate to Sanchez, but he ran a brothel that I knew I wouldn't survive if he sent me there. I'd heard almost nightly that Creed's people cart at least one woman out of there in a body bag because someone went too far.

"Sanchez listened to her. He sent me to the hospital and kept me under guard. After the swelling went down in my face, they did plastic surgery to fix my nose and shattered cheekbones. Also to fix a few areas on my body that had scarred badly. I was in the hospital for months while things healed when Alexis, Sanchez's daughter, came in with her guards and two men I didn't recognize. I soon found out one of them was Creed."

I feel Drae tense under me, but I keep going.

"He said that I'd be perfect for what he was looking for and said he'd talk with the guards outside to arrange the handoff. Alexis stayed in the room, but as soon as the door closed, she darted quickly to my side, covering my mouth so I wouldn't scream."

"You had better let go of me, CJ."

The dangerously low, calm voice Drae spoke in sends chills down my spine, but I hug him tighter, not letting go.

"No, because you need to hear what she said next. She said she's been working with the Feds to bring down her dad and Creed was in on it. His brothel is a front. The women that were taken out each night were acting. She showed me Creed's badge, and I knew she wasn't lying."

He freezes and then stares at me before smirking.

"How'd you know she wasn't lying?" Thor asks me, but I don't break eye contact with Drae.

"Because Dad forced her to do all of their forgings since she's good at computers and is a damn good artist," Drae says, and I nod.

"They were going to 'buy' me and help me get free of Sanchez. I honestly couldn't believe it, but I listened to the rest of her plan. They got me out, gave me a new name and some money. They said to go to Forest Creek, and that I'd find my brother here."

I feel him tense again and sigh.

"Why would the Feds know where Drae was?" Dragon asks.

"Because they were worried he'd start another chapter like Black Plague."

Silence descends, and I wonder if I've done something wrong by mentioning all of that. Someone clears their throat, and it's only then that I turn around, and Drae wraps an arm around my shoulder.

"Uh, CJ, what does Creed look like?"

I stare at Smoke in confusion, wondering why he'd be asking me that. "He's tall, I'd say probably over six feet tall or close to it. Looks like he could have been a linebacker when he was younger. He's got black hair, blue eyes, and is really tan. Though, he could have been wearing colored contacts. Why?"

"Because he's at the front gate."

Smoke clicks a few buttons and I gasp when a picture pops up on the projector screen and I see Creed waiting outside the gate, standing next to his car.

"Is there a reason that Creed would want to follow-up with you at all, CJ?" Thor asks.

I freeze at the look he's giving me, worried that he's changed his mind and I'm still going to get kicked out of here. I shake my head. "No, he wasn't going to follow-up with me because he didn't want to tip anyone off that he knew where I was. I mean, he took a huge risk in sheltering me for a couple of weeks while the rest of my wounds healed after they rescued me. When we parted ways, he said I probably wouldn't see him again until Sanchez was taken care of. I know he's still alive, so I have no idea why he's here."

Thor continues to stare at me and I shift uneasily, but I'm telling the truth. I have no idea what Creed wants. Drae pulls me behind him, and I see Thor shake his head and sigh.

"I'm not going to hurt her Drae, I just find it rather suspicious that he showed up moments after she told us about him."

"Well, we aren't going to learn anything by sitting in here. Let's go have a little chat with him," Dragon says as he claps Thor on the shoulder.

Chapter 23
Thor

I LOOK OVER AT Smoke and frown. "You don't see anyone else on any of the cameras surrounding the property?"

He shakes his head. "No one. It looks like it's just him."

I frown again. I don't like this. It could be a trap, but Trixie...er, CJ, really doesn't seem to have any reason to be lying about him. "Half of you stay inside the clubhouse in case this is a trap. The rest with me. Ladies, Roy, and Prospects, you stay inside. If shit goes sideways, get to the panic room through the kitchen."

I catch Levi's gaze, and she nods as she pats her stomach, letting me know she's armed. Glancing over at Sasha, she does the same. With one last look at Levi, we both nod, and I turn, leading the others out of Church. Phoenix, Dragon, and Ryder flank me, along with a few others. I notice Bear taking up the post by the door and give him a chin lift in thanks. He'll help keep watch over Wildcat for us.

Walking outside, my gaze zeroes in on Creed before checking our surroundings. I'll give him credit. He doesn't so much as flinch as he stands there watching us approach him. I stop short of the gate and cross my arms as I stare him down.

"Hello Thor, I'm Agent Weber and I'm here to talk with Miss Levi Wallace."

Ice runs down my spine, but I force myself not to react. What the fuck does he want with Wildcat? "And what makes you so sure that she's here, Agent Weber?"

He smirks, and I fight the urge to scowl at him. "She's routed her mail to be delivered to the bar. She never leaves without Dragon, though if it weren't for your cut, I very well would have thought it could have been you she was leaving with. Very good food there, by the way."

I grit my teeth. He's been trailing her, and we didn't notice. I can feel Dragon's anger rolling off him. Glancing at him, he seems to be controlling it, but just barely. Same for my brothers. They've all come to love Levi since she's been here. And with their pledges earlier, I know they'll do anything to keep her from getting hurt again.

"What do you to talk to her about?"

"I'm sorry, but that's between Miss Wallace and me."

My jaw clenches, and I'm just about to tell him to fuck off when small hands loop around my arm. My head whips to her, and I scowl.

"I told you to stay inside," I grit out.

She smiles apologetically and looks over her shoulder. "I know. I asked Smoke to let me listen in, and I decided to come out here to see what he wanted. I won't be having any of you getting hurt or taken in because of someone losing their head. If all he wants to do is talk, then we can talk. Besides, with what's been going on, I'd rather we all talk in the clubhouse than have you both out here with half of our family. It'd be like shooting fish in a barrel."

My gaze lifts from hers and I glare at Smoke standing behind her, but he returns my glare as he steps closer to Levi. I'll be having a chat with him later. I'm about to snap back at her, but her scared, doe-eyed look makes me pause.

She steps closer to me, and her eyes mist over. "I heard Uncle Bear talking with Dad. This could be related to my uncle Sean and what he did to me years ago."

I freeze, knowing that we hadn't talked about that in Church earlier. I'd purposely skipped over that so Roy could talk to her about it. She gives me a tight smile.

"Mom told me what happened a few months before she died. She wanted me to know the truth."

I nod and she gives me a small smile as she turns to head back inside with Smoke right behind her. I look back at Creed and give a chin lift.

"All right, let him in. But if you even think of pulling anything on us, you'll be full of lead before you know it."

"Don't forget blades! If he pisses me off, he'll be so full of steel he'll regret stepping foot in our home!" Levi calls over her shoulder as she flips a blade in the air and continues walking back toward the clubhouse. My brothers chuckle and there's no way I can stop mine, even though I'm pissed at her for this little stunt.

Dragon and I grin as we look at each other and then at Creed. His gaze darts from Levi's retreating figure to Dragon and then to me, no doubt having seen the back of her cut. He pales slightly and clears his throat.

"Noted."

He turns to get in his car and restarts it, pulling through when Bones opens the gate for him. Taking a look down either side of the road behind him, I don't see anyone else, but they could be hiding. Dragon claps me on the shoulder and grins.

"Let's get inside, bro. If Spitfire is going to fill him full of steel, I want to make sure I'm there to witness it in person."

I laugh and turn to follow him.

Creed gets out of his car as we approach and jumps slightly when Dragon claps him on the shoulder, squeezing it. Phoenix steps up in front of him and holds out a hand for his weapon.

"I'm not armed. I left my gun in the console knowing that you wouldn't let me in with it on me." Phoenix gives him a chin lift but still pats him down.

"Let me show you to Church, Agent, and then you can tell us what you want to talk about with our Old Lady," Dragon says as he squeezes his shoulder again. Creed swallows nervously but doesn't put up a fight.

As we walk into the clubhouse, Roy, Bear, and the twins follow us into Church. I chuckle when I see Levi sitting on a table with her legs crossed and still flipping her knife in the air.

"Well, I can definitely say you have the intimidation factor down pat there, Miss Wallace. Especially since I know of your reputation," Creed says as he takes a seat. I give him props for sitting down instead of remaining standing.

"I don't know if you are aware, Miss Wallace, but your uncle, Sean Wallace, is due to get out of prison in two weeks. We have reason to suspect that he will come looking for you when he is released."

"Then why let him out?" Bear asks, his voice laced with anger.

"Because he will have served his sentence, even if I don't agree with him getting a few years shaved off his original sentence for good behavior. He can't be arrested again unless he actually does something wrong. He's angry and blames Miss Wallace for his imprisonment. I've come to offer you protection, but after meeting you, I probably already know your answer, even though I don't agree with it."

Levi smiles darkly at Creed and fuck if my dick doesn't take notice.

"Well now, Mr. Creed Weber, and yes, I know who you are and no, I'm not telling you how I know. I'm not the same little girl I used to be. I'm actually looking forward to seeing Sean try. Him and his partner, Scott Black, a.k.a. Fang, Enforcer for the Black Plague MC."

I smirk as Creed freezes. The documents he'd just pulled out of his briefcase tremble slightly in his hand, and I know she's just shot down what he'd hoped would be his ace.

"If you know they're both after you, I highly recommend accepting my offer. Black Plague is being watched and investigated. They deal in human trafficking among other things. Is that something you really want to risk?" he asks as he stands, leaning against the table.

A dark smirk crosses her face, and I notice a deadly, dark look in Roy's, the twins', and Bear's eyes that match her own. She scoots down off the table, walking toward him, still flipping her blade. It amazes me that she can do that so well and not get a nick on her.

"I'm very well aware of what Fang and his cousins are capable of, *Agent* Weber. Where were you and your protection seven years ago when they kidnapped my mother and me? Where were you when they beat, whipped, and cut me? Where were you when they raped my mother and killed her in front of me? Where were you when they almost succeeded in raping me? My family were the ones that rescued me. Fuck you and your fucking protection!" she yells as she points her knife at him and he audibly gulps.

Shit, please don't let her lose her control. No telling what Creed would do to her if she draws his blood. He's a fucking Fed.

"Where were you when all those women, who look a lot like me, were abducted? Oh, you didn't think I knew about that, did you? See, working in a bar and grill that serves people from all backgrounds, I hear a lot of things. Things that aren't always covered by the news. Maybe you should focus on them. Save them from being tortured, abused, or sold," she snarls as she turns and flings her blade at the wall, anger radiating off of her.

Creed shrinks back a little in shock as he stares at her. Shit... I didn't know she knew about that. Fuck.

He shuffles his papers and puts them back in his briefcase as he clears his throat. "Yes, well, I'll note your answer on the paperwork for my superiors." He stands and turns to go, but then pauses and before turning back to Levi. "Please be careful, Miss Wallace."

His gaze darts to Dragon and me, and he seems to be waging an internal battle.

"Just remember, if they do come after you, they are being watched by the FBI. Now, if they were to attack you, self-defense is an entirely different story," he says, as he gives me a knowing look.

I smirk and when Levi comes over, I pull her close, kissing the top of her head, and Dragon does the same.

Creed's face softens, and he sighs. "If the roles were reversed, and it was my daughter and wife that had gone through that, I'd be right where you all are, too. Just be careful. I'd like to be kept in the loop if at all possible. At the minimum, after you've... dealt with them. I can help take some heat off your back if need be."

With that, he hands me his card and heads toward the door.

"Creed," Levi calls. He turns, and she smiles softly. It's then that I notice her phone is in her hand.

"I think there may be someone here who would like to say something to you," she says as she leans further into my embrace. Confusion crosses his face, but she just smiles. "She's waiting in the main room for you."

Creed looks at me in question, and I give him a chin lift. If Trixie wants to talk to him, I won't stop her. He opens the door and heads down the hallway to the main room, before stopping in his tracks.

"Hi Creed," Trixie says nervously. Drae's standing next to her protectively and he looks like he doesn't quite agree with this.

"Carolina?"

She nods and after a few moments, she rushes toward him, wrapping him in a hug. "Thank you for everything you did for me," she sobs into his shoulder.

"Hey now, don't cry," he says as he pulls back, wipes her tears, and tucks a stray hair behind her ears. "You know Bonnie would have had my ass if I had left you in his clutches, especially after what he did to you."

They both chuckle, and she nods.

"Carolina, what you told us has greatly helped us track his associates down and we're getting closer to closing in on him. Hopefully, it won't be long, and you won't have to look over your shoulder anymore." He glances behind her and smiles. "Besides, it looks like you found your brother."

She nods and turns, pulling Drae closer. "Drae, this is Creed. Creed, Drae."

They shake hands, but Drae's body is still tense.

"Thank you for getting my sister out of there. I've been looking for her ever since she disappeared, but the trail went cold after learning who she'd been sold to. I had no idea where to find her."

"No thanks needed. Just happy we could help. However, when this is over, Bonnie's asked me if she could contact you to see you again, Carolina. Same with Belle. I told them I'd ask you after we had caught Sanchez, but that you might not want to because it could stir up old memories."

Trixie chews on her lip but still nods. "I'd like to see them again to thank them for what they did. Belle and I became really close during my time with you, and I'd like to reconnect with her, if that's okay. I don't want to put them in any danger, though."

Creed smiles. "Everything should be okay. I'll let them know and you keep in touch. Thor has my number. Let me know if there's anything you need, Carolina."

She hugs him again and steps back next to Drae.

Creed turns to me and nods. "I meant what I said. Let me know if you need help keeping heat off your back." With another nod, he turns to leave and Alexei follows him out.

I turn toward Levi, glaring at her but her gaze is still locked on the door Creed just went through.

"Just great. Now I can't kill the bastard," she says, sighing as she runs a hand through her hair. She turns toward me, and her eyes widen in surprise, but it quickly shifts to something I wasn't expecting. Heat. Fuck does that already make me harder than I already was.

"You disobeyed me, Wildcat." I pick her up, flinging her over my shoulder. She squeals in surprise and I smack her ass as I head toward my office, slamming the door shut behind me. Sitting on the couch, I lay her over my legs, keeping one hand on her back near her shoulder blades, I raise my other hand and smack her ass hard.

"What the fuck were you thinking? If that was a trap, you could have gotten taken, shot, or killed!"

She cries out in surprise and then moans. My dick twitches, but I can't have her disobeying me like that again. She could have gotten hurt.

Smack.

"If it was a trap, yeah, I could have gotten shot but not killed. Both Sean and Fang want me alive."

Smack.

"You and Dragon were the ones more at risk. You heard him threaten you both. If it was a trap, he could have easily put a bullet in both of you and then I would have lost you both."

My hand pauses mid-air as I hear her sniffle. I shift her so that she's straddling my lap. Reaching up, I tuck her hair behind her ears and wipe the tears that escaped.

"We feel the same way, Wildcat. It would kill us if something happened to you. That's why I wanted you to stay inside."

"I'm sorry. I'm not used to this. I just got so emotional with both of you out there and I freaked out a little." She pauses as she wipes at her eyes and scoffs. "Okay, I freaked out a lot. I think I scared Smoke with how I was because he couldn't get me to calm down. He said he'd take me out to see you as long as I had cover. He had Alexei, Travis, and Ethan all go out the backdoor and they took up positions in the trees. They had their guns and, of course, were armed with some blades. Travis and Ethan aren't as good with their blade work as Alexei, but they're getting closer."

She sniffles again, and I pull her closer, resting her forehead on mine.

Sighing, I collect my thoughts. While I'm not happy Smoke took her outside, I'm also relieved that he'd ordered cover for us. Something I should have done.

"I'll let this go for now, Wildcat, but in the future, you need to do what we say in situations like this. We got lucky this time. Next time could be different. Just know that Dragon and I will do everything in our power to come back to you."

She nods, and I lean forward, kissing her. The kiss starts out gentle but quickly turns heated. She rolls her hips and whimpers as she continues to grind against me.

"I need you, Ryan," she whispers.

"Up with you, Wildcat," I say as I squeeze her ass before swatting it. She quickly scrambles off my lap and kicks off her boots. Unbuckling my belt, I lower my jeans down to my knees. She takes off her jeans, but before she can climb back onto my lap, I sink my fingers into her pussy. I moan when I find her drenched and ready for me. Licking my fingers clean, another moan escapes as her taste hits my tongue.

"I love how you're so ready for us all the time."

She straddles me, grasping my cock, and lowers herself onto me. We both moan deeply when I'm fully seated in her and she starts moving. I crash my lips to hers to swallow more of her moans. I really don't want her father to hear her as she cums on my cock.

"This is going to be fast, Wildcat. I need you too much."

Her hands grip my shoulders as she bounces on my cock. Her perfect tits bouncing right in front of me as she moves. Breaking our kiss, I push up her shirt and pull one of her tits out of her bra. Seconds later, I capture her nipple in my mouth, biting down slightly on her soft flesh. She whimpers as her pussy clamps down on me and she clasps a hand over her mouth to stifle her cries as she cums. My hands go to her hips as I move her up and down my cock a few more times before I follow her, shooting ropes of cum into her.

She collapses against me, catching her breath. Before long, I can feel our joined juices trickling out of her. Grabbing her ass with both hands, I stand and carefully shuffle-walk over to my office chair, sitting her down. Grabbing a few tissues, I clean her off and then myself, throwing the tissues in the trash.

Pulling my pants back up, I pick up her clothes off the floor, handing them to her. She quickly gets dressed again and pulls out a mirror she stowed in my desk drawer a while back. She's taken to keeping a few things in here for when we can't wait to head home or head up to our room here.

Once she's fixed her hair, I pull her to me, kissing her deeply.

"I love you, Levi."

She smiles up at me. "I love you, too, Ryan."

She grabs something out of the drawer, putting it in her pocket. I raise my eyebrow in question, but she shakes her head.

"Let's go find Nick and I'll explain."

Nodding, I tuck her under my arm, and we head back out to the main room.

Chapter 24
Dragon

I SMIRK AS I watch Thor walk toward his office with Levi thrown over his shoulder, and then freeze.

Roy's here.

Shit. I hope Thor doesn't let things escalate while he talks to her about not listening to him.

Scanning the room, I see Roy and Bear off in a corner, talking quietly. I walk to the bar and Colt hands me a beer.

"Give me two more for Bear and Roy."

He gives me a chin lift and pulls out the kind they both like. I grin. This is another thing I like about Colt and Drae. They both quickly learned what we all like and they often have them ready for us before we even approach the bar. Same for Roxy. Though, they wait to uncap them until we're right there.

Grabbing the beers, I walk over to them and hand them their drinks. "You okay, Roy?"

He sighs and nods as he runs a hand over his face, before taking a long pull. "I didn't know she knew about what Sean did to her," he says quietly.

I nod, picking at the label on my bottle. "Outside, she told Thor that Emily had told her what happened a few months before she died. That she wanted Levi to know the truth."

A ghost of a smile crosses his face as he fingers the necklace that he's worn for years. "That sounds like Em. She always hated having to lie to Levi whenever she asked why Sean never attended family events anymore. It ate at her." He pauses as he stares at the bottle in his hands. "In a way, I'm glad Em told her. Looking back, I should have realized it. That was probably around the time she pulled in on herself for a while. Not even Sasha could get her to come out of her room except to eat and go to school. After a few weeks, she suddenly had a different attitude, and she started training harder."

"You're probably right. There were a few times that I caught her and Sasha out back with her laptop and some rope. They were learning how to tie knots. Then they'd each tie one end around each other's wrist and they'd try to get them undone with one hand. After a while, it progressed to tying both hands behind their back. That was right before Levi and Emily were taken." Bear pauses as his fingers run over a bracelet I'd noticed he'd always worn. One on each hand. I always thought it was kind of odd, but never questioned it.

"Levi had these made. Did you know that?" Bear asks me, as he looks up at me, cocking an eyebrow in question.

Glancing at Roy, I notice he also has the same bracelets. Now that I think of it, they all wear them. Levi, the twins, Ethan, and Travis. What's so special about the bracelets?

Bear stands and then, as he turns around, puts his hands behind his back like they're tied together. With one hand, he twists the bracelet on his other wrist, and it comes apart. My jaw drops when I see a small knife that's hidden inside. It could take a while depending on how thick the rope or zip tie is, but you'd be able to cut through them. He sits back down and chuckles at my shocked expression as he puts the bracelet back on.

His fingers linger on the bracelets before he looks up at me. "I never questioned her when she gave us these. It was maybe a month after Em died. I knew why she'd done it. Granted, it wouldn't have helped her or Em since they were tied up spread eagle, their ropes hooked to chains. But still, the fact that she thought enough about it to make them for if one of us was ever in a similar situation broke another piece of me. She's been through so much in her short life. I hate that it's coming back around to haunt her again. This time, though... This time it ends." His hands clench, and I nod.

"This time it ends," I repeat.

We'd have to be careful, though. Knowing now that the FBI has a lock on Black Plague, particularly Fang, it'll make things more difficult. One way or another, I'll make sure the bastard's gone. Either permanently or locked up for life. I smirk.

I have a few contacts that are currently in prison. An 'accident' could always be arranged.

Roy looks up at something behind me. Turning, I see Thor and Spitfire approaching, each having grabbed a drink on their way over. I pull my woman into my lap, burying my face in her neck.

"You had me worried earlier, Spitfire."

She sighs and snuggles into me, wrapping her arms around my neck. "I freaked out with both of you out there when I kept thinking it could be a trap. Or if one of Fang's men was watching and was armed. I think I might have triggered something for Smoke with my freak-out. He wrapped me in a hug and tried to get me to calm down. When he couldn't, he said he'd take me out to you guys, but had Alexei, Ethan, and Travis all sneak out to provide cover for us should it be a trap. Please don't be mad at him. He was trying to help me."

I sigh. While I'm not happy he did that, at least he took steps to help protect her. "I don't like that he did that, but I won't beat him up for it."

She kisses my cheek and then leans back, digging something out of her pocket. She pauses as she fingers a couple of pouches and then hands one to Thor and gives me the other.

"I want you guys to have these. It's something I had made for my family to help if any of us are captured. I had some made for you guys, too."

She blushes, and I place a chaste kiss on her lips.

Opening the pouch, two bracelets fall out, and I grin as I look back up at her. "Bear was just showing me his. It hadn't dawned on me before then that you all wear these. Thanks, Spitfire."

I kiss her again and her blush deepens. Spitfire looks over at Thor and seeing his confusion, climbs off my lap. She turns around, holding her hands behind her back, twists one of her bracelets, and shows him the little knife. She turns around, re-secures it, and then Thor pulls her into his lap.

"Thank you, Wildcat." He kisses her and then puts on his bracelets as I do the same.

I pause as I look at them, a thought coming to mind. "How long does it take you to make these?"

Levi shrugs. "The longest part is waiting for the blades to come in. I have a guy that I work with for all of my designs. He used to compete with me, and we became friends. Once they arrive, I just have to make the cord and secure it to the blade and sheath."

I look at Thor and he gives me a chin lift, already knowing where my train of thought went.

"Wildcat, would you be able to make a bunch for the guys? I have a feeling things are going to get worse before they get better. We know Fang will stop at nothing to get you, and now we've got Sean in the mix, too. I'd feel better if the guys had this as an advantage for if one of them is taken."

Levi blushes and looks down at her hands, twisting them nervously as she clears her throat. "Well, I'm glad you think that, because I've already kind of got them made," she says as she looks up at him sheepishly.

Bear and Roy bust out laughing at the shocked look on our faces.

"God damn, I love you, woman," Thor says as he captures her lips again.

Roy groans, and I laugh.

"Can you save that for when I'm not around? I get that she's with you both, but there are some things a father doesn't want to see," he groans again as he runs a hand over his face. Levi chuckles as she pulls back from Thor.

"Sorry but not sorry, Dad."

Roy laughs, but nods.

A phone vibrates, and Thor swats Levi's thigh. She gets up and sits back in my lap, taking a sip of her beer.

"*Alexei, what's up?*" He freezes and then glances at Levi, then me. "*Bring it into Church. I'll send Colt out to take your place.*"

He hangs up and runs a hand through his hair and then sends a text, most likely to Colt.

"What's wrong?" Levi asks.

He pauses and dread fills my stomach. He opens his mouth and closes it a few times before sighing.

"A package has been delivered. Addressed to you." He pauses again and a pained look crosses his face. "It's got dried blood on it, Levi. It might be best if you weren't there when we opened it."

Her face pales and I feel her body start to tremble. "You'll tell me what it is, though, right?"

Thor looks at me, and I nod. I know she's been worried sick about the women that have gone missing. I just hope it isn't what I think it is. Thor sighs.

"Yeah, Wildcat, we'll tell you. But you gotta let us handle this. Stay out here with the other women, your dad, and the Prospects for now."

She nods, and he gets up, giving her a quick kiss. I place a kiss on her temple, and she slides off my lap just as the door opens. Her eyes lock on the box and grow wide. Her body starts trembling even more, and I curse the timing of things. Looking over her shoulder, Roy nods at me and then pulls her into his arms. Giving him a chin lift, I follow Thor.

"Church!" Thor bellows. A few brothers look up, surprised, but their faces grow grim when they see the box Alexei's carrying.

We file into Church. Alexei puts the box on the head table and then ducks out after everyone's inside, shutting the door behind him. Thor nods to Patch, and he pulls some gloves out of his kit. Ryder steps forward and takes a pair of gloves as well to help him. Carefully, they open the box and then they step back, their faces clenched in anger. Taking a step forward, I quickly turn away after seeing the contents.

Inside the box is a severed hand with its fingertips burned off, some cut-up underwear, and pictures of women who had all been beaten. They all look like Spitfire.

Patch takes a deep breath and reaches into the box, pulling out the pictures and a note before fanning them out on the table. There are names of ten women on each of the pictures but the eleventh picture... It's a picture of Levi in between both of us sitting on the swing on our back deck.

> *You didn't listen to me, Levi. You were promised to me. You let someone else touch you and take what was mine. I'm taking it out tenfold on others until you return to me. Tic toc, Princess.*
>
> *~ Fang*

Thor roars, his fist crashing into the wall.

A small knock on the door draws my attention, and I turn, seeing Levi enter with her phone in her hand.

"I'm sorry to interrupt, and to enter without you opening the door, but Fang's calling me and I figured you'd want to trace it." Her gaze darts to the box and then the contents, which are now spread out on the table right in front of her. She quickly turns away, covering her mouth. I walk toward her and pull her into my arms.

"I'm sorry, I didn't mean to look. Should I answer or let it go to voicemail?"

"Go ahead and answer, Wildcat."

Levi nods, answers, and puts the call on speaker. *"What do you want, Fang?"*

The bite in her voice sends a chill down my spine. Knowing that she's seen what's inside the package, I have no doubts that she wants to make him hurt for what he's done to these women.

"Now, now, Princess, that's no way to answer the phone. I take it you saw my gift?"

"You're a fucking monster."

The anger rolling off her is intense. Her hands grip the phone so hard I'm afraid it might shatter.

"Well, Princess, you know what you need to do to stop all this. Time is ticking. Tic toc."

The phone cuts off, but Levi still has a death grip on the phone and her eyes are darting around. Her body is tense as she gnaws at her lip.

"Spitfire? Talk to us, Babe."

I hear a chair scrape behind me and am surprised when Smoke kneels down in front of her and takes her hand. Her gaze snaps to him and she nods.

"Did you hear it, too?"

Wait, what?

I turn to Smoke, who looks confused as well about her question. Then, he smiles and I'm guessing that means he understood what she's talking about. He quickly stands, grabbing his laptop before walking over to the pictures. Levi gives me a tight smile and follows Smoke. They each take gloves from the box Patch had set out earlier and start looking through all the pictures.

"Would you like to clue us in, Wildcat?"

Looking up, her gaze goes to each of my brothers.

"Did any of you hear anything else besides Fang and me talking?"

Everyone shakes their head, but then Ryder pauses.

"A grandfather clock and some sort of animal bleating."

Levi nods and returns her attention to the pictures.

"Yes, but there was something else. A muffled voice. I thought I heard 'north' and something like 'mend'."

"Here," Smoke says as he grabs a picture. Levi looks over his shoulder and quickly pulls out her phone. She snaps a picture and then Smoke's phone pings.

"Put it up on the big screen," she says, and Smoke nods.

"You got it, Kiddo."

Levi turns and pulls down the screen as I stare at her in shock. I was damn sure that if anyone had called her that, their body would be full of steel, yet she just took Smoke's nickname in stride.

Add to that, Smoke just gave her a fucking endearing nickname.

Smoke.

What the fuck's going on? Turning to Thor, and then the rest of the guys, they all have the same shocked looks on their faces.

After a few clicks, a picture of one of the victims lights up the screen. She'd been beaten to a bloody pulp and has cuts all over her body. What did Spitfire and Smoke see that was so special with this picture?

"There," Levi says as she points to some flowers that are clutched in the woman's hands. "It's a cluster of marsh marigolds. If Fang and his crew are hiding the women near there, then that vastly narrows down where they're located." Levi spins around and snatches Smoke's laptop from him.

Once again, my jaw drops in shock.

Smoke doesn't let *anyone* touch his laptop. He's very particular about his electronics, but here he is looking over her shoulder as she brings up an overview map of Forest Creek *on his fucking laptop.* After a few clicks, she reaches out a hand, making a 'give me' gesture. Smoke pulls his stylus out from a pocket inside his cut and gives it to her without a word. She circles three areas of the map and gives the stylus back to Smoke.

"Why are the marsh marigold's the key to Fang's location?" Tripp asks.

Bear slams his hand on the table as he grins at Spitfire. "Shit. You're right, Little Ninja. Marsh marigolds grow in wetlands. Those three areas are where you'll usually find them around Forest Creek, with the largest cluster in that top area that you circled."

She nods as her smile grows. "I bet if you scout these three areas, we'll be able to find where Fang and his crew are hiding the women. My bet is that it's the northern one, as the marsh does take a notable bend in the forest which matches with the mumbled words I swore I heard. Thor, I'm also betting if you were to give an 'anonymous' tip to Creed, that they'd be able to swoop in and hopefully rescue the rest of the abducted women. As long as we aren't seen, then Fang won't know it was us that tipped off the Feds to their location. Unless he has an inside contact, that is. But something tells me that Creed would keep our names out of his reports."

Spitfire looks between Thor and me nervously as she gnaws her lip, almost as if she's worried about her practically taking the reins and driving a meeting she technically isn't supposed to be in. It also hasn't escaped my notice that she said 'we' and 'our'. It feels like she's referring to everyone as her family, which makes me want to talk to Thor soon about something I've been thinking a lot about lately.

Smoke sends a glare at Thor and me before wrapping my Spitfire in a hug. "Relax, Kiddo. You didn't do anything wrong except for not waiting for a response before barging in. However, based on what we know now, I doubt you're in trouble."

Normally I'd be pissed or annoyed at someone laying his hands on my spitfire, even one of my brothers, but this is weird. Different. Almost like a hug you'd give to a family member. Now I really want to know what happened before she came outside earlier.

I give him a chin lift, recognizing what was happening, and he dips his head in return before turning his attention to Thor. He cocks an eyebrow at Thor, which seems to snap him out of his trance, but before Thor can say anything, someone clears their throat.

"Uh, can I ask something?"

We all turn toward Gunner, who looks like he's barely holding in whatever it was he had to say. Thor gives him a chin lift, and almost immediately, the words fly out of Gunner's mouth.

"*What the fuck, Smoke?* You avoid all women. You don't let anyone touch your electronics, especially your laptop, and here you are hugging our Pres's and Enforcer's Old Lady like it's no problem and you *fucking let her use your computer.* You even gave her a nickname. What the fuck, dude!"

Laughter spills out of everyone since they know he's giving Smoke shit, and the tension I saw earlier in Levi seems to evaporate before she falls into a fit of laughter, too. The laughter from my brothers intensifies when she reaches up and plucks Smoke's baseball cap off his head before putting it on and slipping her long hair out the back. Smoke's face lights up in a smile and he pulls her in for another hug. She turns tentatively to me, with an eyebrow raised in question. I give her a chin lift and the smile that lights up her face is breathtaking.

As the laughter dies down, Smoke clears his throat as he looks down at Levi, who had moved to hug Thor. I give a chin lift to Patch, who is now putting the pictures back into the box and sets it off to the side so that it's out of her line of sight. I'll ask Ryder to try and run some prints after this.

"To answer your question, Gunner, that's what a brother does for a sister who's in trouble."

You could have heard a pin drop at what Smoke was implying.

Levi stares at him in shock before her gaze snaps to me in disbelief and I nod. She looks up at Thor, and when he nods, an ear-piercing squeal leaves her mouth as she dives toward Smoke, giving him a bone-crushing hug of her own.

"I have another brother!"

Chapter 25

Levi

HOLY SHIT, I CAN'T believe it. I knew earlier, when I had practically begged Smoke to let me go outside, something shifted in him. I just had no idea what had changed other than his steel-gray eyes lost some of their hardness. The fact that he just claimed me as his sister blows my mind.

It's true what Gunner said earlier. Smoke avoids women like the plague, but when I first noticed him watching me not too long after I got here, I thought he was worried that I'd screw over the club somehow. As time went on, he almost seemed surprised that I hadn't.

Then there were the few times since then when we passed each other in the halls. He would verbally respond to my 'hello' or 'good morning' instead of just grunting. To say I was shocked when he hugged me as he tried to calm me down while my men and half of my family might be walking into a trap is an understatement. A man who, for some reason, refuses to allow women to touch him, was hugging me and talking soothingly in my ear to try to calm me down.

When Smoke caught onto my train of thought earlier, something seemed to click between us and it's similar to how I am with Alexei and Sasha. We don't even need to talk sometimes because we're usually thinking the same thing.

In all honestly, I'd been warned to never touch his electronics, especially his computer, but today I acted without thinking. Too concerned to find out where the women were being held to even think about the trouble I could be in for touching his stuff.

A knock sounds at the door and out of the corner of my eye, I see Dragon walking over to answer. It takes me a moment to snap out of my thoughts, but when I hear Sasha's voice, I realize she's brought what I asked her to.

I pull back from Smoke and when Dragon comes over with a very familiar bag; I take it.

Thor leans down close to me and whispers in my ear. "Let me say a few things first, and then you can have the floor."

He kisses my temple and then walks forward, banging his hammer against the table to get everyone's attention. When everyone calms down, Thor nods at Smoke and me.

"We'll need teams to go and search each location Wildcat and Smoke pointed out, but remember that at first, it's just a scouting mission. If we are going to give a tip to the Feds, we need to be damn sure we have our facts straight. Ryder and Bones, work with Smoke to see what all you can come up with. We'll meet again to plan the stake out after you've found more out."

Everyone gives him a chin lift and then Thor waves me over. Clearing my throat, I try to stomp down my nerves.

"I don't know if you guys have noticed, but my family and I all wear the same bracelets. One on each wrist. Now, before you all start declaring that I'm offering some pussy-assed, girly-as-shit bracelet to you all, let me first show you what they do."

I hear a few chuckles as I sit the bag down on the table, turn around, clasp my hands behind my back, before revealing the hidden blade inside one of the bracelets. When I turn back around, all but three faces are staring at me in surprise. My men and Uncle Bear have shit-eating grins plastered on their faces.

"Damn, I want one of those, but I hope it isn't as dainty as yours. I'd probably crush it with these hands and then be fucked," Judge says as his shoulders shake with laughter.

"What made you want to make something like that?" Axe asks and I duck my head as I try to push down the memories that are bombarding me.

Taking a deep breath, I look around the room. "I'm gonna take a stab, no pun intended, that you guys know about my Uncle Sean?"

Grim nods come from each of the men, and I nod, thankful that I don't have to repeat what Mom told me had really happened.

"A few months before Mom died, she told me what he'd done and almost did." I pause as an icy shiver runs down my spine. "I pulled away from my family for a while as I tried to process everything, but soon realized that if anything like that happened again, I wanted to be prepared for it. I had previously talked to my friend, Gray, after the attack and asked if he could make me some handmade blades that I could hide on my body and easily throw. We used to compete together and became good friends. Then, I reached out to him again a few weeks later and pitched an idea to him. He agreed."

"Holy shit," someone whispers, and it takes me a bit before I realize it was Timber who was the one that had spoken. "Gray as in Gray Miller?"

At my nod, Timber seems to practically vibrate in his chair with excitement. I have to bite my cheeks to keep from laughing at the sight of a buff, tattooed biker practically bouncing in his seat like a child at their birthday party.

Still, I'm not surprised he caught on to who Gray was since we often talk about my competitions, but now that I think about it, I don't think I ever told him who made the knives that I now use.

"Care to clue us in, asshole, before you shoot through the roof?" Tripp says as he clasps Timber on the shoulder and several of the guys chuckle.

"Gray Miller is a legend. He's been making blades his whole life. When he got older, he stopped going to competitions to focus more on just making blades. They are wicked, but also extremely expensive." He shakes his head in shock and I have to bite the inside of my cheek again to keep from smiling as an idea pops into my head. I think I just figured out what to get Timber when Christmas rolls around. That should give Gray enough time to prepare.

I nod and smile at him. "Well, now you can say you have a Gray Miller blade, Timber, because he makes *all* of my blades, including these and their sheaths. Not to mention the sleeves Sasha and I wear. Once he delivers these blades, I make the bracelets for them. And Judge, to answer your question, the knives that we designed for guys are a bit bigger for that very reason than those we designed for women. I hate chunky jewelry myself, so I tried to keep the bulk down. These are designs that Gray and I worked on and before I came here, only nine were made at that time—for me and my family as well as one for him. Uncle Bear tested some of our earlier prototypes for a rough-size template for men."

I pause as I blink back my tears, thinking about the memory shadowbox I had made after Grandpa passed away, which also holds his bracelets. Taking a deep breath, I shake myself internally as my gaze automatically goes to Uncle Bear's. He gives me a tight smile, no doubt knowing where my mind went.

"The reason why I had asked to have these made was so that if I was ever restrained again, or anyone in my family for that matter, that we'd be able to cut through our restraints so long as we can reach at least one of the blades. Well, and as long as the restraints aren't made of metal.

"After being here for a couple of weeks, I reached out to Gray and asked if he'd make blades for Thor and Dragon as well as all of you. A little bit ago, I gave Thor and Dragon theirs. I didn't ask for any for the bunnies, though just so you know I do have a set for Roxy because we've become very close, and plus, I don't consider her a real bunny. Also, until today, there were only two other bunnies that I could barely stand to be around. To be honest, I'm still a little wary, but time will tell on that subject. I don't know if we should give sets to the rest of the bunnies or not. I'll leave that decision up to all of you. Same for the Prospects, but just remember that Alexei already has a set. And since they are living here for now, I should probably tell you that both Travis and Ethan have these, too.

"I won't take any offense if someone doesn't want one and if you do, but there isn't a band that fits you, I can get that rectified fairly quickly." I pause as I start to pull out the bracelets and lay them on the front table. Almost immediately, the sound of chairs scraping on the floor can be heard as each one of them rises and comes up to pick out their bracelets. A chuckle escapes me as a few of them eagerly unsheathe the blades and are taking a closer look at them.

Thor steps up beside me and drapes an arm over my shoulder, pulling me close to him. "Thank you for thinking of them, Wildcat." He leans down and gives me a chaste kiss.

"Of course, Hun. They're my family and I wanted to do something that might be able to help them if anyone's ever able to pull a fast one on us."

The room once again goes silent, and I turn back toward the guys in surprise before they erupt in cheers. Seeing all the guys excited for the bracelets cements in another thought that Gray had mentioned when he delivered them. But I need to talk to Thor and maybe Phoenix about that first.

In the end, no one needed a different band, since I had purposely ordered extra for that very reason and made bands of varying lengths based on rough calculations from looking at everyone's wrists. The rest I'll ask Thor to lock up in his office for when another brother patches in or if another Old Lady is welcomed into the fold.

"Hey, Kiddo. What do you use to make the bracelet bands?"

I turned toward Smoke, surprised by how closely he's inspecting the band. "A smaller paracord that also has a lot of metal wires on the inside. I didn't want them to be easily cut off. I went with the smaller paracord so that they wouldn't be as bulky as the larger paracord would be. However, if you would like the larger paracord, I could easily make one up for you."

"How would you feel about letting me watch you make one sometime? I've also been toying with an idea of how to get an extra type of tracking device for us in case we're captured, and they take our cuts. If it's possible, I'd like to see if you could add them to your designs."

I pause as I think through what he's suggesting. I could possibly do a wraparound design that might possibly secure the device to the cord, but then I pause as the rest of what he said catches up to me. There are devices in their cuts? Does that mean there's one in mine too?

"And since I can guess where your mind just went, yes, there are a couple of trackers in your property cut. I'm gonna guess Thor and Dragon were planning on telling you tonight."

I shake my head and smile. "That's not a problem, Smoke, and it actually helps ease one of my worries. As for the bracelet, yes, I can make one as you watch, and I was toying with the idea of doing a wraparound design that we could secure the tracker inside, but I've never made one like that before. I don't know how bulky that would make the bracelet. However, if that idea doesn't work, maybe we could talk to Gray. Take a trip up to his shop and see if there are any other options we could discuss."

"Road trip! I vote road trip!" Timber excitedly cries out, which has everyone laughing at him again. That man is such a goofball sometimes.

When everyone has their bracelets and has practiced a few times, Thor calls the meeting closed. As each of them walk by us, they give me a hug and thank me for thinking of them. I have to bite my tongue multiple times to keep from crying.

Going down memory lane is messing with me and making me more emotional than ever.

When it's just me and my guys left in Church, they come over to me and each give me a quick kiss.

"I'm gonna head to the kitchen to see what all we need to restock up on."

"Sounds good, Wildcat. We're gonna chat with Smoke real quick to make sure he's okay and everything."

That pulls me up short and now I'm suddenly nervous that I might have done something to make him uncomfortable. I knew something bad had happened to him a while back with a woman he'd been dating, but still, I wanted to also make sure he was okay. I gnaw on my lip, looking over at Smoke as he leans against the bar.

"Would you be able to let me know if I overstepped at all? Now that you mention it, I'm worried if I had and misread him."

Dragon shakes his head slightly as he smiles down at me. "I don't think you did, but we'll let you know if there are any issues, Spitfire."

"Thanks." Reaching up, I give them each another kiss. "Just don't go razzing him too much for claiming me as his sister." I wink at them, which has them both laughing.

As I turn to head to the bar, Thor smacks me on the ass. I jump and mock glare at him, which has them laughing even harder before they start whispering. God, I love these men.

Chapter 26
Smoke

"THANKS, KIDDO," I SAY as I kiss Levi's forehead and give her a hug. The smile that lights up her face reinforces the fact that I did the right thing by letting her into my life.

I had tried to stay away from her like with the other women, but everything she does draws me in further. The way she cares about my brothers, and how she watches over the bunnies that she gets along with. Even though she doesn't like the other bunnies, she's still cordial to them, even if they are talking about sex and how Levi can never fully satisfy Thor and Dragon like they could.

However, the day that changed everything for me was when she had heard I was sick a week or so after she arrived. She brought me some of her homemade chicken noodle soup, not knowing that I was missing my mom's homemade chicken noodle soup. It actually ended up being better than my mom's, not that I'd ever tell my mom that, even if she was still alive. When Levi came in later to collect the dishes, she saw that I'd polished it off and probably heard from Patch that my vitals were better. She continued to bring me the soup for another week until I was on the mend and able to keep down a normal meal.

Ever since then, I've watched her and slowly felt my walls lowering around her. In a way, I'm glad that Levi's helping me in being able to trust women again. Maybe I'll still be able to find the happiness she has with my brothers. While yes, she's very beautiful, I've never felt aroused by her at all. She's always been like a sister to me. And now she is.

"You're welcome," she says, though it doesn't escape my notice that she's trying to blink away tears. She's been through the wringer today emotionally, so I'm not surprised that everything's getting to her. Especially if my suspicion is true.

As I walk out into the main room, I'm surprised to feel a weight lessen from my shoulders. Looking over my shoulder, I can't help but grin as I see Levi with Thor and Dragon. Those three really are perfect for each other.

At the bar, I grab a beer from Colt, intent on heading up to my room to check a few of my programs before tonight's party starts. I also want to try an idea that I'd had for piggybacking into Black Plague's video feed so I could see everything that they're able to see. While I'd considered making a replay loop of past data that we could use to try to throw them off, I quickly dismissed it. They probably have someone staking out somewhere and watching us. If their intel doesn't line up with what was being seen on the cameras, then they'd know we did something to the feed.

"Hey Smoke, you got a second?" Thor calls out just as I'm about to head upstairs. I give him a chin lift and follow him into his office. With Dragon right behind me.

Shit. I hope they aren't mad about what I just did. Dragon didn't seem too upset, but I'm not sure about Thor.

"What's up, Pres?" I ask as I sit down on the couch in front of his desk. Dragon plops down next to me and takes a long pull from his bottle as Thor settles into his desk chair.

"We just wanted to check with you and make sure you're okay."

"Yeah, I'm good, Pres. I'm not in any trouble by not talking to you guys first about claiming Levi as my sister, am I?" I look between them, and for the first time in a long time, feel uneasy around both of them. I didn't want to cause any problems in the club.

Thor and Dragon both shake their heads.

"Nah, brother, you aren't in any trouble or anything. Though I will say I was shocked that you did that and to top it off, let her use your laptop," Thor says as he laughs.

"Same, bro. I mean, before Spitfire came here, I'd never seen you say anything remotely positive about a woman before. Shocked the shit out of me when we talked the day after she came, and you said you thought she was perfect for us."

He shakes his head in disbelief and I look over at Thor, raising an eyebrow in question to Dragon. Thor shakes his head subtly. Honestly, that surprises me, but I'm glad he hadn't told anyone.

Clearing my throat, I stare down at my bottle, surprised at myself for wanting to tell Dragon. Shit. I should probably tell Levi, too.

"Is it..." I pause as I clear my throat again. "Is it okay if Levi comes in here? I think it's time I share something, and it wouldn't hurt if she knew."

Thor gives me a chin lift while Dragon looks between us both, confused.

"I'll go get her. I think I'm gonna need another beer for this." Standing, I pause when I get to the door. "You guys need a top-off?" They both give me a chin lift, and I head toward the kitchen since that was where Levi was headed after leaving Church.

As I round the corner, I'm surprised that all the bunnies are actually in here for once and are actually fucking helping Levi, Roxy, and Sasha take inventory. Having Levi here is going to change things for the better, I think.

I clear my throat and when Levi looks up; her face once again lights up into a bright smile. "Hey, Smoke. Can we get ya anything?"

"Actually, I was wondering if you would have some time? I'd like to talk to you a bit." Her body tenses slightly, and she gnaws at her lip.

Shit, I bet she's worried I'm mad at her.

"Sure," she says before turning toward Roxy. "Will you be okay without me for a bit? I'll come find you after we're done."

The ladies all wave her off.

"Go girl. And don't look so nervous. It's probably just a chat so you both can learn more about each other," Roxy says as she shoos off Levi.

"Добро пожаловать в семью [Welcome to the family], Smoke," Sasha says as she raises her beer bottle at me. I have no idea what she just said, but I still find myself raising my drink back at her. Levi follows me out into the hall, and I steer her toward the bar.

Giving a chin lift to Colt, I set down my now empty bottle. "Refills for Thor, Dragon, and me," I say and then pause as I turn to Levi. "You want a drink, Kiddo?"

"Sure. Can I have a Coke please, Colt?"

Grabbing the drinks, I guide her toward the office, and her nervousness seems to skyrocket.

"Um, Smoke... are you mad at me by chance? I'm sorry for touching your laptop without asking first."

Grinning, I shake my head. "Nah, Kiddo, I'm not mad and you're the only person I'll let touch my laptop. I want to share something with you and figured Dragon should probably know too, since I just claimed you as my sister."

"I take it Thor already knows?"

Giving a curt nod, I feel my body tensing up. I don't want to relive this shit, but I also don't want to start off our relationship without her knowing what happened. No, I want everything out in the open from the start. I knew Levi was different from Lillian at the get-go and wouldn't purposefully screw anyone over, but some things are just hard to shake.

Once in the office, I shut the door and feel my chest warm when Dragon reaches out for Levi and pulls her onto his lap. I hand out the refills before retaking my seat. Taking a deep breath, I exhale heavily, staring down at the label on the bottle.

"I had a daughter."

Levi's sharp intake has my gut twisting even worse, but they need to know.

"I was seeing someone, and I thought it was getting kind of serious. Even more so when she found out she was pregnant." I pause as the memories wash over me.

"Each doctor's appointment that she had, I made sure I was there with her. Then we'd stop by the baby store and pick up a few more things for her. Money was kind of tight back then since we were also planning to build a house soon, so we decided to get the baby things gradually. At the time, she was living in Rixen, and I was living here at the clubhouse, but I spent almost every night with her. We had planned to rent one of the apartments the club owns until the house was finished and had it all lined up to move in a month before she was due.

"Lillian went into labor six weeks early. I was here, finishing putting together the baby crib in the apartment, then was planning to propose to her that night at dinner. I got the call from the hospital that she was admitted and in the early stages of labor. The fucking hospital called... not her..." I grit out as I feel my anger rising.

A small hand lands on my arm before the cushion next to me dips as Levi leans against me. Surprisingly, having her there lessens my anger a little. Not much, but I no longer feel like I'm on the verge of doing something stupid, like killing my fucking bitch of an ex or that asshole.

"When I got to the hospital, they immediately brought me back... but there was another man in the room. A man I didn't know that was holding my baby. They were both crying, and I didn't know what was going on."

"What the fuck is going on? Who are you and why are you holding my daughter, asshole?" It was then that I noticed Patch came into the room along with Thor. Wait... how did they get here so fast?

Lillian's crying gets louder and the man goes to her, pulling her in for a hug.

"Give me my daughter and get the fuck away from my girlfriend," I say through gritted teeth. I want to punch the fucker so hard, but don't want to hurt Mae. How dare he hold my girls?

The longer dipshit holds Lillian, the more my chest aches as my mind reels at why this asshole was in Lillian's room and why he was holding my girls in an all too loving manner.

"Give me my daughter, then get the fuck out of here. I'd like to be alone with my girls."

The man straightens, and though he pales a bit at seeing me and my cut, he doesn't budge. He's a good foot shorter than me. His blond hair was slicked back, though it looked greasy, and from his round belly, he either loved to eat or loved to drink too much.

"Not until you calm down. And I would like to ask you to refrain from using that language around my wife."

I felt like I'd been sucker punched in the gut. My gaze cuts to Lillian's left hand, which now has a gold band around the finger. The box in my pocket feels like lead.

"You've been cheating on me? When did you get married to this pencil pusher?"

Lillian shrinks back at my tone, but I need to know what the fuck had happened and why.

"I... I was going to tell you tonight. I can't do this anymore, Jax. I've tried telling you that I didn't think the club would be a good place for our daughter to be around."

"It's Smoke. You no longer get to use that name." I pause as I pace, running my hand through my hair as I try to calm my anger. Both Thor and Patch stand protectively by the door, most likely to keep security out if I lose my shit.

"So, let me get this straight. You decide to cheat on me even though we're having a baby together, get married behind my back, and then decide to just 'tell me tonight'? And quite honestly, this is the first I'm even hearing about you not wanting to raise Mae around the club. One would think that in a relationship, if someone is unhappy, they'd speak up about the issue. Not let it fester and apparently lead to this fucked up mess!" I bite my tongue on telling her that I was about to propose tonight. I'll take the ring back to the jeweler later.

Running my hand angrily through my hair again, I notice for the first time that there hasn't been a peep out of Mae. Normally babies are louder or want to nurse a lot. At least that's my observation of how my cousins have been.

"Can I please hold my daughter, if she even is my daughter?"

Lillian dips her chin. "She's your daughter... but she... she..." More tears pour down her cheeks and once again, dread fills me.

Is there something wrong with Mae? I didn't care what was wrong with her. I'd make sure she would have any medical attention she'd need.

Dipshit walks over and places my little pink bundled girl in my arms, and I immediately know my life has forever changed in a blink of an eye. And not in the way you'd think.

She's cold.

"She... she was stillborn."

This didn't make any sense. I'd left Lillian's just this morning, and yeah, I wasn't going to unwrap that right now, but I'd left to finish getting our apartment put together. The crib was delayed and I wanted to make sure it was ready for whenever Mae came into the world.

As always, I rubbed Lillian's stomach and said goodbye to Mae as well. She kicked and moved around like usual. Unless something happened to her since then?

"The cord somehow got wrapped around her neck," dipshit says, and though I hate his guts right now, even he was crying.

Refusing to let go of Mae, I purposely ignore Lillian and dipshit, and give Patch a chin lift. I'll address them later, but right now, I have to take care of my little girl. She comes first.

Patch walks us through everything. The birth certificate. The death certificate. And even though the originals are normally given to the mother in these situations, I take them. Thankfully Lillian didn't fight me on it, but I would have had Patch give me them anyway. At my request, he also took a picture of Mae and me so that I'd have something to remember her by.

It finally comes time for me to give Mae to Patch so she can be prepared for burial. It kills me that I'll never get to see her grow up, get married or have kids. My future is in Patch's arms as he walks her down to the morgue.

The room is suddenly too hot. The tension in the air was palatable. Turning to Lillian, she shrinks back at the hardness of my gaze.

"How long?"

At least she has the decency to look guilty. "I... um..."

"How long, Lillian?"

"Four months."

Once again, the air feels like it was knocked out of me.

Three months ago was when we had signed paperwork for the apartment. She signed the paperwork even though she'd been seeing someone else behind my back.

Suddenly, everything starts to make more sense. The timeline of her excuses for getting together, blaming it on wanting to sleep. Though, I'm sure some of that was true. But then there was the week she suddenly told me she'd be gone for.

"Three weeks ago. That wasn't a trip to your parents' house. Was it?"

She looks down at her hands and shakes her head.

"We got married on the 8th and stayed at a beach house. We were going to wait to do a real honeymoon after little Mae arrived." Dipshit smiles smugly before he leans down and kisses her forehead as she wrings her hands together.

That's what we were going to do.

Turning to face him, he pales slightly as my ire is focused solely on him now. "And who the fuck are you, anyway? And don't give me that shit about swearing, since your wife is the home wrecker in this scenario." I pause at her surprised look and smirk darkly at her. "I was the faithful one, Lillian. You're the home wrecker by opening the door and letting him in."

"I told you—"

"Don't even try that, Lillian. We both know you never said a word about being upset or unhappy about me being a part of the club. Hell, you always had fun whenever we went there for parties. We were even in the final stages of getting the blueprints done for our house when you decided to start cheating on me."

Dipshit clears his throat and stands a little taller. "I'm Preston Cole. I own the car lot downtown. Lillian wanted to be married before our little Mae arrived," he says as he looks down at her. She smiles shakily up at him before looking back at me.

Fury rises in me at what he's implying, and the little bitch says nothing. Doesn't correct him.

"You were going to try to prove I was an unfit parent and take my *daughter from me. Weren't you?"*

"Like I said, the clubhouse isn't—"

"Just shut the fuck up, Lillian. I'm tired of your lies. You were actually excited when we met with Timber to build a house in the compound." I turned toward Preston, who seems like he might be realizing things aren't measuring up with what his dear wife *had told him. "You can have her. Just be careful that she doesn't cheat on you, too."*

I turn to open the door, but don't miss her hurt face. She's not the one hurt in this scenario. She doesn't get to pull that shit. And if she's thinking I'd fight for her after what she just pulled, she's dead wrong.

Before I shut the door, I turn back to her. I have to get it off my chest, otherwise, I'll never forgive myself for not saying it.

"Just so you know, Lil. I would have left the club for you and Mae. All you had to do was tell me." Once again, she falls silent, the shock evident on her face as Preston looks between us nervously before I shut the door. Ending that chapter of my life.

"Three months later, she came back here to see me. Told me she'd messed up. Fell for Preston's lies. He cheated on her, and she wanted me back. I told her to go pound sand, and to never come around here again." I sigh heavily, not wanting to tell the rest, but needing to get it off my chest.

"For the first few years, on major holidays and the anniversary of her birth and death, I'd end them all the same. Me staring down the barrel of my 45. After a few minutes, I'd put it away. Never pulled the trigger, not even to play Russian roulette. Even though I wanted to be with her again, I knew she'd be pissed as fuck if I did something like that."

A small gasp has me looking up at Levi. She fully crawls off Dragon's lap and kneels on the couch cushion between us before placing her hands on both sides of my face, almost as if she was making sure I couldn't look away.

"If you ever get that feeling again, come and find me. I will help you through it or anything else that may be bothering you enough to do the same thing."

"It's been... fuck, almost eighteen years since I did that, so I doubt I'll be doing it anytime soon."

"Still, if something does happen, promise me you'll find me before you even think of picking up a weapon. You hear me, Jaxon?"

The fact that she used my first name makes my chest tighten further, and that's when I see the fear in her eyes.

"I promise, Kiddo."

Her body visibly relaxes and then she pushes me back slightly before crawling into my lap, hugging me tightly.

"Can I see little Mae's picture?"

I pull back from her and reach inside my cut for the laminated picture I always keep on me. Hell, I have one in my wallet too, as well as on my nightstand.

"She's so pretty," she whispers as her fingers trace over the picture.

"That she is. My little Mae Rose."

"...Is ... Is it okay if I get a copy of this? I'd like to put it up in our house. ...If that's okay with you?" She gnaws on her lip.

I'm not even sure if she knows but her gnawing on her lip is her biggest tell that she's nervous or stressed. I stare at her in shock before wrapping her in a tight hug.

"Yeah, Kiddo, I'll get one printed off for you."

I hadn't even realized Thor and Dragon had left until I hear the click of the door latching. Levi pulls back and wipes the tears from her cheek.

"When it's just us or us at the house, can I call you Jax? Or would you prefer I still call you Smoke?"

The tightness in my chest from reliving my memories seems to evaporate as I look down at my sister. "You can call me Jax—you don't even need to call me Smoke if you don't want to. Even here in the clubhouse. You're my sister, so you can call me whichever you prefer."

Once again, a smile lights her face before it turns mischievous.

"So... I can call you a little shit if you're acting up and call you out on stuff," she says as she giggles, which turns even louder when I start tickling her.

"Little smartass. Just remember who's older in this relationship."

"Yup, just tell me when you need me to get the walker for you, *big* brother."

Immediately, she darts off my lap, but she isn't quick enough. I pull her back and tickle her some more. Something I always used to do with Nikki, my little sister by blood. Which reminds me...

"Hey, sometime I'd like to take you to meet my sister, Nikki. My parents died a few years ago, so other than her and my niece, well and now you, they're the only other family I have besides the club."

"I'd like that... But... do you think she'll be mad that you claimed someone else as your sister?" Her body tenses slightly and I shake my head as I push a lock of hair behind her ear.

"No, she'll be fucking ecstatic to have another sister, as well as someone else to gang up on me with." Levi chuckles and I feel her relax into my hug.

"Let us know when and we'll come over. I want her to meet Thor and Dragon, too. Well, actually you should talk to them about what they want you to call them when we're in a private setting."

"I'll do that. But I think there's something else I'd like to ask you since Thor and Dragon stepped out."

She pauses and nods as she sits up, leaning back so she can look at me better.

"Did you get sick after caring for me not too long after you came here?"

She pauses, and then her brow wrinkles as she thinks. "Yeah. I had to go in and get some antibiotics because my head cold led to an ear infection. Why?" She tilts her head as she looks at me, and I realize she has no idea.

I shift slightly to pull out my phone and ask Patch to stop by the office, along with asking Thor and Dragon to come back.

"Jax, you're really making me nervous. Why were you asking that—"

She's interrupted by the door opening as everyone enters, though Patch looks excited as fuck. I just hope he shuts up and lets me talk first. Thor shuts the door.

"The reason why I asked if you got sick was that you've seemed different lately. You're eating more, and I've noticed you seem almost nauseous at times before reaching for some fruit or crackers. You've also seriously cut back on your coffee, and sometimes you wrinkle your nose as you try to drink the one cup you've been drinking. Plus, you've seemed more emotional lately, not in a bad way," I quickly added when her shocked look turns into a glare. "It's just that things seem to trigger you quicker than before."

I pause to let her think about what I said, though I'm sure I'll pay for the emotional comment later, and then eventually see her nodding in confirmation.

"It's just, I noticed those things before... With Lillian. Before she found out she was pregnant."

Silence meets my words as I look between Levi, Thor, and Dragon. Out of the corner of my eye, I see Patch nod as he pulls a box of tests from inside his cut.

"Actually, Levi, I was going to talk to you as well. I'd noticed the same things Smoke just mentioned. You could be pregnant."

Chapter 27
Levi

Holy shit!

Both Patch and Jax think I might be pregnant? My hands automatically go to my stomach. Yeah, I had to get antibiotics, but then again...

Shit.

We didn't use condoms when we started having sex again after I got better.

Oh, fuck!

Are they ready to be fathers? Looking up at Thor and Dragon, I take in their shocked faces.

"I-I'm sorry! I completely forgot that antibiotics could mess with my pill. I didn't—"

My words are cut off when Thor pulls me up off Jax's lap and kisses me. Fuck, my toes are curling at his kiss, making me want to run back to the house. Or kick everyone but Dragon out of here. Wait... Dad's still here. Nope, not going to do that.

After a moment, Thor pulls back, and then Dragon's kissing me just as deeply. We both moan, and then I hear Jax groaning behind me.

"Okay, enough with that! There are things a brother doesn't want to hear his sister doing."

Dragon pulls back as everyone laughs and his hands grasp my chin lightly.

"Spitfire, it's okay if you're pregnant. I'm fucking excited as shit that you might be pregnant. Yeah, it's a little sooner than we talked about, but that's okay. As long as our baby and you are healthy, that's all I want."

"Same for me, Wildcat. A healthy baby and healthy mama are what I want."

I look over at Patch, who's holding the tests out toward me. Tentatively, I take the box and can't help my hands from shaking. Fuck, I'm so nervous.

Shit.

My dad's here. I *do not* want him to find out yet.

"C-Can we head up to our room here in the clubhouse? I'd rather not announce anything until we know. A-and maybe confirmed?"

Dragon takes the tests from me and tucks them into his cut. "No worries, Spitfire. Let's head upstairs for a bit and then we can make sure everything is good for tonight."

"Crap! Did anyone call the caterers?"

Thor and Dragon glance at each other before Thor pulls out his phone, texting someone. "Roxy said she called in pizza for everyone, so we're covered. It'll be here in about an hour and a half."

Jax pulls me in for a hug as he kisses the top of my head. "Let me know what you find out. Meet you guys out in the main room in a bit, okay? I should probably let Roy know what I did," he says with a wink, which has me chuckling despite my nerves.

"I'm going to guess he already knows, but yeah, I'm positive he'd like to hear it from you."

He walks over to the door, but then pauses as he looks back at me. "What was it that Sasha said earlier?"

I grin as I walk over and hug him again. "Welcome to the family."

The grin he gives me is blinding before he hugs me tightly again, kisses my forehead, and heads out to the main room.

Taking a deep breath, I nod to my guys and head out. As we make our way upstairs, my nerves start to skyrocket again. Am I ready to be a mother? Are the guys *really* ready to be fathers? What will people say when they find out we have kids that have two dads? Will they get bullied at school?

I shake my head, knowing it's just nerves getting to me. Besides, if I really am pregnant, our kids will be so protected and loved that we'll be able to get through anything that comes up.

Once in our room, I look around, making sure I don't see anything out of place. My nerves are still high after hearing that Black Plague was able to get cameras inside the clubhouse and our house, too. I can't wait to bring those fuckers down.

But in the meantime, I really did *not* want them finding out I might be pregnant. Who knows what they would do then?

As if sensing my train of thought, both of my guys pull out the scanners and walk around the room. Not finding anything, Nick pulls the tests out of his cut and hands them to me.

"Whether they're negative or positive, we'll always be happy to have kids with you, Wildcat."

"And if they are negative, then we'll just have to practice more, Spitfire," Nick says with a wink, which has all three of us chuckling.

"Okay, give me a few minutes to read the instructions, and then I'll open the door after I've got them ready."

They both give me chaste kisses before stepping back. Taking a deep breath, I will myself to walk to the bathroom and shut the door.

I can do this.

I've watched a few of my friends' kids' before, though if this is real, it's not like I can give them back when they are being little assholes.

Take a deep breath, girl!

You can do this, and you've got your men with you every step of the way.

But do I?

What if they don't like being a father and decide to dump me? To dump us? After these few weeks together, I don't know if I can do this without them. I've come to depend on them, and even though we've had ups and downs, I don't want to ever leave them. I love them.

Mentally, I smack myself. My nerves are going overboard. I know my men love me and won't leave me.

First things first. I need to find out if these damn tests say if I'm pregnant or not. Before I can even open the box, a knock sounds at the door.

"Spitfire, don't take the tests yet. Patch dropped off a container and said that if you can give him a sample, he'll take it in and test it right away. That way, we'll know for sure sooner rather than waiting to get you into a doctor."

Setting the tests down on the sink, I step out to grab the pee cup and duck back into the bathroom. Reading the instructions, I strip out of my underwear and pants, thinking that will be easier.

With all three, yes three because I'm so fucking nervous, tests peed on, and a sample ready for Patch, I put my clothes back on before flushing and washing my hands.

Opening the door, I sit back down on the toilet lid. Nick takes my sample and heads out to the hallway, most likely to give it to Patch. I hug my stomach as my nerves kick into overdrive yet again as I wait for the allotted time to pass. Ryan kneels, grabbing my hands, and a moment later, Nick comes back to join us.

"Hey, Baby Girl, what's wrong?"

"I'm just so nervous, Ry. Will I be a good mom? What if I'm a terrible mom and our kids end up hating my guts?"

Ryan wipes a tear from my cheek as he pulls me into his arms. "Baby Girl, I know for a fact that you are going to be a fantastic mother. How? Because I've seen how you've cared for your family as well as our brothers here at the club. Also, how you've been with the bunnies. You're caring, always thinking of others, and when faced with a problem, you do your damnedest to figure out a solution."

"Agreed, Spitfire. You're going to be an awesome mother, whether it's nine months from now or a few years from now."

Nick pulls me into a hug and then shifts slightly so that Ryan can hug me again, too.

A few minutes later, my phone beeps that it's time, and I pull back before picking up the first test. Then the second. And then the third.

I'm pregnant.

The next thing I know, Nick wraps me in his arms as he steps back into the bedroom and spins me around before kissing me senseless.

"We're pregnant," he whispers when he pulls back and rests his forehead against mine.

I feel Ryan at my back and then he wraps his arms around my waist, resting his hands on my stomach as he nuzzles my neck.

"I can't wait to meet him... or her," he whispers, and I chuckle when I feel both of their bodies tense. Most likely at the thought of having a daughter. I pull away from both of them and glare, pointing my finger at them.

"If we do have a girl, you both need to make sure you don't go all macho-dad on her. You need to let her discover herself without being smothered to death. I know she'll be protected like hell since she'll have so many uncles, but promise me you both won't go alpha-asshole on every guy she talks to."

Their bodies remain tense for a bit before they both relax. I have to bite my cheek to keep from smiling, but I really don't want our daughter to rebel if they did that. If we end up having a daughter, that is.

"We'll try, Spitfire, but it will be really hard. Especially with how hot as fuck you are. If our daughter is anything like you, she'll have men lined up down the street."

Then they both look at me, and the heat in their eyes has my panties damn near combusting.

Ryan picks me up and my legs wrap around his waist as his lips slam down onto mine. A moan escapes me as he rolls his hips and my core is instantly on fire. Reaching down, I pull on his shirt, but then growl when I realize I can't pull up his shirt with how he's holding me.

"Off," I say as I tug on his shirt. The need in my voice has Ryan quickly releasing me, and we all strip. The only article of my clothing that doesn't just get tossed to the floor is my cut, which I put on the dresser. I've noticed how the guys treat theirs and I don't want to disrespect them by not treating the cut they gave me with respect.

Once all my clothes are off, I reach out to Ryan but pause as he picks up my cut back up and holds it out to me.

"Put this back on, Wildcat. We want to fuck you wearing only this." The growl in his voice makes goosebumps break out all over and tingles run down my spine. He spins me around and rubs his cock against my ass.

"Nick's going to fuck your tight pussy and I'm going to take your sweet ass. You ready for one of us to claim this ass, Wildcat?"

Fuck, that sounds hot. Yes, I definitely want that! They bought some butt plugs a few weeks ago to get me used to having something in my ass and to get used to their size. I've been dying to have one of their cocks in my ass ever since.

I slip my cut back on but leave it slightly undone since I know my men love seeing my boobs bounce while they take me. Immediately, Ryan picks me up. My legs wrap around his waist again and his hands squeeze my ass hard. His lips crash down on mine and I moan, moving my hips so that my pussy's rubbing against his cock. God, I need his cock in me!

A whimper escapes when he lifts me away from him, but then I notice he's lowering me down so that I'm straddling Nick's head and his cock is bobbing slightly in front of my face. Yeah, I'm definitely okay with this plan. My body hums in anticipation as my men are almost as good with their tongues as they are with their cocks. His tongue darts out and he licks me from clit to ass before fucking me with it.

"Oh, fuck," I moan, and can't stop my hips from bucking. I fall down to my hands and take as much of his cock in my mouth as I can while grinding myself on Nick's face, his beard tickling my thighs.

"That's right, Enchantress. Take your pleasure from him, ride his face. Suck his cock and get him all lubed up."

I shiver as Ryan peppers kisses on my neck. His large, rough hands run over my ass cheeks. Suddenly, he smacks my ass hard. The force drives my hips down harder on Nick's face and I moan as his cock slides further down my throat. Thank fuck, I don't have a gag reflex.

While Nick's cock is still deep in my throat, I swallow. He moans, and his vibrations push me even closer to the brink. He sucks on my clit, and right as someone's thumb enters my ass, most likely Ryan's, he gently bites down on my c lit.

"Oh my God..." His cock slips from my mouth as I cry out.

My thighs clench, trapping Nick in place while his skilled tongue continues to lick my juices. Violent shudders rip through my body and black dots dance across the edges of my vision. Fuck, I don't think I've ever cum that hard before.

I've barely caught my breath when hands grip my waist and I'm picked up, flipped, and am now facing Nick. It always surprises me how they're able to maneuver my body as if I only weighed a hundred pounds when the reality is I weigh way more than that.

Reaching down, I hold his cock as I lower myself until he's fully inside me. His large hands land on my hips, squeezing tight as he raises me and then slams back into me. Resting my hands on his chest, I close my eyes as he continues to slam into me.

"Fuck, I love your tight pussy, Spitfire, and I love seeing your sweet tits bouncing as you ride my cock."

Cool gel runs down my ass and I moan as Ryan's finger presses against my backdoor. I shiver when he kisses up my neck and then when he bites down on my earlobe and pinches my nipple, he slips a finger inside my ass.

"Fuck!" My nipples seem even more sensitive than before, but damn, does it feel good.

"I've been dreaming of taking your tight ass ever since you became ours, Wildcat."

While both of them love my ass, I've noticed Ryan is more of an ass man, and Nick's more of a boob man.

I shiver as he pumps his finger faster and his bites along my neck and shoulders become more forceful. When he adds another finger and starts stretching me, my breathing becomes more erratic and Nick increases his speed as he leans forward and sucks on my nipple.

"Oh my God! Don't stop! Yes, yes, yes, right there!"

Ryan adds a third finger and right as Nick bites down gently on my nipple, I detonate, damn near blacking out. But when Ryan pushes me forward, I know I'm about to get what I've been dying for the past few weeks, so I focus as much as I can on not blacking out. I am not missing a second of this.

Nick lays back down and kisses me as he cups my breasts, teasing my nipples. The feeling of Ryan's cock pressing against me has me tensing at first before I force myself to relax. It stings a bit, but I know it'll feel good soon.

"Fuck, Wildcat, don't move," Ryan grits out in an almost pained voice and I instantly still, not realizing I had been moving. After a few seconds, he slides in a few more inches and goes slowly until he's fully seated.

"Oh.... I feel so full," I gasp out.

And then they start moving.

"Oh, yes, yes, yes. Fuck, go faster."

Both of them pick up speed—when one pushes in, the other pulls out.

I don't even recognize the sounds coming out of my mouth—all I can do is feel. My body seems to be on stimulus overload as my men bury their cocks in me. Their rough hands roam over my body, teasing my nipples and grabbing my breasts and ass. Fuck, these men are going to be the death of me.

Ryan's hand snakes up to my throat as he pulls me tight against him. "I need you to cum soon, Enchantress. Look down at Nick and see what you do to him."

My eyes snap open, and as I look down at Nick, his face is set, like he's trying to not cum yet. His eyes are hooded, and they've darkened to nearly black with need. His hand moves between us and I moan when he starts rubbing my clit. Ryan's grip tightens a little around my neck and fuck, does it increase everything that I'm feeling.

His tongue snakes down the exposed side of my neck and when he gets to the base, he growls and I swear I feel them both get harder.

"Cum now, Enchantress. Soak Nick's cock." He bites down on my neck and I cum, even harder than earlier.

My body sags and I can't seem to be able to move my limbs. If Ryan didn't have a hold of me, I would have slumped down onto Nick's chest, or possibly the bed. I know neither one of them would have let me get hurt or fall to the floor.

Leaning my head back against Ryan's chest, I close my eyes as I try to catch my breath. "Why the fuck did I wait that long to try that with you guys? We are so doing that again."

I can feel both of their chests shake as they laugh and when they both slide out of me, I feel so empty and I don't like it. Once again, I can feel their chests shake with laughter and my eyes snap open before I scowl at them. Ryan scoops me up, but I still continue scowling at Nick over Ryan's shoulder.

"I do believe, we might have a sex-crazed Enchantress on our hands now, Ry." Nick smirks but I barely notice because my gaze is no longer focused on his smug face. No, it's focused on his cock that's already hard again. I lick my lips, wanting a taste of him.

Ryan sets me down in the bathroom and smacks my ass as he turns on the water. "Later, Baby Girl. We were pretty rough on you and I wish we were at the house so you could soak in a tub, but that'll have to wait for later."

I pout and this time it's Nick that smacks my ass.

"Later Spitfire."

I huff but pull out a couple of hair ties and twist my long locks into a messy bun on the top of my head so it doesn't get it wet. I don't have a blow dryer here, plus it takes forever for my hair to dry, and I don't want to mess with that right now.

Once the water is warm, I step underneath and then move aside for the guys to get wet. Though as we're all lathering up, I can't help but let my gaze roam over their bodies.

"Wildcat."

"Spitfire."

Fuck, their raspy voices make my skin break out in goosebumps and a shiver runs through me. I bite my lip when I see them both fisting their cocks. As they rinse off, I watch as the soap runs down all of their taught muscles and I wish I could run my tongue over them. Not to mention tracing all their ink.

When I step under the water again, I close my eyes as I rinse off, wishing it were their hands instead.

One of them curses behind me and then the water is no longer running over me, but I can hear that it's still on. Opening my eyes, I realized they'd aimed it at the wall, but then one of them grabs my hips from behind and pushes down on my upper back. With a quick glance up, I realize Nick's in front of me and my hands grasp onto his hips to steady myself as I swirl my tongue around his crown and down the vein of his cock.

Moments later, Ryan's cock is pushing into me, and I moan, thrusting back hard against his hips. Fuck, I can't seem to get enough of them today. If this is what pregnant sex is like, then I am totally on board with claiming my men as often as I can.

Again, they both curse and speed up. Nick grasps my bun to hold me in place and starts thrusting his hips, practically fucking my mouth. My fingernails dig into Nick's thighs as they both take me roughly.

As I feel another orgasm building, I also feel both of their cocks swell. Reaching down, I start massaging my clit. Ryan smacks my ass and starts pistoning his hips faster. The sting coupled with what they were already doing sends me over the edge. Seconds later, both of them cum with a roar.

All of my nerve endings seem to be on fire, and as my legs give out, Ryan's strong arms wrap around my waist, pulling me against his body. Nick steps forward and kisses me while Ryan peppers kisses along my neck and shoulder.

"I think it might be time to get clean again," Nick says with a wink.

He reaches behind him, squirts my body wash onto the loofah, and starts washing me. By the time he and Ryan have washed my front and back, my legs finally feel like they can support me fully. One at a time, I do the same to them, along with a wink when my hands run over their cocks. Later tonight, maybe they'd be up for another round, but right now my pussy needs a break.

Once we're all clean, we dry off and get dressed. Ryan's phone vibrates and I glance at the clock. Shit, we've been in here for almost an hour. I hear Ryan texting and as I look back at him, I hope nothing else has come up while we were up here. There's been enough chaos today.

His face lights up, and then he hands me his phone. It's a text from Patch.

My test!

Nick looks over my shoulder and the next thing I know, he's gently cupping my face and kissing me. When he pulls back, Ryan does the same. Looking back down at the phone, I can't believe it.

It's confirmed.

I'm pregnant.

I'm gonna be a mom.

Chapter 28
Dragon

HOLY SHIT! I'M GONNA be a dad. Long ago, I'd given up hope of ever having a family. That is, until Levi came into our lives.

I can't help it. I pick Levi up and hug her as I spin her around before kissing her again.

When I pull away, she's quickly back in Thor's arms as he kisses her again. Breaking the kiss, she looks down at Thor's phone in her hand. She doesn't notice when he comes around to stand beside me.

We take a knee and she looks over in surprise before gasping, dropping the phone as her hands cover her mouth when she sees the box we're holding.

"Spitfire, you mean everything to us, and now even more so because our family is growing. You're our heart, and without you, we'd be lost."

"You're our world, Wildcat, our reason for fighting."

"Will you marry us, Spitfire, and be our wife?"

She starts bouncing on her toes and then holds out her hand. "Yes! Yes, I'll marry both of you."

I slide the ring on her finger and everything seems to settle in place. Our mom's ring is a silver three-carat princess-cut diamond surrounded by smaller diamonds. Both Thor and I got her two matching silver bands, but with different gems in each band—emeralds and sapphires, her two favorite gems.

Unfortunately, both of us can't marry Spitfire, but both of us plan to say vows to her. I finally got Thor to accept that she should marry him, which is why I got to ask her to be our wife.

MC life is dangerous and there's a higher chance of landing in a shallow dirt grave early in life because of your enemies. With Thor being the President of our club's chapter, as well as the MC as a whole, Levi and our kids will gain extra layers of protection should something happen to both of us. Not that I want anything to happen to us, but our parents' deaths have had me thinking of this more and more as of late and I wanted to ensure she'd be taken care of.

She launches into our arms, kissing Thor before me. Reluctantly, I pull away but I'm betting Spitfire needs a rest since we were pretty rough on her. When her feet touch the ground, a concerned look crosses her face.

"Should we announce the baby now or wait? I, I don't..." she pauses, and her eyes get misty.

Tucking a lock of hair behind her ear, I'm pretty sure I know the line of thought her mind was going down. "I'm thinking we should at least tell the others at Church. I'm not sure about the Prospects."

I frown as I think about it more. In no way will I use Levi as bait, but the pregnancy news could cause Fang to do something irrational and out of character. And I know it will be hard as fuck for her not to talk about the baby with Sasha or Roxy.

My gaze locks with Thor's and he gives a slight chin lift. Hope he's thinking along the same lines as me. He looks down at Levi, and my gaze follows. She looks between us and frowns.

"What are you both thinking?"

"That if we announced your pregnancy, Wildcat, that could be the thing that drives Fang over the edge. We'd have to go on high alert and a semi-lockdown. Maybe even a full lockdown."

"What's a semi-lockdown?"

"Where you can only leave for work, doctor, or essentials like food and shit," he says.

"And bullets," I mumble, even more worried about her safety now that it's not just her in danger. It's my kid. *Our* kid.

Levi's gaze cuts to mine and she steps back before she starts pacing and flipping a blade. It's something we learned early on that she does when she's trying to figure something out or is really stressed. After a few moments, she nods and faces us.

"Let's announce both, but let's space them out. Hear me out," she says when she notices my scowl, and I'm sure Thor has a matching one.

"News that I'm engaged to you two will make Fang irrational, but to announce both at the same time may have him jumping the gun *way* too early. We want to catch both Fang *and* Uncle Sean. Let's announce the engagement tonight and then maybe I can talk to Creed and see *exactly* the day Uncle Sean will be released. We could release the baby announcement the very next day."

I can't help the grin that spreads across my face. My little Spitfire is a fucking genius. I look at Thor and see a matching grin on his face.

"They'll both be so fucking mad—"

"That they'll probably crack pretty soon after the news breaks," I finish for him. We both beam down at Spitfire.

"And it also gives us a little time to make sure our defenses are up to par," she says with a dark smile.

I pause at that and then pull out my phone, checking my calendar. Holy shit, it's perfect. I smirk when I looked back up at Levi and then Thor.

"Well, thanks to Spitfire, we just happen to have an event coming up two weeks from now on Saturday with our Junction Creek brothers."

"The competition," they say in unison before relief fills their faces and they grin. It'll be easier to pass off the get-together since it was planned in advance almost a month ago. It's not uncommon for chapters to stay awhile after a party, so nobody should be tipped off at the change. And it will give us extra men if things go south.

Thor's typing a text message and then pockets his phone as he smacks Spitfire's ass.

"Come on, Wildcat, let's go share the news."

"Wait, we need to tell Patch and Jax to stay quiet on this for now."

"I just told Patch, and he'll delete his messages after he gets them. I'll tell Smoke later cause no one will suspect anything when I pull him off to the side to talk."

She grins, kisses both of us, then practically skips out of the room. Fuck, I love this woman.

We catch up to her and as we near the base of the stairs, Thor whistles. As everyone quiets down, I step forward and take Levi's right hand.

"I know today's been a fucking whirlwind, but I have some news before we head out back to start the party." He pauses as he looks at Spitfire and takes her left hand. "She said yes!"

He holds up her left hand, showing them the ring, and cheers erupt throughout the room. Seconds later, I hear chairs scraping against the floor and I know without even looking, the women are about to bombard her. Kissing her temple, I step aside and walk over to the bar.

"Congrats, Dragon," Colt says as he hands me a beer.

"Thanks, man."

As I take a drink, I look around for Roy and see him talking with Thor. Turning back toward Colt, I nod over in their direction. "Grab me one for Roy and Thor."

"You got it." He reaches under the counter and pops the tops before placing them on the bar. Grabbing the beers, I push off the bar and head their way. My brothers clasp my shoulder in congratulations as I pass and once again, I feel fucking grateful that Spitfire came into our lives.

Roy gives me a chin lift as I pass him his beer. He takes a pull and levels me with a hard stare. "Congratulations, Dragon. Like I just told Thor, you hurt her and I'll kill you."

"If that ever happens, I'll pull the trigger myself."

He dips his chin and takes another pull, but he isn't looking at either of us. Following his gaze, I realize he's watching Levi and the girls.

"I wanted to run something by you guys before I talked to Levi about it." He pauses and I turn back to him, wondering what the hell is eating at him when I see the contemplative look on his face.

"You both know I'm the sole owner of the bar and grill. It was supposed to go to Sean and me, but when he pulled that shit years ago, my dad and uncle changed both of their wills to state I would get both of their shares in the restaurant when they died. Levi's currently listed as next in line, but with her about to marry you guys, I was thinking of changing it up a bit."

My stomach drops. Levi would be crushed if he cut her out. "Levi will be so fuckin pissed if she can't take over after you. She's been dreaming of running that place since she was a kid."

Anger courses through me that he'd even think of not giving that place to her when he retires.

"I'm not cutting her out, but I was thinking of a joint ownership between her and the club. She's going to need to take some time off soon and I would feel better knowing the club will step in when it's necessary and she wouldn't have to stress about it."

I freeze and damn near spit out the beer I'd just drank.

He knows.

He smirks at both of us before turning his attention back to Levi. "I was wondering when you two would figure it out." He pauses and gives each of us a dark look. "Now, I want you boys to be honest with me. Are you marrying her for her or because of—"

"Please don't say anything yet, Roy," Thor says quietly to him.

"As for your other question, we asked her because we love her. Now about the other..." I pause as I give him a pointed look. "We're going to announce it at the competition."

Roy seems confused at first, but then I see the moment everything clicks into place.

"Good. I think he'll take the bait."

Thankfully, he doesn't say anything more. He clasps both of us on the shoulders and walks over toward Levi.

A few hours later, the party is in full swing. The bunnies are out in full force, but thankfully, none of them have bothered us.

Well, I shouldn't say full force. Trixie, er CJ, asked if she could stop servicing my brothers but will still help with the other duties. That and she'll do more chores than usual to make up for not being there for the guys. Especially since she now knows her brother is in our club. Thank fuck Prospects aren't allowed to be with the bunnies. If they had hooked up, I'm sure there'd be a lot more emotional shit they'd need to work through.

With what we learned today, Thor and Levi had no problems with the change. Fuck, if I was Drae, I'd be pissed as fuck if my sister still hooked up with the guys, especially if it was out in the open. Tonight, CJ's behind the bar learning the ropes from Roxy.

"What's got you thinking so hard, Babe?" Levi sits on my lap as she hands me a fresh beer. Thor, Phoenix, Smoke, Bones, and Roy are also sitting around the fire pit.

"Was just thinking about the changes and thank fuck none of the bunnies are trying anything tonight."

"No shit. They'd be stupid as fuck if they tried anything after today's announcement," Bones said as he takes a pull from his beer.

"I—"

The backdoor of the clubhouse opens and I groan. Looks like the hang arounds have started showing up.

My body tenses as a flash of blond comes out the door.

Nicole.

My ex-girlfriend.

Based on her outfit, or lack thereof, I'm pretty sure I know what's going to happen at some point. With a sigh, I pull Levi closer and give her temple a kiss. There's no way I'm going to let that bitch ambush Levi.

"Spitfire, wanted to let you know my ex, Nicole, just walked out here. Blond hair, black skirt and blue... whatever the fuck you call that scrap of cloth over her tits."

She tenses but then relaxes as she sits up straighter before she shifts slightly on my lap. A subtle nod tells me she's located her.

"So, Kiddo, who's all gonna throw with you in a couple of weeks?" Smoke asks her.

"Dragon, Timber, Tripp, Gunner, Sasha, Alexei, and Bones. Then from Junction Creek, there's Reaper, Punisher, Beast, Razor, Loki, Cannon, Drake, and Nathan. Eight people on each team. We'll tally up each person's score after each round and the ones with the lowest amount is eliminated. Then we'll keep going till there's only one remaining."

"Does everyone bring their own knives?" Bones asks.

"I sent some home with Reaper when they were here last time. Between Alexei, Sasha, Travis, Ethan, and me, we have plenty for the other guys here to practice with."

I zone out what they're talking about and look around. My neck itches like someone's watching us. No one seems to be causing trouble, but I don't know some of the hang arounds very well and, as with any open party, there are other women from town here hoping to snag a brother.

Not being able to take it anymore, I pat Levi's thigh. "How about you sit with Thor, Spitfire? I'll be back in a bit."

She looks down at me and frowns before she nods. Pulling her down to me, I meant to keep the kiss short, but when her fingers run through my hair, fuck did I want to get lost in her. Reluctantly, I pull back, but she follows me, tucking her head into the crook of my neck.

"She did something back behind the food tables and it looked like she put something on a tree directly across from that spot."

I freeze, and it takes everything in me to not just grab the bitch and demand answers. Spitfire pulls back and gives me a quick peck. She slides off my lap and sits in Thor's. I turn toward Smoke, who is frowning as his gaze bounces between Levi and me. I gesture for him to follow me and we both stand. Walking over to the coolers, I grab us each a new beer and then led him over toward a cluster of trees that are sort of across from the food table.

As we walk, he steps closer to me.

"What's going on, Dragon? I saw that look when she whispered something to you," he asks quietly.

"Remember my ex, Nicole?"

He grimaces and nods slightly.

"Levi saw her putting something on the trees somewhere over here and also doing something behind the food tables."

"Fuck. Can't we catch a fucking break?"

"Fuck, I hear that," I growl. I want to catch these fuckers so Levi won't have to keep looking over her shoulder, worried that Fang or Sean will get her. Nearby, I notice Ethan frowning and after a moment, he heads our way.

Once we get over to the trees, I carefully glance around but don't see anything.

"Hey, Dragon, got a question for you," he asks me.

"What's up?"

"It's about the competition coming up. I volunteered to help the others set it up. We were trying to figure out where you guys would want to put it."

Why would he ask me instead of Levi? She'd know how much space they'd need.

"One of the spots is to put up a large backing and then the targets right up against that long section of the clubhouse wall. We'd make sure the windows are covered so they won't be accidentally hit."

I follow where he's pointing, but I don't see anything other than the double windows, though I think he's pointing to the left set of windows.

"Or we would go off to the side of the clubhouse," he pauses as he points off to the right, but he isn't pointing beyond the clubhouse. Shifting slightly, I think he's pointing to where we have the trash and recycling bins on the corner. What the hell?

"Then the last spot would be if we went back here, but we'd need to mow to make it work," he pauses as he takes a handful of steps to my right, and points out to the field and then back to the tree line before he gives me a pointed look. Stepping a little to his right, I follow where he had pointed first and then to the trees.

That's when I see it.

A camera planted in a knot of one of the trees. Glancing back at the other two locations, there are probably other cameras there, too.

Fuck, we really need to get a step ahead of these assholes.

Keeping up the charade, I rub my chin as I look between all three spots. "Those could work. Did you talk to anyone else for their input?"

"Yes, Sir. Alexel, Drae, Travis, and I were trying to figure out possible spots to get things started. Colt wanted to meet with us tonight, but he's got gate duty."

Well, I'll be damned. Ethan and Travis aren't technically Prospects yet, but they sure are acting like one already. That and Drae seems to be stepping back up, not to mention, Levi's brothers all seem to have eagle eyes as well.

"Let me talk to Levi to see how much space they need in front of the targets and then we'll settle on a location. Good job, keep up the good work," I tell him as I clap his shoulder.

He gives me a chin lift and walks back over to Alexei and Travis, who give me subtle chin lifts as well. They talk for a bit and then split up, going to different areas of the backyard. Alexei nods to Smoke and heads inside.

"He'll be a good addition, both of them, plus, they seem to have a good eye," Smoke says, and I nod in agreement.

"Fuck, you're right, we need to do that still tonight before everyone gets shit-faced." I pull out my phone and send a quick text to Thor.

With another glance around, I spot Nicole over by one of the firepits. She's talking to some guy, but she's glaring at Levi who's still in Thor's lap.

"We need to keep an eye on her, Smoke. See if she did it or someone else."

He clasps my shoulder and grunts. "We'll see to it. Keep your phone handy."

With a nod, I head toward the clubhouse to grab another drink, but my favorite, *Rebel Kent*, is out. My phone dings and I fish it out of my pocket as I toss my empty in the recycling bin. It's from Thor.

> Thor: Grab two cuts out of my office—we'll do it in 5. Then we'll talk locations.

Normally, my position wouldn't allow me to have keys to where Thor keeps the cuts and patches, but being his brother has perks. Not to mention Dad was the President before Thor took over. Pocketing my phone, I head inside. Maybe Roxy has more *Rebel Kent* stashed behind the bar. It's my favorite beer from *3 Sheeps Brewing* and I know she makes sure to always have a stock of what we all like.

Chapter 29

Levi

I'm getting pretty tired of that bitch, Nicole, glaring at me and then practically eye fucking Thor and Dragon. God, we really could use a fucking break. Today has already been a long ass day.

I glance over to where Dragon and Smoke walked off to and see Ethan heading my way. He turns to walk behind us and slows his pace a bit before he reaches us.

"**Здесь три камеры** [There's three cameras]. **Я скажу** [I'll tell] Colt," he says quietly.

Shit, that means I missed one. Thank God he's been learning Russian from Alexei and Sasha. Travis has no interest, but Ethan does. Ethan could only say a few words before and now he's able to say a ton of sentences. Giving him a chin lift, I lean back into Thor.

"I missed one. There are three and he'll tell Colt. Fingers crossed she won't give him the slip."

He grunts as he watches Travis' retreat. Hopefully, by giving Colt Nicole's description, he'll be able to keep her from leaving. Thor pulls me close and kisses my temple.

"Wildcat, would it be alright if you taught me Russian? I know Dragon wants to learn, but I was also thinking Phoenix and maybe Smoke, too? Could be handy in instances like these."

I shift slightly on his lap, reach up, and run my hands through his hair as I lean close to his ear.

"**Да** [Yes]. **Но я думаю, что я воздержусь от нескольких фраз** [But I think I'll refrain from a few phrases]. **Нужно держать вас в тонусе в спальне** [Need to keep you on your toes in the bedroom]."

Pressing a kiss on the corner of his mouth, I can feel him harden underneath me. Sitting up fully, I grin when his eyes darken.

"Whatever the fuck you just said, I wish I could take you back to the house or upstairs right now, but we gotta do a few things first."

He clears his throat and shifts slightly, pulling out his phone. He taps something out quick and the action has me remembering I forgot to ask Smoke something.

Shifting slightly, I pull out my phone and send him a quick text.

> Levi: Smoke—Did the package I ordered arrive yet by chance?

> Smoke: Damn, I forgot to tell you earlier. It came early this morning. I'll bring it later.

> Levi: Thanks!

He replies with a thumbs up emoji and I grin. Guess we'll be tying up loose ends tonight, or possibly tomorrow, depending on what the guys want to do.

Wait, that gives me an idea. Quickly I type it out to Smoke, hoping he'll be able to dig into it, or Alexei, to see if it's a good idea or not. Until then, I'm just going to keep quiet on it.

A few minutes later, the backdoor opens and Dragon comes out, holding two boxes. Shit, is it what I think it is?

Turning to Thor, I raise an eyebrow in question, and when he grins, I can barely contain my excitement.

Seconds later, Ethan comes back by the firepits, and Thor pats my hip. Standing, he gets up and heads over by Dragon. I motion for Ethan to take the seat I had been in earlier and just as I'm about to ask him something, someone whistles loud.

Turning, I see Thor and Phoenix standing over by the door, and I can't help but grin.

"Earlier, we held Church to discuss a couple of requests that were entered. We voted and came to a decision. Can Travis and Ethan please come forward?"

Ethan looks at me nervously and it takes everything in me to just shrug and not give it away.

When they're both up there, Phoenix pulls both boxes from behind his back and gives one to each of them. From here, I can see both of their faces and when they open them, they both break out in huge smiles.

Cheers erupt from the crowd when they slip into their Prospect cuts.

"Welcome to Steel Archangel's, brothers," Thor says and does that man-hug thing where they clasp hands and kind of bump shoulders with both Travis and Ethan.

Out of the corner of my eye, I see movement, but when I turn to look, I don't see anything. Did I just imagine it?

"Spitfire, I have to do something, but I need you to know that I love you and I need you to trust me."

My body tenses and a feeling of dread washes over me. I'm pretty sure I'm not going to like whatever it is that he's talking about.

"What's going on, Dragon?"

He sighs and leans down, kissing my forehead. "I can't tell you that just yet, Spitfire. Stay near Thor for right now." He dips and gives me a chaste kiss before heading back into the clubhouse, with Ryder and Phoenix following close behind.

I'm not sure how long I stare at the backdoor, but the next thing I know, Sasha's wrapping me in a hug.

"**Что не так** [What's wrong]?"

"Dragon's **что-то задумал, что, я уверен, мне не понравится** [up to something I'm pretty sure I won't like]."

"**Хочешь, чтобы я последовал за ним** [Want me to tail him]?"

I pause, but then shake my head. "**Нет** [No]. **Это то, что мне нужно сделать** [This is something I need to do]."

With that, I start walking across the yard to the back door. I can hear heavy footsteps behind me, so I hasten my steps. Someone calls out to me, but that only drives me to move faster. I can hear several curses behind me and my chest aches when I hear Thor's voice among them. I whip open the door and dart inside.

That's when I hear it. Giggles so high they're sickening. Following the sound, I make my way through the kitchen, and even though every Steel Archangel I pass tries to get me to turn around, they give up when my blades came out. When they step back, the pity in their eyes has my gut in knots.

As soon as I step into the common room, my steps falter. Nicole's draped all over Dragon, rubbing her chest against his arm as she's whispering something in his ear.

How could he do this?

I must make a noise or something because she looks over her shoulder and I want to carve up her smug fucking face before they turn the corner. Black dots dance across my vision and the next thing I know, I'm being tugged toward the front door.

Sasha leads me outside, and as we walk, the scene keeps replaying in my head. Why the fuck would Dragon allow her to do that when it was just today that they asked me to be their Old Lady and I agreed to marry them? Was it all just a joke? My gaze catches on my ring and I try to swallow the bile that rises.

Soon, Sasha leads me up the steps to Uncle Bear's house and unlocks the door. He gave both of us keys years ago in case we ever needed protection. She pulls me toward the living room and then down onto the couch. I flop down, numb, and pissed. She doesn't say anything but sits down next to me, leaning on my shoulder.

I sigh as I rub my hands over my face.

"What'd he do and do I need to sink a blade in him?"

Even though I know she's dead serious, I can't help the strained chuckle that escapes. Sighing again, I pull out a blade and twirl it, needing that calm feeling of the cold steel dancing around my fingers.

I fill her in on Nicole, what I'd seen her do, and then the rest of what Dragon said and did.

"...So, let me see if I have this right. He says he has to do something but asks you to trust him and reminds you that he loves you. Then he let that skank rub all over him as he went to who knows where with her?"

Groaning, I lean back against the couch. "Yeah. I know there are rooms off that hallway, but there are secure rooms downstairs, too. One of them is their interrogation room. Thor showed me once since there's also another panic room down there. He wanted me to know my way around in case I needed to help get people to safety if we were cut off from the other panic rooms."

"Wait, there's another downstairs area?"

Nodding, I bite my lip as I try to step back and look at everything from another person's perspective. Dragon seemed really tense and now that I think about it, seemed pissed about what he was going to do when he was talking to me. When Nicole was hanging on him, he didn't act like he enjoyed it or wanted her attention. Instead of his usual swagger, he was walking rigidly. Even though she had a hold of his arm, both of his fists were clenched.

"I think... I think he was trying to lure her into the basement. We need to know who sent her and why she planted the cameras."

"Yeah, but there are other ways of getting her into the basement!"

"I completely agree. I mean, they asked me to be their Old Lady and to marry them today and I said yes to both! Even if my guess is right, I'm so fucking embarrassed and humiliated by what he did and that he could do that today, of all days.

"Every one of them talks about how much they respect each other, but I feel fucking disrespected right now. How could he even think of doing that with her, even if it was just a ploy to get her into the interrogation room? Even if he never meant for me to see what he did, he could have at least told me what he was going to do instead of finding out about it this way. Why couldn't they have just told me what was going to happen? Then I wouldn't have been disrespected and embarrassed in front of their club, and who knows how many people from town?"

I close my eyes and will my tears to not fall. I feel her get off the couch and then I hear her in the kitchen. When I hear the sound of something heavy being set down on the coffee table, I open my eyes and groan.

"I can't drink Sash," I say automatically before I realize my mistake. "Fuck..."

Her eyes narrow and I avoid looking at her.

Fuck me and my big mouth.

"And exactly *why* can't you drink?"

Sighing, I know there's no way out of this. She can be fucking annoying if she knows someone is keeping a secret from her.

"If I tell you, you have to promise not to say anything." She rolls her eyes. "I mean it Sash! If word gets out before we're ready to announce it, it could seriously mess up our plan to get Fang and Sean."

She huffs and holds her hand over her heart as she holds out her pinky finger on her other hand. I hook my pinky finger with hers as I place my hand over my heart and look at her expectantly. We've been making pledges like this to each other since we were kids.

"Fine. I, Sasha Petrov, swear not to tell another soul unless you give me permission to do so."

She drops her hand and now she is the one who's giving me the expectant look.

"I'm pregnant."

As soon as the words are out of my mouth, I automatically cover my ears right before she releases an eardrum-shattering squeal. Sometimes I swear this girl's gonna make me go deaf.

Then she pulls me up and gives me a bone-crushing hug. When she finally releases me, I laugh as she dances around the room excitedly before she comes to an abrupt halt.

"Wait... do Thor and Dragon know?"

My stomach feels queasy and I sink back down on the couch. "Yeah, they were with me when I found out."

"So... when you three went up for sexy times and then you came back down engaged?"

My face flames and I seriously hope no one heard us.

Sasha laughs. "Don't worry, no one heard anything. You just had the look of someone who's been freshly fucked."

When she plops down next to me, I can tell she's angry, but I'm no longer worried that she'll sink a blade into him. Well, maybe a little worried.

"That makes what Dragon did even worse."

"Yeah, it does," I whisper and angrily swipe away a tear that escapes.

"So, why are you waiting to tell everyone about the baby?"

"If we had announced both at the same time, we're worried Fang will lose his shit and come after me right away. If that happens, Sean will most likely be in the wind as soon as he gets out while he plots his next move. We need to get them together if at all possible. Our plan is to announce our baby news the day after Sean's released, which just so happens to be the weekend of our throwing competition with Reaper's crew."

"**Хорошо** [Good]. You'll have better protection with his crew here."

I nod and go back to twirling my blade.

A few minutes pass before she gets up, picks up the beers, and heads back into the kitchen. My hand falls to my stomach. Today's been a fucking roller coaster and right now, I can barely keep from marching back into the clubhouse and demanding to know what the hell's going on.

I'm not sure how much time passes but I'm pulled from my thoughts as Sasha places a huge bowl of popcorn in my lap and sets down a couple of glasses of orange juice on the coffee table.

"Let's watch a movie and forget about tonight for a little bit. What do you wanna watch?"

I don't even have to think before I blurt out my choice. "*Boondock Saints*. Then the second one."

Sasha laughs and does a little happy dance as she goes over to the movie cabinet. We love watching these movies and having some eye candy doesn't hurt either. Especially since I'm pissed at my men, but I'll let them stew a little before I demand answers.

Chapter 30
Dragon

Levi's going to fucking hate my guts for this, but we need to get Nicole down to the interrogation room without her tipping off whoever the fuck she's working with. Especially after everything Smoke dug up on her. Since we couldn't all go into Church without alerting her, we communicated via text. No one else had a better idea and I seriously want to beat the fucking shit out of Judge for suggesting this.

Knowing that Nicole's been watching me all night, I head back into the clubhouse, figuring she'll follow me. As I'm walking through the kitchen, I hear the back door open and then the click of heels against the wood floor. Her steps pick up as she tries to keep up with me and I'm seriously hoping she just follows me and doesn't touch me.

A moment later, I try to repress a shiver when her hand grabs my wrist and then she's practically plastered to my arm.

"Hey, Dragon. I was wondering when I'd be able to get you alone," Nicole said as she bats her eyelashes.

"What are you doing here, Nicole?"

Anger lights up in my veins at the memory. Biting my tongue, I have to remind myself to hold things in check and not blow this.

Late last year, Nicole and I had started dating. A few months later, I'd gotten a call from Thor to get my ass to the hospital because Dad had collapsed and, in my panic and haste to get there as quick as possible, I'd forgotten my Steel Archangel's hoodie in her apartment. Later that afternoon when I went back to get it, I caught her in bed with another man. I grabbed my hoodie and ended things with her. I would have loved to have beat the shit out of the asshole if I hadn't needed to get my ass home to shower quick, grab us all some clothes, and then head back to the hospital.

My body shivers again in revulsion when she plasters herself to me even more.

"I was wrong. Is there someplace we can go to talk?" she asks as she runs a finger down my chest.

I swallow the bile threatening to rise and change directions so I can lead her down to the basement.

I tune out what she's saying and right before we round the corner, I hear a gasp and feel Nicole shift to look over her shoulder. Fuck, I'm probably going to have a knife in me at some point in the near future. Either from Levi or her siblings. It takes everything in me not to push Nicole off me, turn around, and take Levi back to our house. Dammit. This shit better not take long, so I can explain this whole mess to her.

Rounding another corner, I make sure no one's behind us, even though I know the guys will stop anyone from following us. Even Levi, unfortunately. At the dead end, I lift a picture that we'd attached to the wall with a hinge and press my hand to the scanner. The wall slides forward a few inches and then slides to the right. Once we're through, I hit the close button and the wall slides back into place.

Descending the stairs, I stop at the steel door on the landing and press my hand to another scanner. Once the door opens, I close the door behind me, making sure it's secure, and make my way down the hall to the interrogation room. Timber and Tripp are already waiting inside to help me secure her if need be, and Smoke's probably already down here to record any information we get from her.

One last time, I scan my handprint outside the interrogation room and wait for it to unlock.

"You guys have a lot of security down here," she says and for the first time since she came up to me, she seems nervous.

"Yup, there's a reason for that," I say and let the unspoken words hang.

Actually, our security's so heavy for many reasons, but this is the only room she'll be seeing down here. Hence why we were okay with having her see the security measures. Once the door opens, I spin and toss her over my shoulder before entering.

"Mmm, kinky," she says, her voice husky as she smacks my ass.

Fuck, this needs to end soon.

Walking to the center of the room, I notice both Tripp and Timber already have rope in their hands. I sit her down roughly on the chair and immediately grab her wrists, wrenching them behind her. Tripp hands me some rope and I get to work binding her wrists together. A moan escapes her, and another shiver of disgust runs through me.

"Didn't realize you'd be bringing friends along, Dragon."

"Shut the fuck up, Nicole," I bite out.

It's then that she realizes she's not going to get what she wants and the reality that she's in danger sets in. She starts throwing her body around and kicking out her heels, trying to stab at us with her heels.

"Quiet down, Barbie Doll, no one can hear you down here," Timber says, his voice tight as he snags one of her legs, rips off her shoe, and then restrains her leg to the chair. Tripp grunts and swears, but he finally gets ahold of her other leg and secures her. Fuck, I think she nailed him in the balls with her heels.

Once her wrists are bound, I pick up the last length of rope and tie it around her middle, securing her to the back of the chair.

My phone pings and once I've got her secure, I dig it out of my pants.

> Thor: She secure?

> Dragon: Yeah, so get your ass down here so we can get this done. I think Spitfire saw us, so I'd like to get home pronto.

> Thor: Fuck. We're already shutting down the party. No idea where Wildcat is. I didn't realize she wasn't by me until it was too late.

My anger at this whole fucking mess grows as I re-read his text and I stomp over to the wall, leaning against it as I try to figure out how I can make Spitfire believe we couldn't figure out a different way to go about this in the short amount of time that we had. Nicole had been checking her phone a lot, which had us on edge that she'd slip away before we could grab her.

"Dragon, what the hell is going on? Untie me!" Nicole yells as she tries moving around to loosen the knots.

Fat chance she'd be getting out of those. Dad followed Grandpa's lead and was in the Navy for a while. When we were kids, he shared his knot-tying skills with us, among other things. When we were older, both Thor and I joined the Navy and continued the tradition.

"Shut the fuck up, bitch, or you're not going to like what happens next," Tripp snaps at her.

She growls as she twists her wrists and then hisses. "Untie me this instant, you assholes!"

Not wanting to get a headache from her screeching, I walk over to the cabinets that hold our tools and grab a piece of cloth. Walking back over to her, I give her my coldest glare and let her see the dragon inside of me. Fuck, I wish it was a man that'd done this so I could unleash the anger inside of me right now. She shrinks back and at least has the sense to look guilty.

Timber walks up next to me and pries her mouth open. When she sees the bandana, she tries to get out of Timber's grip, which has his grip tightening on her. Quickly, I tie it tightly around her head, gagging her, for now at least, mostly silencing her annoying voice.

Her muffled screams go on for another ten minutes before the door unlocks and the rest of my brothers file into the room, led by a very pissed-off Thor. Once the door closes and locks, he paces around her in a circle. Her head pivots to try to keep him in her line of vision.

Stopping in front of her, he levels her with an icy glare that has her shrinking back.

"When we remove the gag, you're going to answer our questions. If you spout off bullshit or keep screaming, the gag will go back on and you'll be punished. Is that clear?"

She hesitates and when his face darkens, she nods. Thor motions for Tripp to ungag her. He limps over to her and yanks it off before standing behind her, ready to put it back on if need be.

"Why'd you plant the cameras?"

"I-I don't know what you mean. I didn't plant anything," she says as she plasters on an innocent look.

"We know you did. We have proof."

She scoffs and rolls her eyes. At the same time, she sits up taller, having regained some of her composure. "Sure you do," she says sarcastically. "You guys had a huge party tonight. Anyone could have planted cameras."

"Who did you come with tonight?"

"No one. I called an uber."

"Who are you working with?"

"Get off that train of thought, or are you too stupid to hear what's coming out of my mouth? I didn't plant anything and the only one I work for is my boss, Skippy, down at B3."

Skippy used to solely own the B3 bar, which stands for Beer, Bikes, and Babes, but then about ten years ago or so, his wife and daughter were in a nasty car accident. They ended up with more medical bills than they could handle. So much so that they were looking to sell the bar. The Steel Archangel's made him a deal. We'd buy out seventy-five percent of the bar and he'd keep twenty-five percent. However, at the time, our club was smaller, and we didn't have the manpower to manage the bar, so the offer also included that he stay on as manager with a salary and benefits.

"Ah, yes, Skippy. I had a conversation not too long ago with him and I've got to say, you've pissed off the wrong people, Barbie."

A surprised look comes over her before it turns into confusion. "I don't know what you're talking about."

"Is that right?" Thor asks her before turning back to Smoke. "Smoke?"

Smoke pushes away from the table and starts pacing around her. "Yes, I've had a lot of talks with Skippy. Seems he's got a thief working for him. Would you know anything about that?"

The color drains from her face, but she shakes her head. "It's not me. I've never stolen anything."

"Huh, that's not what we hear. Inventory numbers are frequently off. Tills are off. And when it comes to distributing the tips, some nights are much lower than others." He stops in front of her as he stares down at her. "None of that rings a bell?"

She shakes her head again. "N-No."

Fuck, this is going to take a while, and it's already after 1 am. I wish I had gone with my gut and told Spitfire what we were going to do regardless of the vote. Fuck, I hope she's still awake when we're done.

Three fucking hours later, we give up for the night, having gotten no new information. We'll let her stew for a while. Axe and Alexei offered to take the first watch. Normally I'd just have Prospects watch her if we weren't in the interrogation room, but we always have to have at least one patched member in here when we have guests.

Hopping on my bike, I head for the house with Thor not too far behind me. I'm fucking pissed at Judge, but right now, I'm more worried about Spitfire. I'm bone tired and want to curl up with her. If she'll let me, that is. Fuck, I hope she's not that pissed. I park and make my way up the porch before unlocking the door. Besides Bear, the other guys that have houses don't lock their doors since we're inside the compound, but ever since the incident with Monica, Thor and I have been locking our doors.

I hang my cut up and slip my boots off, putting them in their cubby hole or whatever the hell Levi calls that spot. Making my way upstairs, I try to keep quiet so I don't wake her up. Heading into the bathroom, I do my business and then strip down to my boxers.

Walking back into our bedroom, I pull back the covers, but that's when I notice the couple of decorative pillows Levi had gotten are still on the bed. Using the light from my phone, I realize the bed is empty.

Where the fuck is she?

Turning on the light, I curse when I see the room is empty and quickly pull my pants back on. Ducking into my old room, I flip on the light, but it's empty too. Same as Thor's old room. Fuck.

Is she with Sasha?

Praying I don't get my ass beat further, I check each of the empty rooms before knocking on Sasha's door. Getting no answer, I open the door and, using the light from my phone in case they are asleep, I check the bed.

Empty.

Flicking on the light confirms it. Racing downstairs, I check every room, but there's no sign of her. Did she leave? Did she go to Roy's house?

Digging out my phone, I ring Smoke just as Thor comes inside and stares at me in confusion. I switch my phone over to the speaker so he can hear what he says, too.

"Spitfire's not here—calling Smoke."

He curses and I start pacing the living room. Where the fuck is she and why isn't Smoke answering? Finally, after the sixth ring, he picks up.

"Whatcha need, Dragon—was about to go to bed."

"Levi's not here. Can you pull up her tracker?"

He curses and then I hear some muffled noises before the distinct sounds of keys clicking away comes through the line. *"Guessing my sister's pissed at ya, huh?"*

"Yeah, well, if the others would have fucking listened to me in the beginning, this could have ended differently, and she would have known what was going to happen from the start. Now she's probably pissed as fuck, and I'll end up with a knife in me."

He grunts and I run my hand through my hair. *"Don't have to tell me. I was pissed they went that route. She's at Bear's house. Looks like Sasha's there too. Colt and Ethan are showing up on the screen walking around the house as well."*

I'm pulling on my boots as soon as I hear Bear's name. Then the rest of what he said registers.

"Who notified Colt and Ethan they were there?"

"My guess is Sasha told Colt, but I'd have to pull their phone logs. Do you want me to?"

Sighing, I shake my head as I slip back into my cut and stalk out the front door with Thor right behind me. *"Not right now, but if I find anything else out, I'll let you know. Thanks, Smoke."*

He grunts and hangs up. Seconds later, I'm out the door and heading over to Bear's house.

"I'm putting a fucking vote in that we don't pull shit like this again," I mutter, but I know Thor's pissed about how this all went, too. At least he has the guts to look guilty. He could have fucking overridden the vote, but he didn't.

Taking the porch steps to Bear's house quickly, the door opens just as I'm about to knock.

"Kinda figured you'd be here before long," he says as he lets me pass with a fist bump. Looking over my shoulder, I catch the glare he gives Thor. Behind him trails Colt. At least Bear's on my side, though it shouldn't surprise me. He was just as pissed as I was when it was brought up that we shouldn't tell Spitfire.

"If you guys are going to take Levi, I can take Sasha back to my room at the clubhouse," Colt suggests.

I give him a chin lift in thanks because I'm pretty sure it might get loud once Levi wakes up in our arms. And it's probably not going to be the good kind of loud.

Walking into the living room, I notice the girls are cuddled up against each other on the couch as they sleep with a blanket covering them. However, judging by her creased forehead and the fact that every now and then her body jerks slightly, she isn't getting good sleep.

My gaze wanders around the room and based on the junk food on the coffee table, it looks like they had a movie night and the TV screen saver shows they watched Boondock Saints. Nice.

"I can—" Thor starts, and I turn and cut him off with a glare.

"Don't even fucking start with me, Thor. I don't even know the next time she'll willingly let me touch her, so I am going to pick her up, carry her home, and hold her until she wakes up and probably stabs me. ...Actually," I pause and pull out my phone, quickly tapping out a text. "There, Patch is on standby, just in case."

When I turn and start to carefully remove the blanket covering them, I can hear both Colt and Bear's quiet laughter. I wasn't joking either—I'm almost damn positive I'll be bleeding tomorrow, I mean later today.

Kneeling, I gently get my arms under Spitfire and wait as Colt kneels next to me and does the same with Sasha before we both lift at the same time. Once again, I give Colt a chin lift and start my way back home.

About halfway there, she shifts in my arms.

"Why Dragon?" she asks sleepily.

The fact that she's using my road name makes my chest ache even more. Fuck, that probably isn't a good sign. Sighing, I bend down to kiss her forehead. "I was outvoted and Judge's idea was the best one proposed."

"Outvoted how?" She rubs her eyes and yawns, but at least she's still talking to me and I'm not bleeding yet.

"Let's get inside before I tell you the rest." I pause and then lean down closer to her ear so she'll still hear me. "Just in case they planted others around that we didn't catch."

She looks up and locks eyes with me. After a few moments, she nods and then curls back into my chest.

I hasten my steps even though I'd rather slow down and keep her in my arms. But I know she'd probably get pissed if I did that and then my chances of being injured increase.

As we near our porch steps, Thor darts around me and opens the front door. I head straight upstairs and set her down on our bed. Walking over to my nightstand, I pull out two scanners and hand one to Thor. We both start checking the room and the surrounding hallway. Out of the corner of my eye, I notice Spitfire has scooted back and is now sitting cross-legged on the bed, hugging a pillow to her stomach as she waits for us to finish.

Once we're finished, I walk over and sit down next to her. My fingers itch to reach out and take her hand, but I'm not sure if I should take my chances.

When she reaches out and threads our fingers together, some of the weight on my shoulder's releases, and my body sags in relief.

"Even though I'm dead tired, I know I'm not going to get good sleep until I know why it was decided to break my heart and stomp on it the same day you guys asked me to be your Old Lady. The same day you asked me to marry you. The same day we found out our family is growing. Why?"

Fuck, we really screwed this up. Now, this day will always feel tainted because of this shit with Nicole.

"Well, technically this all started after midnight, so it's not the same day," Thor says softly, and the glare Spitfire pierces him with is damn fucking frightening.

"It's close enough, Thor! Now I want details, or I'll be waking up Jax to get them myself from the call and video logs."

Spearing Thor with a glance, I hope he keeps his mouth fucking shut so I can say what I need to.

"We noticed Nicole checking her phone a lot after eleven o'clock and were starting to get worried. Since we couldn't all go into Church, we decided to do a group text. It was noticed by several brothers that she was always keeping an eye on what I was doing, who I was talking to, or where I was going. The guys all know she's my ex, so that, coupled with her always watching me, prompted someone to suggest that I lure Nicole down to the interrogation room."

I don't go into further detail about what's down in our hidden basement cause I know Thor's already given her a tour and added her handprint in case she or anyone else needs to access our third panic room.

"No one else had a better idea, so we agreed to go with that plan. However, it was not a unanimous vote for how we'd act it out, Spitfire."

"I take it you won't tell me who voted which way?"

"Sorry, Wildcat, but that should probably be kept unsaid."

She sighs and shakes her head.

Clearing my throat, I continue. "I voted to tell you what we were going to do so you wouldn't worry. It was suggested not to tell you so your reaction would be more real and would spur Nicole on so we'd have an easier way to capture her. The latter vote won out."

She's silent for a few moments as she picks at the edge of the pillowcase in her lap. "Does anyone have an issue with me being both of your guy's Old Lady? To be your wife?" she asks quietly.

Silently I curse my brothers for making her doubt herself, I pull her into my lap even if she may still shank me. I bury my head in her neck and hold her tight.

"No one doubts you, Spitfire. Everyone was just worried about getting her downstairs before she could have alerted whoever the fuck she was working with."

"If no one doubts me, then why couldn't I have been in the loop and helped out? I did four years of theater in high school; I do know how to act when it calls for it. I mean, it seemed like everyone was trying to prevent me from going into the clubhouse when they realized that was where I was headed. Then inside, the guys still tried to get me to turn around and only stepped back when my blades came out.

"Seeing all of them trying to pull a fast one over me felt like a huge disrespect to me not only as a person, but also as your Old Lady, as your fiancée, and even though they don't know it yet, the mother of your baby. Add onto that, but by disrespecting me, it's also disrespecting you guys. I get that you all can't tell me everything, but you could have told me to follow you, but not too close behind Nicole, and then play along to get her downstairs."

Her voice is almost a whisper at the end and fuck, does it break me.

"I'm sorry, Wildcat. Honestly, I think because this whole shitshow blindsided us, we were left scrambling to figure something out as quick as possible. I'm not making excuses, just letting you know my opinion. And I didn't overturn the vote because then they'd be questioning if I was playing favoritism since it would affect you," Thor says quietly.

Shit, I didn't think about that. That would be a fast way to lose respect in the club.

Thor scoots closer and takes her hand in his. Thankfully, she doesn't pull away.

She looks at him for a while before turning to look at me. "I need you both, as well as the rest of the guys, to know that just because I'm a woman, I'm not fragile. I'm not made out of glass that will easily shatter when met with a roadblock. I'm also going to put it out there, that while I may not agree with what the club decides sometimes, I will do what's needed to protect my family. I just ask that you never pull a stunt like this again." She pauses as she looks between us again. "Think about it this way. If you had a sister and a different club decided to do to her what you all did to me tonight, how would you react?"

My grip tightens around Spitfire as rage burns in me and I know without even looking at him that Thor feels the same way.

"Exactly. Now you somewhat feel what I felt tonight. I want you guys to remember that feeling and honestly, tell that to the guys too. I'm sure at some point there will be more girlfriends or Old Ladies and wives, so I don't want them going through what everyone put me through tonight. Our world is tough enough as it is. Let's not add even more hurdles on top of it."

"We'll talk to the guys, Wildcat."

Spitfire nods and then yawns. "Good, now let's get ready for bed. I'm beat."

She crawls off my lap and scoots off the bed before going to her dresser and grabbing some clothes. I slide off the bed and start stripping, but pause when she clears her throat. Looking over at her, she's standing by the bathroom door, gnawing on her lip.

"This week, I expect everyone in the clubhouse for supper. Starting tonight. If I find out they eat elsewhere, there'll be even more hell to pay."

The hard edge in her voice makes my chest tighten. The thought of us getting off kind of easy about this shit show is instantly thrown out the window. Fuck, I'm not sure what she has planned for payback, but I have a feeling none of us are going to like it.

Chapter 31
Levi

Later that morning, I wake up to an empty bed and a note on Thor's pillow.

Morning, Wildcat. We're at the clubhouse to question Nicole again. Left a bit before 9 am. No need to worry about breakfast today—we sent the Prospects out for donuts. There's a box down in the kitchen for you. We also scanned the rest of the house and it's clean. Text us if you need anything.
-Love Ry

My mouth starts to drool at the mention of donuts and then a little giggle escapes when I see Nick's messy handwriting at the bottom saying he loves me, too. While I am glad my guesses were correct, I'm still pissed at them about last night. This morning. *Grrr.*

I quickly get up and grab clean clothes before stripping on my way to the shower. Once the water's warm, I hop in and take a quick shower. I'm frickin starving and those donuts are calling my name. Oh, and coffee. Can't live without my coffee. Even if this baby doesn't seem to like it.

As I dry off and get ready, my mind wanders to what we talked about last night. They told me about the talk with Nicole and I'm not surprised they haven't gotten anything out of her yet. She has to know the guys won't seriously hurt her, which has me looking forward to the task I have planned later today.

Grabbing my phone off the nightstand, I text Sasha, and almost instantly; I hear a knock on the front door. A second later, my phone pings.

Sasha: Was already sitting on your porch with Roxy, waiting for you to get up. **Так что поторопитесь и откройте дверь уже** [So hurry up and open the door already]!

Laughing, I slip my cut on, grab a notebook from the bookcase, and race downstairs. Unlocking the door, I let them in.

"Sorry, ladies! It was a late night last night."

Sasha raises an eyebrow at me, and I shake my head. I'll wait until they're inside. They follow me into the kitchen, and I make a beeline for the coffee pot, happy to see my men made me a pot and put it on the warmer.

Coffee in hand, I sit down at the table and flip open the box. Grabbing a sprinkled white frosting donut, I moan as the delicious fluffiness hits my tongue. I quickly inhale the first one and reach for a second as I open my notebook.

Roxy clears her throat.

"So, what really happened last night? I know what I saw, but spill. What's going on?"

Sighing, I take a sip of coffee. "What we talk about *cannot* leave this house, understood?" I tell them as I tear off a piece of donut and pop it into my mouth. Roxy nods and even though I know Sasha's answer, she nods as well.

"The bitch's name is Nicole. Apparently, she's Dragon's ex. We caught her planting cameras or something around the backyard last night."

I pause and when I glance at Roxy, her face pales and her hand holding her donut freezes, halfway to her mouth.

"Damn, we just can't catch a break, can we?" she mutters right before taking a huge bite of her donut.

"Apparently not."

Taking another sip of coffee, I fill her in on what happened. Both are even more pissed when I share what the guys told me last night. Well, as much as I can tell them, anyway.

"**Хорошо** [Okay]! Tell us what we can do to help plan," Sasha says as she leans back in her chair and pulls a notepad out of her bag.

Roxy looks between us, confused. "Help plan what?"

Sasha and I lock eyes and I'm sure my wicked smile matches her own. Time to have a little payback.

A little over an hour later, I lock up the house and we head to the garage. Opening the garage door, I see Alexei and Colt are already waiting for us on their motorcycles. Sliding into my SUV, I send a quick text to Thor and Dragon that we're heading into town for supplies and that we have two Prospects with us.

I don't wait for an answer as I back out of the garage and head for the gate. We've already done our research, so we know what stores we're going to have to hit.

First up is a nice Asian grocery store. As a bonus, it's frickin' huge, so I'm hoping we find a lot of goodies in there. Both Colt and Alexei park their bikes and, after a quick glance around, signal for us to get out of the SUV.

Once inside, I grab a cart and can't help my giddy feeling as I start perusing the shelves. I've been here before, so I know the general layout. However, I've never really shopped for the items on our list before, so I have no idea where everything is or if they even have them. We may have to improvise a little.

What surprises me though is when Colt grabs another cart and starts humming the Mission Impossible theme song as he and Alexei start grabbing things off the shelves. Turning to Sasha, I raise an eyebrow in question, and she squirms a little.

"I may have already filled him in on what you most likely would do and then sent him a text with some tweaks. Also, you know I can't keep anything from Alexei. He knew we were up to something with a single glance this morning."

"That's right, Levi, and we have a few contributions ourselves. However, if you tell anyone we actually helped, we'll both deny it to our graves," Colt says, as he pins me with a look.

I laugh and then give them copies of the list.

As we're wandering the aisles, I do my best to ignore the stares we get. While most of them are directed at the guys, which irritates the hell out of Sasha and surprisingly, Roxy, a lot give me curious or hateful glares that turn even darker when they see my engagement ring and the back of my cut. I'm guessing the latter is when they realized who I was seeing and the fact that they claimed me.

As for the curious stares, I don't know how many people in town were at the party last night, so I have no idea if any of them saw what happened. With a sigh, I try to focus my concentration on the list.

It takes a few hours, but we find almost everything we were looking for between the Asian, Mexican, and regular grocery stores. Thankfully, we have three large refrigerators in the kitchen, so we maneuvered stuff around so that our surprises will be solely in one fridge. When we aren't prepping a meal, they'll be padlocked. Right now, Roxy and Amy are prepping some of the easy stuff for supper. Since we don't know how long this will take, we went with an easier dish for tonight.

Grabbing my bag off the counter that I'd packed earlier, I lead the way from the kitchen to Jax's room with Sasha right behind me and knock on his door.

"Come on in."

Turning the handle, I enter and close the door behind us.

"Hey, Jax, I was wondering if I could grab what came in yesterday."

Surprisingly, he grabs the large box and opens it without question. He pulls out two devices and as he's putting one on, a knock sounds on the door. Before I can speak, Jax beats me to it.

"Come in."

Panicking slightly that it's Thor or Dragon or both of them, I'm relieved when it's only Patch.

"Here," Jax says as he hands one of the devices to Patch. Jax turns to me and smirks, most likely noticing my confusion.

"Need to have a patched member down there with you, Levi, and I figured it would be better having Patch there as well in case we need his skills."

I freeze, knowing for a fact only Sasha knows what I'm planning, and we didn't say anything in our texts about it. How did he guess my plan?

"Smoke's right and besides, I was wondering when or if you'd be pulled in."

"Uh, about that… Thor and Dragon don't know," Jax says as he stares down Patch. They share some sort of silent communication and Patch sighs. How the hell did Jax know about this?

"Dammit. I don't like them not knowing about this, but are you sure you want to do this, Levi?"

Relieved that he doesn't seem like he'll stop me, I nod. "Yes. We need her answers and I bet you guys didn't get any new info today out of her, did you?"

Both of them shake their heads.

"All right then. Shall we get the party started then?" Sasha laughs and twirls a blade as she grins.

"You're going, too?" Patch asks her, almost sounding like he's resigned about this.

"Of course. Bitch is messing with our **семья** [family]."

Patch sighs again and puts on the device.

"Okay, Kiddo, lead the way. Hopefully, no one will notice us."

"I've got that part covered," I say and wink at him. Sasha quickly texts our change in plans and Patch groans, but he still follows us out of Jax's room.

Even though I know I have coverage, I carefully walk through the hallways until I reach the dead end and lift the picture. Scanning my handprint, the door opens and once it closes again, Sasha whistles.

"I know this doesn't really need to be said because I know you, but for Jax and Patch's sake, you can't tell anyone outside of the club about that entrance or what you see or hear down here."

"You don't have anything to worry about. My lips are sealed."

We make our way through the other security checkpoints and finally into the interrogation room.

The smell is the first thing I notice, and the second is that there's a plastic tarp underneath her. Looks like she didn't get a bathroom break and was forced to sit in her own filth. I take a moment and thankfully; the smell doesn't trigger any nausea.

Good. With this being just day two of knowing I'm pregnant, I'm not sure what all my triggers will be yet.

Jax dismisses Drae and hands a confused Bones a third device that I hadn't seen him grab earlier. Nodding toward Jax, he turns and starts to set everything up for the translators. Looking over, my gaze locks with Sasha's and, without a word, we both turn and start opening the cabinets. I start pulling some tools out and putting them on the table. Every now and then, I'll pull out a tool, look it over, and put it back. I already know I won't need it, but Nicole doesn't. Periodically, I can hear her whimpering and I have to force myself to school my features, even though a part of me is happy at hearing her suffering.

When all my tools are out, I pull off my ring and slide out of my cut in case this gets bloody, setting it down on the bench next to Jax. I'd already made sure to wear clothes and shoes that I didn't care about. Plus, I've got an extra stash of clothes and shoes in my bag if need be. My hair is already pulled into a high ponytail that's been braided and then wrapped into a bun so that it'll be out of my way.

Slipping on some gloves, I note Sasha's doing the same as we walk toward Nicole. Then both Sasha and I walk around her in opposite directions, our hands clasped behind our backs.

"**Интересно, когда она сломается и задаст свой первый вопрос** [Wonder when she'll crack and ask her first question]?" I ask, and with a quick glance at Jax, he gives me a subtle chin lift that lets me know the translation devices are working.

Good.

"**Наверное, не намного дольше, сестра** [Probably not much longer, sister]. **Я имею в виду, что она сидит в своей собственной грязи, которая не может быть удобной** [I mean, she is sitting in her own filth which can't be comfortable]." Sasha replies.

"**Очень верно** [Very true]." I tap my chin, making it look like I'm contemplating something. My hope is that our Russian will throw her off but also provide us another way of talking since I highly doubt she knows the language.

We don't say anything else as we continue to walk around her. After a few moments, Nicole whimpers and I bite my cheek to keep from smiling.

"What are you going to do? I know you can't hurt women. The club's against it. I've already told them I don't know what they're talking about. Let me go, please," she says, looking up at me with pleading eyes.

Not going to work.

This bitch isn't going anywhere.

"See, that's where you're wrong, Nicole." I pause when her eyes widen and I'm guessing she didn't think I'd know who she was. "While yes, every man that's in this club did pledge to not hurt women and children. But you know, I think you're missing an even bigger piece of the puzzle, bitch."

She pales and swallows loudly.

"W-What's that?"

I stop pacing behind her and pull on her hair until her head doesn't tilt anymore, and then I apply a smidge more pressure. "I'm a woman and there isn't anything in their bylaws that says a woman can't interrogate a woman... guest."

Her eyes widen and I take a closer look at her, determining her weak points. Finding appropriate ones, I walk over to Jax.

"**Камеры** [Camera's]?"

He reaches into his bag and pulls out a black metal box before handing it to me.

"**Сигнал был отключен** [Signal's been cut]?"

He gives a curt nod, which I return, and pivot on my heel. Nicole's looking like she's about to piss her pants again as her gaze bounces back and forth between Sasha and me.

Casually, I walk back to her and stop in front of her. "Now, I want you to tell me why you planted these?" I ask as I open the metal box, showing her the three cameras.

"I-I didn't. Just like I told Dragon and the others."

"Is that so?"

Nicole nods, and I hand Sasha the box before walking around her. When she twists to keep me in her line of sight, I make my move, snatching one of her hoop earrings and yanking hard, ripping it out of her ear.

A scream rips out of her and she glares at me. Patch moves from his perch by the door and grabs a wooden bin before walking toward us and placing it on the floor off to her side, but within her line of sight. Ah, so that's what those boxes are for. Also, a sick part of me loves the idea of keeping the trophies we remove from their bodies within their sight.

Dropping the earring into the box, I don't speak and let the noise of it falling in the box fade before I walk back over to her. Her gaze stays glued to the box, and I can tell her body's trembling slightly.

And I've only just begun.

"Let's try this again. Why'd you plant the cameras?"

Her gaze focuses back on me and swallows. "I... I didn't plant—"

Another scream rips from her throat as I yank her other earring out. I walk over to the box, and like before, drop it inside, letting the sound of the metal hitting the wood fade before speaking again.

"Want to try again?"

She just stares at me, and I turn, picking up two needle-nose pliers. I hand one to Sasha, then I motion for her to follow me as I walk behind Nicole. She twists her head to the left and right, trying to see what we're doing, but she isn't going to be able to see this due to the way she's tied up.

I kneel, making sure to avoid the puddles on the plastic, and when I grab one hand, Sasha grabs the other. Nicole tries to fist her hands as she starts thrashing around.

Secretly glad that she's fighting me, I find the fleshy part above her clavicle bone and apply pressure until she cries out, loosening her grip. Sasha does the same until she loosens her grip on her other hand.

Locking eyes with Sasha, we both nod. In sync, we place the pliers over the tip of her fake acrylic nails. Squeezing down, we start to bend the nails backward.

She screams but doesn't give us any information, so we keep bending her nails till they break and then rip them off before moving to the next ones.

After we've ruined three nails on each hand, we're lining up to grip her pinky nail when she speaks up.

"I was paid to plant them."

I don't remove the pliers or lessen my grip. "Keep talking."

"I don't know who she is, though. She told me where to put them—"

She's cut off by the door opening and I'm relieved it's just my men, but then I start to panic slightly that they're going to be pissed at me for this.

Once the door is shut, they take up positions on opposite sides of the room and lean against the wall, though they are close enough that they can see what I'm doing behind her back. Jax gives each of them a translation device.

"Carry on, Wildcat," Thor says, and the weight that was on my shoulders lessens. Dragon smirks at me and gives me a chin lift.

"You were saying?" I ask Nicole.

She doesn't answer me as she stares at Dragon, so we continue bending her nails back. She screeches and when I rip off the fourth nail; I move to her thumb.

"S-Stop!"

Once again, I don't remove the pliers or lessen my grip.

"She told me where to place them and then to see if I could charm my way into someone's bed. Then I'd plant more overnight."

"Where are the other cameras? How many?" Thor asks.

She doesn't answer, so we continue until the last nail has been broken and torn off.

Getting up, I walk over to the table and make a show of inspecting the weapons. "Идиот [Idiot]. You know, things will be much easier for you if you'd just answer when you're asked a question."

Picking up some brass knuckles, I slip them on each hand, even though they are a little big. Hmmm, I should probably order some smaller ones if I'm ever gonna have to do this again. I'll probably have some bruises later since they are a little big, but it's a small price to pay.

Walking back up to her, I place a finger under her chin and tilt her head up. "Answer him."

She presses her lips together, refusing to answer. Pulling back, I land a punch to her ribs, followed by one to her chest. Normally I'd never tit-punch another woman, but this bitch needs to learn you don't mess with my family. And that means I'll do anything to protect them.

Nicole glares at me as she pants but doesn't say anything.

A few minutes go by with me, punching her ribs, tits and even twisting her nipples painfully. Bitch made it easy for me by not wearing a bra.

Still, she doesn't say anything.

Deciding to take another route, I go back to the table and set the brass knuckles to the side. I thought I saw something in her hair earlier, so I'm hoping my theory is correct.

Picking up the pliers again, I walk behind her and remove her ponytail holder. Running my hands through her hair, I feel a grin forming when my fingers run over little clusters of hair.

Perfect.

I part her hair so that there's a row of extensions visible and twist the rest up into a messy bun on the top of her head. Picking up a section, I wrap the hair around my hand and then grip it with my fist. With the pliers, I clamp down on the bead and pull slightly. Her body stiffens and I wonder if this will be what it takes for her to crack.

"Where'd you stash the remaining cameras?" I ask again, and when she doesn't respond right away, I start getting pissed.

Since I can't see her face, I glance at Sasha, who's taken up point in front of her.

"**Сделай это** [Do it]," she tells me.

Gripping hard with both hands, I yank out the extension. Nicole screams, shouting obscenities as she tries to curl in on herself.

Lining up again, I clamp down on the bead, and at Sasha's nod, I rip another one out. This time, part of her skin comes with it.

I repeat the process two more times, and I'm lining up to grip another bead when I hear her faintly say something.

Sasha reaches out with her blade, places it under her chin, and lifts her head up. "Repeat."

"They're in a bag we hid in some brush around a cluster of trees behind some houses."

"**Мне нужна карта** [I need a map]," I tell Jax, who's already looking through a container holding a bunch of cylindrical tubes that are attached to the wall.

That's convenient. *I wonder how many times they've had to use those?*

Finding the one he wants; he unscrews the lid and pulls out the contents. He brings it over, standing a few feet in front of Nicole, and then he and Sasha unroll it. It's a laminated overview of the entire compound. Walking around so I can see her face, I watch her as she looks it over. Jax hands me a marker.

"Which house is closest to where the bag is hidden?"

There're only four houses so far, but she takes a moment to look at the whole map again.

"It's between the third and fourth house. Then it's back a bit into the woods."

I uncap the marker and point to the middle area between our house and Bear's. "Around here?"

"Yes."

I make a small 'x' on the map. "Tell me how far back, approximately." I inch my way further up the map, waiting for her answer. After a couple of seconds, I have it.

"Around there, I think."

Making another 'x', I circle it. Jax takes the other side of the map from Sasha and then walks to another table. Patch joins him and plops down tools on the corners so it won't roll back up. Sasha approaches Nicole and places her blade under her chin again.

Focusing back on Nicole, I try hard not to let my emotions take control. "What's the bag look like?"

Nicole hesitates, and I draw my ka-bar. Sasha lowers her blade until it's at her throat.

Her gaze bounces between us both. I lightly run it down her face, not enough to draw blood, but enough to up her fear factor. After a couple seconds, I see the moment she caves.

"It's a small camo backpack. There's a metal box inside containing ten more cameras."

"Where were you going to hide the other cameras?" Thor asks.

"I-I was supposed to put them along the edge of the tree line, facing the houses. Two for each house. The other two, I was supposed to put in both guard shacks so they could have a clear line of sight when people leave. As well as getting the codes to the gate. They know they change daily."

With a quick glance at Jax, he gives me a chin lift and then his fingers fly across his keyboard. If there is a bag out there, I'm sure we'll know soon.

I try to stamp down my anger, but it must still show to some degree because Nicole pales even further and tries to lean as far back as she can from me.

"Who are 'they' that you talked about?"

Her eyes widen, and even though Sasha's knife is to her throat, she shakes her head, then winces as the blade digs a little deeper, and more blood trickles down her throat.

Time to up the ante.

Chapter 32

Levi

I STALK BACK TO the table, sheathing my blade in the process. Slamming down the pliers, I walk straight toward the metal restraints. I'd noticed the cutouts in the ceiling and walls, so I know there's a way to secure her for what I have planned.

Grabbing four restraints, I pick up a steel pipe and feel a dark grin growing as I round the table. Nicole's body starts to tremble, but still, she says nothing.

I'm about to walk back over to her, but Dragon and Thor are quickly at my side.

My anger starts to rise. Surely, they've done worse before than restrain someone and use a pipe on them. So why would they try to stop me?

They both grin darkly and my anger instantly fades.

"We'll help her get into a more comfortable position for you, Spitfire."

Dragon leans down and gives me a chaste kiss, but judging by the heat in his eyes, he has no qualms about me taking the reins with Nicole. That itself is a huge relief—I was worried they'd be pissed at me for doing this. Well, they may still be pissed that I didn't tell them first, but after last night, they don't have a leg to stand on.

Walking behind Nicole, Sasha yanks her head back by her hair and puts her knife back at her throat. When Sasha gives my guys a chin lift, they start untying her ankles. As soon as one is free, she kicks out at Thor, damn near kicking him in his balls.

Sasha yanks back harder on her hair and the shift causes her blade to bite into her skin while at the same time, my blade is once again drawn. Seconds later, I'm in her face, the blade at her cheek. I smirk when I see the trickles of blood running down her throat from Sasha's knife.

"Если вы попробуете что-то подобное снова, это будет последнее, что вы сделаете [If you try anything like that again, it will be the last thing you do]."

Even though she doesn't understand me, her eyes widen as her face pales. She doesn't fight when the guys attach the cuffs to her legs and then to the metal rings they pulled out from the walls. Someone then lowers a hook from the ceiling. Both Sasha and I keep our blades on her as the guys start untying her wrists.

When the cuffs are secured to her wrists, the other ends are attached to the hook. As the chain starts to retract, Sasha lowers her blade from her throat and loosens her grip on her hair, but still keeps a hold of it. Stepping back a few steps, I keep my blade pointed at her as the chain pulls her into a standing position, and then up a little more so she has to stand on her tippy toes. Good thing she's a little shorter than me.

Stepping closer to her again, I once again place my blade against her cheek. Looking her in the eye, I trail my blade down her cheek, just hard enough to slightly cut into her skin.

"I'm getting tired of you not answering our questions when we ask them. Maybe what you need is a little more incentive."

"Может быть, ей нужен курс повышения квалификации по манерам [Maybe she needs a refresher course on manners]?" Sasha asks, and I grin darkly.

"Да, я думаю, что вы правы [Yes, I think you're right]."

Nicole's body starts to tremble slightly at the harsh, dark tone of our voices.

Since my blade has now tasted blood, I hold out my right hand, palm up, toward Thor. He relieves me of it, and I make a show of testing the steel pipe's weight.

Without warning, I swing hard at her right kneecap.

The screams that rip out of her have my ears ringing slightly. Resting the pipe on my shoulder, I wait for her screams to subside and for her to catch her breath.

Once she finally calms down, I ask again. "Who are 'they' that you talked about?"

She shakes her head wildly. "N-No, if I say anymore, t-they'll kill me."

I shrug. "You're going to die today anyway, bitch. Might as well tell us, and we'll shorten your interrogation."

At the moment, I'm only about seventy percent sure she should die tonight, but she doesn't need to know that.

Yet again, she shakes her head wildly.

Quickly, I land another hard swing to her left kneecap.

I sigh heavily as I shoulder the pipe and I don't even have to act to put on a bored face as I wait for her screams to subside. I'm getting tired of her not spilling the rest of the information.

When she's finally breathing normally, I notice she's lost control of her bladder again. She's glaring at me now, and I smirk as I slowly walk toward her, trying to avoid her puddles of piss.

Lifting her chin with the pipe, I ensure her eyes stay focused on me.

"Going to answer me yet?"

She hesitates, even though I can tell she's in a shitload of pain. When she presses her lips into a thin line, I grin darkly.

"**Мне понадобится твоя помощь в следующей части, сестра** [I'll need your help for this next part, sister]."

When I crouch and hold the bar between her legs, Sasha cackles evilly as she grasps the other end of the pipe. Nicole's eyes grow wide, and her body starts to tremble.

"**Сейчас** [Now]."

Both of us stand, slamming the bar into her crotch in a literal bone-crushing blow.

Nicole screams and then I see her eyes roll back as her body sags.

Sighing again, I turn to get some water but notice Dragon already has a bucket in hand and it's filled with water. When did they fill that?

He winks at me and when I step back; he dumps the contents on Nicole. She gasps and coughs as she comes around.

Walking forward, I stop a few feet in front of her and rest the pipe on my shoulder.

"Ready to talk now?"

She emphatically nods her head.

Finally, we're making progress.

"Who are 'they' that you mentioned earlier?"

"T-The woman who p-paid me to plant the c-cameras and her boyfriend, F-Fang, along with his three b-brothers."

While I had figured they were behind this, it still sucks to hear her confirm it.

"Describe the woman since you don't know her."

"...S-She's a little shorter than me. M-Mousy brown hair that h-hits her shoulders. Really s-skinny looking. M-Maybe around thirty?"

I wonder if that description matches the woman who helped Korso earlier. I wasn't able to get a good look at her in the photo they shared in Church. Glancing over at Smoke, he gives me a nod. Guess the description matches.

I turn back to Nicole. "What were they going to do after placing the cameras?"

"T-They were going to w-watch to learn your r-routines and hope that they'd be able to s-sneak in and capture both you and b-blondie here as well as another w-woman you're close to. Somehow, they k-know how to get into your compound undetected. H-However, if all three of you women were to go into town together, they'd ambush you, kill your guards, and k-kidnap you."

"Then what?"

"They m-mentioned something about t-tying up loose ends at the c-cabin, picking up their f-friend, and taking you home. They also m-mentioned something about going b-back to where everything started."

My mind whirls as I try to figure out what they mean by 'back where everything started'. Shaking off that thought, I refocus on Nicole. Her breathing's becoming more of a wheeze.

Lifting her chin with the pipe, I make her look into my eyes.

"Do you know what would have happened if they had kidnapped us?"

She shakes her head. "T-They just told me that you'd s-stolen something from them and g-gave it to the Steel Archangel's. They n-needed you to get it back."

Fury rages in my veins. "I didn't steal anything from them. My own uncle sold my virginity to Fang. If they get their hands on us, they will torture and rape us before eventually selling or killing us."

Her eyes widen and her body starts to shake even more. Tears pool in her eyes. "I-I didn't know. I swear I-I didn't know!"

Pausing, I notice her breathing is getting harsher. Fuck, I need to finish this. "What about at B3?"

"I'm the r-reason the numbers are all off. I d-don't think anyone else was doing the same thing."

"Why did you do it? Both the cameras and stealing from B3?"

Her body slumps slightly as she hangs her head. "I n-needed the money. M-My grandpa's the only f-family I have left. He's in a n-nursing home and needs expensive m-medicine for his treatments. If I d-didn't come up with the m-money, they were going to have to t-transfer him somewhere else. I can't afford to s-send him anywhere else. This was the c-cheapest place I could find."

My heart breaks a little at her admission, but it doesn't excuse what she did and would have done.

A hand lands on the small of my back, jarring me out of my thoughts. Dragon looks down at me in concern. Seconds later, another hand wraps around my waist.

"Your grandpa will be taken care of," Thor says.

"C-Can you please not tell G-Grandpa how or why I d-died? It would k-kill him. P-Please."

I nod and relief floods her face.

Glancing up at Thor, I raise an eyebrow in question. "**Есть другие вопросы** [Any other questions]?"

He shakes his head, and when I look around the room, everyone else shakes their head 'no'.

Handing the pipe to Dragon, I take my ka-bar back from Thor. Walking around Nicole, Sasha joins my guys and all three of them walk to the front of the room till they're standing at the edge of the plastic.

Grabbing her hair, I keep her head steady and slice my knife across her throat. Blood spatters on the plastic and I push down the bile in my throat. Giving her a wide berth to potentially avoid getting more blood or bodily fluids on me, I walk over to the others and watch as Nicole takes her last breaths. Her body sags and a sliver of guilt at what I'd done eats at me, but I push it aside. It was necessary to protect my family and myself.

Patch walks over to her, and with a grim nod, confirms she's dead.

"Wildcat, how about you girls use the shower back there to clean up? We'll handle Nicole." He leans down to kiss the top of my head, but I pull back.

"Nope! I need to clean myself off before either one of you kisses me." Instead, I blow them a kiss which has them smiling. Ripping off my gloves, I toss them onto the plastic.

Making sure I don't step off the plastic, I pick my bag up off the table and carefully hold it away from my body.

Jax hands me another bag and puts some cheap flip-flops for me and Sasha on the ground. "Here, Kiddo, put your clothes and shoes in this bag. We'll burn everything when we're done."

"Thanks, Jax." Slipping out of my shoes, I leave them on the plastic and slide my feet into the flip-flops.

As I pass my guys, Dragon swats my ass. I roll my eyes at him but can't stop my grin. His grin is blinding, but I also see his face pinched in worry. Hopefully, after this week, he and the rest of the guys will learn not to pull shit like this again. Either that, or he's worried about how I'll cope with what I've just done. It's probably a little of both.

Ducking into the bathroom in the back of the interrogation room, Sasha and I quickly strip, putting all our clothes in the paper bag. I definitely got messier out of the two of us, but I get not wanting to take the chance that some of Sasha's clothes could be saved. We don't want anything traced back to us.

"Shit! It's almost 4 pm. We gotta hurry," Sasha says, and I glance up at the clock.

"Fuck. Hopefully, the other ladies are doing okay with the prep work."

I hop into the shower without waiting for the water to warm up. Lathering up, I make sure to scrub every inch of my body. Then, because I'm paranoid, I do it again.

"Shit, I should have taken my hair out, out there," I mutter as I begin taking out my bun. Poking my head out of the stall, I toss the hair ties in the bag before I begin the huge task of washing my hair.

My hair has always been hard to take care of and tame because it's so thick and gets frizzy so easily. It seems like it takes forever before all the soap runs out of my hair.

Finally, when I think I've scrubbed everywhere and gotten everything out of my hair, I shut the water off and start drying off before getting dressed.

Running my fingers through my hair, I try to tame my locks and put it up in a messy bun as best as I can. I should really stock a few things down here to make things easier next time.

That thought causes my brain to stutter, unlike before. Why does that thought hit me harder now than earlier?

Probably because you aren't wrapped up in the moment anymore.

I look at my reflection in the mirror, but it's still the same ol' me staring back.

Sighing, I rub my temples. Am I really okay with doing this for the club when needed?

I don't even have to hesitate.

Absolutely.

They're all my family and I'll do what's needed to keep them safe.

Sasha bumps my shoulder while watching me. "You okay?"

"Yeah." Sighing again, I nod. "Yeah. I think I am. We got what we needed out of her. Hopefully, the guys found the bag before Fang and his minions planted the other cameras."

I frown as I lean against the sink while she finishes getting ready. "What did she mean by 'going back to where it all started'?"

Sasha shrugs and I gnaw on my lip as I try to think back to if I had ever seen Fang growing up, but nothing's coming to mind. Did he mean back at college, since that was where we started going out? He can't mean that run-down cabin they took Mom and me to before. Dad and Uncle Bear made sure it burned down to the ground that night seven years ago.

Sasha picks up our bag of soiled clothes and I push those thoughts to the back of my mind for now. I can think about it later.

"Never mind. Let's go give the bag to the guys and then help the girls finish supper," I say, and can't help the grin that forms.

Sasha smirks and winks at me as she opens the door. Hopefully, we can pull this off tonight before the guys realize what we're planning.

"This is everything," Sasha calls out as we walk the perimeter of the room. The guys moved enough plastic that we wouldn't have to touch it. Nicole's body has already been lowered down to the ground and it looks like the guys are cleaning the tools. I slip my engagement ring and cut back on, surprised when a feeling of calmness flows through me at having both of them back on.

"Just set it down on the plastic and we'll take care of the rest," Dragon tells me. Looking around, I notice that Bones has left, but my guys, Patch, and Jax are still here.

"In that case then, we're going to go and finish helping prepare supper," I say, but then Thor snags my wrist, pulling me close.

"Earlier, I was torn about whether or not we should ask if you'd be willing to do this. However, you are *never* to sneak down here again without telling me first. That said, thank you." He pauses as he looks me over and studies my face closely. "Now, how are you doing, Wildcat? Where's your mind at on this?"

"Understood." I exhale heavily. "Honestly, I think I'm okay. I haven't had a lot of time to process it, but I really do think I'll be good." I pause, needing him to know the reasoning behind my actions. "I meant what I said earlier. If doing this when we have women suspects is what I need to do to help protect my family, then I'll do it."

"You mean, we," Sasha says as she wraps an arm around my shoulders. "You don't have to carry this burden alone. I'll be right there with you."

"Are you sure?" I ask at the same time Thor says, "You don't have to."

"**Конечно** [Of course]! Besides, it will be better having both of us being able to do this. Especially since I bet your men won't let you do this once the baby gets much bigger. Levi, you know you can trust me to never say anything about this. Besides, I have a feeling I'll be part of the MC life for good before long," she says with a wink and my chest warms that she's okay and she'll be sticking around.

"If you do need to talk to someone about what we do down here, then search me out and we'll talk. Though you do have a point on the baby," I say and then wince. "Sorry—I forgot to tell you guys that she knows. She brought out booze after this morning's mess and without thinking, I told her I couldn't drink. She swore she wouldn't tell anyone. Wait, does Alexei or Colt know?"

Sasha shakes her head. "I don't think Alexei suspects anything, but it's going to be very hard to keep the secret if he asks me point blank. You know how we are with the twin thing. And the same goes for you, Levi. I'm here if you need to talk as well."

"If Alexei does do that and happens to find out about the baby, please stress that he can't tell anyone until we announce it at the competition," Thor says, spearing her with a hard look.

"He wouldn't do anything to jeopardize our **семья** [family]. If he finds out, he'll keep mum on it. Now come on, Levi. We need to go help finish prepping supper."

She tugs on my hand and Thor lets me go after placing a quick peck on my lips. Not to be outdone, Dragon swoops in and kisses me as well.

Saying goodbye to Jax and Patch, we head upstairs and leave them to handle Nicole. I'm not sure how they're going to dispose of her body, but maybe it's best that I don't know. I'm sure at some point I'll ask, but not right now.

In no time, we're back in the main room. Rounding the corner into the kitchen, I'm surprised it's just Roxy in here cutting onions.

"Hey Roxy, sorry about taking so long. How's everything going food-wise?"

"No worries, girl. Sarah and Amy helped me prep the 'you know what' and they're in their milk baths in the fridge." She pauses as she looks up at the clock. "We put them in there about forty minutes ago and they should soak for an hour or two in total from what I've read. Since we only had the onions and salad left to do, I told the ladies I could finish that up. Unless you want another side to go with it?"

While I want to teach the guys a lesson, I also want to make sure they don't go hungry. At the same time, I don't want to give them too many 'extras' that they don't eat everything. Walking over to the fridges, I peek through them to see what all we have. "Let's add a bit of bacon that's been diced up over the 'you know what'. I remember Dad eating them that way all the time."

Roxy crinkles her nose and shivers. Sasha laughs at her look of disgust.

"God, I can't believe people actually like that stuff," Roxy whispers since a lot of the guys are out in the common room.

"What do you think about potatoes and gravy as the other side dish?"

"Oh, yes! Gotta have potatoes and gravy. Pleeeease?" Sasha begs as she gives me puppy dog eyes.

I laugh as Sasha practically drools. I swear the girl could have potatoes and gravy at every meal and still not get sick of it. At my nod, she damn near skips over to the pantry and grabs a sack of potatoes while I start pulling out what I'll need to cut up for the salad.

A bit of guilt creeps in that the Prospects are going to have to go through this too even though they didn't know anything about what was going on. However, there isn't a good explanation I can give that wouldn't end up in shitty chores for the Prospects in retaliation. Thankfully, Alexei and Colt were good sports about it, and Alexei warned Colt to make sure he has Rolaids or Tums on hand this week.

Chapter 33

Dragon

IT TAKES US AN hour to prep Nicole's body since we brought in Alexei, Travis, and Ethan to show them how we handle this. While some MC's may not agree with having Prospects help with this sort of thing, we've implemented harsh punishments should we find out a Prospect that doesn't make the cut ever spouts off about what we have to do sometimes. Harsh as in they'd be lying in a dirt bed harsh.

Once we explained that and they all swore their agreement, we went through our sterilization process. We took turns showering and showed the guys where they could store extra clothes down here for when this happens. In the meantime, they used some spare club shirts and sweats.

As we walk upstairs, I try to push down my irritation that Spitfire thought she had to go behind our backs to question Nicole. After this morning's bust, I had thought about asking her if she'd be willing to do it as Thor had, but I also didn't want her to feel pressured into doing it. Then again, maybe her way was better.

Sighing, I head to the bar and Drae hands me a drink. Seeing Bear over by the pool tables, I head over to him.

"Hey Dragon. Wanna play?"

"Sure. Rack 'em up."

He starts racking the remaining balls on the table and I go around to each pocket, pulling out the rest. Grabbing a cue stick, I chalk the end.

Bear reaches into his cut and pulls something out, popping it in his mouth before offering me one.

"Rolaids? What the hell, brother? Worried that much about a game?"

He grins and shakes his head. "Trust me on this. Take one and you'll get through supper better because of it."

I stare at him, confused, and when he offers it again, I take one. "What do you mean?"

"Let's just say we're all well-versed in each other's methods of payback."

Turning, I look through the pass-through, and from what I can see; the girls are prepping onions, potatoes, and salad. What could be so wrong with that? When I turn back around, Bear's shoulders shake with laughter.

"Didn't notice the padlock on the last fridge, did ya?"

Slowly, I turn back around, and it isn't until I get further into the common room that I notice it. Turning back toward Bear, he laughs again.

"And don't get any bright ideas about picking the lock to see what's in there. They've no doubt wrapped everything in such a way that they'll know if something's been tampered with and then there'll be even more hell to pay."

He shivers and I swallow thickly. Fuck. Is this why she insisted we all be here for supper?

An hour and a half later, we're all lounging around the common room when someone bangs on a pot.

"All right everyone, we're going to be doing things a little differently for supper tonight. Please take a seat and dinner will be out for you shortly. If Prospects not on bar duty could come and help carry out plates, that would be much appreciated," Levi calls out across the room.

I catch Thor's gaze and notice him swallowing thickly. Honestly, I'm a little glad he's getting squeamish. Glancing around the room, everyone except for her family members seem oblivious to what's about to happen.

Everyone heads to the bar where Drae's handing out drinks. Grabbing a beer, I find a table and sit down. I wonder if the ladies will also be eating the same thing as us? Hell, for that matter, will the Prospects too?

Between the bunnies, Prospects, Sasha, Roxy, and Spitfire, they make quick work of bringing out plates. I'm surprised there are domes on them. I didn't even know we had them.

When all the plates are passed out, each person takes a table and Levi comes to ours. She starts it off by pulling the dome off Thor's plate and then goes around the table removing the rest of the domes.

"Enjoy," she says with a smirk before putting a piece of paper face down on the table and walking off to help some of the bigger tables.

It takes me a bit before I realize what's on my plate.

Liver and onions with bacon sprinkled over the top. For sides, there's a salad and potatoes n' gravy.

I have to bite my lip as I look over at Thor, who's staring at his plate like it's going to kill him. Fuck, he hates liver and onions. Dad always loved it and we had it at least a couple of times a month. I actually like liver and onions, and now that I think about it, this may be one of the few things Thor and I disagree about.

Looking around the table, Judge, Patch, and Bones are also staring at their food. Figuring I think I may know what's on the piece of paper, I pick it up, determined to mess with them some more. Serves the fuckers right.

"Tonight, we have pan-seared liver and onions topped with bacon bits, along with a side salad and potatoes n' gravy. Bon appétit," I say in as much of a foreign accent as I can muster.

Thor and Judge glare at me. At the table next to us, Bear and Alexei are trying their hardest not to laugh as they glance between us. Guess they must have heard me.

Cutting into the liver, I take a bite and damn near moan. *Holy fuck, that's good.*

"Fuck, this is better than Mom's. Eat up, Thor 'ol boy. Don't want to hurt our Old Lady's feelings by not eating her food."

He glares at me, and I'm sure I'm going to pay for taunting him later, but I don't give a fuck.

Slowly, everyone around me starts to dig in. The response is a mixture of praise as much as some gagging going on.

While I'm aware that this is some sort of fluke that I actually like this meal, I'm sure there'll be others this week that I'll be glaring at as hard as Thor's glaring at his meal right now.

I notice that most of my brothers are trying to eat their liver along with a bite of onions or potatoes. It's then that I notice those two helpings are larger than the liver and salad servings. Even though I know she's trying to teach us a lesson, at least she gave them side dishes instead of just the liver. That would have been fucking hell for those that don't like liver if she only served the liver and onions.

I finish my meal in record time and take my dishes into the kitchen. The ladies have been eating in here tonight and I quickly realize why. They have fruit salad, potatoes n' gravy, and a chicken breast with veggie stir-fry.

When they realize I'm in there, they're giggling quiets down and Levi seems surprised that I'm already finished. After putting my dishes in the dishwasher, I walk up behind her and hug her from behind.

"Spitfire, that was better than my mom's. Can you make that for me again sometime?"

She pulls away slightly and squints as she studies my face. "You liked it? Are you serious or just joshing me?"

"I loved it, Spitfire, seriously. Thor, on the other hand..." I trail off on purpose and look out the pass-through just in time to see him gagging slightly. Levi giggles and leans against me.

"Yeah, Babe, I'll make it again for you. My dad loves liver and onions this way. At first, I didn't like it, but over time, I grew to like it as well." She pulls me close and whispers in my ear. "Though it'll have to wait a bit as I've found out the smell of it cooking is a trigger for me."

I stare at her, confused, until she rubs her belly slightly and then it sinks in. I wrap her in a hug, kissing her cheek.

"No worries, Babe. I don't want to add more stress onto you."

She turns, kisses my cheek, and then pats my arm. "Now scoot. The ladies and I are discussing wedding stuff. Later, I need to talk to you and Thor about what you both want, but we figured we'd start on other details for right now."

"Babe, I'd marry you today if I could, and I bet Thor feels the same. Whatever you want, you'll get. This is only happening once, so I want it to be what you want."

Levi practically melts in my arms, and I'm surprised to see a lot of the women wiping a tear or two. Do men no longer react this way to marriage? Fuck, maybe I am a bit old school in this, but I paid attention to Mom when she told us about her wedding and a few of her friends' and sisters' weddings.

"I wouldn't mind getting married sooner rather than later, but I think my main problem might be the dress. I don't know how long it'll take to find one I like and then, when I do find it, how long it will take to alter it if need be."

"Do you want to have the ceremony in a church, or would you like something outdoors?"

"Probably outdoors. Oh! Do you think we could have it here?" Her eyes are sparkling with excitement and fuck does that floor me.

"Yeah, Spitfire, I'm sure we can have it here. You know, I think Reaper's actually an ordained minister. He did it so he could officiate when his cousin got married. Maybe he could officiate for us. If he's still licensed, that is."

Levi jumps off her stool and hugs me. "Yes, I'd love to have him marry us if he's still licensed!"

Laughing, I squeeze her tight and place a chaste kiss on her delectable lips. "Let's ask him when he's here next."

"Okay. But now you really have to scoot! We need to get back to planning."

Laughing, I smack her ass lightly and head back into the common room. Fuck, I can't wait to marry this woman. Well, she'll actually be married to Thor, but we'll still say our vows as well.

Chapter 34
Levi

THE WEEK GOES BY quicker than I anticipated.

The guys all quickly caught onto why they were getting such unusual dishes and after the second supper, they all came forward and apologized to me. I guess Thor and Dragon really did tell them about the 'think of if your sister had had this happen to her' analogy because they all referenced it.

On Monday, we served sautéed sweetbreads, bruschetta, salad, and baked potatoes.

Tuesday was a tofu stir-fry with peppers and onions, rice, and salad. Seeing bikers eating a vegan meal will forever be ingrained in my brain. I'm pretty sure no one liked it, but it was fucking hilarious to watch their faces.

Wednesday was beef tongue, mushrooms, rice, and baked potatoes.

Thursday was a vegan lentil curry, rice, salad, and roasted broccoli and shallots.

Today is Friday and I'm pretty sure I'm going to piss off all of them, but I swear they'll be happy in the long run. Though I've decided that tonight will be the last of their 'punishment'. Tomorrow we'll go back to regular meals.

Sasha and I are outside manning the grills. The rest of the ladies are cooking up our surprise in the kitchen. We've closed the pass-through and created a 'wall' of curtains using PVC pipes so the guys can't see into the kitchen.

We only have a few more minutes on the grill, and then we'll be ready for supper.

"Sasha, give me a couple minutes and I'll come out with the large serving pans after checking in with the other women."

"**Молодец** [You got it]."

Quickly, I slip inside and, after making sure none of the men are peeking, I open the curtain, enter the kitchen, and close the curtain.

"How's it going, ladies? We're almost done out there."

"They finished resting about five minutes ago and we're almost done plating them up. The au jus sauce is in that pan, ready to go, and the veggies have…" Roxy says and then pauses as she looks at the oven timer. "Three minutes left to go. Mashed potatoes n' gravy are already ready, and the Prospects are filling the coolers with beer."

Thank God we have four ovens, otherwise, this would have been a nightmare.

The backdoor opens and I hear Sasha calling out for me.

"Okay ladies, the first round is done so we'll get that ready. Keep going and when all of us are done, we'll get the guys in the backyard."

They all voice their agreement as I pull four serving pans out from the closet as well as the aluminum foil.

Rushing back outside, I quickly help Sasha get the meat off the grill before we tent them and carry them into the kitchen.

"Hey, Wildcat?" Thor calls out from the common room.

"Ladies keep going. I'm going to see what Thor wants. It's probably our guest."

Giggles fill the room and it's hard to keep a smile off my face as I quickly go out into the common room.

"What's up, Hun?"

"Ethan says there's a guy here to see you? Name's Carter?"

"Oh yes! He's the new vet in town. He put up a few fliers around town asking for donations for the animals that get surrendered for various reasons. I told him to stop by and I'd see what we could find for him."

"Wildcat," Thor growls.

"What?" I say innocently.

"This better not be a ploy to get us to agree to adopt a dog."

Shit, why didn't I think of that as an excuse?

"No, no, it's not. Though I really do want one," I say as I bat my eyes at him. He curses under his breath and I have to bite my cheek to keep from laughing.

He stomps out the front door, and I rush back into the kitchen. The ladies help me carry the serving pans out to the common room and the rest of the ladies follow us.

We've just set them in place when Thor comes in, followed by Carter.

I whistle to get everyone's attention.

"All right everyone. It's finally Friday, which means there's a party tonight." I pause as cheers erupt throughout the room. "So, come on up and grab supper."

Once the guys all crowd forward, the ladies and I start removing the aluminum foil when, all of a sudden, they stop in their tracks. You could hear a pin drop.

They all stare at the overdone steaks. Their gazes bounce back and forth between the steaks and me.

"Am I correct in assuming that you've all learned your lesson?"

Instantly I'm bombarded with damn near yells of agreement, and I can't hold it in anymore. I bust out laughing, which triggers the rest of the ladies' laughter as well.

"Spitfire, why are all you ladies laughing so hard?"

Damn, some of them look downright pissed right now. Maybe I pushed a little too far tonight.

"Because," I start as I wipe a tear from my eye. "These are steaks we bought off a butcher to cook for Carter for him to give to his animals at the vet clinic. It's going to be chopped up and mixed in with their gravy and some other cooked veggies. Come on into the kitchen for your *real* dinner. It's prime rib tonight."

Carter is looking around, extremely confused, I might add, and I wave him back. "Come on Carter, there's enough for you, too. We'll get this packaged up for you, and if you want to stick around for a while, we'll put the steaks in the fridge for you."

He gives me a hesitant nod, and I make a point to seek him out later and fill him in.

The guys damn near stampede into the kitchen and I'm glad the other girls moved aside our make-shift PVC pipe curtain dividers that we used.

"Oh, wait. If I'm going to stay for a bit, I need to get Bastion out of the car."

"Bastion?"

"Yeah. I got a call from a friend that works in a vet's clinic a few towns over. He had a retired police-trained pitbull that had been surrendered when his owner passed away. Bastion won't listen to anyone else's commands and is refusing to eat. My friend called me to see if I might be able to help him."

"Oh, my God! By all means, yes, go get him and I'll dig out a can of food that we got for a donation as well in case he changes his mind. Meet me around back. I'm sure Bastion would like to sniff around where he'll be for a while."

Carter smiles and heads back outside. Damn, if I didn't already have my guys, I'm sure that smile would have melted me.

Turning to walk down the hallway, the guys are practically blocking the way. "Excuse me gents, I need to get something quick for Carter."

They step to the side and I'm able to slip through. Quickly, I head straight to the pantry, ripping the plastic surrounding the cans of dog food, and dig out two bowls. Turning, I pause when I notice Dragon and a few of the others watching me.

"What's with the dog food? I thought it was for donation?"

"Actually, Carter just said that he came from his friend's clinic. They had a retired-police force pitbull whose owner recently passed away. He's been refusing to eat. They were hoping that Carter would be able to help Bastion to the point where he was at least able to eat again. I figured we'd try some of the food to see if he'd change his mind and eat."

"Well, damn, Spitfire. I hope Carter's able to help the poor guy."

Nodding in agreement, I grab a water bottle out of the fridge and head out back.

Carter rounds the corner and I damn near fall in love with Bastion. His coat is a beautiful brindle coloring with white socks on each paw. I'm relieved to see that his ears aren't cropped. I hate when people do that to their dogs.

Seeing me, Carter leads Bastion over to me and I'm surprised that he's able to keep the leash fully relaxed. Then again, he said Bastion was a police dog, so he must be very well-trained, so I guess that shouldn't surprise me. When they reach me, Carter stops, and Bastion sits next to him, even though Carter didn't say a command.

"Hello, Bastion." I hold my hand out for him to sniff, which he does before he licks my hand. I can't help the giggle that escapes from the feel of his tongue on my palm.

Bastion gets up, leaves Carter's side, and sits next to me. I look up at Carter, confused.

"What just happened?"

He smiles and hands me Bastion's lead. "I think I know, but let's try it out first. How about we go over by the firepit, and you try feeding him?"

"Um, okay. Come on, Bastion. You hungry?"

Bastion gets up quickly and starts wagging his tail as he gives me a huge doggy smile, making me laugh again. I lead him over to the fire pit that's a little further from where the others are milling about. I don't want Bastion to feel spooked.

Crouching down, I'm about to set things down when I notice he's sniffing the air like he wants to inspect what's in my hands. First, I hold out both bowls, and when he stops sniffing them, I place them on the ground. I repeat the process with the can of food and water bottle. Once he sniffs everything, he sits down. I guess that means everything passes his test?

Pulling the tab on the food, I dump the contents into one bowl and then crack the seal on the water and fill the second bowl. Setting the bowls beside the chair, I stand and then sit in the chair next to Bastion while loosely holding his lead.

Almost instantly, he starts to eat, and I turn to Carter, shocked.

"What the hell just happened? I thought no one could get him to eat?"

"That's what they said, but somehow, you got him to eat. I think Bastion just adopted you."

I stare at him, shocked. "What?"

"Keep in mind that I don't know everything they train dogs for on the police force, but I think when he left me and went to you, that was him sort of claiming you. Add to that, you picked up on what he wanted, and let him sniff what you had in your hands. We'll see what he does when he finishes, but I'm pretty sure he's picked his new owner."

Dumbfounded and still shocked, I turn my attention back to Bastion, who's already finished his food and is currently drinking the water. He gets up, goes to the other side of my chair, sits down, and rests his head on my leg.

Slowly, I reach out and pet his head. His eyes close as he leans further into me.

Carter's shoulders shake with the laughter he's trying to hold in.

"Hey Wildcat, Dragon told me about Bastion. Were you able to get him to eat?"

Bastion's ears perk up and he gets up, sitting in front of me as he looks straight ahead at Thor. A low growl rumbles out of him. Does he think he needs to protect me? Thor stops, but his gaze bounces between Bastion, Carter, and me. Dragon joins us and stands next to Thor.

I stand but keep a hold of Bastion's lead, and slowly sidestep around him since he was practically sitting on my feet. Walking toward my guys, I hug and then kiss Thor before hugging and kissing Dragon.

Looking back at Bastion, I hope he's able to see how relaxed I am and that none of the guys here are a threat to him.

Surprisingly, Bastion walks up to Thor and sits in front of him. He holds his hand out, and Bastion sniffs it before licking his palm, just like he did with me. Then he does the same to Dragon. However, that isn't near as surprising as what happened next.

Bastion comes back over to me, grabs the lead that's dangling loosely in my hand with his teeth, and walks back over to where I was sitting and lays down.

"Um, what just happened?" Dragon asks and Carter laughs.

"I'd say Bastion just adopted you three."

Thor groans but Dragon practically runs over to Bastion, sits next to him, and starts petting him.

"Are you not a dog person, Thor?" Carter asks and Thor sighs.

"I'm more of a cat person and as you can see, Dragon's more of a dog person."

"Well, I know for a fact that cats don't bother Bastion. His owner also had three adult cats and they all got along."

"How is he with kids? Someday we might have them around here and I don't want anyone to get injured," I ask and try not to give away that I'm pregnant.

"His owner had her grandchildren over frequently and he was good around them. If they pulled on his ears or tail, he'd growl but wouldn't snap at them."

I look up at Thor, hopeful, and he lets loose a resigned sigh. "Since it looks like he's already claimed us, let's see how tonight goes when he meets the rest of the guys."

A happy squeal escapes me, and I jump at Thor, hugging him tight and peppering his face with kisses. "Thank you!"

He laughs and lands a passionate kiss on my lips.

A throat clears behind us, and when I pull away, I notice Carter's trying to look anywhere but at us.

"Sorry. How about we head in and get some food? Dragon, do you want me to grab you a plate since you seem pretty content where you are?"

He laughs and nods. Smiling, I head into the clubhouse with Thor and Carter. I can't wait to introduce Bastion to everyone.

Chapter 35
Thor

It's been a week since our last punishment supper, and I think the guys all got Wildcat's message loud and clear.

Bastion has been settling in nicely and follows Levi everywhere. A couple of days after he came here, the son of his previous owner, Matthew, who's also in the police force, came by to teach us the commands that Bastion knew.

While Matthew was skeptical of us at first because of the club, he quickly warmed up to us. Later I found out that was because of how calm Bastion was here and around everyone. If we had been doing anything illegal, like running drugs, Bastion would have been able to sniff them out and alerted him. Thank fuck we aren't into that. Though, I don't think Bastion would have claimed us if he had smelled anything of the sort.

We also found out that neither Matthew, his siblings, or any of their spouses and children were able to get Bastion to eat after his mother's death. Their local vet was also at a loss for what to do and Matthew's family wasn't able to afford to keep him on IV nutrients long-term. It seemed like Bastion had given up the will to live. In the hopes of finding someone that could help him, they made the heartbreaking decision to release him to a no-kill shelter, hoping that finding someone new to bond to would help bring him back from the ledge. Even though I was hesitant at first about adopting him, I'm glad he was able to bond to Wildcat. I would have hated to see Bastion, or any animal for that matter, succumb to his grief.

I also spoke to Matthew about a few things I'd noticed with Levi. Her anxiety has been through the roof, but somehow, Bastion's able to sense it and nudges her whenever it gets bad. She'll start to pet him and then her body will start to relax. Apparently, Bastion was also trained to pick up on certain signals, like Wildcat's anxiety, and react accordingly. Since he can no longer wear his police dog vest, Matthew brought us a service dog vest just in case we needed it for her.

Unfortunately, her anxiety today is worse than anything we've seen so far. Probably because today's the day her uncle Sean is being released from prison. Also, the fact that yesterday we heard back from Creed about the location where Fang had been holding the women. Somehow, Fang had been tipped off, and they were gone by the time Creed and his men showed up, but there was proof they were there recently. Recent as in they'd left probably only a couple hours before Creed got there even though our scouts didn't see anyone leave.

Sighing, I glance over at Levi again. I wish we could have brought Bastion with us. We're on our way to Wildcat's first doctor appointment and she's been constantly wringing her hands together ever since we left the compound. Today, we're in our truck and we've got Ryder, Smoke, Travis, and Ethan, riding point. Reaching across the console, I take her hand and intertwine our fingers together.

"Wildcat, it'll be okay. I'm sure the baby is healthy. Plus, we can talk to the doc about if Bastion will be able to come to future appointments."

She sighs and squeezes my hand. "I don't know why I'm so nervous," she whispers. "I have this really weird feeling and I don't know if it's just nerves about our baby, Uncle Sean, or Fang. Or something else entirely. Or even, all of the above."

Looking in the rearview mirror, my gaze locks with Dragon's. In our short time together, we've heard stories about Levi's feelings and usually, how things go to shit not too long afterward. We'll have to be even more careful now that we're in town.

We pull up in front of the doctor's office, which I'm happy to see is not too far from the hospital if an emergency comes up later in her pregnancy. As I park; I glance around. There are a few people out and about, which isn't too unusual for 8 am on a Friday. No one's acting suspicious at least. Getting out, I walk over to Levi's door but Dragon's already opening it for her and shielding her back.

When she steps up onto the sidewalk, my brothers and I all surround her as we make our way inside. We get a few stares as we walk, but Levi's safety is top priority right now.

We head straight in and Levi continues to the check-in desk. Dragon and I follow her, while the others break off and sit down in the chairs along the back wall of the waiting area. We get quite a few stares from the women here already waiting, but at least no one hassles us.

The lady at the check-in desk, whose badge says her name is Daphne, looks like she's about to drool all over herself, but as we get closer, I scowl when she's practically eye-fucking us.

"Hello, how can I help you?" she practically purrs and leans forward, pushing her chest out. Can't she see that we're obviously with Wildcat?

"Hello, Daphne. I'm Levi Wallace and I would appreciate it if you'd stop eye-fucking my fiancés. I have an appointment with Dr. Rowen."

I bite my cheek to keep from laughing, but Dragon's not as successful. Both of us wrap our arms around her waist and kiss her temples. Daphne's face turns red and she glares at Wildcat before turning and angrily typing on her keyboard.

"Insurance card and driver's license?" she asks, her voice clipped in irritation and annoyance.

Wildcat pulls out her wallet and hands her the cards. Actually, that reminds me, I need to get her on our insurance.

While she gets the rest of Wildcat's information, Daphne keeps sending us flirty looks, which pisses me off more. It's our first time here, and I don't really want to make a scene unless it's necessary. But if she keeps this up, all bets are off.

Daphne opens a file drawer, pulls a few forms out, scribbles a few things on them, and hands Levi the clipboard. She smiles smugly at her before her gaze roams over Dragon and me hungrily once again.

Fuck, I really want to put this woman in her place.

Daphne bats her eyelashes at us, and Wildcat clears her throat. I have to really bite my tongue not to go off on her. Daphne's gaze returns to Wildcat, and she scowls again.

"Fill these out. You can give them to your nurse when you're called back."

"Thank you." Even though she's polite, I can tell her voice is tight with anger.

We walk over to sit near my brothers, whose shoulders are shaking with laughter.

"God, I'd love to gouge her eyes out," Levi mutters. Sitting down next to her, I drape my arm over the back of her chair, and she starts filling out her health history.

I lean over and whisper to Smoke. "Keep your eyes peeled. Wildcat started having some weird feelings on the drive over here."

His face hardens and his eyes darken at the thought of her in danger. Though I know part of his anger is also because his sister, Nikki, works as a nurse here. That's part of why we chose this place.

Levi and Smoke have gotten really close this past week and even had some video calls with Nikki and her daughter, Sadie. Both of them are going to be coming to the clubhouse this weekend to get to know Levi better. It will be their first time coming to the compound.

Smoke turns to look around and I know he's probably wishing he had his laptop so he could run security.

Glancing down at Levi, she's still filling out paperwork and reading through some of the notes that were given to her. I turn, about to ask Ryder something, when I feel Levi's body tensing.

"That fucking cunt," Levi hisses before she jumps up to her feet, storming back over to Daphne, who's talking with an older nurse. Dragon and I are quickly on our feet, following her. What the hell did that bitch pull now?

They both look up at her when she stops in front of the station, surprised.

"I want to speak to the head OB doctor," Levi demands as she stares down Daphne.

"What seems to be the problem?" the older woman, Doris, asks.

"I have an appointment with Dr. Rowen today to see how everything's going with my baby since we recently found out I'm pregnant. However, included with the patient health history paperwork, Daphne here, gave me paperwork to finalize setting up an abortion." She pauses as she holds up the paperwork, and I hear a thunder of boots behind us. Both women pale when my brothers are instantly at our backs.

"To top it off, some information was already filled in for me. The part where it asks if I've given consent is already checked off, which I did not check. The area where it asks for the father's name has 'father unknown' already filled out. And where it asks for my occupation, 'club slut' is already filled out. The reason for wanting an abortion is already filled out as being because 'I have no idea who the father is and I have mental health issues'. Oh, and the signature on the bottom, as well as the rest of the paperwork, *is not in my frickin' handwriting!*"

Rage fills me as I take the paperwork from Levi and notice that it definitely is not her damn near perfect cursive handwriting. No, this handwriting is barely legible.

"Get us the head doctor. Now," I demand as I stare down Doris.

"There's no need for that, gentlemen. The paperwork must have been mixed up by accident. It happens sometimes," Doris says in an overly sweet manner, though her body posture and facial expressions say another thing entirely.

"It wasn't. We saw Daphne get the papers out of the filing cabinet, write on them and hand them to Levi. There was no mix-up," Dragon says icily.

"If you're going to take that attitude with me, young man, then I'll be calling security to escort you out of here," Doris says as she glares at him.

"The issue is not with my fiancés. It's with your nurse, and pretty soon, you as well. Now, I want to speak to the head doctor. Neither of my fiancés are leaving and neither are our other family members. Bring us the head doctor. Now," Levi demands.

"I'll get Dr. Rowen," another nurse who'd recently entered the nurse station said, though I notice she sounds fucking happy to be getting him for us. Do they normally have issues with these two women?

A few minutes later, the nurse returns along with a doctor and another woman trailing him.

The doctor steps forward, offering a hand, and I'm relieved its Dr. Rowen.

"Hello, everyone. I'm Dr. Rowen."

"Levi Wallace," Levi says as she shakes his hand. "These are my fiancés, Thor and Dragon, as well as my brother, Smoke, and a few other members of our family."

Dr. Rowen looks between Levi and the other nurse, that I now see has a name badge of 'Nikki' on her scrubs. When Nikki nods at him, he smiles and almost seems... relieved? Is this Smoke's sister or is there another Nikki working here?

"What seems to be the issue, Miss Wallace?"

"The vast majority of the paperwork I'd been given is fine. Normal patient history and such. However, the last few pages were paperwork I *did not* request and was filled out by Daphne." She pauses and hands him the clipboard. "You can tell from the previous pages that our handwriting is nothing alike."

His face hardens when Wildcat's done talking and then he turns, leveling an icy stare at Daphne, then at Doris. He flips to the beginning of the paperwork and looks through everything. When he gets to the last page, his jaw ticks repeatedly.

"Stacy, please take these and make copies for me. Quickly. Nikki, call Trent and Zach."

"If you have these hooligans under control, Dr. Rowen, I'll see to the other patients for the time being."

"Doris, stay where you are," Dr. Rowen says politely, but I can tell his words are clipped.

No one talks and I notice Doris and Daphne are looking rather smug with themselves. Daphne continues to practically eye-fuck every one of us while we're waiting. It takes everything in me not to fucking snap at her.

A few minutes later, two bald-headed men, who look like they're twins and could very well have been linemen back in the day, come down the hallway.

"Thank you for coming, gentlemen. Doris and Daphne are being let go. After they gather everything at their desks, I need you to escort them to the lockers so they can collect their things. Then escort them off the premises."

"Wha-what? I didn't do anything wrong!" Doris cries.

"Doris, you have been reprimanded time and time again about allowing this to happen as the charge nurse as well as Daphne's mother, since she's the one that usually starts these messes. This is *not* the first time someone's been given abortion paperwork when they never requested it. You may be my late mentor's widow, but I will not allow this discrimination and harassment to continue in this office."

"You're punishing us when sluts like her shouldn't even be allowed to reproduce? She's obviously pulled one over on these guys to score herself not one, but two of these bikers. She doesn't even know which one of them is the father!"

"Daphne," Doris hisses, but Daphne ignores her.

"No, Mom. Dr. Rowen is ruining Dad's practice. He's continuing to let filth like her in here, not caring if the child ever knows the father, and is just going to be leeching off of us normal people when they go on food stamps! For all we know, she could be screwing all the Steel Archangel bikers!"

My anger's damn near boiling as Daphne continues to spew her hate. Glancing at Levi, she's beyond pissed and is clenching her hands repeatedly, something I've learned she does when she knows she shouldn't reach for a blade. Fuck.

"Dr. Rowen, if we could please move this along, I really don't want my fiancée to continue to listen to this hate. It can't be good for our baby or for her to get this worked up."

His gaze cuts to Levi, who must also see her veins about to pop as she resists going after Daphne. He gives me a curt nod.

"Zach, Trent, take them both away."

"About time," Zach mutters as he removes Doris' badge and hands it to Dr. Rowen. Trent does the same with Daphne's badge, before they escort them both, screaming down the hallway.

Dr. Rowen steps further out into the waiting room.

"I apologize for this outburst. We will be with you all shortly." He turns back toward us. "Nikki, if you could please take Miss Wallace and her fiancés to their room, I will be in in a moment."

He steps over to Stacy to gather the copies and talks with her quietly.

Nikki nods to Smoke before leading us down the hallway. She gets Levi's weight and height and then brings us into a patient room.

Once we're in the room with the door shut, Nikki wraps Levi in a hug.

"I'm so sorry that this is how we met the first time in person, but I can't tell you how happy I am to see those fucking bitches walked out of here!"

Levi laughs along with Nikki, but I can tell it's strained.

"Now, let's get you settled in and fill out a few more questions I have for you. I'll wait to take your blood pressure and check your pulse until you're able to calm down a bit more."

It's surprising to see how fast she can flip into nurse mode.

"Thank you so much, Nikki. I was secretly hoping you'd be my nurse today. Actually, is there any way I can request you as my nurse going forward? Besides not knowing if there are any more Doris or Daphne's still employed here, I'd love to be able to have you by my side as your niece or nephew grows bigger."

"I'm sure Dr. Rowen will allow it as long as I'm not already tied up with other patients. Besides, you helped him get rid of two of our major pain in the asses. They seem to think they can play God here just because Doris' late husband, Dr. Dalton, was the head doctor here for years. He was super religious and would only take clients that he knew were of 'good standing family values'. If any of the other doctors took patients with 'suspect origins', they never heard the end of it. They usually didn't last longer than a year because of Dr. Dalton." Nikki rolls her eyes.

"There are many other reasons why women get pregnant, but if they aren't married to a man first, then he wouldn't treat them. Until Dr. Rowen started here, most pregnant women I know usually went to nearby towns to see OB-GYN's there."

She scoffs, but I can see the anger behind her words. Fuck. Did this Dr. Dalton mess with her when she was pregnant with Sadie? I'm not sure who Sadie's father is, but I know he isn't in the picture according to Smoke.

Nikki switches back to nurse mode and takes notes on Levi's family history. Just as she finishes, there's a knock at the door, and Dr. Rowen enters.

"Levi, Thor, and Dragon, I sincerely want to apologize for what happened with Doris and Daphne. I hope they haven't deterred you from using me or the rest of my staff, though if it has, I know quite a few surrounding doctors that are accepting new patients."

"Thank you. Dr. Rowen. We'd like to stay here if at all possible. Though to be honest, if you had kept Doris and Daphne here after that fiasco, I would be going elsewhere," Levi says, and Dr. Rowen sighs.

"I am extremely sorry that you had to experience that. They've been given several notices, but I honestly think they thought they were above the law. They can't continue to harass patients because of who they're seeing or how they got pregnant."

He pauses as he shakes his head, but then seems to snap out of his train of thought.

"So, Nikki tells me that you just recently found out you were pregnant. Is that correct?"

"Yes. My brother, Smoke, as well as our friend Patch, who's a nurse in the hospital's ER, suspected I was pregnant a couple of weeks ago. I then took some home tests, and they came back positive."

Fuck am I glad she didn't mention Patch running that test for her. I know he did it under the radar and I don't want him getting into trouble because of us.

Dr. Rowen's gaze bounces back and forth between Nikki and Levi, who absolutely look nothing alike. Whereas Nikki is taller, skinnier, and blond, Levi is a bit shorter, curvier, and has flaming red hair.

"Smoke is my chosen brother, not blood brother, which also extends to his sister and niece. Blood isn't the only family tie. I mean, I'm sure people have blood family that they wished they were never related to." Levi pauses, and I can't help but squeeze her hand, knowing she's thinking of her uncle Sean. She clears her throat and continues. "I have a lot of chosen family members, but that also means our baby, and any future babies, will have a large family that loves each other regardless of their origins."

Dr. Rowen smiles and nods. "I completely understand where you're coming from. Now, switching gears, based on your last period, it looks like you could be about seven weeks along. Nikki, if you could please get her out a gown and blanket? I'll ask the technician to come in to give you an ultrasound. Then I'll be in to answer any questions."

"Doctor, is it okay if Nikki stays here for the ultrasound? I'd like her to see our baby if at all possible."

"Of course. Would you like your brother to come back too?"

Levi looks over at Nikki, raising a brow in question.

"He didn't get squeamish with Sadie, so I'm sure he'll be fine."

"Then, yes, if Smoke could come back here as well, I'd appreciate it."

Dr. Rowen nods and steps out of the room. Nikki opens a cupboard and pulls out some square paper things.

"I'll step out and go get Jax so you can change into the gown. The opening goes to the back. Your bra can stay on, but your underwear needs to come off. Once the technician is here, Jax and I will come back in if you're ready."

"Thank you, Nikki."

"No problem, girl. Can't wait to see my niece or nephew! Thank you for letting me watch," she says as she gives Levi another hug, then steps out.

Levi slips off her boots and strips. Fuck, just seeing her mostly naked has me wanting her again.

"Later, Ryan."

Smirking at her, I blatantly rearrange myself.

"I don't know how you two are getting turned on right now. I'm in a fuckin paper gown," she huffs as she sits down on the exam table and lays the paper blanket over her legs.

Leaning forward, I give her a chaste kiss even though I'd rather kiss the fuck out of her, but this isn't the time or place for that. "I get turned on all the time when you're around, and now you're growing our baby, Wildcat. That's even sexier."

"Same, Spitfire."

She rolls her eyes, but her smile gets bigger at our words. A few moments later, someone knocks.

"You can come in," she calls out.

Nikki comes in with Smoke right behind her and another woman. Smoke comes over and stands next to me. Why the hell is he crowding over here when there's plenty of room over by the technician?

Wildcat must see my confusion because she bites her lip and her shoulders shake with laughter.

He smirks at me as he shakes his head. "Don't really care to see my sister's pussy, Thor."

Wait, what?

"Isn't it done with a wand and that gel shit over her stomach?" I ask.

Wildcat shakes her head.

"This early in the pregnancy, we have to do a transvaginal ultrasound," the technician says as she pulls out a long wand and puts a condom over it.

I must make a face because everyone laughs, even the damn technician. Looking over at Dragon, he seems just as confused as I am.

"Relax, guys. This is normal. I promise," Nikki says.

"Alright, time to check on your baby."

Wildcat lays down and puts her feet up in those stirrup things. The technician puts the wand inside her, then clicks a few buttons and knobs. A whoosh sound fills the air and the screen lights up.

I have no idea what I'm supposed to be looking for. All I can see is some white stuff and black areas.

The technician's forehead creases and she clicks a few more buttons. She must reposition the wand because the image changes slightly.

"Well, based on your babies' size, you are seven weeks along and their heartbeats are strong."

I blink as I stare at her. Did she just say what I think she said?

"Wait, did you just say babies? As in more than one?" Levi asks in shock.

I grin when the technician nods.

"Yup, you're pregnant with twins. Congratulations! I'll get you some pictures printed off where you can see both of them."

"Oh my gosh, congratulations," Nikki cries out and hugs Levi.

"When would she be due?" Smoke asks.

"Well, a full-term pregnancy would be February 9th, but since you're having twins, you'll most likely go into labor early. I'm sure Dr. Rowen will cover that with you in a bit."

Wildcat's staring at the screen in shock. I reach over and squeeze her hand. She turns toward me and smiles, her eyes misty with tears.

"We're having twins," she whispers and rubs her stomach with her other hand.

"We're having twins," Dragon and I say back to her in unison. I turn to Dragon, who grins and claps my shoulder. When I look back at the screen, the technician is labeling two black dots as Baby A and Baby B.

Holy shit.

I lean forward and kiss her belly.

After a couple of minutes, the technician hands Wildcat the pictures.

"Congratulations again. The doctor will be in shortly."

Levi nods absently as she stares at the pictures.

Smoke leans down and kisses the top of her head. "Congrats, Kiddo. We'll step out to give you some privacy."

"Thank you and thank you for being here with me." Levi sits up and pulls him in for a hug, which irritates the fuck out of me. She's practically naked under that thin sheet of paper.

"Settle down, caveman," Wildcat says as she shakes her head. She hugs Nikki one more time and then they leave.

"Holy shit," Levi says as she exhales loudly. Both her hands cradle her stomach. "It's really sinking in now. I'm a mom and there are two little jellybeans growing in me."

A worried look comes over her face and she bites her lip.

"What's wrong, Spitfire?"

"Having twins means I'm going to get huge. Are you guys going to still love me when I'm as big as a house? Things don't always go back to normal after you have kids. I'll probably have stretch marks and saggy skin, and..."

I cut off her rambling with a kiss. She moans and her free hand comes up to grasp my wrist. When I pull back, Dragon kisses her. When they separate, I place a hand over her stomach.

"Levi, none of that is going to change how I feel about you. I love you, Wildcat. And I love our babies."

"And that includes any shape you're in. I love you for you and already love our babies like crazy."

The smile that lights up her face is absolutely fucking gorgeous. I kiss her again but pull back when I hear a knock.

"Come in," Levi calls out.

The door opens and Dr. Rowen comes back in, smiling. "Congratulations. I heard you're having twins."

Levi nods as she looks down at the pictures again. "Thank you."

"Your due date is February 9th, however since you have twins, you'll most likely go into labor early. I can never tell you exactly how early, though. As your pregnancy progresses, we'll monitor your babies closely to make sure everything is going according to plan. I've already written you a script for prenatal vitamins. I'd like to see you again in five weeks. Do you have any questions?"

"Can we still have sex? We won't hurt the babies?" Dragon asks.

Wildcat smacks his stomach as she huffs. Honestly, I was wondering the same thing. Dr. Rowen smiles, though he seems to be trying not to laugh.

"Yes, you can still have sex. Though, as Levi gets into the later stages of her pregnancy, make sure to choose positions that don't put pressure on her belly. Also, laying on her back could put extra weight on her internal organs. As long as Levi's comfortable, then you should be fine. Of course, if there's any vaginal bleeding, then you need to call us so you can be seen right away. And that's for any time you have vaginal bleeding—not just during sex."

"Thank you, Dr. Rowen," Levi says.

"Any other questions?"

When we shake our heads, he gets up.

"Well, then I'll leave you to get dressed and will see you again in five weeks. Congratulations once again. One of the nurses will schedule your next appointment on your way out." He shakes both Dragon's and my hands, pats Levi on the knee, and then leaves.

Wildcat hops off the table and starts getting dressed again. Seeing her naked again has me instantly hard, and I groan as I adjust myself. There's no way I'm taking her in a doctor's office.

She quickly gets dressed, but then pauses as she's lacing up her boots again.

"Shit. We're going to need double everything. It's a good thing you guys built a big house."

"We built it that way hoping we'd be able to have a lot of kids, Spitfire."

She pauses, her gaze bouncing between us.

"There are six bedrooms besides ours. You guys want six kids?" The last bit is barely a whisper, and I hope we haven't freaked her out too badly.

"We'd love that many, but you're the one that will have to carry them, Wildcat. How many kids do you want to have?"

"I've always wanted three or four. It was really lonely being an only kid. Not that I'm blaming my parents or anything. I know they tried to have more. It just didn't work out that way. Though if we do have six kids, you realize we're going to have to practically soundproof our room, right?"

Shit, she's right. Levi's definitely not quiet during sex, and I've honestly wondered if Sasha can hear her sometimes.

Once she slips on her cut, we leave the room.

On the way out, she schedules her next appointment, and I immediately put it in my phone calendar, sending the meeting to both of them.

The guys come over and start teasing her on our way out.

"So, is it just one or two buns in the oven? I'm betting two since your men are twins. Smoke here won't tell us shit," Ryder says.

"It's not my news to tell, jackass," Smoke says as he thumps Ryder up against the back of his head.

"Gah, you all are acting like children," Levi mutters.

Travis throws his arm around her shoulder. "Yeah, but you know you love us and wouldn't have us any other way," he says, giving her puppy dog eyes. She smacks his stomach with the back of her hand.

"I should probably have my head examined cause, yeah, for some reason, I do. Alright. I need to get this prescription filled. Let's walk over to the pharmacy, as that's the one I usually use, and then head home. I need to make sure everything's good for the party tonight."

We all surround Levi and head outside. I listen with half an ear as I look around. I don't like the idea of walking, but it's not even two blocks down the street.

As we're walking by a café, I hear a couple of distinct pops and then grunts.

Pulling Wildcat close to my side, Dragon's instantly on her other side, both of us shielding her as we quickly run toward the nearest car.

More shots ring out, and then my shoulders burning like it's fire.

"Fuck!"

A quick glance shows blood trailing down my arm but at least it isn't at an alarming rate.

"Thor!" Levi calls out.

"Fuck, get down, Wildcat!"

I pull my gun as I scan the rooftops. Screams erupt from other people as they duck for cover as more shots are fired.

"Stay down, Spitfire."

"But you're both shot! Shit, so is Ethan!"

I pivot toward Dragon and see he's been shot in the leg. Ethan is behind the car next to ours and it looks like he's been shot in the arm. Shit.

"Where's the fucker at? I don't see him," Ryder hisses as he peaks through the car windows.

Carefully, I look over the trunk but can't see anyone.

More shots are fired, and I quickly duck back down. Tires squeal and I can hear a car racing away from us as sirens approach.

"Who the fuck was that?" Smoke grits out as he holsters his gun and puts pressure on my shoulder.

"Fuck, that hurts."

"Good, that means you're alive, asshole."

"Wildcat, are you hurt?"

"No, I don't think so. The blood is from you guys."

I wince when Smoke applies more pressure. Pain radiates down my arm as my vision blurs and I can see little black dots. Fuck, I cannot pass out.

Looking over Wildcat and my brothers more closely, I think we're the only three shot. Both Travis and Ryder are on their phones, most likely calling in the cavalry.

"Ryder, have Alexei bring my laptop," Smoke shouts at him. Ryder gives him a chin lift and after a few moments, he hangs up.

I try to slide my cut off, but I can't do it one-handed.

"Travis and Smoke, help me get my cut off so they don't cut it off me. I don't want to go to jail for killing the fucker that cuts it."

Travis is quickly by my side and I groan when he tugs a little too hard, jostling my shoulder.

"Sorry, Pres."

They quickly have my cut off and I wince again as Smoke applies more pressure. The sirens get louder and then screech to a halt.

Chapter 36

Levi

HOLY SHIT!

Someone just shot at us! In broad fucking daylight!

Dragon winces as I press harder down on his thigh. He shifts slightly and reaches into his pocket.

I snatch it out of his hand as soon as I see it's a bandana, which I quickly wrap around his thigh and tie it tightly.

"Mother fucker," he hisses.

"Sorry, Babe."

"Don't worry about it, Spitfire. It's going to take more than a bullet to take me down." He winks at me, and even though I know he's trying to lighten the mood, I'm not having it and smack his good leg.

"I'm not in a laughing mood. I could have lost you or Thor or the others. *We* could have lost you."

His face softens, and he cups my cheek. "Spitfire, I will do whatever it takes to keep all of you safe. Even if it means taking a bullet for you." He pauses and then smirks. "Besides, we're the Steel Archangel's, Babe. Your own men of steel."

This time I can't help the little chuckle that escapes, despite being fucking pissed. He knows I love the song, *Man of Steel* by Brantley Gilbert. He pulls me to his chest as the sirens stop and what sounds like an army of boots running toward us.

"Ma'am, I need you to step back so we can get closer to him."

I look up at the paramedic, but I can't seem to make my body move. A hand grabs my arm, and I'm pulled up and into a hug. I see Thor's cut in Jax's arms and tears start falling. Wiping my hands on my jeans, I take it in my hands, clutching it to my chest, while trying to not get blood on his patches. I don't feel any of Thor's weapons in his cut, so I'm assuming someone else grabbed them.

Paramedics are hovering over Thor, and when he stands to get on the gurney, he sways slightly. To my right, they already have Dragon on a gurney and Ethan is getting on his.

Glancing up and down the street, other paramedics are treating a few people who seem to have been cut from the glass of shot-out windows, but there doesn't appear to be anyone else shot. To my left, a pregnant woman and a toddler are getting checked out, and fury rises in me that they could have been hurt worse than a few scratches.

This was targeted at us.

"Come on, Kiddo. How about you ride with Thor? I'll ride with Dragon since I know you don't want him out of your sight. Ryder and Travis are gonna follow us to the hospital. Ethan said he was okay enough that he doesn't need anyone to ride with him, but Phoenix still said he'd go with him. The others are on their way."

Numbly, I follow Thor to an ambulance. I'm about to step up to get inside when a hand lands on my arm.

"Ma'am—" the paramedic starts and then shuts up at my glare.

"I'm his Old Lady as well as Dragon's Old Lady," I say as I point at Dragon who's being loaded up in the ambulance next to us. "I am going in one of these damn ambulances, whether you like it or not."

He glances down and his face pales when he sees the 'President' badge on Thor's cut.

"Okay, but you have to stay out of the way. Climb in on the left."

I climb in and as soon as I'm seated, I take Thor's hand. He pulls my hand up to his lips and kisses it, despite my hand being covered in dried blood. He frowns as he keeps hold of my hand and looks me over closely.

"Are you sure none of the blood is yours?"

I look over my arms and hands, but there aren't any cuts. The blood that's on my jeans looks to be all from my hands because there are no cuts in the material. The only pain I have is some throbbing in my hands and my knee.

"The blood appears to be all Dragon's. My knee is a little sore from when I went down hard on the cement. Same with my palms. I'll be fine. You, Dragon, and Ethan are the ones I'm worried about."

He lifts my hand again and kisses it before he winces as the ambulance hits a bump in the road.

The ride is mostly silent except for when the paramedic asks Thor questions. It makes me realize I need to learn more about Thor and Dragon's medical history. I didn't know their blood type was AB+ or that they're both allergic to penicillin.

He shifts slightly, reaches into his back pocket, and pulls out his wallet.

"Here, Wildcat. Carry this for me, so you have our insurance information." He glances down, seeing his cut in my arms. "Keep it safe for me."

"Always, Hun."

Minutes later, the ambulance comes to a stop and the doors open. I get out so they can get Thor out easier. I follow him in, but a nurse stops me.

"Come on over here, Sweetie. You can wash your hands quick. You're not hurt, are you?"

Shaking my head, I swallow the lump in my throat. "I just banged my knee and scuffed my palms when we went down hard on the cement. I'll be fine."

"Okay, let me know if you need an ice pack for your knee at all. Once you're washed up, I'll show you to the nurses' station where we can start getting his information. I'm Allison, so if you have any questions, you can let me know."

"Is there any chance my fiancés can be in the same room? Ryan and Nick Gilbert?"

She gives me a surprised look and then laughs. "Damn, girl! Good for you. I'll see what I can do for you when they go upstairs for observation, but I can tell you that while they're here in the ER, we won't be able to accommodate that, the rooms are too small to fit two beds inside."

I nod, already having half expecting that answer, but I still wanted to try. "Is there any chance I could also be kept up to date on my friend, Ethan Mills? He was also shot. They're all in the same MC, Steel Archangel's."

She looks around before stepping in close. "I'll see what I can do since you aren't family. If I can't, I'll send Luke to come by for a visit."

I stare at her for a minute as I scrub my hands and arms before I remember Patch's real name is Luke Morgan. He said that most people in the ER know he's in the club and that his road name is Patch, but he wanted us to know his name if they got stuck with a new person or if someone was giving them issues.

Shaking my head, I give her a small smile. "Sorry, I forgot that's what Patch's real name was. I'm Levi Wallace, by the way."

"No worries. Nice to meet you, Levi, though I wish it were under better circumstances. I think Luke got pulled in with your man. Something about helping his President?"

"Ryan, or Thor as that's his road name, is the President of the MC. His brother, Nick or Dragon to the club is their Enforcer, and Ethan just started Prospecting with them last week."

"Damn, shot after only being there a week. Talk about a rough start."

"Yeah, it is."

Drying my hands off, I follow along behind her as that thought sinks in. I hope Ethan doesn't change his mind about Prospecting because of this. I can tell he already loves being in the club.

After giving the nurse Ryan and Nick's insurance information, they give me some paperwork to fill out, but the damn pen starts shaking in my hand. No matter how much I try to calm down, I just can't seem to.

Someone takes the pen out of my hand.

"I got this, Levi," Phoenix says as he pulls me in for a quick hug.

"Thank you, Phoenix."

He kisses the top of my head before he pulls back and starts filling out the paperwork for me.

Arms surround me, and I recognize Jax's cologne. I sink into his embrace before a thought hits me.

"Did anyone call Ethan's parents?"

"Yeah, Alexei's on the phone with them now."

"Shit, did you call Nikki? I bet they heard everything."

He sighs and nods. "Yeah, they know, and I promised I'd give her updates on everyone. They all went into lockdown as soon as they realized it was gunshots."

Thankful that they're alright, all I can do is nod as I feel myself drifting. Not able to concentrate on what everyone is saying, I tune them out and trust Jax to have my back.

After a few minutes, we're shown to the waiting room, which is overflowing with a sea of leather that has become my family. There are a few other families in here and they're warily watching us.

Seeing us approach, we're instantly bombarded with questions. Thankfully, Phoenix and Jax take over, answering what they can. I'm so close to tears again that if I had to repeat what happened, I'm sure I'd be a blubbering mess.

Sasha pulls me into a hug, then quickly pulls away, looking me over. "You're not hurt, are you? I brought you guys a change of clothes in case it was needed."

"No, it's not my blood. They both shielded me from the shots. Ethan, too."

She pulls me back into another bone-crushing hug, and I can't help it.

I break down.

I could have lost both of them today. I could have gotten hurt or our babies. Fuck, if I lost any of them, I don't know what I'd do.

A few hours later, we're all still in the waiting room sitting on extremely uncomfortable chairs. I shift in my seat, which causes me to wince. Dammit, my ass is going numb from sitting here so much.

The police came shortly after we got here, and those of us that were there gave our statements. They'll be back later for Thor, Dragon, and Ethan's statements once they are out of surgery and are awake. After they left, Phoenix told me Reaper's crew is heading down today instead of tomorrow. He called them when he got word of the shooting. They should be arriving in an hour or so.

Jax has been itching to look at the camera feeds to figure out who it was that shot at us, but I know he won't do it here. There are too many eyes that can wander in here, and the chance that he'd be caught on the hospital's cameras hacking into any cameras in the area is high.

My gaze once again goes to the vending area off the waiting room and I finally cave. I need some caffeine. I know their coffee will probably be beyond horrible, so I settle for a Coke.

Digging out my wallet, I pull out some cash and get my drink. Turning around, Dad's leaning against the doorframe with a concerned look on his face.

"How's my girl holding up?"

Shrugging, I open the bottle and take a sip. "I'm trying not to go ballistic or crazy. I want updates, but they don't have any yet. I want to cry. I want to target practice. I want to spar. I want to find whoever did this and make them pay."

Knowing I can't take out my anger here, or say anything incriminating, I take some deep breaths, then a few more sips of my soda as I try to calm down. It won't help anything if I lose my shit here.

Dad tugs me closer to him and wraps an arm around my shoulder, kissing my forehead.

"I'm sure you'll get answers soon. Your new family will make sure of it. One way or another."

He kisses my forehead again, and I nod, once again grateful that he doesn't have an issue with me being engaged to two men and adding to the fact that they're part of an MC.

Taking in my new family that's scattered around the room as we wait for news, I have no doubt we'll find out who's behind this. In a way, I hope it's Fang and Uncle Sean. If it's someone else, that will seriously complicate things. Other than maybe Tiffany or Monica, I don't know who it could be.

Behind me, a door opens, and I turn around. A nurse is walking down the hall toward us and her eyes widen at seeing the waiting room full of bikers.

"Family of Nick and Ryan Gilbert?"

"That's us," I say walking quickly to her. "I'm their fiancée."

"To which one?" she asks, scrunching up her nose.

"Both of them."

Her eyes widen with shock before morphing into a look of disgust.

Phoenix comes up to me and wraps an arm around my shoulders. "I'm Phoenix, their brother. And yes, she is with both of them. Now, can we get onto the more important topic of how my brothers and her Old Men are doing?"

I bite my tongue to keep the slew of words I want to say at bay, even though I really want to lash out at her. It's none of her business who I see.

She purses her lips and looks down her nose at us. "They are both out of surgery and are in recovery. I'll be able to take two people per patient back to see them. Once they wake up and are cleared, they'll be taken upstairs for observation."

Ryder and Smoke step forward to go with us.

"Give me one minute and I'll take you back." She pauses as she looks around the room. "Family of Ethan Mills?"

"We're also his family. Here are his parents, Clint and Helen," I state as they both rush up next to us. Helen clutches my hand and I give her hand a squeeze. I've always loved Ethan's parents and I hate that he was hurt protecting me.

"How's my boy?" she asks.

"He is also out of surgery and in recovery. Once he's awake and cleared, he'll also be taken upstairs for observation."

"Oh, thank God," Helen whispers as she leans into Clint's embrace.

"I can take you all back now."

We follow her along the corridor and when we reach the doors of the ER, the nurse swipes her badge. The doors swing open and I'm instantly looking around, trying to find my men.

I don't have to wait long. After passing two rooms, the nurse drops Clint and Helen off at Ethan's room. Seeing his face settles some of my fears. I'll check in on him later. His parents need to see him first. Also, I know Helen will text me as soon as he wakes up.

A couple of doors down is Nick's room. I race to his side, sliding my hand into his. Reaching up, I brush some of his hair out of his face and lean down, kissing his forehead. Resting my forehead on his, I feel a piece of me settle. His steady breathing and the steady beep of his heart monitor reassure me that he's okay.

Kissing him again, I step back and wipe away some tears. "I'm going to check on R—Thor real quick. I just... I need to put eyes on him," I tell Phoenix.

His lips kick up at my slip and he gives me a chin lift. "Don't worry, I'll stay with him. If he wakes up, I'll text ya."

Giving him a hug, I step out and look for Ryan's room. Allison sees me from the nurse station and waves me over.

"Hey Levi, how are your men doing?"

I'm sure she knows how they're doing since she works here, but I still appreciate her asking me.

"Dragon's still resting, and I was looking for Thor's, I mean Ryan's, room."

She waves me over as she walks down away from me and steps out from behind their station.

"He's on the other side of the unit. I've put in a request for them to be put in the same room when they go upstairs. Luke is also trying to get your friend, Ethan, into a room close to them. Something about being able to provide better security for them."

"Yeah, they're going to have someone standing outside the rooms on watch. I'm not sure how that'll go with the hospital staff, but the guys said they'd work it out with them somehow."

She looks around and leans in close when we stop outside Ryan's room.

"If they give you any fuss, have them page me. I have some clout here and can pull a few strings if need be for you."

I look at her in surprise. "You'd be willing to do that for us?"

She grins as she waves me off. "Luke's a friend of mine, so I know his club is one of the good ones. My dad is one of the department heads here. If they won't let you have guards, I can see if he could come and speak with the club. If there's a viable reason for wanting guards, I'm sure he'd be okay with it."

Relief fills me and pull her in for a hug. Even though we just met, my gut says I can trust her. Especially since she's close friends with Patch. "Thank you, and yes, they are a good group of men. Also yes, there's a very good reason for needing security."

She pulls back, grinning, and puts her hand on the door handle. "I'll get you my contact info inside. Now, let's see how your man is doing."

"Yes, please!"

She laughs and opens the door.

Seeing Thor in bed, alive and breathing, has a weight lifting from my shoulders. Both of my men and my brother are safe and alive.

Allison shuts the door behind us and starts checking Ryan's vitals. As she does that, I walk over to his good side, grasp his hand and lean down, kissing his forehead. When I pull back, I wipe my tears and a little chuckle escapes when Allison hands me a tissue box.

"Thank you."

"No worries, Sweetie." She pauses as she looks over at Ryder and Smoke before getting back to work.

I have to bite my tongue when I see how Ryder's looking at Allison. Wonder if he's caught the love bug? Allison is a beautiful woman. She's a little shorter than me, maybe five foot five or so. Her black hair is tied back into a messy bun. She's got a curvy figure, a bit curvier than me, but not unhealthy or anything.

Allison's jotting down notes on the computer about Thor, oblivious to Ryder's staring.

Or maybe not.

Her cheeks are getting a little pinker the longer Ryder stares.

"Now, like I just told Levi," she says as she clears her throat while continuing to type. "If you get any hassle about posting guards, have me paged or text me. I can pull a few strings to get one of our department heads to come down and talk to you. If you have a valid reason for posting the guards, I doubt he'd object."

"Why would you do that for us?" Smoke asks skeptically.

She turns to look at him. "I'm friends with Luke or Patch, as he's known to the club. From what I know about your club, you all are good men."

"Yeah, but why put your neck out for us?"

"I have a feeling something is going on to have three people from your club shot in broad daylight. Based on your guys' reputation, I'm guessing none of your guys fired first, especially since Levi was with you. So, my guess is that someone's pissed off at you for some reason. Now, are you through interrogating me, or do you have more questions? Luke warned me the one called Smoke would probably start running background checks on any nurse that would be looking after any of his club members if they were ever hurt in the future. Judging by your vest, that's you. So, any more questions?"

I bite my lip, but I can't fully stifle my giggle. Ryder's shoulders are shaking slightly from his laughter. The corner of Jax's lips tip up, even though he glares at me for giggling.

"Sorry, Jax, but she totally called you on that one."

I can't help it. Laughter spills out of me, which gets louder when I look back at Allison, only to find her staring down Jax with her eyebrow raised.

"That's it for now, but we may have more questions later if we do run into a snag. And it's a cut, not a vest."

Allison nods and pulls a notepad out of her pocket, jotting down some information, tears off a sheet and then hands it to me.

"Here you go girl, since I have a feeling you won't be leaving till your men and your friend do. Give me a holler if you need something. It shouldn't be too much longer before all of them wake up."

"Thank you, Allison."

She gives me a quick hug and with a nod to the guys, she hurries out, but not before I can see her blushing.

Without a word, Ryder follows her out.

I shake my head but smile. "I have a feeling we may see more of Allison in the future."

A groan has me quickly turning back to Thor.

"What's going on?"

Chapter 37
Thor

JUDGING BY THE SMELL, I'm not in the clubhouse or our house. The smell of bleach is too strong.

There's a beeping noise that's making my head hurt. Voices are murmuring around me and then laughter rings out.

Levi's laughter.

Everything comes rushing back to me. The doctor's visit. Finding out we're having twins. Walking down the street and then being shot at.

Shit, Levi!

I open my eyes, but the lights are too bright, and I instantly close them.

Why is there laughter?

"What's going on?"

Levi gasps and then I feel her small hand slip into mine.

I try opening my eyes again, blinking rapidly.

"Thor!"

My eyes settle on her face and my heart breaks at seeing her red-rimmed eyes, tears running down her cheeks.

"You're not hurt, are you?"

She shakes her head no and I breathe a sigh of relief.

"How's Dragon? Ethan?"

"Ethan's parents are with him and last I checked; he was still sleeping off the anesthesia. Same with Dragon. Phoenix is with him right now. Are you in any pain? Shit, we should let the nurses know you're awake."

She hits a button above my head and I wince when a loud voice crackles over the speaker.

Moments later, the door opens and a nurse with a bubbly smile comes in with Ryder right behind her.

"Glad to see you awake, Mr. Gilbert. Are you in any pain?"

"Fuck yes I am, and I have a massive headache."

She walks over to some bags hanging nearby but fuck if I know what she's doing. Looking back over at Levi, she's fighting a smile as she watches the others. What the fuck did I miss?

"Good to see you awake, Thor. You missed Allison raking Smoke here over the coals earlier." Ryder grins at me, but his eyes keep going over to the nurse.

Huh. Does he have a thing for her? Levi smirks at me and winks.

"Good, he needs to be kept in line every now and then," I grunt out.

Smoke scowls at me and flips me off.

"Get those lips down here, Wildcat."

She smiles and blushes, but leans down, kissing me. It's not as deep as I need right now, but maybe I can get her to kiss me again after everyone leaves.

"How long have I been out?"

Levi's face falls. "A little over three hours. Reaper's crew is on their way down here and should be here in less than an hour or so."

"How you holding up, baby mama?"

She blushes as she wipes more tears away. "Better now that you're awake. Hopefully, Dragon and Ethan wake up soon."

"Try not to stress too much, Wildcat. It can't be good for the babies."

"Wait, babies?" Ryder asks as he stares at Levi. "Holy shit, I was right!"

Wincing, I look over at Levi, giving her what's hopefully an apologetic smile. "Shit, we were going to wait to announce that part tonight. I'm sorry, Baby Girl."

She leans down and kisses me again. "It's alright, Thor. And yes, Ryder, we found out this morning that I'm pregnant with twins."

Allison squeals and then winces when she sees my own wince. "Sorry, Mr. Gilbert. I got so excited I forgot about your headache. Congratulations and Levi, come here and get a hug."

She pushes past Smoke and Ryder, quickly giving Levi a hug. I'm not sure what happened while I was out, but I'm guessing I'll be seeing more of Allison if

Levi becomes friends with her. Suddenly, Allison pulls back as she looks at Levi's stomach.

"We didn't check you out or anything since you said you weren't injured, and you didn't mention being pregnant. Are you sure you don't need to be checked or get an ultrasound?"

"We had actually just come from Dr. Rowen's office, my OB-GYN, earlier this morning. He did an ultrasound there. We were walking down the street to the pharmacy when the shooting started. I didn't get shot or cut by broken glass. The worse was my knee and palms like I told you earlier. I wasn't jostled badly or hit or anything, so I don't think we'd need to do another ultrasound. Then again, I'm not the expert."

"I'll talk to the attending physician to get her input on it and let you know. Now, I'll be back in a few with some medicine for Mr. Gilbert. Then I'll check on your other man and your friend. Holler if you need anything."

"Thank you, Allison."

Allison waves her off, but then scowls as Ryder gets up.

"Just gonna check in on my Enforcer and Prospect. Wondering if they're awake yet."

She scowls at him again and leaves with him close behind her.

"I'll step out to give you two some privacy and check on Ethan. I'll text you, Kiddo, if either wake up as I know you'll want to see them."

"Thank you, Jax."

He gives her a quick hug and a kiss on the temple. I know he's now her brother, but I still find myself fighting a growl at any man besides Dragon and me kissing her.

He smirks at me, and Levi rolls her eyes.

Once he leaves, I pat the bed next to me. Instead, she walks on the other side of the bed and pulls a chair closer. That's not going to fly.

"Wildcat, I need you next to me. Get your fine ass up on this bed. Please."

"Hun, there isn't enough room on the bed for me to sit beside you and there's no way I'm going to ask you to move. You just got out of surgery. Let the meds kick in—oh my God, Ryan, stop it! You're going to pop a stitch!"

I hear the door open, but I ignore it as I try to scoot my way closer to the left side of my bed.

"Mr. Gilbert, please stop moving. You could injure yourself further!"

I grit my teeth at the pain that rips through me.

"I need my Wildcat to be next to me. Those fuckers could have shot or killed her and the babies. I need my baby mama next to me. I need to hold you, Baby Girl."

Glancing down, I've only managed to scoot a few inches and my head is already spinning from the increased pain.

Tears are streaming down Levi's face as she holds my hand. She sniffs and then pulls out her phone. After a few seconds, it dings, and she puts it back in her pocket. She glares at me, and if she had a weapon on her, it would have been pointed at me. I know she has a gun and a few blades in her purse, but she wouldn't pull one of those in front of someone else in the hospital.

"You are not to move another fucking muscle, Ryan Gilbert! Patch will be here soon and between the three of us, maybe we can scoot you over a few more inches. But don't you fucking dare pull a stunt like that again! You went white as a sheet doing that!"

Seeing fresh tears fall down her face, I cave, even though I know I won't be able to do anything for a few more minutes, anyway. That fucking hurt like hell.

"I'm sorry, Wildcat, I just need to hold you for a bit. I'm going crazy about not being able to touch you after this fucking fiasco."

"I'm the same way, Hun, but I don't want to hurt you."

Hearing a sniffle, I turn toward Allison, who's wiping her face with tissues.

"Sorry. Ignore me. I hope someday I can find someone who loves me like you two love each other. You two are a perfect match." She pauses as she blows her nose, and then a small chuckle escapes her. "On the other hand, I just remembered you said you're also seeing his twin brother. Maybe you need an award for handling two of him."

Laughter sounds from the door and Levi spins around startled, before relaxing, but I can't see who it is.

"Our Queen definitely needs a fucking medal. Not only does she put up with this asshole and his brother, but all of us assholes at the club. Let me guess. Numbnuts over here decided to move too soon, didn't he?"

Levi sighs and nods. I debate snapping at him for the 'numbnuts' comment, but decide to let it go for now.

"Yup, your friend here desperately wants to hold his woman after what happened. His heart rate is increasing even more, so he's getting anxious or near an anxiety attack. Honestly, I'd feel the same way if I was in his position. His lower body's still on a chuck pad, so that will help with friction. If you can help pull his lower body, I'll stabilize his upper body as best as I can."

What the fuck is a chuck pad?

Patch rounds the bed and then lifts the blanket slightly, exposing some of the mat or whatever the hell is underneath me. Is that what they are saying is called a chuck pad?

"If you ever fucking talk about me being this close to your ass or dick to anyone, I'll shoot you myself."

"Noted. Now help me move so I can hold my woman. My anxiety is going through the roof at not holding her after almost losing her and the babies."

"Babies? You're having twins? Oh fuck, what if they're girls?"

I glare at him and notice the women trying to hold in their laughter. "If my babies are girls, I'll be stocking up on lots of ammo, and at least they'll have lots of uncles to scare off horny teenagers. But Wildcat, I won't be having ruffle butt babies! I'm the President of an MC for fuck's sake."

Both women bust out laughing at that, and a sliver of fear runs down my spine. Fuck, now she'll probably get some of those ruffle butt underwear, or whatever the fuck they're called, I remember my younger cousin wearing years ago just to piss me off. If we have a girl, that is.

"Fuck, if that happens, I want pictures, Levi. Didn't happen if there's no proof!"

I turn my glare on Patch, which only has him laughing harder.

I'm stewing as they laugh, but then they try to get themselves under control when my heart rate monitor keeps beeping faster. Fuck, they aren't helping my anxiety. If I didn't need Patch's help, I'd punch the fucker. Finally, their laughter dies down.

"Let's try sitting the bed up a bit. Once you have a good hold on him, Allison, Levi can lower the bed down slightly so that there's less resistance against the bed."

Wildcat grasps my good hand, giving me a squeeze before letting go so Allison can come closer to me on my good side. Patch shows Wildcat what buttons to push when they give the word. They raise the bed. After I take a few deep breaths, I grit my teeth and nod, giving the okay to start. Allison helps stabilize me.

"Lower the bed, Levi."

Even though I know Allison's trying to prevent jerking when Patch moves me, I still curse at the pain that radiates through me when my body jolts.

"Bed up now, Levi."

The bed raises and when my back touches it fully, Allison releases her hold on me.

I take a few deep breaths as the pain washes through me. After a few moments, I hold out my arm and Levi instantly sits down and curls into me.

My body instantly relaxes, and I can slowly hear the heart monitor's rate lower and even out.

"Well, shit. Guess I need to keep that in mind for any other Steel Archangel that comes in here and has a woman."

I look at Allison in confusion and Levi shifts so she can see her better as well. Both her and Patch are watching the monitors.

"What?"

"If your numbers wouldn't have gone down shortly after waking up, we were going to have to give you something for high blood pressure. As soon as Levi laid down by you, it instantly started dropping along with your heart rate. I know Nick, er, Dragon's numbers are high, so when he wakes up, we'll definitely need you to be with him shortly afterward to see if his numbers drop as well."

"Are Ethan's numbers high? He doesn't have a girlfriend, at least that I know of anyway," Wildcat says.

"His numbers were normal the last I checked his chart, which was before you went into Dragon's room. He was still asleep though, so we'll see how he is when he wakes up."

"Now, since we just jostled you a bit and your numbers spiked so much, Thor, we're going to restart your observation time. Allison already kicked your meds up a little, so those should be hitting your system soon, but they may take a bit to kick in though. In about a half-hour, we'll check on you again and if you're okay, you'll be sent upstairs. Allison already arranged for you and Dragon to be in the same room, and I pulled strings to get Ethan in the room right next to you, but they're still fighting me on guards."

"Allison, do you—"

"Yup, hold that thought," she says to Wildcat.

She walks over to the phone and dials someone.

"Who's she calling?"

"Her dad's a department head here and said she might be able to pull some strings to help with the guards," Wildcat says.

I turn and look at her, rubbing her arm. "That means we're going to have to tell him what's going on with your stalkers, Baby Girl," I whisper, but notice Allison's eyes widening when she hears the word stalker. In essence, that's what Fang and Sean are. I just hate everything they're making my woman go through because of their fucking obsessions.

"I know, but he'll get the cliff note version. I don't want to go into too deep of context."

She kisses my chest and then sits up but stays on the bed next to me. Allison seems really rattled and I pray they haven't said anything incriminating to the cops yet. I'm sure the others already gave their statements. Shit, I hope Creed doesn't show up. That might make things worse.

"You have a stalker?" she asks when she hangs up.

"Yes, I do. Two of them and they're working together. I need you not to say anything to *anyone* about this. The cops don't know because the Feds asked us not to tell them. Please. I know we just met Allison, but you said you're friends with Patch, too. Please, don't tell anyone about my stalkers. I don't want you or anyone else getting tangled up in this."

"The FBI is involved?"

While I know the Fed thing is complete bullshit, well, at least the part of not telling the cops, but maybe mentioning that will be what gets Allison not to say anything. She nods in response to Levi's confirmation and I breathe a sigh of relief.

"I've known Luke since we were in diapers. Our moms are best friends. I know he wouldn't get tangled up in anything illegal, so I trust you. I won't say anything to anyone, but you might have to tell my dad about your stalkers. He'll question why you don't have cops for guards then. If you point out that the Feds don't want to bring unwanted attention and left you in the safety of the club, then that means they are your appointed guards per the FBI."

I look at Patch, who's grinning and rolling his eyes at Allison. I hope he hasn't told her too much about the club. While it's true we aren't into anything illegal, we do sometimes put down people who are a threat. Then again, she just laid out a perfect argument for us with her dad, so maybe she does know a little about us.

"Wait, back up. You've known Patch since he was in diapers? I need pictures, girl!" Levi looks over at Patch with a mischievous glint in her eyes.

Allison laughs at the look of horror on Patch's face.

"Don't you even think about it, Alli! I won't be bringing ice cream, cookies, and wine when the next asshole breaks your heart if you betray me like that."

"You do realize, I can get you as much booze and ice cream as you want, right? Plus, I know someone who makes melt-in-your-mouth cookies, too," Levi whispers as she puts an arm around Allison and grins wickedly at Patch.

"See if I save your men's ass again, Levi. Ouch."

Levi winks at me and goes over to hug Patch, while Allison howls with laughter.

"You know I'd never turn your friend against you, jackass. So let this be a warning if you neanderthal's don't listen."

Allison is laughing so hard she's crying when there's a knock at the door. Levi comes over to sit by me on the bed again, holding my hand, while Patch gets the door.

"Hello, Luke. Is Allison still in here?"

"Yup, and she's laughing at my expense, yet again, Mr. Thatcher."

"Why am I not surprised? Alli, Sweetheart, I take it these are some of the men you wanted me to talk to?"

Allison nods as she tries to contain her laughter. Patch rolls his eyes and steps in for her.

"Mr. Thatcher, I'd like you to meet Levi and Thor, or Ryan Gilbert, per his paperwork while he's here. Thor is my President. Dragon, or Nick Gilbert per his paperwork, is our Enforcer. Ethan Mills is a new Prospect for us. All three of them were shot this morning. Levi is engaged to Thor and Dragon. She has a couple of stalkers and we suspect they were the ones to start the shooting earlier today, but we don't have evidence of that yet. I heard there were others that were treated at the scene for cuts from broken glass, but that was it."

"Then why aren't the cops posted as guards?"

Levi clears her throat. "Mr. Thatcher, that's because the Feds are involved, and they were already on the trail of both of my stalkers when they started targeting me. Seeing how protected I was with the club, they thought it would be safe to leave me under their protection, especially since I was dating, well, now engaged to two of their members. They didn't want extra protection to make me an even bigger target."

"What happened this morning, then?"

"I recently found out I was pregnant and had my first appointment with my OB-GYN, Dr. Rowen, this morning. Four others from the club went with us to the appointment. When we left, we were headed to the pharmacy to fill my script for prenatal vitamins. About halfway there, the shooting started."

Wildcat dips her head, tears rolling down her cheeks. "My men and their brothers protected me until we could get behind some cars for protection. They were shot, protecting me and our babies."

I looked over at Mr. Thatcher and know we aren't going to have a problem. I can tell by the look on his face that his heart is breaking over what could have happened to Levi.

A phone rings, and Levi jerks. She pulls it out of her pocket and inhales sharply. "It's Creed."

Thank fuck I had her program in his number after he gave it to us. He must have heard what happened, but I still hope he doesn't come here. That could tip things off even worse with Fang and Sean.

"Step into the bathroom, Levi, and shut the door. You'll have more privacy in there," Patch tells her.

She squeezes my hand and does as Patch said.

"Who's Creed?" Mr. Thatcher asks.

"He's our FBI contact," Patch says and turns his attention to me, letting me take over.

"Mr. Thatcher, what I say to you cannot leave this room. Allison has already agreed not to say anything. I'm not threatening you, so please don't take it that way. I'm just trying to protect you."

He glances at Allison who nods to him and then to Patch, who also nods. He turns back to me.

"If my daughter and Luke trust you, so will I. You have my word."

"Thank you. Wildcat has two stalkers after her, and one is her own uncle, who's sold her to the other stalker."

Allison inhales sharply and goes to her dad, hugging him. He bends down and kisses the top of her head.

"Her uncle just got out of prison, today actually, for crimes he committed against Levi when she was six. I won't go into detail about that, but on top of wanting her, he also blames her for being sent to jail for almost seventeen years. We're trying to track the fuckers down, but this appointment could not be missed, so we had to step outside of our compound. They must have been watching us, even though we didn't notice a tail, because they knew where we were."

"Either that or you have a mole."

Fuck. I hadn't mentioned the rat possibility to anyone else, but to have someone else think that gives me pause. I don't think a patched member would betray us, but you never know. Same with Levi's family. If one of them had, she'll probably kill them outright. Either that, or Fang and his crew were able to put up more cameras, even though we confiscated the other bag. They don't need to know all of that, though.

"I'm not going to lie, but that has crossed my mind. Even more so after getting shot."

Patch looks back at me, raising an eyebrow, but I'm not saying anything now. I'll wait till there are no loose ears around.

The bathroom door opens, and Levi comes out, wiping more tears off her cheeks. Shit, she looks even more stressed than before.

"What'd Creed want, Wildcat?"

"First, to make sure we were all okay. I could vouch for you since you're awake, but I haven't been texted about the others yet, so they must not be awake yet. He had wanted to visit us tonight, along with Smoke and whoever else we deemed necessary, as he has some information for us. However, because of the shooting, that'll be postponed. He asked that we let him know when everyone will be released, and I agreed, saying I'd text him a time when we have it."

I can tell by the set of her jaw that there's more, but we'll talk about that later, too.

"Levi, I'm very sorry about your situation, but there will be no issues with guards as long as they stay out of the way of our staff."

A knock at the door has him pausing and we turn to see Smoke entering. He raises an eyebrow at me, and I motion him in.

"Smoke, this is Mr. Thatcher, Allison's dad. Mr. Thatcher, this is Smoke, our tech guy as well as Levi's brother."

They both shake hands.

"I hope I'm in time to ask something about the guard situation?"

"Yes, of course. I was just telling Luke and Thor that there would be no problems with guards. I'll talk to the appropriate people and you'll be fine as long as you stay out of our staff's way."

Smoke's eyebrow raises and he gives me a quick glance that has my stomach tightening before refocusing on Mr. Thatcher. "That's partially my concern, Sir."

"How so?"

"Well, I think we may have another problem. Sir, I just witnessed a situation that suggests you have some rats. I need the names of each of your nurses or doctors that will be treating my brothers so I can run a quick check on them."

"Fuck," Levi hisses and her gaze locks with mine.

She gives me a subtle nod. If she's saying what I think she's saying, fuck is right. This is not good. Not good at all.

Chapter 38
Levi

I'M SO FUCKING PISSED right now, I can hardly see straight. Someone I've trusted for years appears to have betrayed me. I want to give him the benefit of the doubt, but I need to first ask Smoke to verify his phone records.

Not only that, but Creed gave me pictures of two women who work in this hospital who have been seen with Fang around town recently.

Now I'm even more worried about my men and my brother while we're in the hospital. Why the fuck can't we catch a fucking break?

Refusing to focus on that right now, I clear my throat. "Mr. Thatcher, how many people are normally allowed to stay overnight?"

"Usually just one person per patient unless there's a child involved."

I nod and try to plot who I want as backup here and at the compound.

"Now, Smoke, was it? What do you mean, I may have some rats of my own?" Mr. Thatcher asks.

"First off, Ethan did wake up about ten minutes ago and would like to see you when you're able to, Levi. He just wants to put eyes on you for himself to see that you're safe." He gives me a look that makes me question if he knows what I now know.

Smoke pulls out his laptop and brings up two pictures. They're the same ones Creed sent me which means he must have also warned Smoke. Or something else triggered Smoke's suspicions.

"I noticed a couple of nurses were acting weird outside Ethan's room from the window. Thankfully, I'd relieved his parents a few minutes earlier so they could go and get something to eat. I warned Ethan not to give me away to the nurses and ducked into the restroom on purpose before they saw me. I heard them through the door that I'd left purposefully cracked open."

"What do you mean they were acting weird?"

Smoke clears his throat and gives me an apologetic look.

"They were arguing as they compared vials of something, but I couldn't tell what they were holding. Their arguing was what got my attention, and I quickly slipped out of sight of the window. Then they were looking around like they were trying not to be noticed before moving toward his door. It was then that I'd slipped into the bathroom.

"Once they were inside, they started talking to Ethan since he'd recently woken up. At first it was normal health care routine until it wasn't. They were trying to convince Ethan to turn and switch sides, otherwise they'd pump him full of medicine and he'd be dead in an hour.

"When it seemed like they were going to give him the meds, I flushed the toilet and quickly opened the door, pretending I didn't know they were in there. I caught them as they were about to insert the meds into his IV but the one administering it quickly stuffed the vials into their pocket. I was able to catch their names on their badges. Ryder's in there with him now and I've instructed him that for now, only Patch can administer medicine, and it has to be unsealed when it's brought in the room. I haven't told his parents yet, for obvious reasons."

Mr. Thatcher's face pales, and he slumps into a nearby chair.

"I just got off the phone with Creed, Jax. He knew about the nurses last night, but he only just got word of the shooting a little bit ago, so he called me as soon as he heard to warn me. The pictures you have match the ones he sent me."

I hand him my phone, praying he won't say anything about the other pictures right now.

He flips through the pictures, and when his gaze meets mine, I can't hide the betrayal. Tears stream down my face once again. He'd been one of my best friends since high school. I thought of him as a brother. How could he do this to me?

Thor pats the bed next to him after Jax hands me back my phone, and I crawl in, burying my face in his chest, willing it not to be true even though the proof is there. Both in video and audio. The hate in his voice as he spoke about my men broke me. It was even worse when he talked about our baby being the spawn of Satan because I was with two men. He wanted to rip it out of me because I was going against God's wishes for how I was living.

I mean, yeah, his parents are super religious, but didn't he understand going to Fang was even worse? Add on my uncle and it's two crazy ass psychos we have to deal with. He would rather have them rape me and God knows what else because I'm engaged to two guys and am now pregnant?

"I'll have the rosters drawn up and you'll have them momentarily. How do we deal with these two nurses? Do I need to call the cops or does your FBI contact want to deal with them?"

"Call Creed, Jax. Give him your new information. He told me to let you guys know that he's in the area, so he'll be able to move in if it's enough proof."

"Then it's a good thing I've been wearing a fucking camera since we left the compound," he mutters.

I quickly sit up, staring at him in disbelief. Did his cameras capture who shot at us? Did he get clear enough pictures of the two nurses along with their badges?

"With this being your first out-of-the-ordinary-trip out of the compound, I figured they'd be watching us. I just didn't know where they would be or when they'd approach. You're my sister, Levi, even if it's not by blood. I'll protect you till I take my last breath."

Sliding off Ryan's bed, I walk over to Jax and am instantly wrapped in a hug. I can't stop the tears that come, even though I'm sure I'm soaking his shirt.

After a few minutes, I pull back and notice Mr. Thatcher is now gone, along with Allison.

"We need to talk about the other part now, Kiddo."

Sighing, I nod glumly. "Do you have your jammer?"

"Yup. Thank God Alexei thought to grab it."

I take a deep breath, pull out my phone, and unlock it. Jax takes it from me as I move the table closer to Ryan so he can see the picture better on Jax's laptop once he copies over the files. Patch steps up by the head of Ryan's bed. Smoke sets up his jammer once the files transfer to his computer.

I crawl back into Ryan's bed again and curl up with him, needing his strength for this. "Just do it, Jax. I already saw and heard it."

He sighs heavily, but he's only seen the pictures, not the video. "First, here are the pictures of the two nurses Creed sent Levi."

He shows one picture and then flips to the second.

"This is where things turn on its head," he says as he looks at me sympathetically.

What follows are pictures of Travis with Fang on multiple occasions, both before and after he became a Prospect. Some were even of him in his cut when he was meeting Fang. Then there are the ones where he's focusing on me, watching me. I don't know how Creed got photos from inside the compound, but I fully intend to look into that.

Then it's the start of four videos.

Each one is worse than the last.

One part that hits me especially hard is when he says my mother would be ashamed of me. Fang grins evilly at that. Did Travis forget Fang was the one that ultimately killed my mother?

I don't know why Creed didn't tell us of Travis' betrayal earlier, but maybe he has a reason. Still, it's not going to save Travis from my wrath. Or Creed for that matter. He'll be getting an earful from me the next time I see him.

Ryan is practically vibrating with rage underneath me, and I don't blame him. I know exactly what I'm going to do to Travis when I get my hands on him. And no, the Feds aren't getting him, no matter what they say.

Travis is mine to deal with.

No sooner had the last video ended that my phone pings with a text.

"Looks like Dragon just woke up, Kiddo, and he's asking for you."

I glance up at Ryan, who sighs but nods.

"I've had you for a while, Wildcat, and even though I want to keep holding you after that shit, he needs you too."

"Don't make a plan without me for Travis cause he's mine, no matter what Creed fucking says. And I know just the thing that I'll be ending it with. Bring him to the sticks and keep him there."

"The sticks?" Patch asks.

I sigh, not understanding how they haven't come up with a nickname for it yet on their own. "Jammer still working?"

Jax nods.

"The interrogation room, idiots. You guys should have thought of a nickname for that place a long time ago, so for now, unless you have a better idea, I'm calling it 'the sticks'."

Groans surround me.

"What you'd rather I call it 'bum fuck Egypt'? Cause if that got out, I don't really want to have anyone on our asses for that nickname."

They groan again, but Ryan winks at me and then winces as he shifts slightly. Shit.

"Patch, can we extend that medicine gag to Thor and Dragon, too? At least until they get those bimbo's out of here?"

"Shouldn't be a problem."

"If it is, enlist Allison if you really do think she won't talk. My gut says she won't, but you've known her longer than me."

"She wouldn't. Should I send her to Dragon's room so you can talk to her first?"

I pause. "That's probably a good idea. Jax, come with me for a bit just in case I need you."

Thor snags my hand, and I look back at him.

"Wildcat, I need to know what you're thinking with Travis. How far do you want to go down the rabbit hole?"

I let him see the full weight of Travis' betrayal in my eyes. The hurt. The pain. The anger. The rage. The need for vengeance.

"I considered him as a brother. He betrayed me in one of the worst ways imaginable. You'll all get to play and I'll help a bit every now and then. Probably more so with the dragging out of information by pressing his buttons since I know all his buttons after having known him for years." I pause and an evil grin spreads across my face. "It's the device I had made after our last guest. He'll get the same treatment as my stalkers."

Thor's dark grin deepens and he gives me a chin lift. I had run my idea past him first and when he gave me the go ahead, I made him swear not to tell anyone but Dragon so that it'd be a surprise for the others.

Then suddenly, it feels like someone's poured ice water over me. "Um, how much did he help with the exit of our last guest?"

Curses ring out and I'm getting even more nervous now.

"All the new Prospects were down there to help get her ready, but Dragon and Ryder were the ones that took her out under the stars," Thor says.

"If he knows we're onto him, then he's probably no longer in the waiting room. If he's skipped out, then we need to find him fast. He could go to the cops." I pause and grab my phone. "Hold that thought," I say as I dial Sasha.

It doesn't go through. Dammit, the jammer.

"I know it's a risk, but I gotta do this to figure out if he's still in the waiting room. In this scenario, it'll be more likely that I'm calling Sasha because I'm freaking out, but I'll have her speak Russian."

"Travis doesn't know Russian?" Patch asks.

"No, he's never shown an interest in learning. He may know a word or two from repeated use, but I think that's only if it's spoken slowly. Sasha can rattle off Russian so fast he wouldn't be able to decipher it."

At Thor's nod, Jax disables the jammer and I dial Sasha again. This time, it goes through.

"*Hey, Sasha.* **Наш рыжый брат все еще находится в приемной с вами, ребята** [*Is our red-headed brother still in the waiting room with you guys*]? **Говорите только по-русски** [*Speak in Russian only*]."

"**Да, он все еще здесь** [*Yes, he's still here*]. **Но он вел себя нервнои много проверял свой телефон** [*But he's been acting antsy and checking his phone a lot*]."

"**Держите его там как можно дольше** [*Keep him there as long as possible*]. **Если он уйдет, скажите нам и попытайтесь преследовать его** [*If he leaves, tell us and try to tail him*]."

"**Что происходит** [*What's going on*]?"

"**У нас может быть крыса** [*We may have a rat*]."

She gasps, and I know she's probably as heartbroken as I am.

"**Не действуйте по-другому** [*Don't act any different*]. **Если кто-то спросит, просто скажите, что вы беспокоитесь о парнях** [*If anyone asks, just say you're worried about the guys*]."

"**Хорошо, как дела** [*Okay, how are they*]?"

"*You mean Ryder never came out?*"

"No."

Shit, I slipped into English, but this part should be okay.

"Thor's been awake for a bit. I just got a text that Dragon is awake." I hesitate about Ethan because of what Smoke said and switch back. **Наш шатен проснулся** *[Our brown-haired friend is awake]*. **Тем не менее, скажите любому, кто спрашивает, что он все еще спит** *[However, tell anyone who asks that he's still asleep]*. **Я постараюсь поймать его родителей, чтобы они пока ничего не говорили** *[I'll try to catch his parents so they don't say anything yet]."*

"Oh, thank God." I hear her sniffling and I know it's a combination of good and bad news cry.

"I gotta go, Sasha. I'll keep you posted."

"Okay."

I hang up, grateful that she didn't really give anything away. Or me for that matter. I signal Jax to put the jammer up again and sigh. He nods at me when it's ready.

"Travis is still in the waiting room, but Sasha says he's been antsy and checking his phone a lot."

"He needs to be sent on a task. Where's Phoenix?"

"Last I knew, he's with Dragon. What if we head over there, bring them up to speed quick, and then send Phoenix your way?"

"Do that and then I'll talk to him about what to do going forward. We need a brother in each room and then at least one outside each door. Preferably two. Especially until Creed gets here and gets those bitches out of here."

"The vast majority of us were in the waiting room earlier, so we shouldn't have a problem manning the rooms. Don't forget, Reaper's crew will be here soon if they aren't already. Phoenix asked that they go to the clubhouse since we left a skeleton crew there," Smoke says.

"Good. Now, give me a kiss, Wildcat, before you go."

The smirk he gives me makes my knees weak. I lean down and kiss him, intending to keep it brief since Patch and Jax are in the room. As I start to pull back, his hand grasps the back of my head, and he pulls me back down to him, kissing me hard enough to make my toes curl.

"Thor, quit kissing my sister so we can deal with these assholes."

A giggle escapes at Jax's exasperated voice and, with one last peck, I pull back.

"Let me know when you get cleared to go upstairs, Hun," I say, and he gives me a chin lift. Squeezing his hand, I turn to head to Dragon's room.

Chapter 39
Dragon

My anxiety has been through the roof since I woke up. I need to see my Spitfire. To hold her. To make sure she's safe with my own eyes.

A nurse, whose name is Allison, came in shortly after I woke up and, once she verified who I was, told me that Spitfire is in Thor's room with Patch and Smoke talking about some new information they received from Creed.

Both Phoenix and I shared a worried glance. How the hell does she know about Creed?

She warned us to not accept any new medicine or let anyone tweak my medicine unless it was her or Patch. Then she left saying that she'd send Spitfire to my room as soon as she saw her.

That was ten minutes ago.

I'm going out of my mind waiting to see her.

"I'm going to knock you out if you don't fucking relax, Dragon."

"Fuck you, Phoenix. If your woman was shot at today after finding out you're having twins, then you'd be fucking freaking out until you saw her, too."

He tilts his head in agreement and then shakes his head. "I still can't believe you got her to agree to marry both you assholes and to top it off, she's knocked up with twins."

"Yeah, we're lucky bastards, that's for sure." I can't help but grin at that. We are so fucking lucky to have her in our lives.

The door handle jiggles and I notice Phoenix cross his arms, one of his hands inside his cut. The door opens and I'm relieved when I see a flash of red hair and then Levi's rushing to my side. I wrap her in my arms, breathing in her sweet jasmine scent. Finally, I feel my body start to relax.

"Yup, I'm definitely gonna have to remember this if any of you guys are ever in here again," someone says, and I look up to see Allison smiling as she shakes her head and continues to watch the monitors.

It's then that I notice Smoke is in my room as well and damn, does he look pissed.

I pull back and try to scoot over more to my right to make room for Spitfire. It hurts like fuck to lift my leg, but I grit through the pain.

"God dammit, you two are way too much alike sometimes! If you move like that again, Nickolas Gilbert, I will shoot you myself. You went white as a sheet, just like Ryan did."

"Well then, it's a good thing I was able to move over enough. Get your sexy ass in this bed so I can hold you, Spitfire."

She rolls her eyes, but comes around the bed and lays down, resting her head on my chest.

"Okay, everything is looking good. Thankfully, your numbers didn't spike as bad as Thor's when you tried to move. I'll be back to check on you later."

"Thank you, Allison," Spitfire calls out, but Allison waves her off.

"Not a worry, Levi. I'm going to go check in on your friend."

When she leaves, Levi stiffens in my arms as Smoke pulls over the table and puts his laptop on it.

I'm about to ask something when Levi covers my mouth and mimes me not to talk. I nod and she removes her hand, but not before I lick it. She shivers and I can't help but grin when I see her squirming a little.

Once Smoke sets up some sort of device, he exhales heavily.

"We have a lot of new information that was just handed to us. The first is that these two nurses threatened Ethan a bit ago that if he didn't switch over to Fang's side, then they'd pump him full of drugs and he'd be dead in an hour." As he speaks, he brings up the images of two women on the screen and I frown.

"How do we know that?" Phoenix asks.

"Two ways. One, Creed sent these pictures to Levi when we were in Thor's room. He knew about them last night, but it wasn't until he heard about the shooting that he called Levi to warn her. Two, I caught the bitches about to pump

Ethan full of whatever the fuck was in those syringes if he didn't switch over to Fang's side."

What the fuck?

"That's not everything, either. Levi, do you want me to take this, or do you want to do it?"

Shit, it must be bad if he isn't calling her 'Kiddo'.

Spitfire sighs and sits up. "Creed thinks we have a rat." She pauses and I'm instantly furious that we trusted someone only to have them betray us. "Based on the pictures and videos, I'm inclined to believe him." She pauses, and her jaw ticks as her eyes harden. "Phoenix, after we catch you up on this, Thor wants to talk to you about how to get him down to the sticks."

"Sticks?"

"Levi's nickname for where our last guest stayed," Smoke tells us, his lips kicking up a bit in the corner as he glances over at Spitfire.

She huffs and rolls her eyes. "If you guys can come up with a better one, then by all means, change it. I'm surprised you don't have a code for it yet myself."

"Who's the rat and how do you know? Why did Smoke ask you if you wanted to lead this part?" Phoenix asks, his eyes narrowing on her.

Oh, fuck no. "Phoenix, back the fuck off."

He ignores me and still continues to glare at Spitfire. If I could fucking get up right now, I'd be so up in his face.

"Creed sent me some pictures and four videos. I don't know how he got pictures from inside the clubhouse, but he did."

"Levi. Who. Is. The. Rat?" Phoenix asks again, his voice is lethal, but Spitfire doesn't back down or cower from the tone of his voice or his hard stare.

Even though she's pissed as fucking hell, a single tear still streaks down her cheek.

"Travis."

My mind is still reeling from Travis' betrayal.

Phoenix left as soon as Smoke and Spitfire filled him in on everything. As pissed as I am, I'm worried as fuck about Spitfire. This is three times now that she's been betrayed by a family member, two of those times by the same person.

She got back a few minutes ago from checking in on Ethan and is twirling a pen she got from somewhere as she stares up at the ceiling tiles.

"Spitfire, talk to me, Babe."

She takes a deep breath and sighs. "My mind is replaying things, trying to figure out when things shifted for him. It can't just be me being with you and Ryan that made him flip his switch. Something else must have happened, but what?"

I'm about to say something when her phone rings.

"Hey, what's up Sasha?"

Her brow creases and then she snatches the pen out of the air before shooting to her feet.

"Fuck. Okay, stay with the club. Did you already let Thor know?"

Fuck, fuck, fuck. What the hell is going on?

After a few moments, she nods. *"Okay, bye."*

She hangs up and takes a few deep breaths. "Travis left. Gave some bullshit reason that his parents needed him for something."

"Fuck, the little snake is running."

"Yeah, he is," she grits out, her fists clenching and unclenching as she paces.

"Come here, Spitfire."

She shakes her head.

"Give me a few moments and I will."

"Nope. Get that sexy ass over here and lie down with me."

"You better not be thinking anything sexual, Nick. You were shot today," she shakes her head and rubs her temple, but she keeps pacing.

"Oh, I'm definitely thinking sexual things about you, Spitfire, but even my dumbass knows now isn't a good time for that. Now, get your sexy ass in this bed before I get up and drag your ass over here."

She rolls her eyes and crawls in bed with me, but not before smacking my shoulder. "Nothing strenuous for you for a while, Mister," she says as she snuggles up to me.

I hold her for a few minutes as my mind goes back to Travis. Levi was on the right train of thought earlier. What changed that caused him to switch sides? Or was he always working with them?

"When did you say Travis and Ethan moved to Forest Creek?"

"Both of their families moved here at the end of our freshman year. Their houses sat empty for about a month after they were sold. We later found out that was so they could finish out the school year at their previous school."

"So then, when you were around sixteen or so?"

"Yeah, I was the last to turn sixteen that summer.

"Did they know each other before they moved here?"

Levi pauses as she thinks and then shakes her head. "No, they didn't, and they didn't live near each other before they moved, either. We actually met them through Alexei because all three of them were playing baseball that summer."

Worry begins to set in that my suspicion could be true. "And you all went to the same college?"

"Yeah. It was the closest one that wasn't a community college. I didn't want to move away too far and none of us wanted to pay out-of-state tuition. They had a decent business program for me, so that's why I chose it. The twins both had full art scholarships there, and Ethan had a partial scholarship. I was actually surprised that Ethan and Travis both chose Wisconsin University because Berkers College of Art & Design actually has a better architecture program."

Fuck, yeah, I wouldn't want to pay out-of-state tuition either. That shit is expensive. Wait.

"Did they say why they chose Wisconsin University over Berkers?"

"Ethan didn't get any scholarships to Berkers, but he did to Wisconsin University. That's why he made the choice he did."

"What about Travis? Why did he choose Wisconsin University?"

Her brow furrows. "I honestly don't know now that I think about it. The guys would sometimes razz him for following us like a lost puppy dog. His response was that he followed cause someone had to keep us out of trouble." She laughs and shakes her head.

"What?"

"It's just that Travis is actually the least responsible one out of all of us. Honestly, I think it's his parent's fault. Mr. and Mrs. West are old school in their thoughts, where a woman's place is in the house and pregnant. They hated how independent Sasha and I were and were very vocal about it. After meeting them that first time, we never met again at his house. They are extremely religious, and I'm not saying that's a bad thing, but they are very over-the-top extreme about it. And as if those aren't enough reasons, they are also among the top five, if not the top wealthiest, families here in Forest Creek. Travis is spoiled rotten.

"When we were living in the apartments, Alexei and Ethan would always complain about how much of a slob Travis was. He got a bit better in that aspect over the years since the guys forced him to carry his own weight in that regard, but still. It was annoying and sometimes I felt like we were his keepers."

"Where did they live on campus?"

"In the same apartment complex as me. There was only one three-bedroom apartment available, and the rest were all single apartments. The guys rented the bigger apartment together and Sasha and I got our own apartments, even though we wanted to share one if possible. Shortly after we moved in, we met Sam, who was next door to me. He hung out with us a lot. Remember the group of us in those pictures Fang sent that were from our apartment? The other guy that was with the five of us a lot? That was Sam."

I chewed on my lip. "Can I see your pictures on your phone again, Spitfire?"

Her brow creases, but she pulls out her phone and unlocks it. "Yeah, but is there something that you're looking for? What are you thinking?"

"I have an idea, but I'd rather see the pictures first to see if I'm wrong. I don't want to say something unless I have a pretty good idea I'm right."

As I flip through the pictures, occasionally Spitfire would laugh and tell me what they were doing when they took the photos.

Shit. I think I'm right. And that makes me fucking pissed that I missed it. Either his feelings have changed, or he's gotten damn good at hiding them.

I stop and back out before scrolling back to the first one that caught my eye before laying the phone down on my chest. Fuck, do I want to punch that little traitor even more now. Exhaling heavily, Levi sits up and faces me.

"What?"

"I think he likes you. Hell, maybe even loves you, Spitfire."

Her jaw drops in shock before she starts laughing. "There's no way he loves me like that. He's like a brother."

"The way he looks at you in these pictures isn't in a brotherly way, Babe."

"What? No, he doesn't. Besides, I'm nothing like the girls he would date or hook up with." She pauses and then shakes her head.

I lift the phone and show her the first picture. They're around a campfire and Levi and Sasha were making silly faces while they roasted marshmallows. Off to the side, Travis has a lovesick smile on his face as he stares at Levi.

"He could be looking at either of us in that picture."

"All right, then what about this one? Or this one? Or this one?"

I keep flipping through the pictures and I see it slowly sinking in before she snatches the phone out of my hand and flips through more pictures. After a few moments, she drops her hands in her lap in frustration.

"No. Travis has always gone after skinnier women with big boobs, though she always has blond or red hair, but that's the only similarity to us. They were always the types that would do whatever he said. Honestly, I always wondered where he found them because if they were at Wisconsin University, then they had to be getting an MRS degree cause, wow."

She grimaces as if she's remembering the women.

Pieces are definitely clicking together and I'm not liking where this is going, but before I can say anything, the door opens and Patch walks in. He looks between us and pauses.

"Am I interrupting anything?"

"Yeah, but it's okay cause I'll be bringing it up to the guys in a bit."

"Okay," he says, drawing the word out a bit as he stares at me for a moment. "I was just going to let you know that you're clear to be moved upstairs. They'll most likely keep you overnight to make sure there are no infections that pop up or other complications."

"Are Thor and Ethan cleared to move upstairs yet?"

"Yup. Thor's already on the move. I verified that his meds and everything were correct and put a nurse I trust with him. Smoke's keeping a lookout for him right now. Allison just started prepping Ethan and I'll get you ready. Levi, can you grab his things out of the cupboards over there?"

As Patch double-checks my IV bags, I notice he isn't dressed in his scrubs anymore.

"You off the clock now?"

"Yeah, but since I figured we'll all be talking soon about what happened, I offered to help take you upstairs to free up one of the nurses down here."

I watch as Spitfire bundles up my stuff into a plastic bag and I hate when she puts my cut in the bag. I don't feel right not wearing it. She gives me a tight smile when she's done. I pray I'm wrong about Travis' intentions, but my gut tells me I'm right.

Chapter 40
Thor

FOR THE LAST COUPLE of hours or so, the rest of our brothers have cycled through to talk to us and checked in on us. They wheeled Ethan in here so it would be easier to talk to everyone. I'm so damn fucking tired, but I know we aren't even close to being done discussing this shit.

Creed had been talking to Smoke over in the corner most of the time and I'm betting Smoke gave him the other evidence from his cameras. Creed left about ten minutes ago.

Wildcat's been edgy and talking quietly with Sasha the whole time. I've noticed Dragon looking over at her worriedly as well as Patch, which has me wondering what the hell is going on.

For our guards, Alexei will be in our room with Judge and Bear outside. Timber is going to be in with Ethan. Gunner and Axe will be outside his room. They'll sleep in shifts until we're let go, which the doctors think could be tomorrow morning.

Finally, everyone leaves except for the guards, Patch, Sasha, Colt, and Phoenix. Ethan's still in the room too and he and Alexei have been sucked into whatever conversation the women are having.

"Okay, will someone please tell me why you two are acting jittery and nervous?" I ask, my gaze bouncing between Dragon and Wildcat.

"I think we might have missed something," Dragon hesitantly starts. He looks over at Wildcat and her shoulders fall.

"Will someone please fill in the rest of the class?" My tone comes out snappy, but dammit, I'm tired, in pain, and I've barely gotten to touch Wildcat since she came in here.

"Dragon thinks Travis either likes or maybe even is in love with me," Levi says quietly.

They fill the rest of us in on what they talked about down in the ER as well as showing us the pictures.

"Over the years, I'd noticed that he would always watch both Sasha and Levi closely whenever we were together. He never mentioned to me that he liked either of you, but it looked like he did," Ethan says.

"Same here, but his gaze always lingered longer on Levi. There were times where it was downright creepy in high school and I called him out on those," Alexei says as he shivers.

"Creepy how?" Levi asks in disbelief.

Glad someone asked cause if they didn't, I sure as hell was going to.

Alexei runs a hand through his hair, shifting a little like he's nervous. Or really uncomfortable. "A couple of times when we were swimming."

However, he doesn't elaborate on what Travis did, though I can imagine. I've seen Wildcat in a bikini and damn, was the sex hot that night.

Ethan clears his throat, also seeming uncomfortable. "You weren't the only one. I shoved him into the pool more times than I can count in hopes you wouldn't see him hard."

Levi covers her face as her cheeks heat. "Thank you for that. I would definitely not have wanted to see his boner. I always saw him as a brother, well, not any more of course. He's cute, but not my type."

Sasha nods in agreement.

"Alexei and Ethan, I hate that I even have to ask, but I just want to get it out in the open. Both Levi and Sasha are in relationships. That's not going to cause any issues with either of you, is it? Neither one of you are gonna turn into a psycho because they aren't with either of you?" Phoenix asks and I give him a minute chin lift in thanks.

Almost in sync all four of their faces screw up and all of them slightly shudder, as a resounding 'nope' sounds from all four, again it's almost in sync.

A few guys chuckle at their reactions, and I let out a breath I hadn't realized I'd been holding.

"These two are my brothers, and I'd only have an issue with whomever they date if she is a manipulative, lying bitch." Levi says.

"Same," the others say in agreement.

"Well, the three of you look extremely beat. How about we let you rest? I'll get to work on looking through other cameras to see if we can get a better picture of whoever shot at us. I already put in for background checks on the nurses, so I'll let you know about those as I get them back," Smoke says.

"Sounds good," I say as my phone dings. I look at the text and grin. "Creed has those two nurses in custody."

"That's a relief. Alright, we'll get out of your hair for a few hours. Later, when we bring you guys food for breakfast, we'll bring fresh clothes and shit for all of you," Phoenix says, and the others get up to leave.

Patch holds back by Ethan's wheelchair and then gives us both a chin lift. "Let me or Allison know if you need anything."

"Thanks, man," I reply.

Once the door is shut, Levi's posture slumps. She looks dead on her feet, even though it's only nearing ten o'clock. It's been a shitty fucking day. Not the finding out we're having twins part, but the rest of it.

"Sleep, Levi. I'll keep watch," Alexei tells her.

I pat the bed next to me and she nods. She goes over and gives Dragon a quick kiss. He looks about ready to pass out, too, and I'm not far behind. Walking over to me, she gives me a kiss and then lays down next to me.

"Love you, Wildcat."

"Love you too, Thor."

"Love you too, Spitfire," Dragon calls out sleepily, and Wildcat giggles.

"Love you too, Dragon." After a few beats, she raises a hand. "Love you too, Alexei."

He chuckles and lays a blanket over her. "Love you too, Levi." He pauses and looks up at me. "As a sister."

I grin and give him a chin lift, letting sleep take over.

The next morning, I'm sore as fuck, but I can at least move without wanting to pass out now. The first few times I got up to use the bathroom last night were really tough.

We're getting dressed and I'm struggling with my shirt big time when I feel Levi's hands on my back.

"Don't get mad. I'm only intervening because some tape isn't fully sticking to your skin and is catching your shirt. Give me a minute to fix it."

She grabs the roll of tape off the IV pole and runs back around behind me since I'm stuck for now and it's killing me to hold this position. Her soft hands on my skin has me instantly hard. Fuck, it sucks not being able to taste or have sex with her like we used to.

"Don't even think about it," she says as she lightly smacks my ass.

She steps away and I finish pulling on my t-shirt. It sucks that I can't ride my motorcycle for a while. Dragon has to wait at least a week before he can ride, but it helps that he was shot in his right leg. If it was his shifting leg, then it would be longer. I have to wait at least a couple weeks before I attempt to try and ride since I was shot in the shoulder.

"When the hell do we get to leave? I'm itching to be back home," Dragon complains.

"Just waiting on the discharge paperwork. I've got everything packed up so as soon as we have the papers, we can leave," Levi says as she grins, but it doesn't quite reach her eyes.

We're all cranky because of not sleeping very well, but I also know she's been worried sick ever since Creed called her yesterday.

Patch brought my truck over this morning, which miraculously didn't have any broken glass or bullet holes in it, and Colt drove his SUV for Ethan. Half of our club as well as half of Reaper's crew are here today to escort us home. We're all paranoid as fuck about Fang or Sean trying anything on our way back to the clubhouse.

Reaper walks over to me when Levi goes over and sits next to Dragon on his bed. "How you doing, Thor? Like really, how are you doing?"

I sigh and shake my head, talking quietly. "In a shit ton of pain. Thank fuck Levi put on more gauze than the nurse first told her to since the stitches are right by the edge of my cut. Fucking surprised the bullet missed my cut in all honesty. Also, I'm fucking pissed at Travis' betrayal and I fucking want him, Sean, and Fang so bad I can taste it. I want this over for Levi, too. It's been a couple of months of looking over her shoulder constantly and the stress can't be good for the babies."

He grins and nudges my good shoulder. "Can't believe you two are settling down and having babies. Fuck, I wish your parents were still alive to see this."

I can't stop the smile that crosses my face when Wildcat looks up at me, smiling widely. She must have heard him razzing me. "They would have loved her and our babies to pieces. Damn, I miss them."

A knock sounds before the door opens and a doctor comes in.

"We have your paperwork, so you both are free to go. I know the nurses went over a lot of information for you. Remember, if you experience any redness or oozing around your wounds, you could have an infection and will need to be seen. Remember to keep the stitches dry in the shower. I understand one of our ER nurses is a member of your club, correct?"

"Yeah, Luke Morgan. He's over in Ethan's room right now," I tell him.

"Good, if he's there, he can take a look at it and determine if you are indeed fighting an infection. Do you have any other questions?" Seeing us all shake our heads; he claps his hands together. "In that case, I'll get out of your hair, and I hope you have a smooth recovery."

After he leaves, Wildcat picks up her purse and backpack while Alexei grabs our bags. As we're leaving our room, we notice the doctor talking to Ethan, so we wait a few minutes for him to finish.

"Thank fuck we can get out of here finally," Ethan mutters as he leaves his room.

"Completely fucking agree," Dragon replies.

"Language, there are children in the hallway," Wildcat hisses.

"Sorry, Mom," Ethan says teasingly. Her hand snaps out quick as lightning, smacking him up alongside the back of his head.

"Ouch, Levi. Quit hitting the invalid," he says, laughing.

"Don't make me go Grandma Mills on your butt."

We all laugh when he immediately straightens up and looks around nervously.

"That's not funny, Levi. Grandma is fu—flipping scary on a good day."

Minutes later, we all load into the vehicles. In my truck, Levi is riding shotgun, Dragon and I are in the back, and Patch is driving. I reach forward and squeeze Levi's shoulder. I can see from the side mirror that she's chewing on her lip nervously while looking around like a hawk.

"We'll be home soon, Wildcat."

She doesn't answer except for a hum as Patch backs out into the street and waits a few moments for the group that'll go in front of us before he starts to drive.

Luckily, there aren't very many turns between here and the compound, but there are a lot of traffic lights. We have a group in front of and behind our truck and the same with Colt's SUV in case we do get separated by the lights. I just hope it's not by much. We're better protected the closer we are together.

We're most of the way home when Levi screams as she grabs the oh shit bar. "Floor it and brace! From the left!"

Patch quickly glances left as the truck revs, but we aren't quick enough. A red truck runs into the truck on Dragon's side. The truck lurches again when someone else hits the front end of the truck. We must hit something else cause the truck lurches yet again and then we're rolling.

When we finally stop, we're hanging upside down.

"Wildcat! Are you alright? Wildcat! Dragon! Patch!"

Two male groans answer me, but nothing from Wildcat.

My vision is blurry, and it takes me a bit before I realize Wildcat isn't moving. Shit! Please let her be alive!

"Spitfire! Babe, answer us," Dragon calls out as he tries to get himself un-buckled.

"Shit. Let me get unbuckled and I'll help get her down," Patch says.

Someone tries opening my door but they can't. A face appears in the busted-out window and it takes me a moment before I realize it's Reaper. "Help Levi." He nods and then he's gone, quickly replaced with Phoenix.

"She's alive but unconscious, with cuts on her forehead and arms," Patch yells.

"Thank fuck!" both Dragon and I say in unison.

"First off, anything in pain besides your fucking shoulder?" Phoenix asks me.

"Think my head hit the window and a few cuts from the glass. Other than that, just my shoulder and it's worse than before, but I don't see any blood so far."

"Alright, let's see if we can get you out of here."

It takes a bit of maneuvering since I feel like I've been hit by a freight train and I can't support much weight with my shoulder fucked up.

After a ridiculous amount of time, I'm finally able to crawl out my window after Phoenix busts off the rest of the glass shards.

Once I'm steady on my feet, Phoenix steps aside and a paramedic is instantly in my face, guiding me to a gurney.

"Where are you hurt?"

"Help my fiancée first. She's unconscious and pregnant."

"She's already being helped, Sir, and I heard one of your friends say she's pregnant, so the paramedics treating her already know. Now, where are you hurt?"

"My left shoulder hurts worse than it did when we left the hospital a bit ago. I was shot yesterday. So was my brother, Dragon, who was also in the backseat."

"Fuck, that's a definite rough couple of days," the guy says and I grunt in agreement. Rough as fuck, that's for damned sure. He cuts up the sleeve that I gestured to and looks at the stitches.

"Well, at least you didn't pop a stitch, so that's a plus. None of the lacerations I can see need stitches and you aren't bleeding anywhere else it looks like. Anything feel broken?"

"No, just sore as fuck and I have a headache."

His hands feel around my head and I wince when I feel pain at my temple.

"You've got a decent-sized goose egg but no lacerations to your head that I can see. Now follow my light with your eyes. Don't move your head."

My eyes follow his flashlight even though my entire body vibrates with a need to check on Wildcat.

"You don't appear to have a concussion. Let's check your other vitals."

While he's doing that, I'm finally able to look around. It appears someone hit Colt's SUV but both he and Ethan appear to be unharmed. There are a couple of bikes on the ground. I think they're part of Reaper's crew because I don't recognize them.

"Beast and Punisher have minimal road rash, but otherwise, they're okay. It appears that once again, you guys were targeted," Phoenix quietly tells me as Devil, Reaper's VP, approaches us.

"Since you guys were still being checked out and since he was with her, Reaper rode with your Old Lady to the hospital. He said he'll text when he has an update."

I turn and curse when I see an ambulance speeding away. "Fuck. Do I need to get checked out at the hospital too, or can I go check on my fiancée?"

Dragon comes over, limping slightly, followed by Patch.

"You really should go in to get checked out—" he starts to say when I interrupt him.

"But are we required to?"

"I'm actually an ER nurse," Patch says as he shows the paramedic his badge. "How about I'll stay with them and if any of us show any signs that we need to come in, we will. I can have another ER nurse friend be with us, too, in case I start to show symptoms. Is that enough for you to let us go?"

After hesitating, the paramedic nods reluctantly. "Yes, you're free to go, but make sure you get in to see someone as soon as something pops up or if new injuries present themselves."

"Thank you," I say, ripping off the blood pressure cuff.

We walk, or I should say limp, back over to the truck. Timber's holding the duffle bag that was on the floorboard by me as well as Levi's backpack and purse. They are all a bit torn up, but still in one piece.

"I called Smoke, and he's already getting into the cameras for evidence. Drae and Judge are coming with SUVs since Colt is still talking to the police about his SUV and your truck is totaled. A cop already talked to me, and I mentioned your fiancée was headed to the hospital. Once you guys give your statements, we'll be able to leave," Timber says.

"Then let's go give our statements," I bite out. Fuck, I really need to get to the hospital and check on Wildcat.

Twenty fucking minutes later, we're piling into the club SUV's when my phone rings.

"Whatcha got, Smoke?"

"The ambulance carrying Levi and Reaper never made it to the hospital."

"What?" I roar, fury running through my veins like lightning.

"They pulled into a parking garage, but it never left. I'm tracing the other vehicles I saw leave now to try to figure out where they went. Get back to the compound."

He hangs up, and it takes everything in me not to throw my phone.

"What happened?" Phoenix asks, his voice deadly.

"The ambulance didn't go to the hospital. Get back to the compound. Hopefully, Smoke will have more information when we get there."

Dragon roars and kicks a piece of debris.

Fuck, please let Wildcat and our babies be alive.

Chapter 41
Levi

Fuck, my entire body feels like I've been run over. I try to open my eyes, but that just makes my head pound worse when light burns my eyes. Something trickles down my face and I move to wipe it away, but I can't move. Fuck... I'm restrained.

Fear instantly fills my veins before I try to push it down. Freaking out won't help me at all right now.

Slowing my breathing, I keep my eyes closed and listen. There's some shuffling nearby and in the distance, I can hear a woman screaming.

"Levi, you awake? No one's in here, but someone is outside the door. I think. Whisper if you can hear me."

"Reaper, is that you? I'm awake, but my head hurts like a son of a bitch. It hurts to open my eyes."

"Yeah, it's me Half-pint. The glass cut you pretty bad on your forehead and you've got a nasty bump. Does anything else hurt?"

"I think it's just pain from being tossed around. Did they do anything else to me while I was out? And I'm not that short!" I whisper yell at him.

He chuckles softly. "Glad to see you still have your sass. Can't speak for when I was knocked out, but since I've come to, no, they haven't. They gave you something in the ambulance, but I didn't think anything of it till they stuck me with something, too. I've been awake for a while now. It's either near dusk or near dawn from the little I can see through the gaps in the boards covering the windows. They must not have given me enough to keep someone as big as me out long enough."

I nod at that. Reaper is a big man. Not as big as Uncle Bear as he's about half a head taller than Reaper. I wince when pain shoots up my ribs and then again when I gasp for breath.

"My ribs might be bruised. Laughing hurts and it hurts to breathe deep."

He curses. "I'm sorry I failed you, Half-pint."

I start to shake my head and then stop when my head spins and I get a little light-headed. "It's not your fault, Andre. The fault is with whoever took us, which is most likely Fang, my uncle Sean, Travis, or all the above."

"Andre?"

"Yeah, if you're gonna call me Half-pint, then I'm calling you Andre. Like that wrestler, Andre the Giant. He also played Fezzik, in *The Princess Bride*."

He chuckles and shakes his head, but doesn't comment. I slowly blink, trying to clear the black dots dancing around the edge of my vision. After a few moments, the pain from the light, thankfully, doesn't shoot straight through my skull anymore. Slowly, I raise my head and look around.

We're in some sort of dilapidated cabin, and the windows are boarded up. A single light bulb hangs above us. Memories assault me, but it can't be the same cabin from when I was almost sixteen. I watched as Dad and Uncle Bear torched the place.

Turning, I see Reaper to my left, who's also tied up. Fuck, I wish I had just sent them the bracelets instead of wanting to wait until this weekend to give them to him and his crew. However, whoever tied him up is an idiot because the rope used around his ankles isn't over the crossbar support of the chair. It's under it and he's already trying to lower it.

Glancing down, I notice that there is rope around my ankles too, but it's not that tight, and it's also under the crossbar support. I can actually wiggle my ankles a little and I keep that up as I feel around for my bracelets.

"Levi, they didn't take your bracelets. You should still have them on."

I pause at that and my head whips toward him, which I instantly regret when pain lances through my skull for moving so fast.

"How do you know about them?"

"Because yesterday, Phoenix gave us ours when he got back from the hospital. Everyone took one when he showed us what they can do. Can't thank you enough right now."

Relief flows through me at that. "How far through are you?"

"Almost halfway, but I'm tied up more than you are."

Looking down at his hands, from what I can see, he's got four lengths of rope leading up his wrists, but at least they look like single layers, for the most part anyway. I spread my fingers and try to feel how deep and high the ropes are, and I breathe a sigh of relief when I only feel a couple single layers that are similar to the times when Sasha and I tied each other up and practiced how to get out of them. I send up a silent prayer, hoping that this goes easily.

Shimmying a little, I push my wrists together more until I can feel one of the bracelets. Twisting, I carefully hang onto the cord until the blade is in my hand.

"Got it," I whisper and get to work cutting through the rope.

I'm about halfway through my ropes when I hear heavy footsteps from up above us.

"Shit," I whisper.

"Get it balled up as safely as you can in your fist, quick. Pretend you're still out of it. No matter what they do, stay strong Half-pint and don't give them anything."

"Stay strong, yourself," I whisper back. His grunt tells me he'd heard me.

I let my body slump and work to slow my breathing as I carefully gather up my bracelet, praying I don't cut myself in the process.

"Any movement?" I hear from outside the door, and my blood runs cold when I recognize Fang's voice.

"Not a peep," someone else replies, but I don't recognize the voice this time.

"Move," Fang says.

The door unlocks and then it quickly shuts. I force myself not to react when he steps up close to me. His shoes squeak and I'm guessing he crouches down because the next thing I feel is him lifting my chin slightly. I let my head naturally roll a bit when it feels like it wants to so that I hopefully appear to be zonked out yet.

He lets go of my chin and my head painfully bobs back down.

Fuck, does that hurt.

He walks over to Andre and must get a similar result because I hear the sound of his steps crossing the room again before the door opens, shuts, and is locked.

Even though my mind screams to start cutting the ropes again, I wait, making sure no one else decides to come back into the room.

We're not that lucky.

I can hear multiple footsteps walking toward our room and then the door is unlocked again.

I gasp when ice water hits me and curse when my wet, heavy hair blocks part of my view, including Andre. Someone else must have helped him carry in the buckets but the door shuts again before I can see who it was.

"Rise and shine, sleeping beauties," Fang's voice rings out. I glare at him as I painfully try to catch my breath.

He props a bucket on his hip, cocking his head as he gives me a feral grin. "Miss me, Princess?"

"Not in the slightest," I grit out.

Fang backhands me, and I bite my tongue to keep my cry from escaping, remembering that he thrives on the sound of pain.

"While we wait for my brothers to get back from sending those pussies on a wild goose chase, I think it's time we get reacquainted again. While I had wanted to do this to those two pussies you let touch you, I'll start with your friend Reaper here. Are you screwing him, too?"

Hoping that Fang wouldn't hurt him more, I answer honestly. "No."

An evil smile lights up his face. "Good, then you won't mind if I kill him then."

I struggle harder, which makes Fang laugh again right before he punches Andre in the face.

"Don't say any—" Andre says before Fang lands another punch to his face.

"I didn't give you permission to speak, asshole."

Fang walks around Andre and I force myself not to look at his hands and draw attention to the ropes.

"Now, before we get to the good stuff, I gotta get a few things out of the way." He walks to a nearby table and picks up a knife.

Walking back over to Reaper, he starts whistling as he starts cutting off Reaper's 'President' badge. Both Andre and I struggle harder, but when I feel the ropes loosen a bit more around my wrists; I try not to wretch them around as much so that Fang doesn't notice. It's still not loose enough to slip my wrist out, but it's closer than it was.

Andre's 'President' patch falls to the floor and in the next sweep of his blade, he slices up the length of his cut.

A growl escapes me at seeing his cut mutilated and disrespected. Andre is furious and pulling at his ropes so hard that the vein in his neck is bulging.

Fang pays him no mind as he cuts Andre's shirt, revealing his chest. Slowly, he starts slicing into his skin. Tears roll down my face as I cry out.

"You know what you have to do to get this to stop, Princess. All you have to do is say the words."

"Don't—"

Fang stops cutting and punches him in the face again. "I didn't give you permission to speak!"

Andre's eyes plead with me not to say anything, so I clamp my mouth shut even though it's killing me.

Fang goes back to carving up Andre's chest when the door flies open again, but Fang doesn't stop.

A man who looks like his face has been beaten in repeatedly comes in carrying a woman over his shoulder. Her legs are bound and ice slides down my spine. Behind him trail two other men I don't recognize until someone steps into view that I do recognize.

Travis.

However, what pisses me off even more is that he's wearing a different cut with the road name, Diablo, on it.

He grins evilly at me as his eyes rake up and down my body, then scowls when he sees my face. "That better not have been your handiwork, dear brother."

Does he mean brother as in club brother, or like an actual blood brother?

My gaze darts between Fang and Travis and I can't help but jump a bit when the first guy unceremoniously drops the bound woman hard on the table. She groans in pain around her gag. It's then that I see that her wrists are taped together in front of her. I keep a close eye on the three new people, but more ice slides down my spine when I see their cuts. Archer, Joker, and Korso.

A, J, and *K.*

Fuck...

"That's from Shorty not hitting the truck where he was supposed to. He's paying the price, don't you worry. I did have to backhand her, though, for being mouthy."

Travis shrugs. "At least he's paying for his mistake. As long as she can still have a dick in her mouth later, then that's fine." He turns back to me and grins darkly again. "I see you recognize everyone now."

My gaze goes back to Fang's brothers. All three of them closely resemble Fang, but there are differences. Archer's right eye is milky white. Joker's the one that was carrying the woman before. Korso's face is even worse than Joker's and it looks like his nose was broken more than once.

Travis turns and walks over to the woman, rolling her so I can see her face. "Now, while we weren't able to get Sasha, Roxy, or our traitorous cousin, Carolina, this little beauty will be our stand-in for showing you what will happen to you later."

Bile rises in my throat as the woman's eyes widen in fear.

Quickly, he slices through the tape around her wrists, and she struggles. The other men step forward and her wrists are quickly secured again but this time, to metal chains attached to the table. He does the same thing to her ankles, but she's a fighter and nails him in the balls before her ankles are quickly secured to the table as well. Travis backhands the woman and grips her face hard.

"You will pay for that, you worthless cunt."

I don't recognize the Travis in front of me, and he sure as hell isn't the same Travis that I knew.

He rips her clothes off her as she screams for someone to help her.

Reaper grunts and when I glance over at him, I see a larger trail of blood sliding down his arms. My eyes widen when I see his chest. Fang's carved the club initials into his chest. And he hasn't stopped there. He continues to cut into Reaper's skin, and some of them look deep.

A cry has my attention snapping back to the woman. Travis is carving BP into her stomach.

"No, no, please don't! Please don't!"

I struggle harder against my ropes, but with this many people in here, I know I'll be dead before I can free or help any of us. It's then that I see the back of Travis' cut. He's seriously part of Black Plague? Then my stomach sinks when I remember him saying CJ is his cousin. Fuck. Is he seriously Fang's brother like he said before? As in blood brother?

Archer approaches me, and I glare at him when he places duct tape over my mouth.

"They'll be no interrupting this part, Princess. This is part of your punishment for not coming to us sooner. You'll endure the same treatment, but the ending won't be as fast as what hers will be," he says as he and the rest of the men laugh.

"You three can take her while I make sure our Princess watches the whole thing," Travis says as he walks over to me, still holding the bloody knife from cutting up the woman's stomach.

"First things first, time to get this filth off you," he sneers.

He roughly starts cutting off my patches before slicing through the leather, cutting off my cut. Tears stream down my face as the leather falls to the ground. Next, he cuts and rips my shirt off, and the asshole licks his lips as he stares at me in my white lacy bra. Stepping behind me, he pulls my hair painfully and a shiver of disgust runs through me when he licks up my neck.

"You're going to watch them fuck her and you'll pay every time you look away or close your eyes."

Tears stream down my face and I can't help it, my eyes close. A scream rips out of me as I feel Travis' blade sink into my skin.

He tsks me. "Naughty naughty, Princess."

Fuck that hurts!

Please let my guys and the club get here soon.

Chapter 42

Thor

As soon as the gate opens, Drae doesn't waste any time driving through before screeching to a halt in front of the clubhouse.

My door is open before the car even stops moving and I storm into the clubhouse, Dragon right next to me. Bastion is at my other side the next second. I wonder if he senses that Levi's missing.

Seeing us enter, everyone grabs their drinks before going into Church. Even though I want a beer, I know it won't mix with my pain meds. Instead, I grab a Coke, wanting the extra caffeine. I need to make sure my head stays clear.

"Prospects, one of you stays on the computer on lookout. The rest of you rip down every camera that isn't ours and crush them. The jig is up, and they don't need to know our next steps after this."

"You got it, Pres," Alexei hollers out.

The door shuts behind me and I walk up to the front of the room, and fuck if Patch isn't there with a chair.

"I mean no disrespect by this, Pres, but sit the fuck down. You were shot yesterday and were just in a serious accident. You're lucky to have as few injuries as you do. Save your strength for rescuing our Queen and our brother."

Grunting, I gratefully take the chair, but I'm not saying that out loud. Looking around the room, Smoke, Bones, Ryder, and Python are on their laptops.

"Tell us what you were able to find so far," I bark out. It's Smoke that speaks up.

"At first the ambulance followed the path it was supposed to back to the hospital, and yes, it looks like it is a real ambulance. Whoever took it must have stolen the keys and uniforms from the hospital. I haven't heard a peep about the hospital reporting that they're missing an ambulance, but they must know by now."

Smoke clicks some buttons, and an image of a parking garage appears on the wall. I move to lower the screen, but Phoenix beats me to it. I give him a chin lift in thanks.

"This is where they dumped the ambulance. The third-floor cameras are down. I did see it on the second-floor cameras but not on the fourth-floor cameras. Not too long afterward, five cars leave the parking garage from different floors and head in different directions. We don't have clear shots of any of the drivers thanks to ball caps, and they all paid in cash at the exit. We've sent Axe and Razor to do a drive-by and see if they can give us a visual.

"We've traced three cars so far and are working on the other two. The first three went to residential homes and none of the homeowners come up in any of our hits for outstanding warrants or any priors.

"Alexei's helping keep watch at our access points here as well as running a program on another laptop watching to see if Reaper's or Levi's tracking devices suddenly come back online."

"Fuck," Dragon curses.

"He either ditched their cuts and bracelets or he's got a jammer," I say as I think this through. "Wait, when did we lose their signals?"

Smoke levels me with a hard look. "As soon as the doors shut on the ambulance."

Dragon curses again and is quickly on his feet, his chair falling to the ground. I wait and watch my brother, even though I'm feeling the same fury he is, but we have to keep our heads, no matter how pissed we are.

He curses again and punches the wall. Thankfully, he just hits sheetrock instead of a stud. Quickly, I'm on my feet until I'm standing in front of him and grip him hard on the shoulder. Bear and Ryder are leaning against the wall, not too far from us. Fuck, I didn't even hear them get up.

"Dragon, tame your beast for now. He'll be able to get revenge later, but we can't flip our shit right now or go off half-cocked when we don't even know where they are."

He glares at me, but I know he sees my beast barely restrained right now as well. Thankfully, he nods and after a few moments, sits back down. With a chin lift to Bear and Ryder, I retake my seat, but they stay where they are for a few moments before sitting down as well.

"How far are we—"

A phone rings and at first, I'm pissed till I realize it's Phoenix's. We're the only two allowed to have our phones in Church. Well, and Devil, since he's the VP of the Junction Creek brothers.

"*Phoenix.*"

After a few moments, he curses and then hangs up.

"There's a fire in the parking garage and they aren't letting anyone in, so Axe and Razor can't get us a visual."

"Are the cameras on the third floor still out, Smoke?" I ask.

His fingers fly across his laptop again before he frowns. "They're back online and the ambulance is indeed on fire. From the angles shown, there's no one inside."

"Fuck, okay. See what you can get on the other two cars. Is there any recent property that has been bought by Black Plague members or Travis' family?"

"Not by Black Plague, but we're still looking into all the properties that were owned before by the West's."

A knock sounds and Phoenix gets up to answer it. Seconds later, the door opens and Alexei comes in with a laptop.

"Levi and Reaper's beacons just showed back up."

He sits the laptop down by Smoke, who unplugs a cable from his laptop and puts it into Alexei's. The beacons are coming from the forest Northwest of town.

"Isn't that around where we scouted before?" Timber asks.

Smoke's forehead creases as he frowns and pulls up something else on his laptop. "Either we missed something or the entrance is hidden. Since the beacons are still up, I'm guessing the idiots didn't set up the jammer again when they arrived there. Maybe they changed vehicles."

"So, there's no buildings according to satellite images?" I ask.

Smoke zooms out before going in closer and compares the image to whatever's on his laptop. "No. But there used to be an old cabin near there, according to my records. It burned down a long time ago."

"Fuck," Bear yells as he jumps to his feet before pacing, his hands on his head. "That's not where the cabin was that burned down." His voice was low but deadly. "A few miles further Northwest from that spot is where the cabin was that burned down."

He turns and looks at me. "Remember what Nicole said? About going back to where it all started? The cabin that burned down is where we found Levi and Emily. We were the ones that burned it down and all the bodies in it."

"Oh shit," someone says.

My gaze snags on Dragon, who's barely hanging onto a thread of control. Our eyes lock and we both nod. This ends tonight.

"The beacons are moving again," Alexei says, and I refocus back on the screen.

The dots are continuing Northwest, but at a slower pace than before. They continue for a couple of miles before they stop, but the beacons stay lit.

In the background, I can hear keys clicking away before the screen changes again. This time, to an aerial overview.

There's a two-story house on the property that looks to be around a couple of acres. There's a large wrought-iron and brick fence around the perimeter. A long driveway exits the property to the east.

"Who owns the property?" I ask.

"A Robert Smith is listed on the deed. It was bought four years ago. Fuck, the last name had to be a fucking Smith," Smoke mutters.

"Why does that matter?" Gunner asks.

"Because in the US, Smith is the most popular last name," Python says as he sighs.

"How far North is that place from here?" Dragon asks.

After a few moments, Smoke replies. "About twenty miles." The screen changes from aerial to a road map, which he draws on with his stylus. "Right here is the only way in by actual road. So, they either drove or walked through the fields to location A, where the beacons first reappeared, but I doubt they dragged Reaper's heavy ass that far. Once they started moving again, I'm guessing some sort of vehicle was used because the rate the beacon was moving was too fast to be walking and carrying heavy bodies. Someone said Levi was still unconscious when Reaper went with her in the ambulance. Even if Reaper was walking on his own accord and, taking into how fit he is, if he were carrying Levi, he still wouldn't be moving that fast. From location A to location B, they were moving around twenty mph according to my calculations."

"We got a few new things," Python says, and we all turn to him.

"Traced the two other cars. One is tied to another residential house that doesn't have any warrants or priors. The second car is listed as being owned by a Robert Smith with an address of that house. 101 Highland Drive. I don't know how the fucker passed the checks when buying the house four years ago because the information he gave doesn't belong to any US citizen. He doesn't exist. It's an alias.

"Also, there are permit records that state Robert put in a very large basement but then built a modest two-story house over part of the basement. The basement is about three times the scale of the first floor's square footage and it also has a secondary exit point that leads to a three-mile-long tunnel to the Southeast. Since I didn't see anywhere to hold heavy equipment above land, I'm guessing they rented the equipment to do the build."

"If they rented the equipment from old man Meissen on the edge of town, then he would have been adamant about seeing the building permits first. Even though he's known me since I was a kid, every job I do, whether residential or commercial, he needs to see all the papers before he'll rent anything heavy to me," Timber says which makes sense since he's owns a construction business which we also have a stake in.

I lean forward, resting my elbows on the table as I process everything. "Men will need to be stationed at location A just in case someone is able to get into the tunnel to escape. Smoke, you still have your drone?"

"Yeah, but it only has about a half-hour fly time, so I'll need to get close depending on how much surveillance you want me to do."

Everyone starts talking quietly about ideas before Smoke signals that he has something to say. I bang my hammer. Once everyone quiets down, I turn back to him.

"Smoke?"

He grins as he looks at Python and then Devil before he turns his grin my way. "Pres, remember when Levi got the translation devices?"

"Why the fuck would you need translation devices?" Beast asks.

All of my brothers from my chapter grin. After we had secured the other set of cameras Nicole had stashed, we had to tell them how we got information out of her. While I hate how they went behind my back, I was grateful Wildcat and Sasha got all the information out of her. Then Smoke showed the guys the video of what Wildcat was able to pull off before he wiped it from our servers.

"Because it was Levi and Sasha who extracted the information from Nicole when none of the rest of us could. They spoke Russian periodically to confuse and push up the fear factor. It was hot as fuck seeing and hearing my Old Lady doing that," Dragon said, and fuck, he actually adjusts himself at the memory.

"Why am I not surprised that violence turns you on, fucker?" Loki says while laughing.

Dragon just grins and looks over at me.

I will say that, in the moment, I didn't focus on that aspect. I was more worried about how she was going to handle it afterward. However, later, when the guys saw the video, it was definitely hot as fuck to see her taking charge and getting answers.

"You let your Old Lady talk to the guests? And she's okay with that?" Doc asks.

I pause, debating whether or not to tell the truth. We hadn't known she was going to do it. It wasn't until I needed Smoke for something, but he said he wouldn't be able to help me for a while and couldn't give me a timeframe. It was then that I realized I didn't know where Wildcat was. I pulled up our software that logs when people go through our security doors. It was then that I saw Levi's log from entering into the basement and then into the interrogation room or 'the sticks' as she calls it.

"Oh shit," someone says, and I look up to realize it was Punisher that spoke. "Are you telling us your Old Lady took matters into her own hands and went down there to get the info out of the bitch?"

I level him with a glare, but he doesn't seem pissed, more intrigued and... happy? Excited?

"Yes, she did. As soon as I realized where she was, Dragon and I went down there but didn't interfere."

"I knew what she was going to do as soon as I saw what she had ordered. Patch didn't know till the last second that it was unsanctioned," Smoke says.

I glare at him, but he doesn't back down. We had a long talk after that regarding his stunt.

"Let's get back on track," Ryder says, sensing I'm getting pissed again. "Why did you bring up the translation devices, to begin with? What else did she get?"

Smoke grins. "Communication devices similar to what they use in the Secret Service and the military. Don't ask me how she got them, because there's only three people in our chapter that can know besides Levi and that's Thor, Phoenix, and me and even then, she won't or can't give us all the information. Pres, I talked to Phoenix, and he agreed that with what's going on, Devil and Python should be brought in the loop on this one. Reaper will get filled in later."

I grin as relief floods me that my woman was watching out for us, though we're gonna have a talk later about this and any other possible surprises she might have.

Timber whoops. "That's our Queen!"

"Well, fuck, can we get hooked up with her contact?" Razor asks, and the guys laugh.

"Most likely since she also already had those bracelets made up for you guys," Phoenix says and it's then that I realized the Forest Creek guys are wearing her bracelets.

"Thank fuck. Hopefully, they don't realize that, or maybe Travis will forget, and Reaper and Wildcat can use them to get free."

"She does have extra communication devices here, but not enough for everyone to have one. She must have anticipated we might have people from other clubs with us at times, but not this many. Those that will be on the final legs of the rescue will all need to have them, and the rest can be split out as even as possible between the remaining groups," Smoke tells everyone.

"Alright. Settle down everyone," I pause as the chatter dies down. Looking around the room, I give them a chin lift. "Let's plan the rescue, and I want everyone to have it down to a 'T' because no one is coming home in a body bag."

Fists thunder against tables in agreement.

Almost three hours later, we creep into position at location A as some of the last rays of daylight still linger in the air. It's just enough for us to use Smoke's drone but dark enough that no one should be able to see it.

We leave the vans and trucks about half a mile down the road. Bones had found an old service road that got us close to our location and we left the vehicles on the partially covered section of the service road. A handful of men stayed with the vehicles.

Up ahead, I can see lights on in some of the rooms. The others either have the lights off or have heavy curtains blocking our view.

"Alright, Smoke, do your thing."

He gives me a chin lift and walks a few steps away from us. Kneeling, he opens a large case. It takes a few minutes for him to set up his drone before it's off and flying. I watch over his shoulder at the monitor and once again, am impressed with how clear of a picture we're able to get with his setup.

It doesn't take long for the drone to reach the house and he switches to thermal. In this section of the yard, I only see two of our guys, so far, according to the red dots on the screen.

"*Alpha, Golf, what's your status?*" Smoke asks.

"*Two tangos, male, walking around the perimeter. One tango at the front door and one at the gate. Earlier I counted five tangos, male, in the Southeast room on the first floor. About... forty minutes ago, heavy curtains were closed and lost sight. Second floor, lights off, no visible movement. No entries or exits from the front of the house,*" Alexei replies.

"*Northeast room on the first floor has heavy curtains drawn on the North side of the house but the windows on the east side are boarded up. Can't see in, but lights are on. Second-floor room has lights on, curtains shut. No visible movement,*" Gunner says.

"Charlie, Sierra, what's your status?" Smoke asks.

"One tango, male, at the back door. No entries or exits from back of the house. No one's been in what looks to be a study on the first floor, no lights. Three women were bound upstairs in the Southwest room with another tango, male. About forty minutes ago a tango, male, carried one of the women out of the room," Cannon replies.

"Windows are boarded up in the Northwest room first floor. There's a light on, but I can't see enough through the gaps. Lights out in upstairs bedroom, no movement," Smithy says.

"Bravo Team, you're with me. Fan out and give the signal if you see anything," Smoke says. Besides Smoke it's Axe, Tripp, Loki, Python, and Doc in that group.

"Alpha Team, move out," I say and we creep forward, sticking to the shadows. With me are Dragon, Phoenix, Ryder, Bear, Patch, Punisher, Beast, Razor, and Devil. Half will go in the front and half through the back. The ones in the front will clear the first room and then go straight upstairs, since the only staircase is right by that door. Dragon and I will bring up the rear to the rear entrance with Bear since we're both still feeling the effects of our injuries, but there was no way in hell we were not going in.

Phoenix sneaks up behind the tango guarding the back door and quickly snaps his neck before throwing him over his shoulder and dumping his body in the nearby tree line. Bear and Razor make quick work of the two tangos walking the perimeter. For as big and heavy as Bear is, it still surprises me that he can move so quickly and so quietly.

Phoenix and Razor move to the front yard with the rest of their team while we get in position by the back door.

"Front neutralized. Enter in three, two, one, go!"

Chapter 43
Levi

My body is on fire. I have a dozen or so cuts across my torso and even more on my arms and legs. The word slut has been carved into my left thigh. Travis cut most of my clothes off and has enjoyed his painting, as he calls my cuts, while he gropes me. Thank God, I'm still in the chair and not stretched out on a table.

I try to peek over at Andre, but doing so gets me another slice into my skin. Pain blossoms as blood trickles down my thigh. Besides the word slut, they haven't cut too deeply into me, for which I'm thankful for. While I no doubt will have even more scars, especially the slut one, my heart breaks when I remember my last good look at Reaper.

While I know I'm in pain, it's nothing compared to how his pain must be. His chest and arms are covered in cuts and blood as well as a nasty diagonal cut across his face.

They've already killed the woman they brought in earlier after they each took their turn. They left her mutilated body chained up to the table. A 'visual reminder' they said for what will eventually happen to me.

"We'll be back, Princess, after our friend gets some time with you," Fang says cryptically before he kisses me roughly. His tongue begs for entrance, but I clamp my jaw together tight. Unfortunately, it's short-lived.

Pain sears up my leg and I know they've cut deeper than they have so far. I can't help the gasp of pain that escapes, and Fang takes advantage, shoving his tongue in my mouth. I clamp down hard with my teeth on his tongue until I taste blood. His head rears away from me, blood trickling down his chin before he backhands me so violently the chair rocks. Thankfully, it doesn't tip over.

"You'll pay for that bitch," he says and spits some blood on the floor. "I'll make sure it's extra painful when it's my turn," he sneers.

Fang and his brothers leave the room as they all smile darkly. Travis is the only one left in the room and he takes advantage of it by violently groping me. I struggle, trying to get the last bit of rope cut. He's been too busy groping me and licking me to pay attention to my wrists.

"We've got a special surprise for you, Princess," he says as he walks around in front of me and drags his knife across my cheek. I clench my jaw as the blade bites into my skin deep enough that I know it'll scar. Instead of focusing on the pain, I continue to concentrate on the ropes and I almost make it through when the door opens, but I don't take my eyes off Travis.

"I'll just be over here, making sure you don't do anything stupid. Hope you enjoy it, cause I'll be taking my turn next."

He walks over to Andre, grabs his hair, and places his knife at his throat.

"Now, how is my *special girl* doing?"

It's only then that I focus on the other man.

Sean.

Though, as I look him over, I realize the years have not been kind to him. He looks like he's been the subject of a lot of prison fights as his nose has been broken several times. He looks gaunt, his skin stretched taught over his bones. I didn't think they would starve people in prison, or maybe they hadn't, and he lost his food since he doesn't look like he'd last a minute in an actual fight. His brown hair is styled in a comb-over in an attempt to hide his large bald spot.

Keyword—attempt.

"I'd be doing much better if you'd let my friend and me go," I said sweetly, hoping to buy us some more time to get through our ropes.

He smiles darkly and I'm praying even harder now that my men and the club get here fast.

Turning, he walks over to the table with tools on it and picks up another knife. Slowly, he walks over to me and starts to pace in front of me.

"You fucked up my entire life. If it weren't for you, I would have everything and been set up for life. Because of you, I went to jail and had to push off my plans to get your mother out of the picture for good. Her price to pay for choosing Roy over me."

Wow. I did not suspect that bit of information, but I force myself to focus back on Sean and buying time. Later, he'll pay for his hand in what happened to Mom.

"Pretty sure you went to jail because you drugged me and was about to have sex with a six-year-old," I grit out. God, I can't believe I ever looked up to this fucking asshole when I was younger.

Pain radiates across my cheek as he backhands me. Jesus, this backhanding shit is getting old.

"No, I went to jail because someone tipped off the cops. I had it all set up with pretty-boy's dad over there. After I broke you in and trained you, I'd sell you to the highest bidder and be living the high life. Instead, his mom decides to grow a conscience, once again, and calls in an anonymous tip."

"How do you know it was his mom?" I ask, trying to buy more time. I'm almost loose enough that I can slip out my hand. Out of the corner of my eye, Reaper gives me a thumbs up that neither Travis nor Sean see because they're too busy staring at my near naked-body. I need to find a way to get Sean closer to me.

Travis scoffs. "Please, Dad had every square inch of our house on cameras, and all the phones are bugged. She knew the consequences of what she did. Only this time it was worse."

What the hell is he talking about?

"The first time she tipped off the cops about selling a girl was about a year before I was born. That's how our connections grew even more. For her punishment, Dad got into contact with one of his most violent customers. Boar, President of Black Plague. They were already into trafficking, so their lower levels fed our upper-crust ones. Boar got to keep Mom all to himself until she got pregnant. Her punishment was to endure everything Boar did to her and then to raise her rapist's son.

"When she tipped off your family and hence the cops, Dad took her to Boar again. This time, his punishments were rougher, but she did conceive and deliver a baby girl. After Mom healed from the delivery, Dad and Boar beat and trained her into total submissiveness. She had to watch her little girl be trained from the get-go for a life of submissiveness to a master. To watch her be sold after she hit puberty. Now, everything Mom does is a cover for how we run our businesses. To cast us in a favorable light in the public."

Bile rises in my throat at what he's saying and to boot, he's fucking preening at what his mom had to endure. Not once, but twice?

What the fuck is wrong with him?

I stare at him in disbelief and then almost jump when a hand roughly grasps my chin and I'm forced to look at Sean. I mentally curse myself for becoming so distracted that I hadn't even noticed him approach me. Then again, this could be my chance.

"You'll pay for what you've taken from me, the West family, and Black Plague. You'll pray and beg to be treated like his mother was because your treatment will be ten times worse. Once your devil spawn is old enough, they'll be brought into the life and trained from the moment they're born."

At the mention of my kids and the threat of them being thrown into that kind of life, a fire lights in me.

I spring up from the chair, grabbing both of his wrists and squeezing as hard as I can on the wrist that holds his knife. My forehead is right in line with his nose and, when I headbutt him, I hear the satisfying crunch.

Behind me, I can hear the sounds of a shuffle. After a few moments, I hear a few painful grunts and know Andre's taking care of Travis. Finally, Sean's knife falls from his hands and I spin Sean around, kicking the back of both knees until he falls to the ground. Grabbing the knife, I land my weight on his back before wrenching his hands behind him.

Rope lands on the ground next to me and I look up quick enough to see Andre going back to tying Travis' hands. Like me, he's pressing a knee into Travis' back as he secures his hands.

As I'm tying the last knot, footsteps race through the house, and I hear the muffled sound of silenced gunshots go off.

"It's the club, Half-pint."

I glance up and notice he grabbed his phone from the table. He shoves it in his pocket and puts a bit more pressure on the knife at Travis' neck. I grin when I see both of their eyes filled with fear. Though, I am concerned with how much Andre's moving around because of his injuries.

Once the knots are secure, I roughly grab Sean's hair and pull back harshly as I hold the knife to his neck. "If you think the punishment you had planned for me was bad, just wait until you see what the Steel Archangel's will do to you. What *I* will do to you," I seethe quietly in his ear.

Anger runs through me at what these men have done and would have done to Reaper, me, and my babies, but I don't say anymore in case this place is bugged.

I'll make sure their time being entertained is long and painful.

The door to our room is flung open, and masked men pour into the room. Relief floods me when I recognize Uncle Bear along with my men right behind him, despite them being in disguises. Since they haven't taken off their masks, I have to remind myself not to say any of their names out loud.

Dragon scoops me up and Bear hoists Sean to his feet, talking dangerously low to him. Dragon gently sets me down on the chair I was on before, even though I don't want to be anywhere near it. He must see me about to lose it, cause he quickly whips off his shirt and puts it on me. It goes down a little past mid-thigh and thankfully, covers the wounds on my thigh.

"I got you," he says gently as he picks me back up.

"They hurt him so much. It's my fault they got him. If I had protected my head better, I wouldn't have been knocked out," I try to get out, but my voice sounds weird to me and black dots dance on the edges of my vision.

"Shh. Our medic has him. We're going straight to the hospital. I gotcha."

"Call one of the men to get the vehicles up here. Big guy needs blood, and the woman looks like she's going into shock. Have the other medic hop in whichever one they bring," I hear Patch call out, but everything starts to fade before darkness washes over me.

Chapter 44

Dragon

LEVI'S BODY GOES LIMP in my arms, and I start to panic. "She passed out!"

"Fuck!" Patch curses.

When Devil and Punisher both have Reaper's arms carefully stretched over their shoulders, they start to help him walk out. Patch rushes over to Spitfire and feels for a pulse. I notice Thor's off to the side talking to Phoenix even though his eyes never leave us, and I know it's about the dead bodies and hostages, but Spitfire is my focus right now. Thank fuck she has both of us.

"It's a little weak, but she'll be okay. She might have just gotten overloaded temporarily. Get her outside after big guy and hopefully they're bringing the big van. My friend's going to the hospital and will make sure everything is prepped for our arrival."

I follow Reaper, Devil, and Punisher out of the house and am relieved when I see the van that Colt's driving up in is the bigger one with sliding doors. It has two rows of seats, but in the back, we installed bench seats along the length of the van on both sides as well. I climb up into the back section, and so does Reaper, Thor, Doc, and Patch. Both Devil and Punisher give us chin lifts, saying they'll stay to help with our prisoners before shutting the doors. Now that we're in the van and no one can see us, thanks to the tint on the windows, I rip my mask off. The others do the same.

"Reaper, who did this? We have Travis, Sean, Fang, Korso, Joker, and Archer all alive. A little bloody, but alive," Thor asks as he sits down to my left, since I'm still holding Spitfire. He picks her legs up and drapes them over his legs. It's then that I notice the rope burns on her hands and legs. Shit, I didn't get a good look at her torso for the other wounds, so I don't know exactly how bad they are.

"Travis mostly did that to Half-pint, though Sean and Fang did some as well. It was mostly Fang that did this to me, but all of them cut into me some. All of them but Sean and Travis had a go at the woman on the table."

"They didn't... they didn't... did they?" Fuck, I can't even say it.

"I came too before she woke up, so I can't speak about when I was out, but they didn't rape her as far as I know."

As a whole, breaths whoosh out of almost everyone in the van. Levi shifts in my arms as Colt starts driving, and I look down at her, worried that I, no we, might lose her because of this.

"What's our story? Do we have to get Creed involved? If he needs suspects, I vote he gets Archer, Joker and Korso as long as he promises they'll never get out. We get Fang, Sean, and Travis."

Relief floods me. Her words have me thinking she's not leaving. Especially since that was the first thing out of her mouth.

"Tiffany and Monica were bound upstairs too. From the laptop I secured, it looks like they were setting up profiles to sell them," Thor says.

"I vote they stay then, too. Bitches probably helped them get us before the tables were turned," Levi spits out.

Thor shifts next to me and pulls out his phone. *"Creed, it's Thor. Are you in a secure place to talk?"*

Creed must tell him to wait because he doesn't say anything for a bit.

"Do you need suspects?" He pauses and then nods. *"We've got eight, but we'd really like to deal with five of them as long as you can ensure the other three never get out. I can get Smoke to give you the address if you agree to that."*

After a few moments, he nods, agreeing to whatever Creed's saying, and then calls someone else.

"Phoenix. Leave Archer, Joker and Korso there. Secure them and blindfold all of them, not just those three. It'll help that Fang was in another room, so those three haven't seen him yet. But we can't have those three saying much. Same with Travis and Sean. At least we all kept our masks on while we were there. Have someone then take our guests to the sticks along with Tiffany and Monica. Creed's going to meet up with us at the hospital and then he will meet you out there to pick up his three suspects." He pauses and turns, winking at Spitfire.

She grins back at him and leans her head against my shoulder before she shifts and looks over at Reaper. Once again, I feel the nervous tremble in her body as she wrings her hands together and chews on her lip.

"Keep staying strong, Half-pint. You can break down later if you need."

Spitfire nods, sits up straighter, and takes a couple deep breaths, though I don't miss her slight wince. When she opens her eyes, it's like a mask falls over her. She smiles at Reaper, but it's still slightly strained. He gives her a chin lift in response.

We drive most of the way to the hospital in silence except for Patch and Doc talking quietly every now and then as they try to stem as much of Reaper's bleeding as possible.

Colt quickly gets us to the hospital, and as he pulls up, I realize Allison is waiting for us outside the ER doors, along with two gurneys.

The van doors fly open and I slip out of the sliding door while still holding Spitfire, leaving the back for Reaper to get out of since he was closer to it. My feet carry me to the closet gurney, and I carefully lay Spitfire down on it. Behind me, I hear grunts and as I look over my shoulder, they're laying Reaper down.

"Stay strong, my giant," Levi calls out, but I don't miss the tears that are now falling down her cheeks.

A deep but loud and strained chuckle escapes Reaper. "You too, Lil' Sis."

Levi's eyelids start to droop, but she does her best to answer the nurse's questions. Once we're in the room, the nurse tries to get Thor and me to leave, but we don't budge. It's not until Levi informs them that she wants us here that she stops pushing.

Patch tosses me a shirt as he walks up to us. "Here, it's clean. I always keep extras in my locker."

"Thanks, man." I quickly pull on the shirt.

Once the room door closes, they carefully cut my shirt off Spitfire since it's now clinging to her wounds and my stomach bottoms out as I take in all of her cuts and bruises. I'm not sure how I didn't notice it before, but the fuckers carved the word 'slut' into her thigh. Running my hand angrily through my hair, my anger toward these assholes increases. I hope her wounds don't scar too bad, especially the 'slut' one, but if she wants plastic surgery for any of this, we'll get it for her.

I catalog every injury she has, wanting to pay them forward tenfold.

The nurses clean and disinfect her wounds and while I occasionally see her wince, she doesn't otherwise react. Spitfire opted for local anesthesia, so Allison is helping get set up for that. Later, once her wounds have been stitched up, they said they'll bring in an ultrasound to check on the babies.

Spitfire's soft hand slides into mine, and I'm brought back to the present.

"I'm fine, Dragon. I'm alive. Andre's alive. In a little bit, we'll have confirmation on the babies. We will find who did this."

Fuck, I must have been looking murderous for her to slip in that last comment.

"Sorry, Spitfire. I'm just so pissed you got hurt because of those assholes."

"I know, Babe, but I need you to put away that look before they make you leave. You're making a few of the nurses that pop in here really nervous."

Allison chuckles and nods. "Yeah, you were looking downright murderous, there for a bit, but they tended to forgive you when they noticed where your gaze was fixated most of the time." She gives me a sympathetic look as she gestures to Spitfire's thigh.

Taking a deep breath, I try to push down my emotions. They'll get what's coming to them soon enough.

It's a couple of hours later and the ultrasound technician just left. Our little jellybeans, as Spitfire calls them, are doing just fine. Though the doctor suggested we call and make an appointment every two weeks for the next six weeks just to make sure they continue doing well.

The rape kit came back negative, and Spitfire cried when she heard the news before saying 'thank God' a bunch of times. While I didn't say anything, I was right there with her and I know Thor was as well.

Creed stopped by earlier and got her statement while they were stitching her up. Not going to lie, it was pretty badass to see his reaction to her as she answered his questions, conveniently leaving out bits of the truth, as the doctor worked.

Once she was cleaned up, Creed apologized but said he had to take pictures of her wounds for his report.

When he left, the doctor looked at Spitfire in amazement.

"Miss Wallace, I've seen a lot of things in my years as an ER doctor, but I can honestly say, this was the first time a victim gave their statement while getting stitched up and did not flip out at what we were doing or even get mad at the officer."

That got a few chuckles out of everyone in the room and Levi filled him in that she's been training with and throwing knives for years. Thanks to her grandma, who was a nurse, she knows when she can stitch herself up or if she has to go in and have a professional do it. Plus, there was no sense in getting pissed and pissing off the people trying to help her. It doesn't hurt that she has a high pain tolerance as well. The doc shook his head in disbelief and wished her a smooth recovery.

When both Spitfire's and Reaper's bloodwork came back clean, the doctors had to admit that they had no idea what the assholes gave them in the ambulance since there's no trace left in their systems. Our best guess is that it was a sedative.

Reaper's still back being worked on, but they told us they had to put him under because of how much they needed to do to him. We haven't heard any update on him yet. Spitfire's trying her best to not show how stressed and worried she is about him, but we see it. I don't blame her one bit since they both witnessed and endured unspeakable things together.

Thor and I are trying to distract her when Allison suddenly comes storming in along with Patch.

"What's going on?" Spitfire asks urgently as she tries to sit up.

"We're trying something unconventional to help calm your friend down so we can save him," Allison says as she tosses aside Spitfire's blankets. She sets down a set of scrubs and immediately starts helping Levi get into them, being careful of her wounds in the process.

Patch shoves what looks like a larger set of scrubs at Thor. "You'll be able to hold her longer. Get dressed, now. Then wash up. If your pain gets to be too much, we'll bring in a wheelchair for her, but we figure she may need one of your guys' support during this, too."

Levi's face tightens with pain as she lifts her arms to change shirts. Thankfully, the shirt has buttons for the arms since she's still hooked up to an IV. Once she has the shirt on, Allison helps get her hair into a bun on top of her head and then puts a haircap on her.

When Thor's changed and they both scrub up, Patch lifts Spitfire and Allison trails behind him with her IV pole. I follow them, pacing outside Reaper's room nervously since I can't go in. Thankfully, Allison takes pity on me and leaves the door open a crack when she leaves his room.

I can see Thor sitting down at the head of the bed and then Spitfire's soft voice talking to Reaper, or Andre as she's started to call him. My heart breaks when she says it's her turn to be the strong one for the both of them and she'll tell him stories to keep him calm.

As she starts talking, the only machine that I can make sense of, the heart monitor, starts to slow down. The entire room seems to breathe a collective sigh of relief and the doctors continue working and sewing my brother back up.

I stand there for I don't know how long, listening to Spitfire's voice as she talks about anything and everything.

After a while, someone walks up next to me, causing me to jump.

"Levi's been cleared to go upstairs when they clear Anthony. Would it be okay if I left her stuff with you?"

It takes me a minute before I remember Reaper's first name is Anthony, as well as what else she's asking, and I groan. "I'm sorry. I hope you weren't waiting for long to use the room for someone else."

She gives me a gentle smile and waves me off. "The clearance only just came through because we pulled some strings to get them in the same room upstairs. That way she's close in case we need her to work her magic for him again. He'll have a long road of healing ahead of him, and he'll need all the support he can get. Plus, we figured it would be easier for you guys to post your guards."

I head back into the room Spitfire was in and grab her stuff from the cupboard. My heart breaks again when I see her cut ripped to shreds and her engagement ring all bloody. When I have everything gathered, I walk out to the nurse's station. I can at least fix one thing right now.

Seeing Allison is still out here, I go straight to her instead of the bimbos trying to flirt with me.

"Hey Allison, is it possible to get some Q-Tips or something so I can clean off the blood from my *fiancée's* engagement ring?"

She laughs but turns it quickly into a cough. Judging by her slightly shaking shoulders, she knows exactly who I was saying that for.

"Yup, head on over here," she says as she gestures to a sink behind the counter that's toward the other end of the nurse's station. She reaches up into the cupboard and pulls down a few supplies for me.

"Do you want me to clean it for you? Wouldn't be my first one I've cleaned off."

I look around but noticed there were only a couple of other rooms being used back here. "You're not too—"

Her and a couple other nurses quickly shush me, cutting me off from saying 'busy'. I guess the superstition is true about not wanting anyone to say that phrase.

I clear my throat. "Ah, yes, if it's okay."

She nods, trying not to laugh at me, and takes Spitfire's ring from my outstretched hand. As I stand there, I realize we haven't checked in with the guys in a while. I dig my phone out and dial Phoenix as I walk back to Reaper's room and glance inside.

"How are they, Dragon?"

"Spitfire's doing as good as can be expected after everything. She's all stitched up and just got cleared to go upstairs, but they had to pull her in to help Reaper."

"Give me a sec," he whispers, and my guess is, he's getting out of earshot of the others. A few seconds later, his voice comes through the line again. *"How bad is he?"*

"They're still working on him, but his heart rate was skyrocketing, and Patch said they were worried about if his heart would give out from the stress. But since he's so torn up, it's not safe to use the paddles if it does stop."

"Let me guess. They suggested what Levi did for both of you when you both woke up?"

"Yeah. Once they took Spitfire into his room and had her talk to him, his heart rate dropped back down to normal, so she's in there talking about anything and everything under the sun to keep him calm. I swear everyone in the room breathed a sigh of relief when that happened."

He exhales loudly. *"Thank fuck it dropped. Do they know how much longer it'll take to finish stitching him up?"*

"So far, no, they haven't. I honestly don't know how much longer they'll let me hang out in here since I'm outside his room right now. Thor's dressed in scrubs and helping hold Levi steady since she can't move very well right now and they think she might need one of us with her as she talks to Reaper and seeing him out of it. That and I think the pain from everything's catching up to her."

"Your babies okay?"

"Yeah, thank fuck."

"No shit. Okay, I'll let everyone know how things are going so far. I know everyone wants to at least lay eyes on both of them, even if they are passed out before they leave. We'll still have some guards posted both inside and outside your room, as I'm sure you and Thor are probably gonna be running on empty soon since you both were in the accident, too."

"Not gonna lie. I'm starting to feel it now that the adrenaline is wearing off." I pause as I look down at the bag I set against the wall. *"Later we're gonna need to get their cuts reordered. They were ripped to shreds."*

"Tripp's already working on it. Speaking of cuts, we have yours and Thor's for when we're able to see you."

"Thank fuck. I feel naked without it. How's Roy holding up?" Fuck, I hate that everyone's been here practically two days in a row.

"Trying to hold it together. Bear's helping him, but it doesn't help that Roy suspects Bear knows how bad her injuries are and won't tell him."

"Fuck. I'll see if I can find out anything about Reaper's timeline. Hey, I gotta let you go. They're bringing over a wheelchair, so I want to see what's going on."

"Keep us posted," he says and then hangs up.

I walk over to Patch, who's bringing a wheelchair toward Reaper's room. "What's up Patch?"

"Levi crashed. I'm bringing her this so she can sit by his head in case he starts stressing in his sleep again. I'll be right back to get you and Thor settled, since I know you won't leave her back here alone."

"Thank fuck for that. I was hoping they wouldn't make us leave her."

"Nah, I explained it to the doctor, and he understood. Though it helps that he saw what she did for Reaper. Let me get this in there, help get her settled, and I'll be out to get you sorted."

"Thanks, man," I say and go to slap his shoulder but then pull back. "Shit, I don't know where you're hurt from the wreck."

He waves me off, but that makes me worried about how he's feeling. A few moments later, Thor steps out of the room with Patch behind him. Thor rips off the paper scrubs he had slipped over his clothes earlier, and I swear some of the nurses swoon.

Allison stalks over to them, raving mad, and I notice the charge nurse paying attention. I figured she'd be mad as well, but she almost seems... amused?

"Get a fucking grip on yourselves. We are in a hospital to save lives and you ladies are over here swooning over two men that are engaged to the woman in there helping to save their friend. Get yourselves in order before I file a complaint!"

"Oh please, you must be getting in on with that one with how much he was always searching you out," one of them replies snarkily before she bats her eyes at me and waves off Allison's warning.

"No, I'm their friend and quite honestly, I'd rather they came to me than you two because at least I pay attention to the patient's rather than trying to get into her fiancés pants."

"Please, you just think you're all high and mighty because your dad's a department head here," the other nurse says as she rolls her eyes.

"I've had enough. Samantha, Courtney, come with me," the charge nurse says as she walks past them. When neither move but instead stare at her in shock, she levels them with a glare that has my balls shriveling up.

"Luke, Allison, I know neither of you are technically on the clock, but if you could please make some phone calls to the backups? I think we may need them since the others are still tied up with your friend assisting the doctors. Once I'm back down here, I'll relieve you both. Oh, and Luke?"

"Yes, Ma'am?"

"Once you're done making phone calls, sit your ass down, along with those other two men. I recognize them as two of our gunshot victims yesterday and heard that their woman and the three of you were in a nasty car accident earlier today. I'll let you know if we need you to move, but you won't be forced to leave. I know you talked to the doctor about all of them and I agree."

"Thank you, Ma'am."

"Thank you," Thor and I both call out to her. She waves us off before marching the two women down the hallway.

I try to not laugh out loud, but when Patch and Allison both hold up their hands, I try harder to hold it in. When I hear the elevator ding and the doors shut, we all start laughing.

"Fuck, she's a ball-buster, but at least she's fair."

"That she is, but I say good riddance to those two. They try to hook up with guys more than they try to help their patients," Allison says as she shakes her head and heads over to her station. Her ass is barely in the seat before she stands back up and goes over to a row of wheelchairs. She leads two of them our way and Patch goes to take one from her. I smirk when she swerves away from him.

"Nope! These are for Thor and Dragon, but go get one for yourself cause that's where your ass will be when you get done helping me call people."

"I'm not a patient."

"Just get one, will ya?" She pauses as she stares him down with a wicked smile as she wiggles her eyebrows at him. "Or do I need to resort to blackmail? After talking to Levi yesterday, I took some pictures from Mom's photo albums, and I made sure they were embarrassing ones."

The glare he sends her is pure evil, but she just laughs.

"Patch, get your ass a wheelchair," Thor bites out.

Patch sighs but does as ordered.

By the time he's over to us, Allison already has our wheelchairs unfolded, and the wheels locked. Patch leaves his by the wall and walks over to the station.

"Just remember Alli, you aren't the only one with embarrassing pictures. So keep that in mind when you threaten to blackmail me."

She grumbles and flips him off as she starts calling people.

Hooking Levi's bag on the handle, I sit down, and damn near sigh when this feels so much more comfortable than the chairs in the ER rooms.

"Fuck, I told Phoenix I'd let him know any new news when I saw Patch bringing the wheelchair for Spitfire."

I type out a quick message to him and pocket my phone.

"So, they're updated so far?"

"Yeah. I figured it was the least I could do since you were in there with Spitfire. Roy's not taking it well, but Phoenix thinks it's partially because Bear knows how injured she is and is refusing to tell Roy how bad it is."

"Shit, we should have had him brought back while she was still awake. There's no way they'll let him go in Reaper's room with her."

I cringe. "Yeah, I feel bad about that. Honestly, I was trying my damndest to not kill anyone, so I wasn't in the right frame of mind to even register that we should have brought him back."

Thor groans and looks over at Levi's bag hanging off my wheelchair. "We need to get them new cuts ordered."

"I mentioned that to Phoenix, but he said Tripp's already on it."

"Thank fuck."

I lean my head back against the wall and look up at the ceiling. "I know the guys all stepped up to help when Mom died, then when we had to take Dad to the nursing home, and then again for his funeral. But that pales in comparison to how much it seems everyone's been rallying around us these last couple of days."

Thor's silent for a bit and I'm just about to check if he passed out when he speaks up. "I think it's Wildcat. Everyone loves her and honestly, I think she brings out the best in us, too."

"Damn straight she does. Thank fuck, she said yes to giving us a chance."

"I feel the same way."

Chapter 45
Levi

I WAKE UP TO arms lifting me and I try to pry my eyes open. It takes a few attempts, but finally, the sleep slips from my eyes and I start to panic. Where's Andre?

"Easy, Spitfire, I gotcha."

I tense when I feel a soft bed below me and I panic even more. "Where's Andre?"

Looking around, I'm the only one in the room. Where'd he go? I thought Allison said we were going to be allowed to share a room. The last thing I remember was talking to him about camping.

"Relax, Wildcat. They're in the hall waiting for us and the nurse to get you situated and then they'll bring in his bed."

My body instantly relaxes at that.

I had tried not to freak out when Thor carried me into Andre's room at first. However, since I was up higher, I could see over the paper guard they had set up by his head and upper body to try to block the view of them working. Fang and the others had really done a number on his chest, but only a few looked deep. However, there were parts where skin had been shaved off.

I wasn't sure how Andre would react to me talking to him at first, but relief flooded me when his heart rate started slowing down. I talked to him about everything from when I first met the twins, to when I first started throwing Grandpa's knives, to camping, living at the compound, and the babies.

There were a few times that I broke down crying and told him he had to pull through this because I needed my gentle giant. That the babies needed to know their newest uncle.

Fuck, that was hard.

I don't know if he heard any of it, but I imagine he at least heard my voice since his heart rate didn't start to lower until I started talking. Then, because I had to do something with my hands, I ran my fingers gently through his short brown hair.

Fuck, I need him to pull through this.

The door opens again, pulling me from my thoughts, and my tears start falling again when I see the nurses maneuvering his bed into the room. I don't remember what time it was when Thor brought me into his room, but I'm guessing a few hours have passed since the clock says it's a little after 1 am.

Once Andre's settled in, the nurse starts letting both the clubs come in, but they stressed it had to be for a quick visit. First in line is my dad and I'm ashamed to say I hadn't thought to give him updates sooner. I hope the guys did.

He stops by my bed, unsure of how to touch me, even though I can tell he wants to. I open my arms.

"Soft hugs, but don't squeeze. My back is fine, but I had to get stitches on my arms, torso, and a couple on my left thigh. The rest should heal fine on their own or with that skin glue stuff."

"Oh, Sweetie, I'm so sorry you had to go through this again," he whispers, and I nod completely in agreement, but at the same time, I got off easy compared to Andre.

After he pulls back, he comes around the bed on my left side and pulls up a chair, making it clear he's staying awhile.

Sasha's next in line and I bark a laugh at the large duffle bag hanging off her shoulder. She rolls her eyes at me.

"I wasn't sure what would feel comfortable, so I brought you a few options. There are fresh clothes in there for your men, too. One of Reaper's guys grabbed clothes for him, too.

She gives me a hug and sits over on the couch.

The rest of the clubs filter in, and I'm surprised that they all give me a hug. Even everyone in Reaper's crew. I'm pretty sure I've gone through a couple tissue boxes with how much I cried as everyone wished me a smooth recovery.

Andre slept through it all, but after the first person went to pat his leg, Patch warned them to stay away from his ankles as they were rubbed pretty raw from the ropes, though not as bad as his wrists.

Finally, around 2 am, it's down to my men, Dad, Phoenix, Bear, Jax, Devil, Punisher, and Beast.

Dad sighs and stands. "Is it possible to have a couple minutes with just Levi?"

The guys all gave him a chin lift and leave. Both my men give me a kiss and they're the last to step out. I brace myself because I know what he's going to ask.

He sits down on the bed by my feet. "Sweetie, please tell me. What did they do to you? My mind has been running around like crazy, thinking of all the possibilities. I know you weren't raped, thank fuck, but Bear wouldn't tell me, so I know something isn't good."

I run a finger lightly over the bandages on my wrists, swallowing the lump in my throat.

"My wrists and ankles are raw from the ropes and struggling, though my wrists are worse than my ankles. They run almost as wide as the tape is." I let out a shaky breath as I try to laugh and find some good in this. "At least I know the bracelets work. Both Andre and I were able to cut through the ropes."

He gives me a watery eyed smile in return.

Releasing another shaky breath, I carefully untie the top of my gown, lowering it, but stopping just below the last cut above my boobs. I'm not showing him the couple of shallow ones in between my boobs. That's just something I'm not comfortable doing in front of him, for obvious reasons. Tears fill his eyes, and I push myself to keep going.

When I have the top of my gown back in place, I pull the bottom of the gown out from under the blanket and show him my stomach. Lowering the gown, I cover my panties back up and show him my right leg. Once I cover it with the blanket again, my hands pause over the section of the blanket covering my left leg. He stands up and walks around to the other side of the bed, most likely not knowing how far down they go, though he does know about my ankles already.

Tears prick my eyes and I decide to just rip the proverbial band-aid off as I yank the covers up. Dad falls to his knees when he sees what they carved into me, carefully holding my calf as he cries.

The nurses wanted my wound to breathe for a while and to watch for infection, so they hadn't taped it up, but it will get taped up before bed.

Seeing him crying sets off my own waterworks. I bury my head in my hands and I can't help the little jump when his arms pull me into a gentle hug as he sits on the right side of the bed near me. I hadn't even registered that he'd move from my left side, but I imagine it was so that he wouldn't accidentally hurt my leg.

I'm not sure how long we sit there crying, but a groan has my head snapping up.

"Half-pint... Half-pint, don't cry."

"Andre!"

Shoving the blankets off my legs, Dad stands and hovers over me. I hesitantly try to stand, but when I wince in pain, Dad picks me up carefully and sets me down on the foot of Andre's bed.

I take his hand as the guys all come back in, most likely having heard me shout his name, but Andre's gaze is glued to my thigh, and I quickly reposition my gown to cover the scars.

"Glad to see you're finally awake, Sleeping Beauty," Punisher teases him.

"Fuck off, jackass."

"You had us worried, Pres. You better not die on us cause I don't want that gavel," Devil says with a laugh.

The guys give him shit, and I love how my men are always touching me in some way, making sure I'm okay without having to say anything. Though, I know they all notice how Andre's gaze keeps going back to my leg. I just hope that he doesn't bring it up.

About ten minutes later, he sighs, and I swallow the lump in my throat.

"Please tell me that doesn't say what I think I saw, Half-pint."

I look away, again swallowing thickly as I wipe more tears that fall away in frustration.

A low growl has me looking back at him, but I don't stop him when his hand moves to my thigh and carefully moves the gown aside.

The anger in his eyes has his heart rate picking back up, and I quickly recover my leg, taking his hand in mine again.

"You can't get worked up right now, Andre. The doctors are really worried about your heart."

He looks at me in confusion. "What's wrong with my heart?"

I open my mouth and close it, not able to speak as the image of his torn-up chest pops back into my head. Thankfully, Thor clears his throat and takes over, filling him in on what happened.

For a while he's quiet, but I can see the swirl of emotions in his eyes and how he's trying not to tense up but fails. When he winces, I motion to the call button.

"Shit, we need to tell them you're awake. Punisher, can you press his call button since you're right by it? Andre might need more pain meds."

The nurse comes in and balks at how many people are in the room and tries to get them to leave. I'm getting fucking pissed cause she's not listening, and it's working Andre up even more.

"Listen here, Ma'am. We have the authorization to have this many people here for guards inside as well as outside our room, plus my dad and my fiancés. If you have a problem, then by all means call Mr. Thatcher up or our FBI contact, but it's not gonna make a lick of difference except for calling them in the middle of the night and pissing them off because you refuse to listen. The charge nurse on this floor knows about this, so why don't you take your complaints up with her? If you continue to be a stubborn bitch to try and get your way, I'll go find the charge nurse myself and demand another one for Anthony and me. Now, are you going to listen and help my brother, who just woke up and is in pain, or am I getting in a wheelchair and dragging you out of here by your ear?"

The nurse huffs as the guys try to hide their laughter and, out of the corner of my eye, I see Devil leave the room. I hope like hell he's gonna talk to the charge nurse, but I wasn't kidding. I'd get my ass in a wheelchair and go talk to her myself if I have to.

I watch the nurse like a hawk as she increases his dosage a little and checks his vitals. She looks at me when she's done, her face pinched, but she doesn't say anything as she leaves the room.

"Fucking bitch," I mutter and the guys all let their laughter out.

"Now I seriously want to see you dragging her down the hall as we push your wheelchair. All you're missing is a slipper to beat her over the head with," Smoke says as he doubles over in laughter.

"Sash said she packed my slippers, so if she causes more problems, you might just get your wish."

This causes them to laugh even harder and even though I'm laughing with them, the weight of everything is finally crashing down on me.

"I think it's time I get you back in your own bed, Kiddo. You almost just swayed off Reaper's bed." Jax steps forward and I'm confused when he stops my guys.

"Nope. Thor, you can't lift her yet because of your shoulder, and Dragon, I know your leg has to be killing you. Both of you look about ready to fall over like Levi. I think we should wind this down and let all four of you sleep."

My guys grumble but don't fight him.

Once Jax carefully sets me down, he helps me wrap my leg like the nurse instructed earlier and then helps straighten my blankets back in place. My guys are unfolding the sofa bed and I wince when I see how thin the mattress is. Jax must see my wince because his gaze follows where I'm looking and he nods.

"If you're still here tomorrow night, I'll get something so that they're able to sleep better."

"Thank you, Jax."

He waves me off and pulls a chair in between our beds, but against the opposite wall. Guess he's taking first watch inside.

"I'll be back tomorrow to see you, Sweetie. That way, one of them can have the recliner if they need to sleep as they rotate."

Dad hugs me one more time and kisses me on the forehead before he stops by Andre's bed and wishes him a good night.

Punisher takes the first watch outside our room and Devil sits in the recliner.

"Good night, everyone," I call out and settle into my pillow and they all respond in kind.

Even though I'm tired, I can't fall asleep. I try to get comfortable, but I can't.

"Half-pint, you still awake?"

"Yeah, my leg itches and I'm really trying hard to not concentrate on it."

He pauses and I look over at him. He's running his hand over his face and through his hair.

"What's wrong, my giant?"

"I know you probably don't need it, but if you do need help getting plastic surgery to fix your leg, I'll help."

I wave him off. "Nope, not getting that. I learned the first time around to accept my scars. They're proof that I survived something twisted and tragic. Once it heals, I'll talk with Sasha, Alexei, and Axe about a tattoo. There are a few others I've been wanting to get too, but just haven't gotten them yet. I'll use the coping mechanisms that I used last time to help me process things and put them behind me."

"Damn, I hope I find someone like you someday."

"I'm sure you will. You're too good of a man to not have someone special in your life."

He snorts, but I know it's true.

"What else is bugging you? I can tell there's something else."

"It's weird, but I keep getting flashes of things when I know I was out. Well, sort of out of it. I remember them putting the mask over my face, but then I could still feel them stitching me up, but the pain was muted, sort of."

My eyes widen at that. "You weren't fully under?"

"I'm guessing my size was messing with things. In the past, I've never stayed as sedated as much as they thought I'd be when I had to go under. After the first time in the hospital, Doc just took care of me at my house whenever he could, since the doctors at the hospitals kept messing up with the sedation."

"I think if you hadn't needed blood, he probably would have taken you to the clubhouse. He sounded resigned when he agreed with Patch that you had to go to the hospital."

"Yeah, I bet he hated to admit it. But I do remember you talking to me and running your fingers through my hair. After a while, I could tell that you were getting sleepy, but I'm glad they let you still stay in there when you fell asleep. Knowing you were there and that you and the babies were safe staved off my need to rip those fuckers apart."

"I hate that you had to feel everything they were doing to you. Just remember, I'm here for you if you need me. I'm sure our guests will be kept entertained until we're stable enough."

A strained, low laugh erupts out of him before he settles back down.

"And I'm there for you, Lil' Sis. Try to get some sleep, Half-pint."

"You too, Andre."

I turn and am surprised to see Devil watching me. He mouths 'thank you' to me and I smile back at him. I'll help Andre get his spark back, but I know I won't be everything that he really needs. I've seen the way he watched my men and me earlier. He wants what we have, and I hope like hell there's a woman out there for him.

Chapter 46
Levi

It's been two weeks since I got out of the hospital. I ended up having to stay a total of three nights. That first night, I developed a slight fever and an infection in my leg, but it started clearing up not too long after they got antibiotics into my system.

However, it will be a bit before Andre can go back to Junction Creek. Doc offered to stay back with him for a while, saying he was going to need to teach Patch his tricks for taking care of him. It's almost a four-hour drive to the Junction Creek clubhouse, so the doctors want Andre to stay close until his stitches heal a bit more before he drives that far. We offered a room for him and Doc in our house, which they both accepted.

Andre told me that he's struggling with nightmares, and I confided in him that I am, too. I'm pretty sure that's part of why he accepted our offer, but that was also why I initially asked the guys if it would be okay if they stayed with us. However, I didn't tell them about his nightmares. I wasn't going to break his confidence like that, but I think they may suspect that Andre's struggling. I also know that if anyone does find out that Andre's having nightmares, he'd want as few people as possible to know.

Aside from Doc, the rest of Reaper's crew went back to Junction Creek the day after I was discharged. There was a party that night welcoming me back home, and I made sure to send food to Andre and his guards. We're still not sure if other Black Plague members will retaliate and come after us, so we aren't taking any chances and lowering our guard.

Today, Andre's finally okay enough to get discharged. I've visited him every day and made sure to bring him food and anything he needs to keep from dying of boredom. His words, not mine.

He confided in me that he loves to read and I'm not going to lie, we totally bonded on our shared favorite genres. Though he did make me swear to not tell anyone what he reads. To help keep his secret, I made covers for each of the books I bought so he could read without his brothers knowing what they really were. On top of the books, I made sure they had some cards and brought in some movies he told me he likes. Thankfully, there is a DVD player in his room, so I didn't need to bring one in for him.

As Thor pulls his new truck into the hospital parking garage, I try to clamp down on my nerves. Every day that we've come here, we have to drive past the intersection where we had wrecked and where Black Plague were able to finally get their hands on me and Andre.

After the first day and my freak out, my men took different routes to the hospital, but my gaze always went in the direction of that dreaded intersection. I know with time that these feelings will pass and fade, and I'm so ready to be at that point. I've already filled a couple of journals, both blue and black, full of my feelings, fears, and hopes. Someday, I plan to burn them when I feel I'm ready to put it all behind me.

The first day I visited Andre after I was released, he asked me about what I had said that first night. About how I'd use my coping mechanisms from the first time Black Plague had kidnapped me.

"Half-pint, there's something you said the other night that keeps nagging me, but I couldn't bring myself to ask you about it until now."

I sit cross-legged in a chair next to his bed, and other than twirling a pen, I give him my full attention. Ever since our kidnapping, I always have to be doing something with my hands. I can't sit still.

"What's that?"

"What do you do to cope? How do you bring yourself out of those dark thoughts and not let them eat away at who you are?"

"Sometimes I talk to Dad or Uncle Bear about what I'm feeling. Other times Sasha or Alexei. I also spar or throw knives to relieve pent-up frustrations."

Pausing, I get up, grab my backpack that I'd dumped on the empty bed earlier and bring it back over, sitting it on my lap. I pull out my two journals, one with a black cover and one with a blue cover, as well as a pack of colorful pens. Taking a deep breath, I hand him my journals.

"I also keep two journals, and I always have a stack of each color for when I fill one up. The blue one is my everyday journal to chart how I'm feeling. I use whichever color pen strikes my fancy but never black or red for the lengthy daily journal entries.

"On days that are exceptionally hard, I make a note, like this one," I say as I open my blue journal and point down to an entry that has a note written in red in my daily journal. "If I feel like I'm in a really dark place, I'll make a note like that in either black or red ink that says I used the black journal today. That's how I track how frequently I use it. I only use black or red pens for the black journal.

"In the black journal, I write everything down that I'm feeling. Times where it seems like I'm caught in the clutches of darkness and trying to claw my way out. I would write out every dark, and often torturous, action I'd do to my captors. When I found myself crawling out of that dark hole, I'd go out back to our firepit and light a fire. Then I'd rip out those pages and tear them up before rolling them into little balls and throwing them into the fire, letting the fire burn away my hateful and gruesome thoughts.

"At first, the time periods between needing to write in the black journal were usually pretty frequent. Dad had heard of a saying that some therapists use with their patients to gauge how they're doing. He'd ask me 'how long'. Meaning how long has it been since I felt the urge to write in the black journal and I'd always answer truthfully. Over time, the time periods between using the black journal and burning the pages lengthened. Eventually, I'll burn the blue ones too when I feel I'm in a good place to put it all behind me."

He's silent as he flips through the pages, not reading them, but seeing how much I'd written in each one already.

"Can you bring me some journals? I'd like to try it."

Giving him a small smile, I reach back into my backpack and pull out four new journals, two black and two blue ones, as well as another stack of colorful pens. I put everything on the table next to us.

"I wasn't sure if you would want to try it, but I brought some just in case."

Even though he has my journals, he looks up at me, tears in his eyes. "How long?"

I give him a sad smile and answer truthfully. "Ten hours, and it's only that long because I was asleep for most of it. Do you feel the urge to use the black one?"

He nods, his hands tightening around my journals. I hold my hand out for my journals and then hand him new blue and black journals, as well as the pens.

"When you're out of here, we'll have a bonfire where you can burn your pages if you want."

"I'd like that," he says as he takes out a blue and red pen.

He writes something in the blue notebook, first with the blue pen and then the red before he switches to the black notebook and continues writing in red.

I sit back in my chair, opening my black journal, and we both sit there in silence as we write.

I blink as I come out of my thoughts and look around. My cheeks heat when I notice everyone's waiting on me. Even the guys that rode their bikes.

"Get that look off your face, Wildcat. It's nothing to be embarrassed about. It'll take time before these feelings fade and pass. How long?"

They'd taken to using Dad's saying too once I told them about it. My face heats again, but I answer honestly. "Three hours."

Thor reaches over the console and squeezes my hand. Dragon gently squeezes my shoulder from where he's sitting in the backseat. They know the closer we get to our meeting, the more I've been having these thoughts. The need to make them hurt for what they did to us and, I'm sure, countless others throughout the years.

Taking a deep breath, I nod. "Let's go bust Andre out of here. I know he wants to be under the sun again and breathe fresh air."

Climbing out of the truck, we head into the hospital, waving to some nurses that we've come to know over the past few weeks.

Walking into Andre's room, I can't help but smile when I see him pacing impatiently. He's already dressed in his street clothes, and I can tell he's ready to get out of here. He's got his new cut on and I'm itching to wear mine again. I feel naked without it.

"Ready to bust out of here, Andre?"

He laughs, but I don't miss his slight wince. "More than ready, Half-pint. I'm going crazy about not being in a clubhouse. I need to get out of these four white walls."

I chuckle at his exasperated face but completely get it. He's used to being the man in charge and I worry how much it's gonna affect him since he won't be able to ride his bike for a while.

Walking over to him, I give him a gentle hug, which he returns.

"I've got your favorite meal planned for tonight."

Shock is evident on his face before he practically starts drooling. "You're kidding me! Don't tease me now, Half-pint. If you don't have baby back ribs already marinating, then we'll be going to the store as soon as we leave."

"Baby back ribs have been seasoned. I also have some that have been in a marinade overnight. They'll go on the smokers as soon as we get back. We've also got mashed potatoes with gravy, roasted veggies, and corn on the cob. For dessert, I ordered cherry and apple pies from that new bakery in town."

"Woman, if you're not careful, I'll put in a transfer just so I can keep eating your food. I'll make Devil run the Junction Creek chapter," he says as he winks at me.

My gaze cuts to Devil, who's glaring at him. The Junction Creek guys all came down yesterday for Andre's release from the hospital as a surprise for him.

"Nope! You're not transferring. It's bad enough I have to step up till the doctors release you. Not doing this without you, Reap."

The guys bicker back and forth while I walk around the room, making sure everything is packed up.

As I'm looking through the cupboards, I jump when I close a door and Andre's leaning against the wall.

"How long?" he asks quietly.

I swallow thickly. "Three hours. How long for you?"

"Two hours. I can't wait for tomorrow."

"Same. It's like the closer we get, the more I need it."

He leans forward and kisses my forehead. We both chuckle when we hear twin growls.

"I get you claimed her as your sister, but stop kissing our woman, Reap," Dragon tells him.

I laugh as Dragon spins me, kissing me senseless before Thor does the same. Slipping my arms around Thor's waist, I turn and can't help the giggle that escapes at seeing Andre fake gagging. He winks at me, but my heart squeezes when I realize he's deflecting. Shit, I hope he doesn't think this has ruined him for finding someone.

A nurse comes into the room with the discharge paperwork and I'm grateful for the reprieve. When he's ready, I'll be there for him to talk, but in no way will I be pushing the subject.

It doesn't take long, and we're all walking back to the truck.

"Your chariot awaits," Thor teases him.

"Fuck, this is gonna suck to be in a cage for so long. Can we at least roll the windows down?"

"Hey, we're in the same boat you are, man," Dragon groans.

"Ha! I've got all three of you beat. I can't ride my bike or either of my men's bikes until these babies come, since my due date is February 9th, though we all know I'll go into labor sooner than that. Then I have to wait for spring or good weather to ride again. Suck it up buttercups!"

"Shit, I didn't think about that, but yeah, definitely don't want you on a bike with the little jellybeans incubating," Andre says with a wince.

Throwing my hair up in a messy bun, I put my shades on and roll down the windows as Thor backs out of our parking spot and heads home.

The ribs have been on the smokers for a while now, and Uncle Bear and Dad offered to man them tonight. I tried to help the girls with the other dishes, but they banned me from the kitchen, telling me to rest and enjoy the party.

But the truth is, I'm not enjoying the party.

I'm antsy and my fingers itch to throw a blade. Everything in me wants to go downstairs. I know the guys have been 'keeping them company', but I'm ready to end this. Tomorrow can't come soon enough.

With a sigh, I head to Thor's office, deciding now's as good a time as any to do what I had planned tonight. I definitely don't want to do it later when the hang arounds arrive. There've been some new ones lately and I've gotta say, I'm not impressed. They are the cattiest girls I've seen in a while and are downright bitches. That's another reason why I'm missing my cut. I'm tired of having to fight with them about my men.

Unlocking the door, I dig my black journal out of my bag that I'd stashed here earlier and carefully tear out all the pages. While I do plan to rip up the pages and burn them, I hate leaving my journals messy. Folding the pages as best as I can since there are so many of them, I tuck them into my back pocket before securing my bag and relocking the door.

A few of the guys say hello or give me a chin lift on my way to the backyard, but I don't stop to talk. I step into the kitchen to grab a water and then I grab the matches out of the pantry. Sasha gives me a small smile and a hug before teasingly kicking me out again. I'm thankful for the distraction because I don't want the other women to know about this. Not yet at least.

Once outside, I'm grateful not too many people are out here yet. I grab a few logs from the woodpile and make my way to the far firepit.

When the fire's lit, I pull a chair close, putting my back to the clubhouse. Taking the pages, I unfold them and start tearing them up before tossing little balls of paper into the fire. I don't need to re-read them. With how much I've written the past couple of weeks, the memories of what's on the pages are still at the forefront of my mind.

I've just thrown in the last ball from the second page of my stack of papers when I jump, startled at the chairs surrounding the firepit all shuffling closer. I blink out of my thoughts and realize Andre is sitting to my right. My guys, Dad, Uncle Bear, Jax, the twins, and Ethan all sit down as well. My heart melts when I see my family all here for us.

Andre reaches out a hand and I clasp it, holding it. "You're not alone in this nightmare anymore, Half-pint. When I'm here and you or I need to do this, we'll do it together, not alone, you hear me?"

A tear streaks down my cheek and I nod. "Together."

He squeezes my hand, lets go, and reaches inside his cut before pulling out a stack of papers. I'm surprised when the others pull out stacks of their own papers as well.

"Reaper's right. You aren't alone in this, Wildcat. We're all here for you, for each other. You have us to lean on for support, too. We all took a page out of your book, so to speak. So tonight, we're all burning our black journal pages."

A strained chuckle escapes, and I try to blink back my tears. Sniffling, I tear another section off and ball it up before tossing it into the fire.

Soon, we're all laughing when it turns into a competition for most impressive or ridiculous throws and the laughs continue even when the pages are long burned to ashes.

Once night falls, Bones and Loki light off fireworks since Andre had to spend the 4th of July couped up in the hospital.

As I lay on a blanket stretched out on the grass in between my men and watch the array of colors light up the sky, my hands settle on my stomach. The next time I'll be watching fireworks, our babies will be here. A tear escapes as my mind goes back to how easily I could have lost them because of the wreck. Or lost them if my torture had been more severe. How I could have lost Andre if he'd succumbed to his wounds. Those bastards are going to pay for what they did to us.

I feel both of my men's hands taking one of mine and they squeeze as they both roll on their sides, facing me.

"Soon, Wildcat," Thor whispers as he kisses my temple.

"Your beast will have its vengeance soon, Spitfire," Dragon says before kissing me.

Tomorrow can't come soon enough.

Chapter 47
Levi

AFTER BREAKFAST, I EXCUSE myself to Thor's office and lock the door.

Time to get ready.

Thankfully, my hair is already done. After showering this morning and washing my hair, I put it in a high ponytail and then braided it before winding it up into a bun.

Since I helped cook breakfast, I had worn a long sundress that would cover my leg. I found out the hard way that if I was in the kitchen for too long, my stitches would become irritated by the extra heat and increased movement if I had gauze covering them. Ever since then, I try to wear sundresses when I'm cooking so I can let my leg breathe. Then if I'm going to be doing other stuff that day; I change after breakfast and tape on my gauze padding to protect the stitches.

I get to work putting gauze down and taping everything in place. On my thigh, I put extra gauze on as an added protection in case my movements start aggravating the stitches later on. Once all the gauze is taped down, I tape down some cling wrap over the top in an attempt to prevent our guests' bodily fluids from giving me an infection. This was a suggestion the nurses told us to do when my men needed to take showers after they were shot. If it'll help keep the water out, then it should be a good preventative measure to keep bodily fluids out of my wounds.

Clothing-wise for today, I opt for fitted black yoga pants, a scoop neck red fitted long-sleeve shirt to protect the wounds on my arms and over it, a fitted black t-shirt with the club logo on it. The guys ordered me a bunch of club shirts back when I said 'yes' to being their Old Lady. I'd taken it a step further and ordered some other sizes as well for whenever the guys decide to ask someone to be their Old Lady.

Smiling, I pull out the box I'd stashed in here earlier. I'd read a book not too long ago by M F Moody called *Family Justice*. I'm a sucker for mafia and MC books as well as my PNR RH books, but there's one thing from *Family Justice* that I instantly wanted when I read it.

Bethany's heels with a metal needle heel.

Only I wanted mine in a boot version.

It took a while, but I finally found some that would come the way I wanted them and I'm absolutely in love with them. My men are the only ones that know about them so far because they were there when I opened them after they were delivered. Let's just say there was some really hot sexy times with me in just those knee-high boots. However, since I wasn't cleared for sex yet, it was all oral. Not that I was complaining because I love giving my men blow jobs and having them go down on me.

That memory triggers another of Travis cutting up my cut.

Fuck, I miss my cut.

Thankfully, Phoenix said it should be done today. I'm itching to wear it again.

Taking a deep breath, I refocus and slip into my boots. I won't always handle business with these boots, but today I want to. I have a couple of pairs of these boots. Black leather for whenever I want to wear them out and about, and these red leather ones for business. A dark smile pulls at my lips as I think of my other surprises Thor said he'd have secured down there for me for today.

Today is questioning day.

Our guests have been here for a little over two weeks, and in that entire time, I was told no one from the club spoke to them while they were 'entertaining' them. Though I heard my men rained down holy hell on them the day after I was released from the hospital. No bones were broken, but they were definitely bloody and bruised. At least their beasts have been sated a bit.

But mine hasn't and it's itching to come out.

The purpose of these last two weeks was to wear them down just enough where Andre wouldn't be in too much pain before they cracked.

Hopefully anyway.

As the one that was hurt the most, he'll mostly be in charge today. I'm next in line, but I know Thor, Dragon, Jax, and Uncle Bear want in on the action. Alexei and Dad wanted to get in some punches, but I don't know if they'll let them since Alexei's a Prospect and Dad's not in the club. Though Dad has said that he's been thinking about it. Sasha's only allowed to come down because we have two female guests, and our torturing methods are slightly different from the guys' in some aspects. Not to mention, sometimes you just need two sets of hands and I'm not about to make one of the guys be the second set of hands so that they don't have any conflicting emotions regarding hurting women.

Once I'm dressed, I open the cabinet I keep spare clothes in, as well as a few other personal things in case of emergencies. There's been more than once that my men have torn my panties off me in this office that I insisted on keeping a stash in here because I am not a woman who likes to go commando in my pants. No, thank you.

I also installed a long mirror on the back of the cabinet door so I can make sure I'm not walking out too rumpled or with sex hair. Satisfied with my appearance and that my wounds are all covered, I shut the cabinet and head out into the common room.

My men spot me instantly and, based on both of their heated looks, I know they're remembering our sexy times. I am too, for that matter. The guys don't know it, but my doctor cleared me for sex finally, which I'm planning to have happen later today.

The click of my metal heels draws lustful glances from the guys when they take in my appearance, which has my men growling, even though they know none of their brothers would dare try anything with me.

"When did you get those? Those are practically fuck-me boots!" Sasha screams as scrambles off Colt's lap where she was waiting and rushes over, damn near drooling over my boots as laughter rings out when she stumbles in her haste.

"Fuck, Baby, please say you'll get a pair of those," Colt whispers into her ear, but he isn't as quiet as he thinks.

Alexei glares at him and Colt winces as the laughter increases.

"Sorry, not sorry, Lex."

"I like you, Colt, but if you keep talking about my sister like that around me, you'll end up with a blade in you."

"You hurt him, Alexei, and you'll have a blade sticking out of you," Sasha warns him with a scowl of her own.

Arms entwine around my waist and Thor leans in for a bruising kiss. "Fuck, I can't wait till you're cleared, Wildcat," he whispers into my ear, which has me shivering with need. Thankfully, he doesn't press into me like usual since he's on my left.

"You'll definitely be wearing these when that happens, Spitfire," Dragon says before he kisses me.

When I pull back, I decide to put them out of their misery. "Well then, I guess I'll just have to keep them on the rest of the day then."

It takes them a few moments for my words to register, but Dragon gets it first and immediately his lips are back on mine before I'm pulled out of his arms and into Thor's. Catcalls ring out around the room.

"I'm guessing someone just got cleared for sex," Ryder shouts, which has me blushing and my brothers, Dad, and Uncle Bear all groan above the laughter.

"Reaper, you ready?" Thor asks him.

"Fuck yes. You ready, Half-pint?"

"Absolutely," I reply, grinning. I can't wait to use my new toys.

We all file downstairs and into the sticks.

I'm surprised to find the room doesn't reek of feces and body odor, but then I notice all five of them are wet but still fully clothed. I raise an eyebrow at Thor.

"We wanted them to be all squeaky clean for our little chat today, Wildcat."

I can't help the chuckle that escapes and go back to inspecting them, my metal heels clicking loudly against the cement as I walk. All of them have restraints on their ankles that are linked and connected to the walls. The men have their hands bound in front of them and attached to hooks in the ceiling. The women have their hands bound behind them, which are also linked to hooks in the ceiling. Fang and Travis are sporting black eyes, but they aren't swollen shut. All three of the men have bruises somewhere on their bodies in varying degrees of healing. However, when I look over at the women, I'm surprised to see that they also have bruises on them.

"They slipped down the stairs," Sasha says, shrugging with a grin.

I grin back at her, and after slipping on some gloves, I walk over to the wall and press the buttons that will raise the men's chains on their arms, so that their movements are even more restricted. When the chains stop, their arms are bearing most of their body weight, but I let them have a few toes to stand on. For the women, I raise their arms until it's clear they can't raise anymore without dislocating their shoulders.

Last night, Andre and I talked about how we wanted to handle things today, so we'd be in sync. I told him a little about my surprises and he tried to bribe me to tell him more, but I wouldn't budge.

It's a tight fit with both clubs in here, but there is plastic up over the back half of the room's walls since our guests are pushed further into the room than where Nicole previously was.

"Ready for a little payback, Half-pint?"

I grin at him in response and grab two knives from the tool cabinet, handing the larger one to him.

He goes over to Fang, and I go to Travis, sawing off their patches like they did ours. Both of them start thrashing violently when the first stitches are cut. When all the patches are on the ground, I cut his cut to shreds, just like he did mine.

"Sucks seeing something you love ripped to shreds and on the floor, doesn't it?" I hiss as the last of his cut falls to the ground.

"When I get my hands on you, bitch, you'll regret this," Travis seethes.

I laugh and, with my arms open, spin a little. "These people and these four walls are the last that you will ever see before your pitiful lives are brought to an abrupt end. None of you are getting out of here alive."

"Y-You can't do that, Levi. I'm your uncle! I'm blood!"

I get right in his face, trailing my knife down his face. The blade bites into his flesh, leaving a cut that mirrors the one he gave me.

"See, that's where you're wrong, *Uncle*. Besides, us sharing blood never stopped you from kidnapping me, drugging me, and trying to rape me when I was six, did it? Or the plans you had for me? That once you had me, you were going to whisk me away to start training me to be someone's *pet* that you'd sell to the highest bidder."

Yeah, that had been a big mess when Andre and I told everyone what happened at the house after we arrived back at the clubhouse yesterday. I swear I'm going to look into fucking padding to put up on the Church walls, so we don't have to keep patching up drywall. At some point, someone's going to punch a stud and they'll have a broken hand.

I back away from him and give Thor, Dragon, and Andre the floor. They circle around Sean, Travis, and Fang. Both Thor and Dragon are sporting brass knuckles, while Andre still has his knife.

"I'll make this easier for you. The ones that answer our questions won't get punished as severely as the others, but make no mistake, none of you are leaving here alive. It just means that your death will not be as painful."

"Y-you can't hurt us. You said everyone in the club swore never to hurt a woman," Tiffany stutters as she bats her eyelashes, trying to flirt her way out of this.

"See, that's where you're wrong," I say as I walk forward and start circling both of them. "The bylaws state that the male club members have to swear that they will never harm women or children. But you see, I don't have a dick and I wear my balls on my chest, so there's nothing in the bylaws that prevents me from handling women issues when the need arises."

Both women pale, and Tiffany actually looks like she might cry, but I'm not falling for their tricks. Once again, I step back and give Thor a chin lift.

The dark look that comes over his face as he smirks at me makes me break out in goosebumps. Walking to one of the tool cabinets, he pulls out a giant hammer that looks like a hammer that would be befitting of Thor, the Norse God of thunder.

Dragon's right behind him and grabs a coiled length of rope that I quickly realize is a cat o' nine tails whip. The design of the whip looks like it's made of scales that remind me of his vibrant tattoos. The tails are all tipped with metal barbs that look extremely sharp and painful. Some of them have metal barbs up the lengths of the tails, much like the spikes on the tails of dragons you'd see in a lot of fantasy pictures.

I lick my lips as my gaze roams over my men as they circle our three male guests. Fuck, there must be something wrong with me because seeing them like this is sexy as fuck. Either that or it's the fact that I haven't been able to have sex in two weeks.

Maybe a little of both.

"Before we get to the main event, Dragon and I have a little present for you three. You thought you could put your hands on our woman and take her for your own selves and your sick pleasure. That was a big mistake. You're going to get a taste of what Dragon and I like to dole out as punishment. You're going to find out exactly how we got our road names."

Thor hefts his hammer in the air a few times and then swings violently, smashing Fang's right kneecap. His screams ring out through the room and a part of me relishes his pain. Then he does the same to Travis and then Sean.

He looks over his shoulder at me, a wicked gleam in his eyes. "Wildcat, can you lower the chains for their arms?"

I do as he asks, though I am curious about what he has planned next. When Phoenix and Ryder step forward, pulling three tables on casters with two large cuffs mounted on the table, I can't help the grin that forms.

All three of them soon have their wrists secured, the restraints forcing them to keep their palms flat on the thick metal tables. Screams once again ring out as Thor smashes each of their hands with his hammer.

Phoenix and Ryder unlock their wrists and push the tables against the wall so that they are out of the way. Thor gives me a chin lift and I raise their restraints once again.

"I would like to continue, but I'm not the only one that wants your blood today. Dragon?"

Thor steps back, placing his hammer on the table, and turns back toward our guests.

Dragon paces the floor in front of them as he uncoils his whip. When he cracks it, you can hear the tails cut through the air with a wicked crack that sends a shiver down my spine.

"You three touched what wasn't yours to touch. You hurt my Spitfire. My Enchantress. My Queen. We're going to make you pay tenfold for the pain you caused her and my brother."

When he steps around behind them, every one of their heads pivot to try and keep him in their line of sight, even the women.

He says nothing else as his whip cracks through the air. Travis is the first that cries out and then more curses follow from the others. Dragon spends the next few minutes whipping Fang, Travis, and Sean, though he focuses mostly on Fang and Travis. Most likely because one, they were the ones that hurt both Andre and me the most, and two because we don't want Sean to die before he coughs up his information.

Dragon whips Fang's back one more time before he coils up his whip and sets it down on the metal tables against the wall.

His gaze connects with mine and the heat in it has a fire lighting inside me. Yeah, there's got to be something wrong with me to be turned on by my men enacting vengeance on my behalf.

Thor steps forward and Dragon and Andre flank him.

"Now that we have our warmup in, you're going to answer our questions or things are going to get even more painful for you."

Since we're now at the questioning part of our session, I grab one of my boxes from the tool cabinet to start assembling something a friend built for me. I pull out several metal pieces, a few joining pieces, small metal chains, and their remotes. I start screwing the pieces together and assembling as both my men give me dark grins. They're the only two who know all my surprises, though I do notice more than one of the club brothers keeping an eye on what I'm doing. Thor takes my cue and continues.

"Who do you and your father, Sterling, work for, Travis?"

Travis' chains rattle as he tries to stand up taller. "What makes you think we aren't at the top?"

Andre shakes his head as he taps his knife against the tips of his fingers. "Nah, neither of you are smart enough to be the person in charge."

As expected, Travis' face is starting to turn red. His ego is his biggest weakness. I'd given my guys and Andre tips on what gets under their skin and a few buttons to push that are liable to get some sort of response.

"No, I'm thinking the West's have got to be some of the lower grunt men, even if they do have money, but money won't protect them in here," Dragon says.

"And if they're some of the lower grunts in the operation, that would mean Fang's even lower than that, since it appears Travis and Sterling were pulling the strings for their section of the puppet show."

Now Fang's getting red in the face, and I'm wondering which will be the first to crack, Travis or Fang?

"Are you sure Black Plague is actually part of the operation? Or are they the absolute lowest level of grunt workers, getting off their rocks abducting women? Getting pennies for providing the West's merchandise while the West's were bringing in the big bucks to sell to the higher-ups?" Thor asks.

Fang's head whips to Travis and now that Thor's seed of doubt has been planted, I wonder how it will play out?

Travis looks away, and Fang struggles to get closer to him, even though he's chained.

"You rat bastard! We were partners. How much did you skim from my share to fund your cozy lifestyle?"

"Next time get it in writing, idiot. Jesus, all of you are just as dense as a block of wood. Of course, we'd pay you as little as possible. You think you're the only one that supplies us? We have our hands in so many cookie jars that you and your club aren't even going to cause a blip on the radar when all of you disappear, cause guess what? Another one will always pop up, willing to take what they think is big bucks when it's really chump change."

"You really think you're all that just because your last name is West? Or have you forgotten that you're really a Black? If you honestly thought your dear old *daddy* was going to let you climb the ranks with him, you're even more pathetic than me. I've got mayors and officers on my accounts, asshole, as well as my own network of warehouses."

"Please, I have my own accounts. My own warehouses. My own contacts. Each of them are separate from Dad's. If you seriously think I'm solely dependent on that dumb fuck, you're not as observant as you think you are. I mean, your biggest accounts are fucking mayors and officers. But me? I have governors as client's, dipshit. And since Dad's a fucking idiot with computers, I make all his appointments, so I know all of his clients, too. It was just a matter of time before I take over his accounts and remove him permanently."

I try not to pause as I look up at them before catching Thor's eye. He smirks but hides it quickly.

It takes a moment before they both realize what just happened.

"Fuck," they both mutter in unison.

Andre laughs. "Well, that was fucking easier than I thought it would be. Now, both of you are going to tell us who your clients are, where your warehouses are, and who's supplying you with women and children. Half-pint, you want to help me with this next step?"

Putting down my claw, I pick up my knife again. "I'll get a few in on them and then hand it over to others so they can work out some of their aggression. I have more toys to play with later though, so no killing them when you all take your turns."

I'm almost to Travis when Dragon grabs me, pulling me flush against him and kisses me. "God damn, I love you woman."

"I love you too, Dragon, but I need you to let me go so I can get in some slicing and dicing." He smacks my ass but releases me. "Fuck, you're perfect. Don't change, Spitfire."

"Wasn't planning to, Babe." Giving him another quick kiss, I walk over and stop near Andre. "Which one of these idiots do you want first?"

"Depends. Do I get to use one of your surprises?"

"Not yet," I say and pause, laughing when he pouts. "Those are for later, so hurry up and pick your idiot, cause the faster we get their information, the faster you get to play with the surprises."

He perks right up at that.

"Fuck yes! It's Christmas in July," he shouts and hurries over to Travis while I casually walk over to Fang, deciding to start with him first. It won't take much for Sean to break since he's already repeatedly pissed himself from what Thor and Dragon did to him. Even though I'm focusing on the men right now, I know Tiffany and Monica are scared shitless.

"Did you hear that, Pretty Boy? Christmas came early, so you might want to start spilling your guts before I actually spill them for you."

"Don't get too excited, Andre, they still need to be alive by the time we get to the surprises because I know you're going to want to play with the new toys for a while," I say as I start cutting Fang's clothes off.

He groans. "Spoilsport," he mutters and I chuckle in reply.

"Fuck, Spitfire," Dragon groans.

When I look over my shoulder, I wink at him when I realize he is really turned on as he adjusts himself. My gaze flicks to Thor, who's also sporting a pretty big bulge and I smirk. At least I'm not the only one turned on by this. I'm definitely in for a fun time later.

Once I have Fang's clothes removed, I put them in the bag Punisher brings over. His dark grin tells me he's looking forward to his turn, which will be coming up. Turning my attention back to Fang, I take a catalog of his weaknesses as I trace my knife across his skin.

"We could have had so much fun together if I had known you were into knife play, Princess. It's not too late."

Letting my knife dig deeper into his skin, I grin darkly when I see his face tighten in pain. "I'm not a Princess. I'm a mother fucking Queen, asshole. As for my sexual preferences, that's something you'll never know about." I pause but continue cutting into his skin. "For the record, there's nothing 'play' about what my knife and other toys are going to do to you by the time this is all said and finished. Same with the clubs behind me. Now, you might want to start talking about those names and locations, otherwise, I'm going to give you a few things that might bring some memories to the forefront."

When he doesn't answer, I cut into him methodically as I hum, already knowing where and how deep I'll be cutting him. However, since this is only the start of the questioning, I don't go as deep as I'd like to. We need answers before we can kill him.

Knowing his club tattoo is on his back, I save that for Andre to further fuck up, so I get to work on his torso. My knife cuts through his skin like butter and I ignore his pleas, grunts, and gasps since he isn't giving me any information. For someone who had spouted more than once that he likes pain with his pleasure, he seems to have a low pain tolerance. Once his chest and stomach are done, I move onto his legs.

By the time I'm done, he's starting to sound like he'll be cracking soon. Since he still hasn't given me a name, I walk back to the tool cabinet and grab some pliers. I start to walk back to Fang when I purposefully turn back around and grab multiple boxes.

"Almost forgot the trophy boxes."

Andre chuckles along with a few other guys as I deposit three of them onto the floor, making sure everyone will be able to see the contents of the boxes in front of them. Walking back to Fang, I open and close the pliers a few times, and I can see his Adam's apple bob as he swallows.

"Do you want to start talking?"

His lips press into a thin line, but he's already sweating a lot.

"Suit yourself. Your loss is my gain. And I do so love the sound of my trophies bouncing around in those little boxes."

Mind you, when I knew him as Scott, he only had one eyebrow ring and a tongue ring. However, as Fang, he has a fair amount of piercings—on his face, tongue, ears, and nipples. Surprisingly, he doesn't have a cock piercing. Too bad. I bet I could have made the removal process hurt.

I start with one of his four eyebrow rings. Clamping down, I give a hard tug, rip it out, and drop it into the box. He curses at me but still doesn't answer, so I move on to the next one.

After I rip out the fourth eyebrow ring, I let it bounce around in the trophy box before clamping the pliers down on his nipple ring next.

"I bet this will hurt like a bitch if I rip it out." I pause as I give it a tug. "Still don't want to talk?"

He's sweating harder now, and I tug once more, a little harder than before.

"M-Mayer Killeg," he pants.

"Good, now keep talking. What'd he ask you for?"

"H-He wanted boys around t-thirteen years old."

"How many boys did you give him?"

He hesitates, so I pull harder on his nipple ring and twist.

"Eight in the last f-four years."

"See, was that so hard?" I let go and his body sags. Turning around, I address the clubs. "Who wants him next?"

"B-But I told you. You're still going to p-punish me? He said we wouldn't be p-punished if we talked."

I look over my shoulder at him and smile sweetly. "Do you honestly think we're going to stop because you give us one name and what you provided him? We're going to keep going until we get every single answer out of you that we need. If you do cave and give us more information, the one who gives us the most information with the least resistance will not be punished *as severely* as Thor said earlier."

Fang pales and I turn back around, not surprised to see Punisher walking up.

"Nope, my turn to have this guy," Andre says as he switches over to Fang.

Andre's jaw ticks when he sees my marks on Fang. Marks that he recently found out resemble what he and his brothers did to me the first time.

"Well, if you're switching to Fang, then there's one thing I want to do to Travis before you guys have your fun."

Stealing Punisher's serrated knife, since it will do more damage than the one I have, I walk over to Travis. Crouching down by his left leg, I start carving. His curses echo off the walls as I carve 'rapist' in his thigh.

"There, now you can have fun, but not too much fun, big guy."

Punisher grins darkly at me in response. I hand over his knife and walk over to the women.

Chapter 48
Levi

AFTER I PLACE THE trophy boxes in front of the women, Sasha steps up next to me and hands me my knife. We get to work stripping them down before putting their clothes in a bag.

Tuning out the guys, I know Python will catch any conversations we have while Jax will continue logging the guys' conversations. Though it doesn't escape my notice that the translation system is up and running.

"Time for you ladies to get some attention," I say as I trail my knife down Monica's cheek. Pulling back, I circle them, looking for potential weak spots. "Now, how did you wind up bound and gagged in the house Black Plague was using?"

Neither of them talks and they both look wary for if we'll really hurt them.

"**Как вы думаете, с чего нам следует начать** [What do you think we should start with]? **Портить их кожу** [Marring their skin]? **Пирсинг** [Piercings]? **Ногти** [Nails]? **Волосы** [Hair]? **Я думаю, что в этом порядке, а затем несколько сюрпризов** [I'm thinking that order and then a few surprises]."

Sasha laughs. "**Да, но, может быть, немного использовать железный дрын** [Yes, but maybe a little bar work, too]? **Это выглядело довольно болезненно** [That looked rather painful]."

"**Да, да, так и было** [Yes, yes it did]," I reply and grin darkly when I stop in front of them. "Still don't want to talk?"

Monica's lips press in a thin line and Tiffany doesn't talk either.

My grin deepens. "Good, I was hoping you'd take the hard route."

I get to work marring Monica's pale skin, starting light in a few places but then digging deeper in others. I cut with no rhyme or reason but stay away from her major arteries. She's panting and sweating a lot when I decide to switch things up.

"How did you end up bound and gagged in that house?" I ask her again.

She glares at me and I quickly slide my finger through both hoop earrings on her right ear and pull till they rip out, leaving her earlobe in shreds. I drop one earring at a time into the box, letting each one bounce until it stops. Reaching around to the other side, I pause after sliding my finger through the hoops. Her body tenses, but she stays silent, so I repeat the process.

When the last earring settles in the box, I grab a stool and some pliers off the nearby table. I place the stool behind the women and set the other pliers on it for Sasha when she's ready, along with my knife.

Grabbing one of Monica's hands, I start with her index finger, clamping down on her fake nail before bending it backward until I'm able to rip it off along with her original nail. I repeat the process until she's weeping and finally talks.

"Fang promised that when you were out of the way, I'd be able to take your place."

"And how did he promise you'd be able to take my place?"

"Surgery to make me look more like you and a new identity. Even though it makes me sick, I was eating more to fill out my figure to be more like yours."

I walk around to look her in the eyes for this next part. "You do realize that just because you change the package, it doesn't change the contents. My men would have seen through your bullshit attempt and still see your hateful, poisonous soul. From what I've seen and heard, all you care about is yourself and what rank you can slither into so you'd get more power. They would have tossed you aside, just like they did before."

She glares at me but says nothing.

"What did Fang say he'd do to get me out of the way?"

She shakes her head, not answering, so I go back to work on the rest of her fingernails. When I'm done, I decide to strike at her vanity again. It won't hurt physically, but probably mentally or emotionally. Her once blond, long locks look like she attempted to dye them red but ended up with almost a deep strawberry blond that looks so wrong on her.

Setting down my supplies, I dig out another small box from the cabinet and set it down on a small cart that I wheel over it over by Monica. Opening the box, I pull out a mirror and set it up so she can see what I'm about to do. Next are a few pairs of scissors, packets of new hair ties, and some large plastic baggies. Too bad she dyed her hair cause if her blond was natural, I might have seen if we could donate the hair anonymously for wigs.

Running my hand along her scalp, I don't feel any extensions, so I get to work sectioning off her hair. I secure each section with a hair tie about two or three inches from her scalp, as well as a few more ties down the length of the sections to help contain her hair. When all of her hair is sectioned off, I pick up the scissors and start hacking away, cutting off her hair haphazardly and tucking each bundle into the plastic bag, trying to minimize loose hairs that could escape and possibly be missed in the cleanup. She thrashes her body around, but all it does is make the hack job look even worse.

Once the sections are removed, I close the last baggie and toss it in with the clothes to get burned later. Running my hand through her hair, I make sure to turn her head so she can see her new look. She shrieks as she tries to throw her body against mine.

Time for a little more pain. I go back to the table and get the devices I'd assembled earlier.

"My friends made these for me and damn, did they go all out on the design," I say as I hold up the circular claw-like devices, making sure she sees the pointed tips. "See, they can be adjusted based on cup size and then secured around the body." I pause as I lift the chains and then the remote. "Once in place, this little device will let me increase the pressure, add rotation, and even eject prongs to a desired depth that are similar to fishhooks that will imbed themselves under your skin. Now, since your boobs are obviously fake, I can't go too deep at first, otherwise I'd release whatever the hell chemicals are in those airbags into your system, which could send you into shock before we get our answers. So! How about I just get this in place and the fun can begin?"

I start adjusting the claw angles when an arm drapes over my shoulders.

"Half-pint, please say you have some toys I can play with?" He looks at me with puppy dog eyes, and I can't help the laugh that escapes.

"How far are you with your questioning?" I set down the boob prongs, and he leads me over to the guys.

Fang and Travis' bodies have cuts all over their bodies except their cocks. There's a considerable pool of blood already forming under their bodies. Dragon's currently working over Sean, but it looks like he's being careful that he isn't doing anything too deep, since Sean already looks close to fainting.

"We've got a lot of names and locations out of them, but I don't think we've hit pay dirt yet."

"Hmmm," I hum, and my eyes go up to the ceiling. "Too bad we didn't have a track in the ceiling where we could rotate our guests so they could see our play methods on each other. We could even rig places where we could put ceiling panels in place to protect the tracks from the results of our playing."

"Holy fuck," someone mutters, but I don't know who said it.

"Let me get the women set up so we can ask a few more questions. I want the men to see and hear parts of this because they'll be enjoying some of this soon, just a little differently."

"Fuck, show me what you're doing Half-pint."

Walking back over to Monica, I notice she's pissed herself again. Ignoring her pleas and whimpers, since she isn't giving me any useful information, I loop the chain around her neck and secure the ends to each claw. I fit the claw over her breast and attach the second chain to that claw. Looping the chain around her back, I fit the second claw over her other breast, securing the chain and then connecting the two claws together between her breasts.

"Shit, you designed a metal claw bra."

"Yes, I did," I say and pick up the remote. Her not knowing what I'm going to do will increase her fear. Andre peers over my shoulder as he looks at my remote, which sort of resembles a controller for a remote-control car. He whistles when he sees what all the controls are and what they do, since I have each one labeled.

"Now, what was Fang going to do to get me out of the way?"

Monica bites her lip but doesn't say anything. I notice Sasha hooking up Tiffany in the metal claw bra, as Andre called it, and Tiffany is watching Monica and me intently.

I flip a switch and the claws pierce Monica's skin just enough to get a little beneath the surface. She cries out in surprise, which increases in volume when I rotate the dial back and forth, making the claws mimic my actions. Sasha asks the same question to Tiffany in case she knows anything and soon, both of their cries fill the room.

After a few minutes, I stop when I think I hear a muffled voice and signal Sasha to stop, too.

"Either of you feel like talking yet?"

They both nod vigorously.

Finally.

"Once they got their hands on you and took their revenge, they were going to disappear with you," Monica says.

"Disappear where?"

They both shake their heads.

"He didn't say the exact location, but that they had a cabin on a secluded piece of land in Canada. They'd have their fun with you till you gave birth and then make you watch as your baby was sold and then sell you, too," Tiffany says.

"Did they say anything else about the cabin or anything unique about the surroundings?" Thor asks.

Both women scrunch up their faces as they think and eventually Monica nods.

"They mentioned a few times that they needed to make sure they stayed off the radar of the people studying and trying to save the whitebark pine trees."

I glance at Jax and then Python. They both give me a chin lift, so I'm going to take that as good enough information to narrow things down a bit.

"What else did they say? Who were they going to sell us to?"

"They were careful to never say their name around us and only referred to the buyer as 'he', 'him', or 'the client'."

"How long were you bound and gagged?"

"For a couple of days," Monica replies as she glares in the direction of Fang.

"A day," Tiffany replies.

"When did things change? What'd they say?"

"Fang took me upstairs like he did every night, but this time, these two men were in there, as well as Fang's brothers. He hooked me up in some weird contraption that was set up over a bed. It looked like the wooden device people would be locked up in a long time ago with the wood secure around the person's wrists and neck.

"Once they had me in the contraption, my legs hit the end of the bed and my upper body was horizontal over the bed. They cuffed my ankles to the bed. Fang then told me they were going to break me in for my new buyer, Sanchez. They took me, three at once, and made sure they were rough about it. That went on for a couple of days. When they weren't with me, they left a bucket under my legs for when I needed to use the restroom. The last day, they finally let me out, let me shower, gave me food and drink before they gagged and bound me," Monica tells us.

A part of me feels sorry for her, but that feeling's quickly squashed. That could have been my fate if Fang had succeeded in getting away with me again.

"The same thing happened to me, but I was only restrained for a day," Tiffany says.

Walking over to Sean, I painfully grip his chin.

"If you had succeeded in selling me when I was a child, who was the buyer you had lined up?"

He smiles darkly at me, his teeth bloody from his beatings. "You mean you haven't figured it out yet?"

"Oh, I'm pretty sure I have, but I want to hear it coming from your mouth."

"Sanchez was enamored with you when he first saw the picture I sent. You've become his obsession, and he vows he will have you one day."

I pull my arm back, but someone catches my wrist. Anger rips through me as I look over my shoulder and see Dragon holding me. I'm about to let him feel my rage for stopping me when he smirks and winks.

"Spitfire, if you're going to hit him, how about you use these instead? It'll hurt him a lot worse," he says as he holds up new brass knuckles. Well shit, now I can't be mad at him.

"Fuck, you got lucky there, Dragon. I thought she was going to castrate you," Uncle Bear says as he laughs, and a few others laugh along with them.

"Nah, I like his dick and balls too much to do that to him," I say, winking back at Dragon, which has my brothers groaning and Dragon grinning at me.

Slipping on the brass knuckles, I open and close my hand a few times, getting a feel for them before turning and landing a punch to Sean's jaw.

Next, I go to Fang and wrench his hair back painfully.

"Who were you going to sell my baby to?" I purposefully don't let him know that I'm having twins.

"Everything all leads back to Sanchez, Princess. Like Sean says, he's obsessed with you and will take you any way he can. Once your kid was old enough, he was going to start grooming him or her for his personal use, since he couldn't have you when you were a kid. Though he fully intends to have more kids with you. And when he tires of you or you're no longer of use to him, he'd ship you off to one of his brothels like he does his other toys when they no longer interest him."

I rain my fists down on Fang, hitting vital points over and over until a hand lands on my arm. Looking up, I realize it's Thor. Anger, hate, fear, sympathy, and love all swirl in his blue eyes.

A tear escapes and his rough, calloused thumb wipes it away. However, I'm surprised when it's Sasha that speaks and not him.

"**Он попросил меня сказать тебе, чтобы ты задал Трэвису твои последние вопросы** [He asked me to tell you to ask Travis your final questions]. **Тогда вы можете закончить дело** [Then you can end it]."

Taking a deep breath, I compose myself and realize I've done a number on Fang. His face is mostly swollen, but he can still see, and his body is starting to turn black and blue thanks to the brass knuckles. Out of the corner of my eye, I see Travis smirking at me, and turn before walking toward him.

"What did you have to gain from all this, Travis?"

"Wouldn't you like to know?" he asks as his smirk deepens.

However, it falls a bit when he sees my dark smile.

"I was hoping you'd go the hard route." Turning, I look at each of the club members. "I'm going to need a little help before we break out the big finale. I need all three men laying on the ground, legs spread. Any volunteers to get them into position?"

Punisher laughs. "Oh, I think I know where you're going with this and even though it'll hurt like hell to watch, I want these fuckers to feel your wrath."

"Aww, thank you Punisher. I'll make sure you get extra desserts tonight just for that comment." Reaching up, I cup his cheek before placing a chaste kiss on it, which has my men growling but there's no threat behind it.

I retrieve my last couple of boxes from the cabinet and set them down on the table, but I don't open them yet.

When the men are in position and restrained, I walk back over to Travis and crouch down by his head.

"What did you have to gain from this, Travis?"

A smirk is his answer, so I get up and walk over to Sean before landing my metal spiked heel into his balls. Sean's cries fill the air as I grind down on him. Out of the corner of my eye, I notice almost all the guys behind me wince in pain.

"Oh fuck! Please say you have more tips in one of those boxes," Sasha says excitedly.

Looking over my shoulder, I grin at her. "Open the smaller box, and you can have Fang."

I laugh as she squeals with excitement and rips open the box, revealing a few hundred metal spikes that mirror my heels.

Walking over to Travis, I notice both he and Fang have pissed themselves as they watched what I did to Sean. I stand in front of Travis and wait for Sasha to come over. Travis eyes both of us with fear in his eyes, though I can tell he's desperately trying to hide it.

Sasha crouches down in between Fang's legs with her spikes and a hammer. "This is for what you did to my sister and Emily, both when she was sixteen and what you've done the last couple of weeks."

She drives the spike into his balls and I step closer to Travis, driving my heel into his balls. After a few minutes or so, I step back and Sasha does the same.

"Can you guys please get them back into a standing position? It's time to end this," I say as I walk over to the tables.

Andre practically skips over to me and I'm not surprised when I see Punisher right behind him. I let Andre open the box, and he roars with laughter when he opens it up. He pulls out five metal-looking dildos, but I don't think he realizes their potential.

When they pick up a remote, I snatch it out of their hands before they can play with it since they're still holding one of the dildo's. Their faces fall as I point at them.

"If you had turned this on with how you're holding the dildos, you would have seriously hurt your hands."

Both of them quickly place the dildo's back on the table, before their confused stares focus back on me.

"For starters, each dildo is engraved with a letter and that letter is also engraved on its paired remote. Once the dildo is inserted into our guests, there are straps to secure around their waists to keep the dildo in place. For our male guests, there are also these circular attachments that will mimic what the dildos are able to do. The attachments are also engraved."

I make a show of holding it up and am met with whimpers from our guests. Placing the 'A' dildo and 'A' attachment on the table, I make sure to grab their corresponding remote before turning both on and pressing a button. Metal spikes protrude from the dildo and cock ring. Everyone around the table jumps back slightly.

"Shit, those are metal spiky dicks and spiky cock rings," Andre says, his voice mixed with awe and pain.

"Yup, and if you look here," I say as I hold up one that isn't turned on, "you can insert a regular dildo for the vibration and motion effect. There are also straps to keep it in place, but I don't know how long the actual dildos will last with how we'll have to clean them afterward."

Several of the men look from me, back to the table, and back to me. Looks of shock and disbelief on all of their faces.

"What? I've had almost seven years to think of payback for Fang and his brothers, and this was one of my ideas. If none of you want to handle these, I can do it."

That seems to snap a few of them out of their shock.

"Holy shit! Can we keep her? I mean, I know you guys are marrying her, but can we seriously keep her? Like, give her a patch and shit? Make it all fully legit?" Andre asks and this time, I'm the one frozen in shock.

I look around, expecting the guys to all be upset at Andre, but instead, I'm met with smiles. What the fuck?

"Well, it's funny you should ask that Reaper because we had a special session of Church last night," Phoenix says as he grins.

"What the fuck? Why didn't I know about this?" Dragon bellows.

"Because this is a first for the club and Devil and I thought we should take family out of the equation for this question, which includes you two, since you're going to marry her. Same for Bear, Smoke, Reaper, Alexei, and Ethan, since Levi considers you all her family. Thor only knew about it because he's the President of the entire club, but he wasn't allowed to vote or be in the room when it came time."

"Well, are you fuckers going to fill us in on this secret Church session?" Bear growls.

"We were going to offer this to Levi after we were done with these assholes and bitches, but since Reaper brought it up sooner," Phoenix pauses as he looks down at my hands. "You may want to remove your gloves for this, Levi. Maybe even wash up and use some hand sanitizer if you want," he says with a wink as he pulls a familiar box off the top of the tool cabinet.

I practically run to the sink, which has the guys laughing. I shed my gloves, push up my sleeves slightly and wash my hands. For good measure, I also use hand sanitizer before rushing back over to Phoenix.

"Oh, I've missed my cut! I feel naked without it."

When he opens the box, it isn't what I was expecting.

I was expecting my property cut, but this one is different. Instead of 'Enchantress', 'First Lady' is stitched into the patch. With shaky hands, I pick up the cut and turn it around, expecting the rocker to say 'Property of Thor & Dragon' but it doesn't say that. Instead, it looks just like the back of their cuts.

A fully patched member of the club.

I look around at all of them in shock.

"I know that there isn't anything against voting in women in the bylaws even though a lot of clubs frown on it, but I haven't Prospected. This isn't fair to Colt, Drae, Alexei, Ethan, Drake, or Nathan!"

"Sweetheart, we're conceding on the rules a little bit with your case based on your history. And being in the room with you today was a fucking eye-opener, even though our club all saw the video of what you did with Nicole. Honestly, you'd be perfect if we added a second Enforcer spot, but that's a topic for another day. If another woman wants to Prospect with the club, they can and will go through the other steps just like Colt and the others. When we talked to the Prospects about this, none of them were against bending the rules slightly in your case," Phoenix says.

"Besides, Colt pointed something out. While we may have to consider this with future women Prospects, we'll handle those on a case-by-case basis. Now, this wasn't the deciding factor in the least, but you're about to be doing something none of us can do for the next seven to eight months and then squeezing two watermelons out of you. That means you wouldn't be able to do some of the things we normally put Prospects through. It wouldn't be safe for you or the babies. Besides, I bet if those two assholes have anything to say about it, you'll be pregnant again pretty quickly and then have to go through it all over again," Devil says with a smirk.

I twirl on my guys at that. "If you even think of getting me pregnant right away after the twins are born, you're insane and I'll seriously be cutting back on sexy times! Can't we time it so that the vast majority of my next pregnancy is in the winter months, so I don't miss out on riding my bike or on either one of yours? I'd also like at least a year between pregnancies since I plan to breastfeed."

My rant has the other guys laughing, but both of my men look downright afraid of me for threatening to withhold sex from them. Then I see the shocked looks on our guests' faces and I realize I just let it slip that I'm having twins. Oh well, at least they won't be getting out of here to tell anyone about it.

"We'll do what we can to plan winter pregnancies, but we can't make promises, even if we go back to gloving up, Wildcat. And for what it's worth, I'd love it if you were a fully-fledged member. How you've been with the club so far, with Nicole, and now with these asshats, I think you'll fit in just fine with us."

"Same, Spitfire. You're badass enough on your own that you don't need a property rocker. Anyone that crosses you will end up with at least one blade in them. Also, I'd love it if you were an Enforcer with me. We could get up to so much fun together," he says, wiggling his eyebrows at me.

I don't reply to that except for smiling and hugging him, because I think that's a conversation we really need to have in private before it goes any further.

"Alright, we need to focus and get back on track! I accept the patch, but Phoenix, could you please box it back up until we're done with these assholes? I don't want any blood or bodily fluids on my new cut. Now, who wants to do the honors with these guys?"

Andre makes sure I have one of the spikey dicks as he calls them, and then he, Dragon, Punisher, Bear, Sasha and I get to work.

Slipping new gloves on, I take Monica since she attempted to rape Dragon before. Ignoring their cries for a quick death, I shove the deactivated dildo into her cunt and put on the strap, making sure it'll stay secure. Then I insert the regular dildo and secure it as well.

"**Оставьте металлические лифчики** [Leave the metal bras on]," I tell Sasha and then point to a button on the bra remote. "**Используйте это, а затем это, когда я даю сигнал** [Use this and then this when I give the signal]."

She nods and I know she understands my meaning. This is the women's equivalent of the spikey cock rings.

Once everyone is strapped up, but before giving the signal, I walk over to Travis. He has tears streaming down his face.

"What did you gain by doing this, Travis?"

"I was hoping to gain you and negotiate with Sanchez. I've loved you since I first saw you."

For the first time since his betrayal, he actually looks like the Travis I used to know.

"I wasn't yours for the taking. I never saw you that way. Yeah, you were cute, but there was no spark. You were my friend and a man I considered my brother. When you were unable to accept that, you betrayed me in one of the worst ways. Tell the devil I said hello."

Walking back to the table, we activate the devices for the bras and cock rings. The cries that quickly fill the room are deafening. Thank fuck this room is sound-proof.

After a few moments, I hand out the remotes for the regular dildos. Seconds later, the cries increase as their bodies writhe in pain. I wait a couple more minutes and then nod to Sasha. We hit the button that sends the spiked barbs at the end of the rods deeper into their breasts before they start rotating.

When I think they've suffered enough for the pain they've caused, I pick up my knife and walk behind the women. Grabbing their hair, I drag my blade across their necks to speed up the process. Dragon and Andre help with the men.

When Patch and Doc confirm they're all dead, I flip a latch open on the back of the remotes and show the guys how to retract the spikes so they get the devices out without ripping them out of the bodies with the spikes still protruded. Once the devices are removed, we immediately set about cleaning them, but my men ban me from the bleach baths.

"We don't want you getting bleach in any of your wounds, Wildcat. Besides, I don't know what breathing in all those fumes would do to the babies."

I give them each a kiss. "I'll help with other things then, and when they're all wrapped up, I'll get cleaned up. There are tools and instructions in the boxes for the bras. Same for the spikey dicks and cock rings to remove the spikes from their tracks so we can fully clean them and not leave any traces."

"Fuck, you thought of everything, Spitfire."

"Well, I did have seven years to plot, but it was my friends that got it all to work for me."

"Should we be worried about these friends of yours talking to anyone?" Devil asks and I confidently shake my head.

"Nope, because I know all the skeletons in their closets, too. Plus, we have an airtight gag between the three of us. If one of us spills without the consent of the other two, repercussions are listed. Besides, they knew who I had intended to use these on and why. People who end up down here that have done similar things will also get the same treatment. They know these tools aren't for innocents and they're okay with that. They even said if I need more tools designed in the future to let them know."

"Will we ever get to meet these friends, Wildcat?"

"I'll ask them, but I can't guarantee that they'll want to unveil themselves."

"As long as they won't throw us under the bus, then we won't throw them under the bus," Andre says.

I give him a hug and get to work.

Chapter 49

Levi

AFTER WE GOT THE bodies prepped, Phoenix and Devil said they had planned a party tonight for my patching in, and that they already called the caterers so we wouldn't have to cook.

The guys let Sasha and I have the showers first, but I take one look at the small shower stalls and frown.

"Yup, not gonna work."

"I wondered about that with your stitches. You do you and I'll hurry so the guys can get in here for their turns. I can always go up to Colt's room for a better shower if need be. Too bad they didn't plan to have another bathroom or divide it off so that it's like a girls and guys locker room."

"That's not a bad idea for if we ever have to remodel."

As Sasha hops in the shower, I settle on using soap where possible and baby wipes in other areas to clean up as best as I can before slipping into clean clothes.

I learned from Nikki that baby wipes are very resourceful for cleaning up small messes. She still uses them around the house or on road trips, even though Sadie's seven years old.

I leave my hair alone for now, but I use the baby wipes to get off any visible blood or anything that looks of suspect origins. Slipping into some sandals, I bag up my clothes and, in another bag, I put in my boots. The guys taught me a few new tricks for how to handle bloody clothes, so I don't have to burn them unless they are badly or permanently stained.

Walking out, I let the guys know my plans, slip on my new cut and the guys that are clean all give me hugs, welcoming me fully into the club. After giving my guys a kiss, I head upstairs.

In the common room, I'm instantly bombarded with questions about my cut by my brothers, Dad, and the bunnies. Colt, Drae, Nathan, and Drake all come to give me a hug.

"You assholes knew?" Ethan asks as both he and Alexei scowl at the other Prospects.

"Yup, and both Phoenix and Devil told us we couldn't say anything until it was revealed," Nathan said, grinning.

Laughing, I fill them all in on what I can.

When I'm finished, Alexei has a contemplative look on his face.

"I wonder if Sash will want to Prospect? She's said a few times she wished she was a guy so she could join."

Colt's face falls a bit, but he nods. "She'd be a good addition to the club. I mean, she's already unofficially helping you out, Levi."

"Then why the long face?" I ask him, nudging his shoulder. Although I'm pretty sure I know why.

He blushes. "I was going to ask her to be my Old Lady when I patch in. I love her and I know she's the one for me. Knew it as soon as I saw her. If she Prospects, I'll need to wait until she patches in. Though I would have loved to have seen my property cut on her, I'll love it even more if she fully patches in."

I hug him, beyond happy that he and Sasha are happy together. Alexei grins at him and they bump fists. Since Alexei didn't flip out, I'm guessing Colt already talked to him.

After chatting for a few minutes, I take my leave and head to the house.

Locking the door, I leave my backpack holding my clothes and boots by the washing machine and head upstairs. I'll put them in the washer once I'm done showering so I can throw in the clothes I'm wearing now, too.

Turning on the water in the tub, I strip and wait for the water to warm up. Placing a towel nearby, I get in and then down on my hands and knees for the arduous task of washing my thick, long hair. If I didn't love my long hair so much, I would have cut it because of the hassle of cleaning my hair like this. I can't wait for my stitches to fully dissolve. They're about half gone now.

After getting out of the hospital, I first tried leaning over the ledge of the tub to wash my hair. That was an epic failure because I had to use the tub faucet and the weird angles I had to tilt my head put too much pressure on my sore ribs and stitches on my torso. However, since I hadn't planned on getting in the tub at that time, the stitches on my thigh weren't covered. I had to wait while my guys wrapped me up and then I got on my hands and knees in the tub to finish washing my hair.

Later that day, Ryan came back with a showerhead wand that could be moved around as needed. That made things so much easier, even though I still get on my hands and knees to keep most of the water inside the tub when washing my hair.

Once my hair is washed, I wrap it in a towel and then rinse the rest of the soap off the tub before filling it a couple of inches with clean water. Carefully, I soap up and then rinse off. Just as I step out of the tub, the guys walk into the bedroom, their hair still wet from their showers. Fuck, they're so sexy.

Their eyes immediately heat when they see me naked. Nick smirks at me and then walks over to the closet, pulling out my black boots with the metal spike heel.

"It was so fucking sexy seeing you being all badass and dishing out punishment, Spitfire."

Ryan picks up my cut from the dresser and holds it out to me. "When did you find out the doctor cleared you?"

"When I went in for my checkup yesterday. I texted Nikki to tell Dr. Rowen not to bring up the sex topic in front of you guys. I asked if she could find out and text me so I could surprise you. He said that today I would be cleared since yesterday marked the end of the two-week period they were most worried about. I had planned to tell you after we dealt with things, but when I saw you both after changing, I knew I couldn't keep it a secret any longer. Not knowing how much sex would take out of me for the first time after everything, I opted not to tell you before breakfast, so I'd still have all my strength for our... talk."

"It's probably best you didn't say something, Spitfire, cause at 12:01 am, I would have been licking that sweet pussy of yours to get you ready for our cocks."

I shiver and my skin breaks out in goosebumps.

Ryan unravels the towel that's wrapped around my hair. Gently, he helps to dry it. I close my eyes and moan at the feeling of his hands in my hair. I feel a tug on my skin and when I crack open my eyes, I realize Nick's helping to take off the gauze and cling wrap over my stitches.

Closing my eyes, I feel my muscles relaxing as Ryan continues to dry my hair and massage my scalp.

Hot skin meets mine and my eyes fly open. Nick is now standing in front of me, naked except for his boxers. His lips take mine in a passionate kiss as his hands knead my ass cheeks. Vaguely, I feel my damp hair hitting my back, and when Nick pulls back from the kiss, Ryan is now naked except for his boxers.

"Put on your boots and cut but don't button it up. We want to taste those tits of yours again, Wildcat."

Quickly I do as they ask and Nick leads me over to the bed. Laying down, they're instantly on me and latching onto my nipples.

"Fuck!"

My hands automatically go to their heads, and I press them closer, needing them to be harder. They start nipping my skin. I can feel my juices sliding down my thighs. Fuck, I need their hands on me.

As if they could read my thoughts, both of their hands trail hot paths down my stomach and my hips jump when they both push a finger inside me.

I roll my hips against their hands, trying to get the friction I need.

Ryan lets go of my right nipple with a pop and then kisses down my stomach. Nick pulls out his finger, licking my juices off.

"Fuck, I've missed your taste, Spitfire."

Nick goes back to paying attention to my nipples, and I moan when he presses into my good thigh, and starts moving, practically humping my leg. Ryan's tongue swipes up and down my slit before he latches onto my clit.

My orgasm builds quickly, but when I'm about to cum, Ryan backs off, slowing down and moving away from my clit.

"Ryan, please," I whimper when he doesn't speed up after a while.

His chuckle sends tingles through me and then he's spearing me with his tongue, licking up my juices like they were his last meal. He slides in a finger and starts pumping before he latches onto my clit again.

Instantly, my orgasm builds again and when he nibbles gently on my clit, I detonate. He continues to lap up my juices until the tremors mostly fade. When he gets up, my face heats at how much my juices are coating his beard.

"Our woman is a squirter if she's riled up enough, Nick."

My cheeks heat in embarrassment. Nick groans, his hips rolling against my good hip one more time.

"I need a better taste. I'm missing my favorite snack."

He wastes no time diving between my legs, licking me multiple times from slit to ass.

"Oh fuck, yes." I try to push against him harder, but he holds my hips in place.

He repeats the process, only occasionally latching onto my clit for short bursts until he resumes licking me. It's not until I'm begging him for more, my body trembling with need, that he sucks my clit into his mouth and bites down.

"Fuck, fuck, fuck," I cry as I try to grind on his face. A finger slips into my ass and after he bites down gently on my clit again, I detonate.

When I'm able to open my eyes again, Nick's beard is just as juicy as Ryan's but then something being tossed on the bed snags my attention and I moan when I see the lube. I scramble to get off the bed and button my cut.

The guys pump their cocks with their fists, and if I didn't need them in me so badly, I'd take turns sucking them off.

Nick lays down on the bed since he still has some pains in his leg. I straddle him and his cock slides right in. His hands tighten on my waist before he starts helping me move, so I don't put too much strain on my own leg.

"Oh, fuck, oh fuck. Fuck, I've missed your cocks."

They both moan when I start to ride Nick's cock and a moan escapes me when I feel lube dripping onto my ass, then Ryan's pushing in a finger.

"We've missed this pussy and this ass too, Wildcat. Are you ready for my cock to fill your ass? Ready for us to fill you full of our cum?"

My core clamps down and they both moan. The tip of Ryan's cock presses against my ass and I slow my movements, relaxing to let him in.

As soon as he's fully seated, his hands grip my waist tight.

"Give us a minute, Wildcat. This first time will be fast, but we'll make up for it."

I wait and when they start to move, a deep moan escapes.

"Oh fuck. Yes, fuck me faster. Fuck me harder. I need to feel you."

Both of them pick up the pace. Nick unbuttons the first couple of buttons on my cut and my breasts spill out, bouncing as they move.

"Fuck, I love seeing your tits bounce as you ride our cocks, Enchantress."

His hands squeeze my breasts and he twists my nipples. Another orgasm rips through me and seconds later, they're both pumping me full of their cum.

When I catch my breath, I realize they're still hard.

"Ready for round two, Wildcat?" Ryan asks before he licks my neck, takes my earlobe in his mouth, and bites down.

"Fuck, yes. We've got two weeks to make up for."

They both moan deeply as they start moving again. This time, their movements are slower, but my orgasm still builds quickly. I've been without them for too long and my fingers or their fingers and tongues weren't enough.

I clench down on them a few times and they pick up the pace.

Ryan smacks my ass as Nick tweaks my nipples, alternating between them as his thumb circles my clit.

Their roughness is just what I need to have my orgasm peaking. They keep going, thrusting into me as my orgasm continues.

But just as it ends, another one is fast approaching. My limbs begin to tremble and black spots dance across my vision.

"That pussy and ass of yours is greedy for our cum. Milk our cocks, Wildcat."

Their movements become rougher, and Ryan smacks my ass hard as Nick twists a nipple and moves his thumb faster against my clit.

Within seconds, another orgasm rips through me and I swear I black out for a bit because when I open my eyes, I'm laying on my right side, both of them watching me with concern.

"We are so doing this again tonight after the party."

They both chuckle and Ryan goes into the bathroom to run me fresh bath water. Nick helps me to my feet and follows me into the bathroom.

Wetting a washcloth, I clean myself up as best as I can before stepping into the bathtub to clean up again.

Chapter 50
Levi

It's been a few months since my demons were laid to rest. Fall is in full swing and I'm loving the changing of the tree colors.

Our wedding is a week away and today, I have another OB-GYN appointment, followed by my last dress fitting. The ladies and I are getting ready to head into town and I'm so excited I can hardly stand it.

Sasha is my maid of honor. Roxy, Nikki, Allison, and Erin will be my brides-maids. Nikki's daughter, Sadie, is going to be our little flower girl and Axe's nephew, Jordan, will be our ring bearer. His sister, Susie, and her son, Jordan, are coming into town again for the weekend. I'd met her earlier this summer and Jordan is just the sweetest little boy ever.

The guys are having Phoenix as their best man, and the groomsmen are Alexei, Ryder, Jax, and Timber. Reaper's going to officiate for us. I went easy on the guys and just asked that they wear black pants, white button-up long-sleeved shirts, and their cuts. They could wear their riding boots as long as they were clean.

I grew closer to Alli ever since that first day we met in the ER. I still think she and Ryder have something going on, but that's for them to figure out. If he is serious about her, I know she'd have no problems fitting in with the club.

Erin's a much newer friend but is an absolute sweetheart. She's the owner of the bakery shop in town and became fast friends with us, though she's still leery about coming to the clubhouse. If she does come to the compound, we almost always stay at our house for the duration of her visit.

Today, my men are going with us as well as Jax, Patch, Bones, Gunner, Timber, and a couple of Prospects. I'm driving us in my SUV and the guys are all enjoying a fall ride.

Slipping on my cut, I run my hands over my First Lady patch and find myself smiling. I never imagined I'd be in a motorcycle club, especially after what Fang and his brothers did to me when I was almost sixteen. But here I am, a fully patched member, engaged to the President and Enforcer of our club. Dragon's still trying to get me to become our club's second Enforcer. I probably will accept the position, but right now, I just want to focus on marrying my men.

Grabbing my purse and keys, I head out the front door, locking up behind me. Thor pushes off the deck railing he was leaning against.

"Ready, Baby Mama?" he asks me as he leans down to kiss me.

"More than ready, Hun. Sasha's bringing the bag that the doctor will put the note in for what gender our babies are. Did you guys decide who was going to be the ones to fire up the dirt bikes for the reveal tonight?"

"At first, we asked your dad and Bear, but they said they want to watch. Same with Alexei. So, our next thoughts were Ethan and Reaper. They agreed, so they're researching and testing out the best way to do them."

No one wanted to chance their bikes with this, understandably, but then Dad spoke up that he had held onto all our dirt bikes from when we were kids. The downside was that they haven't been touched in years, so Judge took them into the shop to look them over. There were a few wires that needed to be replaced thanks to mice, but overall, they're still in pretty good condition. I have a feeling that at some point in the future, the guys will be building a dirt racing track and they'll get plenty of use again.

Thor sighs as another cheer goes up from behind the clubhouse.

I laugh at his pained expression. "Seems like Ethan and Reaper have some helpers."

"Yeah, and I think they're praying for girls because I've been seeing a lot of pink clouds coming out of the back of the bikes."

I try to hold in my laughter on this one because he seems really nervous about the thought of having girls. "Or maybe they're so certain it's boys that they're trying to use up the pink dust."

He cocks his head as he thinks about it for a minute before he looks back at me. "You don't think that's the case, do you?"

"Abso-fucking-lutely not. I think they're hoping for girls to see how you both will handle them. However, eventually, someone's going to have a daughter someday, so if that's the case, then you can do some karma paybacks later on."

"Huh, I didn't think of it that way," he muses and then sighs again when another round of cheers goes up. "Come on, Wildcat. Let's get to the appointment. The others should be at the clubhouse by now. Nikki and Sadie are going to meet us there. Your SUV is already up there. Judge had Drae change your oil, then sent him off to wash it and then detail it."

I giggle. "I'm guessing he couldn't take it to a carwash to have them do it, huh?"

Thor smirks at me. "Nope, it was all done by hand, Wildcat. Now let's go before I drag you back upstairs and we miss the appointment."

He takes my hand, and we walk to the clubhouse. Bastion comes running from somewhere and joins us on the rest of our walk. He's been a good addition to the club and is very protective of everyone. He's also alerted us of trouble a few times when the club would have parties on the weekends.

Not too long after some new hang arounds arrived, Bastion cornered a couple of them and alerted us. Ryder and Dragon searched the people in question, and each time, they found drugs on them. The people in question were banned from coming back and the drugs were flushed. Though Bastion wouldn't relax until the toilet bowl was cleaned and the bag was tossed into the garbage, and then that garbage bag was taken out to the dumpster.

Rounding the corner to the clubhouse, I sigh when I notice Erin is already in the car waiting for us. I want to know who put those self-conscious thoughts into her head and beat them up. Yes, Erin has curves, but damn are they the good kind. That woman is smoking hot, and I've noticed Phoenix eyeing her appreciatively. It will be interesting to see how things with both him and Ryder end up with their women of interest.

As I step out behind my car, I bite my tongue to keep from giggling because, speaking of the devils, it looks like we have two more additions to guard detail. Both Ryder and Phoenix are on their bikes, waiting to head out. I wink at Ryder since he's closer and I'm momentarily shocked when I notice him blush. Okay then.

"Is everyone ready to go?" I call out.

Sasha squeals and launches herself at me, hugging me until she dips down and talks quietly to my babies. Colt grins at me as he shakes his head before turning to go to his bike, seemingly content that the babies will almost always come first. For now, that is, unless they decide to have kids someday.

"Now remember what we talked about, lil' bikers. Side with Auntie Sasha on the gender." She winks up at me and I bite my lip to keep from giggling.

Sasha stands and pats her cut, making sure she has everything with her. Yup, not too long after I was patched in, she put her name in the hat to Prospect, which was accepted.

A few guys lounging on the deck of the clubhouse raise their beers at me and smile mischievously. They're all on 'team girl'.

I don't think my men know, but there's a bet going around as to what the genders will be. Sasha is rooting for twin girls and that's where my money is, too. It's just a feeling, but we'll see later tonight if it's right or not.

"Alright, ladies, let's get in the car!" I call out. Even though Sasha could ride with the guys, she opted to be in the car for added protection, but I'm also sure a good dose of that is about having more girl time.

Walking to the driver's side, I give Bastion a good scritch behind his ear. "Backyard," I say as I stand and then watch as he bounds off toward the guys back there.

Twenty minutes later, I pull into a parking spot as close to the door as I can get. I still have momentary panic attacks when I come here, but it's gotten a lot better. As I put the car in park, I remind the women of our rule, since Allison and Erin don't always ride as a group with us.

"Remember ladies, don't open your doors till we get the signal."

"Oh, that's right," Erin replies and lowers her hand from the door.

Dragon gives the signal and Thor opens my door. Colt gets Sasha's and Thor grins at me when Ryder gets Allison's door and Phoenix gets Erin's door. Once Roxy exits, since she was in the middle, the guys close ranks around us as we head into the doctor's office. Though, a few men stay outside watching my SUV and the bikes to make sure no one tampers with them.

In the waiting room, we get a lot of looks as the men fan out around the room in groups.

"Hello, Levi! Ready to find out what you're having today?" Elaine asks me as I sign in. Elaine is Dr. Rowen's wife. She was with another patient on our first day, so we never met her then, but she started taking more shifts at the front desk ever since Daphne was let go. We've gotten close over the past few months, and we invited her and her husband, whose first name is Curt, to the party tonight.

"Yes, I can't wait!"

She leans in closer. "I'm rooting for team girl."

Biting my cheek to keep from giggling, I look over my shoulder, but the guys are watching the exit with Jax. I lean in closer to her. "So am I."

She gives me a thumbs-up as I turn and walk over to the guys. As I approach, Dragon gives me a weird look.

"What was that about?"

"She was telling me her guess for what genders the babies will be and I told her mine."

He pouts. "You're still not going to tell us your guesses?"

I mime zipping my lips. "Nope, you'll find out later."

Jax covers his smile with his hand as he tries not to laugh. I don't know how my men haven't found out about the bet yet—it started about a week after Andre got out of the hospital, and I'm pretty sure it was him that started it.

A little blond bombshell crashes into Jax's legs. He grins when he looks down.

"How's Miss Sadie doing today?"

"Good, Unca Jax. I get to try on my pretty dress today and Mama brought my white biker boots you got me."

I can't help smiling when I hear her say 'Unca Jax'. Nikki said when Sadie was younger, she had the damnedest time saying 'uncle' correctly. That problem has since been rectified, but the nickname, for the most part, stuck.

Sadie is a tomboy, wanting to be just like Unca Jax–wearing a leather jacket, t-shirts, jeans, and biker boots. She even has her own helmet. On other occasions, although rare, she'll sport a dress, but it's always completed with her leather jacket and biker boots.

About ten minutes later, Elaine calls us back. Today, all the ladies, my men, and Jax are going to cram in the room to look at our babies. Kind of a pre-cursor to tonight's party.

"Okay, everyone. I'll go get the ultrasound tech and remind him or her, no genital shots while you're looking at the babies. In the end, we'll turn the station slightly to get some pictures that will go with the gender cards that Sasha's eagerly waiting on. Be back in a few minutes," Elaine tells us.

A few moments later, Elaine comes back into the room. Squealing, I quickly take a few steps forward and hug her. I wanted her to be able to see the babies, but didn't know if she would be able to. Turns out she was able to get one of the other girls to cover the front desk so she could be in on seeing the pictures. Between her and Nikki, they are my favorite nurses to work with.

"What gender are you hoping the babies are?" Nikki asks Sadie.

"I hope she has one of each! I don't have a brother or sister yet, so I want one of each for cousins!"

My heart squeezes at the look that crosses Nikki's face, but it's quickly masked.

Sadie kneels on her chair and hugs Nikki. "Someday I hope you can meet a nice guy like how Auntie Levi met Unca Thor and Unca Dragon!"

That thought has Jax turning pale. "Nope, Munchkin. If your mama meets a guy, that's it, just one."

She turns to him, looking confused. "But why? I know Mama would smile more and be happier if she has two someones that are nice. And Auntie Levi smiles almost all the time, so she must be really really happy. I want Mama to be that happy."

Oh, out of the mouth of babes.

On one hand, I want to laugh so much at her unknown innuendo of one of the sources of my double happiness. On the other hand, my heart breaks at how much Sadie has observed in her short life but also how much she wants her mom to be happy.

Nikki hugs her and kisses all over her face, making Sadie giggle. "All I need is you, my little Sadie pie." When Nikki hugs her, her mask breaks and Jax hands a tissue to Nikki, which she readily accepts.

A knock sounds at the door and the technician comes in.

"Yeah, it's time to see the babies!" Sadie cries out, which has everyone laughing and breaking the tension in the room.

The technician smears the gel on my stomach and soon my babies' heartbeats fill the air while she takes their measurements.

"Your babies are right on track for their size, their heartbeats are strong and there's lots of fluid around them."

The knot in my gut loosens at hearing they're still going strong. Ever since I woke up in that house and remembered the crash, I'd been worried sick about if I'd end up losing one or both of them.

"Okay, I'm going to turn away to get the gender checked. If you could please pass the bag over, I'll seal it up for you."

Sasha anxiously hands the bag over to the technician with an envelope. After a few minutes, she tucks the pictures inside and seals the envelope. She staples the bag closed and passes it back to Sasha, who immediately tucks it into her purse. The technician helps me clean the gel off my baby bump before gathering up her things.

"Dr. Rowen will be in in a few minutes. Hope your reveal party is a blast later today!"

"Thank you!" we call out.

Elaine gives me a hug and says she'll see us tonight before slipping outside.

The rest of the appointment goes by quickly and I soon find myself settled back in the car. Time for the dresses.

Three hours later, we're back in my car and almost home. Nikki's following close behind me, and our men are split between front and rear guard. As we near the clubhouse, Thor and Dragon slow our pace earlier than usual and their heads start swiveling, watching our surroundings. Sasha notices the change too and starts scanning as well. I can make out a person outside the gate, but I don't know if they're alone. There's no car. Did he or she walk here? Ensuring our windows are up and the doors are locked, I watch my men for any signal they may give.

When we get closer, I realize it's a woman, and she's gesturing frantically. She turns around when the guys pull off the road in front of the gate and shut off their bikes. I keep my car straight on the road, still in drive and my foot on the brake in case I need to get out of here quickly.

The woman shows some pictures and something in a notebook to Thor and Phoenix. Thor looks hesitantly to our rear guard and then back to me.

He gives the signal to Ethan to open the gate. The guys get back on their bikes, restart them, and pull in. I slowly follow them and take stock of the girl that's waiting just inside the gate. She's skinny but is wearing oversized clothes from the looks of it. She's clean, but you can tell she only has access to very basic necessities. She has a backpack with her as well as an over-the-shoulder duffle bag.

"When I park, stay in the car unless one of the guys tells you to get out. Roxy, since you're in the middle, slide up here and get in the driver's seat, just in case. Keep it running, lock the doors."

I park and quickly get out of the car, patting my stomach to make sure the orientation of my sleeve is correct. Sasha's right behind me as the men fan out.

The woman's eyes widen in fear, but she doesn't back down.

"Why are you here?" Thor asks.

"A-Are you Thor? The President of Forest Creek Steel Archangel's MC?"

"Yes. Now answer me. Why are you here?"

"I need help and I'm looking for my dad. I have information that says he's a member here."

"Why do you need help?"

"I think my stepdad, and maybe my mom, is trying to sell me to someone."

Curses ring out behind me. Thor looks at me hesitantly, and a worried look crosses his face.

He turns back to the woman. "Who's your dad?"

"Jax. Jaxon Witlock."

Grabbing Thor's hand, I spin and find my brother frozen to the spot in shock. Then an angry look crosses his face as he steps forward.

Oh, shit.

"I've only had one daughter, and she died the day she was born twenty-one years ago to the day."

I turn back to the woman, who is shaking her head and holds out some pictures to him when he reaches the other side of Thor.

He takes them, and after a few moments, his hands start to shake. She hands him a notebook.

"I have more information to show you if you want, but after reading Mom's journals, I figured this would be the best place to start."

Jax reads the page and then the next couple of pages. As he reads, my gaze snaps to the woman, who's shuffling on her feet. As I study her, I realize she's almost a carbon copy of him, although much skinnier. Jax closes the notebook and looks back up at her.

"What's your name?

"Mae. Mae Rose Cole."

The end until Steel Archangel's MC: Timber (SAFC2)

Author's Note

THANK YOU EVERYONE FOR reading my book! I hope you loved the members of the *Steel Archangel's MC* as much as I do! Next up is Timber's story as he finds, and later saves, his Sunshine <3

Reviews are very important for authors, especially to new authors! Thank you to everyone that leaves a review, even if it is only a line or two! Keep reading for info on how to contact me as well as other books by me. I'd love to hear from you!

About The Author

R. KNIGHT LOVES READING and writing romance novels, whether it be contemporary, MC, paranormal, reverse harem or menage. If you like strong women surrounded by the men who adore and worship them, then follow me to hear about current and upcoming books that will satisfy your craving!

When R. Knight isn't reading or writing, she's spending time with her amazing husband, two kiddos, two cats and a dog where they live in Eastern Wisconsin. The usual shenanigans involve watching movies, camping, playing board games and/or video games.

https://linktr.ee/Author_R_Knight

www.ingramcontent.com/pod-product-compliance
Lightning Source LLC
Chambersburg PA
CBHW060758030726

47503CB00002B/297